As Natalie coasted past, their gazes locked.

In that fraction of a blink, she memorized everything about him. Eyes the color of coal, chiseled jaw, Olympic shoulders, hard everywhere, all of him bottled into an explosive package.

Boom!

His eyes pierced into her like an arrow's point, took her, owned her.

Dear God! What was this?

A lazy, wolfish, one-sided grin spread slowly across his face.

Just one look and all the mysteries of the universe were answered. Every nerve ending in her body tingled to life as if she'd been asleep for a hundred years and was awakening for the very first time.

It's him!

LORI WILDE

NEW YORK TIMES
BESTSELLING AUTHOR

Love
AT
FIRST
SIGHT

A CUPID, TEXAS NOVEL

AVON
An Imprint of HarperCollins Publishers

AVON BOOKS
An Imprint of HarperCollins*Publishers*
195 Broadway,
New York, New York 10007

Copyright © 2013 by Laurie Vanzura
ISBN-13: 978-0-373-60317-6
www.avonromance.com

First Avon Books paperback printing: June 2013

Avon Trademark Reg. U.S. Pat. Off. and in Other Countries, Marca Registrada, Hecho en U.S.A.

HarperCollins® is a registered trademark of HarperCollins Publishers.

Printed in the U.S.A.

To Esi Sogah, thank you for all the backstage work you do on my books. You are an unsung hero!

Special thanks to both my best friend,
Hebby Roman,
and the most wonderful
mother-in-law in the whole world,
Marie Vanzura,
whose detailed personal knowledge and
interesting tales of life in far southwest
Texas held me captive as I researched that
hauntingly beautiful, unique world.
And to my late brother,
Shawn Blalock,
whose fascination with Marfa, Texas,
became my own.

Chapter 1

Just one look and the earth trembled beneath my feet.

—Millie Greenwood

Dear Cupid,
The most awesomely awful thing has happened. I
have fallen truly, madly, deeply in love.

Awesome because I have never felt anything
like this. I've heard people talk about love at first
sight, but I never believed in it. Then with just one
look—bam! I was a goner. The minute we laid
eyes on each other we knew we were destined soul
mates. Suddenly, our minds are wide open and
the world is the most beautiful place. How have
I gone so long without knowing magic like this?

But that's what you do, isn't it, Cupid? Fling

*your arrow and make people fall in love at first
sight. Drive them crazy. Send them over the edge
of reason.*

*It's awful because I've been accepted into Ox-
ford University with a full scholarship. I can't
bear the thought of leaving my guy behind, and
family responsibilities keep him from joining me
in England. My head tells me that this is a once-
in-a-lifetime opportunity and I can't pass it up,
but I ache at the thought of being so far away
from him. What's the point of the finest education in the world if you can't be with the one you
love? Tell me what to do, Cupid. Go or stay? My
fate is in your hands.*
—*Shot Through the Heart*

Natalie McCleary folded the well-creased letter and
tucked it into the pocket of her Van Gogh yellow sundress. The letter writer's angst settled in the pit of her
stomach. Sometimes, playing Cupid was more difficult than running her bed-and-breakfast, Cupid's Rest.

It had been over a week since the letter had arrived
and she still had no answer for the sender. Her response
had the power to change the entire trajectory of Shot
Through the Heart's future, and she did not take her
duties lightly.

The trouble was, at twenty-nine, Natalie herself had
never been in love. Who was she to give advice to the
lovelorn?

*You're Millie Greenwood's direct descendant, that's
who. It's your obligation whether you want it or not.*

Wasn't that just the story of her life? Obligation. Responsibility. Tradition.

Natalie shook her head and squared her shoulders. *C'mon, don't be resentful.* She'd never been a complainer or shirker and she wasn't about to start now.

The sole of her bright yellow Keds made a slight scraping sound as she scuffed over terra-cotta paver stones. She moved toward the large white wooden box situated underneath the cherubic fountain in the botanical gardens, located in the center of downtown Cupid, Texas. It was just after dawn and the gardens weren't yet open to the public, but in another two hours the place would overflow with tourists.

Mockingbirds called from pink-blossomed desert willows. Over by a prickly pear cactus, a black-crested titmouse gobbled up a fat grub worm. Undisturbed by Natalie's presence, a long-legged roadrunner strolled over the limestone rock wall surrounding the gardens. Locusts started a low-hummed buzzing, tuning up for the encroaching late June heat. Dragonflies hovered over the fountain, and a toad peeked up at her from blue pebble gravel around the firecracker plants. From La Hacienda Grill down the street, the smell of huevos rancheros wafted on the air and mingled with the perfume of fuchsia rockroses.

The morning seemed to be holding its breath, waiting for something to happen. For what, she didn't know, but the notion dug in so deeply that she hesitated, caught her breath, and glanced around.

Nope, no one, she was totally alone.

You're losing it, woman.

She cocked her head, listening, but heard nothing out of the ordinary. Off in the distance an eighteen-wheeler ground its gears as it churned up the mountain. The rhythmic sound of a garbage truck's backup beeper drifted over from First Street, followed by the mechanized wheeze of the lifting arm and the clattering clang of a Dumpster being emptied. From the stables behind the gardens, a horse whinnied.

Home.

Still the same, but oddly different somehow.

Inexplicably, goose bumps spread over her skin. She rubbed her arms with her palms.

Weird.

Junie Mae Prufrock, who owned the LaDeDa Day Spa and Hair Salon next door to Natalie's B&B, would claim that someone had walked over her grave.

Shrugging off the unwanted sensation, Natalie twirled the combination lock on the white wooden box marked "Letters to Cupid" in stenciled red block print. The lock popped open and she raised the lid.

As usual, it was stuffed with letters. She pinched up the full skirt of her shirtwaist dress with one hand, forming a sling to hold the letters as she emptied the box. The dewy morning air kissed her knees. After one-handing the padlock closed, she limped over to the bicycle she'd left parked on the pathway and deposited the letters into the wicker basket strapped to the front.

One swoop of her foot released the kickstand. She slung her leg over the cruiser saddle seat and she was off, pedaling through the back of the garden to the dirt-packed alley that ran between the gardens and the stables.

The wind ruffled her hair, brought with it the scent of horses. A long-tailed flycatcher perched on a telephone line, its split tail hanging underneath it like scissors. She smiled as the sun warmed her face, more at ease on a bike than she ever was on her feet. When she rode, no one could see her limp.

She bumped through the alley, turned left on Murkle Street, and waved to Deputy Calvin Greenwood, who was also a cousin. Calvin was coming out of the Divine Bakery with two boxes of doughnuts in his arms and headed for his patrol car.

Smiling, she waved a hand, paused in the middle of the road.

"Morning, Nat," he called. "Lots of love letters this week?"

"Usual Monday morning. Cupid's got his hands full."

"That's a good thing, right? Keeps our economy rolling." Cal balanced the doughnut boxes in one hand while he opened his cruiser door with the other.

"You can say that again."

"Maybe you should write a letter yourself."

"To Cupid?"

"Yeah."

"Why would I do that?"

"So you'd have a date to mine and Maria's wedding next month."

Natalie snorted good-naturedly. "Cal, there's no such thing as Cupid."

"Shh." He pressed an index finger to his lips. "Don't let that get out. Maria thinks that's how she caught me."

"Any sign of Red?" Natalie asked him about her long-term boarder who'd disappeared four days ago without a word of warning. It wasn't the first time Red had gone missing, so she was trying not to worry too much, but he'd left all his possessions behind.

"Haven't seen him, but you know these war vets."

Calvin shrugged. "They ain't like regular folks. Red can take care of himself."

"But you're still keeping an eye out for him?"

"'Course."

"Now you're just patting me on the head."

"He's a drifter at heart, Natty. I warned you about that when he moved in."

"That's the issue. He doesn't have anyone else to worry about him."

"Your heart's too big, cousin. It can't hold the whole world."

"Doesn't have to hold the whole world. Just my corner of it."

"Funny that he disappeared the day the rent was due."

"If he just left, why didn't he take his things?"

"Tell you what, I'll do some more asking around," Calvin promised. "Now I gotta get to work. Have a good day."

"Don't eat too many doughnuts," she hollered over her shoulder as she took off again, the bike picking up speed on the downhill slope.

She had so much to do that morning—take the letters to the community center for Aunt Carol Ann to sort out, cut fresh flowers for the guest rooms, make sure Zoey got up in time to make it to her anatomy class at Sul Ross, greet the guests at breakfast, order organic multigrain flour before her cook, Pearl, actually followed through on her idle threats to quit, and make a decision about Red. She didn't want to give his room away, but if he wasn't coming back, she needed to rent it out.

Natalie had put off the decisions because she kept thinking that Red would pop back up as he usually did, but something felt different this time. Lately, he'd become more reclusive than usual and he'd taken to wearing a John Deere ball cap and dark sunglasses ninety percent of the time, as if he was trying to vanish behind the thin disguise. Maybe he had just walked away, leaving her on the fence about what to do.

After she finished all those morning tasks, she had to head back to the community center for lunch and the tri-weekly meeting of the Cupid committee volunteers, where they gathered to answer the letters written to Cupid. This Monday she wasn't looking forward to the meeting. The other women were bound to ask why she hadn't already answered Shot Through the Heart's letter.

Why? Because she couldn't think of a single word of useful advice.

Her hand strayed again to the letter in her pocket. She fingered the edges, mentally toying with her reply. She wanted so badly to tell the letter writer that there was really such a thing as love at first sight, but Natalie was having her own crisis of faith.

It was the central conflict she wrestled with every time she answered a love letter. Dishing out advice when she had no clue what she was talking about. She'd expressed her self-doubts to the group, but they'd waved away her concerns.

"Listen to your heart," they always said. "You know the truth, deep down inside."

Yeah? Well, her heart was telling her she had no business responding to the letters, considering that she'd never been in love. She'd wanted to be in love, had imagined it happening to her a thousand times. How could she not, in a town chockful of romantic legends?

She'd dated six men in her entire life, had kissed four of them but slept with none. She'd been holding out for that one special man.

Except he'd never come.

Waiting had been easy enough when she was younger. She'd been starry-eyed and hopeful. Her limp had made her shy and self-conscious, but she was convinced that the right man would see through all that if she only held out for him.

Then the years rolled away.

She'd gotten swept up in running the B&B and riding herd on her sister, Zoey, but she'd kept the faith. But then as the years kept clicking by, she'd started having doubts. What if it was all bunk? What if there wasn't one right man for her? What if she'd missed out on some genuinely nice guys simply because she didn't give them a chance because she'd never felt the magic?

Now, on the precipice of turning thirty, her virginity was an albatross. An embarrassment. How did you bring that up in conversation on a date? *Would you like to be the one to deflower me? Take me for my maiden voyage? Pop my cherry?*

But this was the part that really bothered her.

What if she just got on with her life, gave up her shaky belief in love at first sight and all that other romantic stuff, found a decent guy, married him, and then The One finally came along?

Then again, what if The One never showed up? Was she expected to live her entire life without sex, without a husband, without kids while she waited around on a fantasy?

She was of two minds. Her heart desperately wanted to believe, but at her core, she was a pragmatist.

"Just you wait," Aunt Carol Ann would say. "When it hits, you'll know. There will be absolutely no doubt."

Natalie wished she could get her faith back, but the last few years her aunt's promise sounded as much of a fairy tale as Cupid with his bow and arrow, flying around shooting people through the heart.

"You're too practical for your own good, Natty," Junie Mae told her at least once a month. Usually when they sat on Junie Mae's front porch sipping sweet iced tea spiked with lemon and eating sugar cookies. "You need to brush up against Zoey, see if some of her spontaneity will rub off on you."

That hurt.

Natalie didn't particularly enjoy being the sensible sister, but someone had to be the responsible one and since she was the older one, she'd been elected by default. Sure, she'd love to be like Zoey, twenty-two and still working on finishing her college degree because she'd flakily changed her major four times. Her sister had dabbled in—and ditched—criminal justice, natural resource management, and musical theater. Now she was hung up on the idea of being an archeologist.

Solid career plan, sis.

Her bike clipped along at twenty-five miles an hour, kept pace with her racing mind, until she slowed to round the corner onto Main, and suddenly there he was, big and unexpected.

A naked man.

No, not naked, her brain corrected, catching up to what her eyes saw, just gloriously shirtless.

Speechless, she stopped pedaling.

He was in the empty Piggly Wiggly parking lot, head down, bending over a big black motorcycle as he tinkered with the engine. His torso was leanly muscled, darkly tanned, and glistening with sweat in the early morning sunlight.

The hair on his head was the color of a raven's wing, so black it looked almost blue, and curled unkempt around his ears and down the nape of his neck. His powerful biceps flexed as he worked. A sexy dark blue tattoo graced his left upper arm. His abdominal muscles were taut as drum skins. A pair of black jeans hung low on his hips, and he wore well-used cowboy boots.

His masculinity was palpable and she could have sworn she caught a faint whiff of his scent, aftershave and motor oil and something sensually seductive—danger. But that was foolishness. Danger didn't have a smell, and besides, she was yards away.

His cheekbones, cast in shadows, looked sharp as blades. His chin was pure granite and peppered with stubble. Natalie's practicality vanished as wild fantasy took her hostage with tumbling images—leather tool belts, muscle cars, Desert Eagle pistols, campfires, and mountain lions.

Honest to Pete, she didn't know men could look like that outside of movie reels. Her jaw dropped, and all the breath left her lungs. She stared, stunned.

Natalie saw him in a freeze-frame flash of blind clarity. A click-whirl snapshot caught in time. Her mouth went instantly dry and her heart slam-pumped blood through her ears. Oh my. Oh dear. Oh no. He's here.

He reached for a red rag to wipe his hands, straightening to his full height. He stood well over six feet tall, sturdily built and breath-stealingly impressive.

The moment hung in the air, tremulous as a spiderweb spun under eaves in a rainstorm, but bright, sharp, clear, and unmistakably special.

As Natalie coasted past, their gazes locked.

In that fraction of a blink, she memorized everything about him. Eyes the color of coal, chiseled jaw, Olympic shoulders, hard everywhere, all of him bottled into an explosive package.

Boom!

His eyes pierced into her like an arrow's point, took her, owned her.

Dear God! What was this?

A lazy, wolfish, one-sided grin spread slowly across his face.

Just one look and all the mysteries of the universe were answered. Every nerve ending in her body tingled to life as if she'd been asleep for a hundred years and was awakening for the very first time.

It's him!

He was a stranger to Cupid. She did not know him, had never met him, and yet, in that hushed sweet second, her body knew something that her mind did not. She felt him deep in her center.

At last.

He'd found her at last.

It struck her like a fever, hot and rushed, an emotion so sudden and sweet that her brain fumbled and stupidly came up with the word "love."

Did she dare think it? How foolish to think such a thing of a stranger. No. Not love. Love at first sight was absurd, right?

And yet...and yet...

Panic spread through her as more images fell in on her. His big, black cowboy boots parked underneath her bed, her sunny yellow Keds lined up beside them. Warm quilts on a cold winter night. Silver lightning that lingered—burning and brilliant. His hard mouth crushed against her soft one, tasting rich and decadent as pure dark chocolate.

What did it all mean?

She had no explanation for what she was feeling. It was too blissful. Too good. It scared the living crap out of her.

Thankfully, gratefully, she'd already sped past him. She was too terrified to glance back.

A mirage, she told herself. A dream. Not real. He could not be real.

The blood had drained from her face, leaving her cheeks quite cold. Ghostly. The road flattened, her pace slowed. She tried to get her legs moving again, but they were cement, too heavy to move.

Craziness.

This was sheer craziness. She'd lived in Cupid too long and even though she didn't believe in the love legends, apparently the stories had been like the creeping damp, silently, insidiously closing in on her to culminate in this…this… What the hell was *this*?

She swallowed, listening to the quickening of her pulse, felt the blood rush fierily back to her cheeks, and suddenly, she could not see. Oh, everything was still there—the trees, the buildings, and the vehicles—but the image imprinted on her retina was not of the scenery before her. Instead, his face blotted out everything else, like a full solar eclipse turning high noon to midnight.

Music filled her vision—violins and saxophones, pianos and drums, Vivaldi and Mozart, Pachelbel and frickin' Bonnie Tyler. Colors surrounded him—a rainbow of pleasure—crimson, azure, olive, lavender, saffron.

Could she be having a stroke?

Yes. A stroke. That might explain the wild euphoria, the ceaseless pounding of her heart, the inability to breathe. Why couldn't she breathe?

"When it hits, you'll know." Aunt Carol Ann's words rang in her head. "There will be absolutely no doubt."

Dear Cupid, the most awesomely awful thing has happened.

Dazzled, Dade Vega blinked and she was gone.

He shook his head, wondering if he'd imagined the phantom beauty in yellow on the pale blue Schwinn, looking like springtime in Paris. Why did it feel as if the bottom had just dropped out of his world?

A hard tightening gripped him in all the right places. He scrubbed a sheepish palm over his face. Purposefully, he stepped to the curb and glanced down the street.

Nothing. Nobody.

She was gone, if she'd ever really been there at all.

It wouldn't be the first time he'd had a hallucination, but it would be the first time since the head injury he'd suffered in Afghanistan four years ago.

Ah shit. Man, he couldn't backslide, not after all the progress he'd made. If he was backsliding, it's had everything to do with Red's disappearance.

Funny how easy it was for the past to reach up and punch you in the face when you least expected it.

Honestly, he was half hoping that she *was* a hallucination because that would rightly explain the berserk push-pull between his head and his heart. He felt a

rushing need to go after her, spill his guts, tell her who
he was and how he felt. One look in her enigmatic sky
blue eyes and he felt as if love beckoned him with open
arms, while his soul had dug in its heels and jerked
back, too guilty of damage and sin to believe anything
so good could be true.

He knew better.

Life had kicked Dade in the teeth far too many times
for him to trust it. He'd learned that happiness, by and
large, was a mirage and it was best not to romanticized.

But the woman's image lingered, leaving an indel-
ible imprint, and he found himself thinking about a
soft mattress on a hot sweaty night, sheets tangled up
in their entwined limbs. He could almost hear her calling out his name in ecstasy, and dammit if he didn't
start to get hard.

False, this vision, he knew it, but he could still see
her delicate lightness, her smile, modest and a little shy,
but as welcoming as warm socks on a cold winter's day.
A tumble of soft brown hair floating out behind her like
a cloud as she rode past.

For that instant when she'd looked at him and he'd
looked at her, one lonely soul connecting with another,
Dade had thought, *It's her*.

It was a stupid thing to think, he was well aware of
that, but he'd thought it nonetheless.

Forget it. Move on.

Moving on was the only way he'd survived, another
lesson courtesy of the Navy SEALs. It was harder to hit
a moving target. Red had proven the point. His friend
had stopped in Cupid, stayed, gotten comfortable, and
now he'd gone missing after texting Dade a Mayday
message three days earlier.

Tanked.

The secret code only they understood. It meant *I'm in trouble deep, trust no one.*

That's why he was here in this dead-end, desert mountain town. To find out what had happened to his foster brother who'd also served with him in the SEALs. They'd joined the navy together the day after they graduated from high school, and Red was the only person in the whole world that Dade gave a shit about. Because of that, he'd taken a leave of absence from the security detail he'd been on in New Orleans.

There were no commercial flights into Cupid and since the nearest big airport was in El Paso, two hundred miles away, he decided to simply make the drive. Waiting around in airports made him feel helpless. At least when he was on the road, he was making progress. Unfortunately, he'd been out on an oil derrick in the Gulf of Mexico when the text had come through, and it had taken him this long to arrive.

He was terrified that Red had gone off his meds and was in the grips of full-blown, post-traumatic stress flashbacks. After the Mayday message, Red had not answered any of Dade's calls or texts. Tough as he was on the outside, his buddy was as emotionally fragile as an eight-year-old.

Dade had to be careful. He couldn't afford to assume it was simply PTSD. What if Red had stumbled across something or found himself in some other kind of trouble? He was here to retrace his buddy's steps. The best way to do that was to ease himself into the community and see what he could find out.

First his junkie parents, and then the foster care system, had taught him that trusting people was a damn dumb thing to do, so his plan was to keep his connection to Red a secret until he got the lay of the land and figured out where his buddy had gone.

Which was another reason he was particularly disturbed by his overwhelming reaction to the woman on the bicycle. It simply wasn't smart.

There she was again, clogging up his mind—that pretty oval face, big blue eyes, and full pink lips. He imagined she smelled like honeysuckle. When he and Red were kids, they used to pluck the white blooms from the honeysuckle vines that grew up the wooden privacy fence of their foster home, break them open, and suck out the drop of sweet nectar.

Kissing her would be like that.

Honeysuckle woman, that's how he thought of her now.

For Chrissakes, Vega, knock it off. If she's even real, she's way out of your reach for so many more reasons than you can count.

He might as well wish for the Hope Diamond. He was as equally likely to possess it. Dade pulled a palm down his face, winced at the prickle. He hadn't shaved since the previous day and he haired up fast thanks to his father's Hispanic blood, Satan rest the bastard's soul.

"Screw it," he muttered, and wrestled into the T-shirt he'd stripped off while working on his motorcycle.

The trip through the desert and up the Davis Mountains had messed with the Harley's timing and he'd had to disassemble the gas tank to get to the timing belt. The job had taken over an hour and he'd been putting the chopper back together when she'd ridden past.

He'd stopped underneath the security lamps in the

Piggly Wiggly parking lot because it had still been dark when he'd started the job. Dade packed up his tools, stuffed them in the compartment underneath the seat, and wondered what honeysuckle woman's name was.

Forget her already.

He strapped on his helmet, slung his leg over the machine, reached down to turn on the check valve. Instantly, fuel poured from the tank, soaking the leg of his pants in gasoline.

Dammit!

In his stunned enchantment with the woman on the bicycle, he'd neglected to reattach the hose.

Chapter 2

*Love at first sight is a very scary proposition
when a stranger instantly becomes an intimate.*
                                        —*Millie Greenwood*

After Natalie dropped the letters off at the community center, she made her way down the Main Street sidewalk, past Tilly's Dry Cleaners and Tailoring Shop, Cupid's Bow Tea Room, and Cox Realty—all of which were closed at six-thirty in the morning—before she stopped outside Ticket to Ride travel agency.

Conrad York, the prim, debonair ex-Vermonter who'd moved to the arid climate of southwest Texas on his doctor's advice, owned the travel agency. Every Sunday evening, he changed out the posters in the window, and every Monday morning, Natalie stopped by to see what destination awaited the plucky traveler.

This week, he featured Paris.

Hand to her chest, Natalie stared at the montage of the City of Lights—the Eiffel Tower, the Champs-Élysées, the Arc de Triomphe, the Louvre, Versailles, brightly colored umbrellas over wrought-iron tables at outdoor cafes. She could smell the French bread, hear Edith Piaf crooning "Non, Je Ne Regrette Rien," taste chocolate napoleons, see the *Mona Lisa*, feel the cobblestones against her feet. In Paris it would be so easy to have a wild, passionate affair that wasn't meant to last; the perfect place to re-create herself.

She heaved a little sigh, reached out, and pressed her fingertips against the glass, touching the top of the Eiffel Tower.

Someday. One day. But in her heart, she knew that day would never come.

Loneliness shuddered through her like a cold draft swooping down off Swayback Mountain on a frosty December day. She hunched her shoulders and stared at her reflection in the glass.

A stranger would see a tall, slender woman in a bright yellow dress, wearing an ugly polypropylene ankle-foot orthosis (unaffectionately known as an AFO to those who were forced to depend on them) on her right leg, and unstylish sneakers. They might never catch a glimpse of the haunted expression that lurked beneath the surface of her cornflower eyes. She worked hard to forget the past, but at the most unexpected times it could rise up and clasp her in a sorrowful embrace.

Natalie had been born with the weight of tradition on her shoulders, the oldest daughter, of the oldest daughter, of the oldest daughter of Millie Greenwood, the woman who started it all.

The entire history of Cupid was wrapped up in her family. It was a smaller-scale, but no less heavy, version of being a Disney, a Rockefeller, or a Barrymore. Not a responsibility one could shrug off like a coat. People depended on her. She couldn't afford to be selfish.

For the most part, she accepted her role without complaint, but once in a while it would have been nice to forget who she was, pack her things, and run away.

Fly, fly away.

Flying.

And then there it was. The dark memory clutching at her throat.

It was her ninth birthday and a clear summer day just like this one. Daddy, laughing and carrying two-year-old Zoey on his shoulders, walked across the tarmac of Cupid's tiny private airfield toward the twin-engine Cessna that he'd been flying since he was seventeen.

Zoey giggled and tugged his hair. Natalie had skipped alongside their mother, who swung a wicker picnic basket between them and whistled "Zip-a-Dee-Doo-Dah."

Natalie's hair had been plaited into braids and clipped in place with pink Hello Kitty barrettes. She wore blue jeans with the cuffs turned up, a red shirt with the appliqué of a watermelon on the front, the black buttons shaped like seeds, and a pair of red polka dot Jelly shoes. How she loved those shoes.

It was the last time she remembered being truly, blissfully happy.

Daddy, can I do the flight check with you and Mommy?

Not this time, strap your sister into the backseat. Make sure the buckle is tight.

How come I always hafta take care of her?

Because you're a good big sister, we depend on you. Now do as you're told.

Scowling, she'd taken Zoey's hand and led her toward the airplane steps. Her sister had dawdled, stopped to pick up a Cheeto—the puffy kind—abandoned on the ground.

"Yuck, that's nasty, put it down." She knocked the cheese puff from her sister's hand and Zoey started wailing. Natalie had to drag her kicking and crying into the plane. Their relationship had been pretty well like that ever since, Zoey getting into trouble, Natalie bailing her out, and Zoey getting pissy about it.

She finally got her sister buckled in, and a few minutes later, their parents climbed inside the plane. Mommy settled the picnic basket between Natalie and Zoey. Natalie could smell the bologna and mayonnaise sandwiches with thick slabs of cheddar cheese and dill pickles on them. Her mouth watered.

Daddy took off and climbed into the marshmallow clouds crowning the Davis Mountains; the sound of the propeller engine was a lulling drone. Zoey had fallen asleep in her seat. Mommy and Daddy were teasing each other, and Daddy leaned over several times to give Mommy a quick kiss on the cheek.

Mommy would giggle and kiss him back and say, "Jimmy McCleary, keep your lips to yourself."

Natalie smiled and thought about the chocolate cupcakes with pink icing that Mommy had packed in the picnic basket, and everything was perfect.

The marshmallow clouds suddenly turned black and out of nowhere a gust of wind blew in as the hot air from the desert valley floor mixed with the cool air flowing down the mountains.

The little airplane bobbled.

From his reflection in the rearview mirror, Natalie saw Daddy's face go pale and serious. He gripped the yoke with both hands.

"James?" Mommy asked, her voice coming out thin as string cheese.

"We gotta go back."

Disappointment weighed heavy in Natalie's stomach. "No," she wailed. "We're supposed to have a picnic for my birthday!"

"Hush!" Her mother shot her a fierce look over her shoulder, but there was terror in her eyes.

Natalie's stomach rose up into her throat and she got a creepy, wriggly feeling, the way she did last year when her cousin Melody told her to close her eyes and hold out her hands and she'd give her a big surprise. Natalie had done it, but when she opened her eyes, she'd seen a ribbon snake curled in her palm, flicking its tongue at her. She'd screamed and thrown down the snake. She wanted to scream now, but she was too scared. The plane was bumping and diving and buzzing. Daddy was cussing under his breath, and Mommy was hanging on to her seat with both hands.

"Mommy?"

"It's okay, baby. It's okay."

But it wasn't okay. The plane was going down, down, down, spinning and twirling the way Natalie did when she twisted the chains up on the park swing tight and then let them go.

"James, what is it?" her mother whispered.

"Wind shears." Daddy's voice was tight as he battled the yoke.

Anxiously, Natalie tugged on her braid; the Hello Kitty barrette sprang open in her hand.

Impossibly, Zoey was still asleep.

Daddy fought as hard as he could, but the angry wind pushed down on them, and through the window, she could see the mountain become the ground.

They hit so hard Natalie's teeth jammed together and she bit her tongue. She tasted blood, heard Zoey cry out, but she could not see because everything went black.

Sometime later, she became aware of a deep, biting pain in her right leg and cold rain hitting her face.

Zoey's sobs were soft.

Natalie's eyes popped open and she was startled to find they were upside down in a tree. The top of the plane was gone, the misshapen metal razor-sharp. She was held in place by the seat belt, her hair dangling past her head. The picnic basket had spilled open and bologna sandwiches were strewn across the ground below. She counted them. One, two, three, four.

A chocolate cupcake lay smashed against her lap. The rain washed the icing into a gooey pink smear. She tried to move but the pain in her leg shot up hot and mean through her hip, and she got sick to her stomach.

She glanced around for her father, but she did not see him. Where was Daddy?

Her mother's seat was gone out of the plane, but then she spied Mommy nestled against a tree branch, moaning quietly. That's when Natalie realized that the tree branch was poking right through her mother's chest.

"Mommy?" she whimpered.

"Natalie," her mother whispered. "Are you okay?"

"My leg hurts."

"Can you see Zoey?"

"Uh-huh."

"How is she?"

Why couldn't Mommy see her? She was right there, staring at Zoey. Couldn't she see? "She looks all right to me."

"Natalie?"

"Yes, Mommy?"

"You're going to have to be a very brave girl."

"I'm scared."

"I know you are, baby, but listen to me. Promise me that no matter what happens, you'll look after Zoey."

"I promise."

"Good girl." Her mother's voice was so weak she could barely hear her now.

"Mommy?"

She didn't answer.

"Mommy!" Natalie screamed.

Mommy's eyes were closed and she did not speak again.

The rain came down harder.

Natalie sobbed. She wanted out of this seat. Wanted down from this tree. Wanted her leg to stop hurting. Wanted her mother and her father to take care of everything. Wanted the sweet, happy day back the way it was before the storm took them down.

Daddy was gone and Mommy wasn't talking anymore. It was up to her to fix things. She would climb down from the tree, help Zoey out of her seat, and go get Gram. Gram would know what to do.

The rescue workers found them at dusk. Natalie was on her butt with Zoey in her lap, dragging them over the rough, rocky terrain of Mount Livermore, tears streaming down her face as she fought against the blinding pain. She was going to take care of her baby sister no matter what. She'd promised Mommy.

Later, after she'd gone through surgery to have pins put in her leg that had been broken in twenty-two places, the doctor told her relatives that he had no idea how she'd managed to get as far as she did.

"It must have been excruciating, but the body," he'd said, sounding amazed, "can do miraculous things under extreme stress."

Her parents had died on that mountain, leaving Natalie and Zoey orphaned, but not unwanted. Their loving grandparents and a bevy of aunts and uncles had raised them, but Natalie never forgot her solemn vow to her dying mother. She would always look after Zoey.

Natalie's leg twinged at the memory and she ran a hand down her thigh. That day had marked her forever, set her life in cement. She was ingrained in Cupid, Texas. There was no getting out, no escape, even if she wanted to, but she knew who she was and she accepted it, although once in a while a travel poster had the power to make her yearn for the impossible.

Putting the past firmly in the past, she got on her bike and rode home.

The McCleary mansion was in the older part of town on Stone Street, where the yards were massive, the fences white picket, and the live oaks stately. A decade earlier, when Cupid had rezoned Stone Street from residential to commercial, many of the grand homes that fronted Lake Cupid had been turned into businesses. Junie Mae had morphed Farnsworth House into a hair salon and spa. The old Van Zandt place became a chiropractor's office. The Harris manor was now a tourist information center, and Natalie had converted her house into a bed-and-breakfast.

Transforming the McCleary ancestral home had been an act of necessity. While Natalie came from a long line of well-to-do McClearys, her father, she'd discovered when she'd been old enough to understand, had been something of a spendthrift, and he'd died owing more than a million dollars. There'd been life insurance policies on her parents, of course, but by the time Natalie was twenty, most of the monies had been exhausted and the only asset she had left was the house.

Tourists frequented Cupid, drawn by the romantic legend, the vineyards, the caverns, the mineral springs, the game fishing in Lake Cupid, and MacDonald Observatory, which offered some of the darkest night skies in the United States.

Natalie figured, why not give the tourists a place to stay? Armed with an interest-free loan from her grandmother Rose and advice from practically everyone in town, Natalie had hired a cook, a housekeeper, and a gardener and set about becoming a businesswoman.

For seven years, her business had thrived and she'd thrown herself into being the best hostess she could be; her B&B even garnered a starred review from *Texas Monthly.*

Then the corporations had sniffed out Cupid and everything changed. Hilton bought up land on the other side of the lake and erected a posh four-star resort hotel. Halfway between Cupid and the mineral springs, a developer built lavish vacation condos. The twin projects had siphoned off seventy percent of Natalie's revenue.

Unskilled at anything else, she'd had little option but

to take in long-term boarders. While she kept her three best rooms for tourists, sometimes she felt like she was running more of a halfway house or an assisted living facility than anything else.

She came in through the back entrance of the mansion that was a bastard combination of Greek Revival and Southern Plantation. The house needed a new paint job, but it would cost over two thousand dollars and she just didn't have the spare cash right now.

Soon, she promised herself as the screen door snapped closed behind her.

Oh good, Zoey was in the breakfast nook adjacent to the kitchen, eating a bowl of Cap'n Crunch while she leaned over Lars Bakke's shoulder as he worked the Sunday crossword puzzle from the *Alpine Gazette*. The B&B guests took their meals in the formal dining room where breakfast was served buffet style, but the long-term boarders ate where the family did.

"Eleven-letter word for bogus," Lars said, tapping his pencil against his chin.

"Counterfeit," Zoey supplied.

"Smart girl." Lars painstakingly filled in the cross-word grid, gripping his pencil so low on the shaft that his fingers encircled the lead.

Zoey wore pink short shorts, a pink and white halter top, and white woven sandals that looked familiar. Her straight, chestnut-colored hair was cut in a striking asymmetrical style that looked cute on her, but would have made Natalie's thick, wavy hair look like a drunkard had attacked her with pruning shears.

"You're awake," Natalie said to Zoey.

"Don't make it sound like it's such a miracle. I've got a ten o'clock class."

"I'm surprised you remembered."

"Have you ever had your blood type checked?" Zoey asked.

Natalie blinked. Her sister had such a mercurial mind it was sometimes hard to follow her train of thought. "What?"

"We're checking our blood type in class today."

"No, I don't think I've ever had my blood type checked."

"They probably checked it when you had surgery."

Natalie shrugged. "Maybe. No one told me."

"I'm betting your blood type is sour apple." Zoey loved odd comparisons.

"Oh, I get it. Not a serious question, but rather a sarcastic dig at me."

"It wouldn't kill you to lighten up once in a while." Zoey straightened, polished off her last bite of cereal, and left her empty bowl on the table.

Natalie crossed her arms, stared at the bowl, and then shifted her gaze back to Zoey.

"Okay, all right, I'll take it to the kitchen." Zoey carried off the bowl.

Lars set down his paper, cocked his gray head, his reading glasses dangling low on his nose. "Are you all right, Natty?"

Lars was Natalie's oldest long-term boarder. He was from Norway and had once commanded a tramp steamer. He was in his late sixties, retired from the Department of Motor Vehicles, stood six-foot-five, loved quoting Eric Hoffer, and smelled persistently of pine. Every year his daughter sent him lutefisk for Christmas, and afterward, no one would go near him for a week. How he'd ended up in this arid part of Texas, so far from the sea, was one of the great mysteries of Cupid, although rumor had it that a broken heart had brought him here.

Natalie forced a smile. "Yes, sure, why wouldn't I be?"

"You look…" He paused, and his blue eyes grew pensive. "Like something happened."

"Nothing happened." That is unless you counted falling in love at first sight. *C'mon. Get over that.* She had not fallen in love at first sight. It had been startling sexual chemistry, plain and simple. Really? All these years she'd longed to fall in love and now that it appeared to be happening, she was backpedaling faster than a politician caught sexting.

"Moonstruck," Lars said. His perceptiveness unnerved her. Could he really see it on her? Was it that noticeable?

"The sun's out. No moon to be struck by." Natalie jammed her hands in her pockets, fingered Shot Through the Heart's letter. If she was anything, she was lust struck. But she wasn't even that. Not really. She would never see half-naked biker dude again. He was passing through and she was forever rooted in Cupid.

"Did you meet someone?" Zoey asked, coming back into the room with a sly smile on her face.

"No." It was true. She *hadn't* actually met the guy, but dammit, her cheeks heated.

"We lie the loudest when we lie to ourselves." Lars dished up a Hofferism.

"I'll keep that in mind."

"Have you got a secret boyfriend?" Zoey cocked her head, looked intrigued.

"Are those my Brian Atwoods?" Natalie asked, trying to derail her.

Zoey put one foot behind her as if she could hide her feet. "You can't wear them."

"That's not the point."

"It's just plain weird that you buy designer shoes when you can't wear them."

Natalie hardened her jaw. She knew it was foolish to buy shoes she would never wear. She couldn't explain why she did it. Owning them made her feel...well... *normal*. Other women got to own beautiful shoes. Why not her?

"What's the use of letting them go to waste?" Zoey argued.

"You should have asked my permission."

"Ha! Like you would have said yes."

Natalie sank her hands on her hips. "So you just take them?"

"A man is likely to mind his own business when it is worth minding. When it is not, he takes his mind off his own meaningless affairs by minding other people's business," Lars said.

Natalie raised an eyebrow. "More Hoffer?"

"I met him once, you know," Lars mused, pocketing his reading glasses and getting to his feet. "In a Greenwich Village coffee shop. Fittingly enough, it was called Destiny. Destiny's Coffee Shop. It had flamingo pink and black checkered tile floors. I was young and Hoffer was old but we clicked instantly. Magnificent man."

"How's the boat coming?" she asked to sidetrack him from more talk of Hoffer. Lars was having a handcrafted sailboat built in Mexico, in hopes of living out his dream of sailing around the world before he died.

He shook his head, looked so baleful that she wished she hadn't brought it up. "On hold for now until I can come up with another installment payment."

"How are you going to get the money?"

"I have a couple of schemes up my sleeve."

At that moment, Pearl popped out of the kitchen, the smell of yeast bread, bacon, and French roast popping with her. She wore a V-neck tank top that was two sizes too small for her 44 DDD chest, green Bermuda shorts, and a camo-colored bandana wrapped around her short, spiky, gray hair. Her feet were shod in brown Doc Martens with black ankle socks, and deep, purple-blue veins bulged at her shins from a lifetime of standing at stoves.

Natalie had no idea how old she was. Pearl could have been anywhere from a hard forty to a light sixty. Someone told her once that they'd heard Pearl had spent time in Gatesville prison, but Natalie didn't put stock in gossip, and besides, other than her crotchety attitude, Pearl was a model employee.

"You order that flour yet?" Pearl grunted. "I can't make a decent multigrain pâte à choux without it." The way she said the French word sounded like a sneeze.

"Not yet."

"If I don't have that flour in time for the Fourth of July weekend, I'm quittin'," she grumbled, and waved a red rubber KitchenAid spatula for effect. Pearl was the most cantankerous woman she'd ever met, but she was also the best cook in Cupid. "And I mean it this time."

"I'm on it."

"That's what you said yesterday." Pearl glowered.

"You can discover what your enemy fears most by observing the means he uses to frighten you," quoted Lars.

"You want me to take them off?" Zoey interrupted,

reaching down to unbuckle a sandal. " 'Cause I'll take 'em off if that's what you want."

In the back of her mind, Natalie heard a deep-voiced male narrator say, *Natalie McCleary, this is your life.* It was small-minded of her to get pissy over the shoes. Someone might as well get some use out of them. "No, go, wear them in good health."

"Thanks." Zoey picked up her anatomy textbook from the table and headed out the door. "You're not such a bad big sister."

Pearl took her red spatula and went back to the kitchen, while Lars said something about taking his constitutional along the river and slipped out the back door.

From the other side of the wall came the sound of guests entering the formal dining room. Natalie went to greet her visitors—which included two older women traveling together, a young newlywed couple, and a middle-aged gentleman who said he was writing a book about the Marfa Lights.

The nearby town of Marfa was famous for inexplicable "ghost" lights that appeared in the night sky and defied scientific explanation. It was something of a curiosity. Several movies had been filmed in Marfa, including *Giant* with Rock Hudson and Elizabeth Taylor. Natalie's great-aunt Delia had gotten the movie stars' autographs and they were framed and displayed on the wall in her foyer.

Natalie shook hands, made pleasantries, and suggested outings to the guests. Welcoming people to Cupid was her favorite part of the job.

"So," said the female half of the young married couple. She was a trim blonde with a pert upturned nose dotted with freckles, and earnest brown eyes. "Tell us the story of how the town of Cupid got its name. I heard it involves a romantic legend."

The young woman threw a besotted look at her husband as they filled their plates from the chafing dishes on the buffet. He responded by filching a piece of bacon off her plate. She swatted at him playfully and they laughed in unison. Seeing them together tugged at Natalie's heartstrings. Would she ever have that easy camaraderie with a mate? Maybe. Could be. If this morning was the real deal. How would she know? And what was she supposed to do if it was the real deal? Biker dude was most likely halfway to El Paso by now.

"Yes, please do tell us. We love a ripping good yarn, don't we, Mazey?" one of the older ladies chimed in as she maneuvered to the table, a cane in one hand and her plate in the other.

It was a story Natalie told every day, sometimes numerous times, but no one ever had to twist her arm to get her to relate it again. She was proud of her hometown and her heritage. Besides, the legend was her edge over the four-star hotel and spa condos.

"Well," she said, sitting down with the guests, lowering her voice and glancing at each of them in turn, drawing them into her crafted narrative. "It all started with a hanging."

Chapter 3

Until he appeared I never knew what I was waiting for.

—Millie Greenwood

"Right after the Civil War, when Cupid was still just a settlement, there were three times as many women living here as men. And the few men that were around were either too young or too old for military service," Natalie told her guests.

The sunlight fell across the table. Mazey squinted. Her companion shaded her eyes with her hand. Natalie got up to close the blinds. Cars motored by on Stone Street, and there came the sound of a motorcycle engine.

Natalie's pulse quickened. It was a Harley! How fast could her heart gallop before she had a heart attack? Riveted. Right there to the spot. The Harley came into view. Natalie held her breath.

It was a gray-haired guy with a ZZ Top beard and a red "For Sale" sign posted on the back of his Harley. The local taxidermist, Beau Jenkins.

It was not he. Not her guy.

With trembling fingers, she snapped the blinds closed. Breathe. Crazy. This was craziness. Then again, wasn't that what love at first sight was all about, an illogical craziness that somehow turned completely rational in the face of overwhelming emotion?

"Common problem post–Civil War," said the guy who was writing the book. "All the good ones got picked off."

"There were also a lot of outlaws and deserters roaming the area, and the local caverns often served as a hideout." Natalie limped over to close the cover on the chafing dish of bacon that had been left open.

"Bad boys," whispered the blond newlywed, and gave a little shiver.

Her husband hooked her around the shoulder with the crook of his elbow and pulled her closer to him.

"Because of all the outlaws, there were also a lot of hangings." Natalie rearranged the paper napkins on the buffet table into a pretty pattern. There. Nice and orderly again.

Mazey put a hand to her mouth. "My goodness, how barbaric!"

"Function of the times," said the writer. "Back then, they were free with the noose."

Natalie slipped back into her chair. "Anyway, because of the man shortage and the preponderance of outlaws, someone got the bright idea that a man could be saved from being hanged if a woman from the settlement would agree to marry him."

"Rehabilitation through forced marriage." The writer laughed.

"It's just like in that Jack Nicholson movie *Goin' South*," said Mazey's companion.

"Exactly." Natalie smiled. "We have the movie available on demand. It's the ultimate marriage-of-convenience story. Jack Nicholson doesn't get hanged and Mary Steenburgen gets someone to do her manual labor. And then nature takes its course. Similar story here in real life between Mingus Dill and Louisa Hendricks."

"And it was love at first sight?" The blonde cut her eyes over at her husband. He chucked her under the chin affectionately.

"Hardly," Natalie said. "Mingus was a good-looking man and quite charming. He had a way with women, but his talent got him into trouble. When a husband in Fort Worth caught Mingus in bed with his wife, he came at him with a meat cleaver. Mingus barely made it out the window with his hide attached. The husband was in a blind rage and came after him. In order to make a quick getaway, Mingus snagged the man's horse, took off into the night, and fled to the Chihuahuan Desert."

The writer took a small spiral notebook from his front shirt pocket and started taking notes.

"It turned out the woman's husband was a marshal and feeling vindictive. Mingus was tagged as a horse thief on his wanted poster." Natalie shifted in her seat, and the antique chair creaked.

"Horse thievery was a hanging offense," the writer supplied.

"Sometime later, Mingus showed up here and caused a stir among the ladies, but eventually someone recognized him. One of the women warned him to get out of town, and once again, he barely made good his escape. A posse was hot on his trail," she went on.

"How thrilling." Mazey bit into a cinnamon roll.

The writer took a big gulp of coffee and went back to his scribbling.

"Not for Mingus. He was a lover, not a fighter." Natalie got up again, retrieved the coffee carafe, and topped off the writer's cup.

"Thanks," he said.

Natalie held up the carafe. "Anyone else want more coffee?"

The bride shook her head.

The groom said, "Orange juice?"

Natalie retrieved the hand-squeezed orange juice from the iced bucket on the sideboard.

"Mingus reminds me of Jake Spoon from *Lonesome Dove*," Mazey's traveling companion said. "Remember him?"

"Oh yes." Mazey fanned herself with her free hand. "Jake Spoon was a hottie. I would marry him in a nanosecond to save him from the gallows."

Natalie didn't point out that she was mixing the leading men in her fantasies. She gathered the guests' empty plates and piled them into a stack at the end of the table. "Mingus took refuge in the caverns. He went deep in the cave, took a narrow passage that had never been explored before, hoping it would lead him to safety."

"But it didn't," the bride guessed.

"No. Instead, he came upon a massive stalagmite, tall as a man, and in the perfect shape of Cupid holding a bow and arrow." A strand of hair fell across Natalie's eyes as she sorted the forks, spoons, and knives into separate piles.

"That must have been surprising to come across that in the dark," the young groom said.

Natalie brushed aside the errant lock of hair. "Mingus took it as a sign. He'd heard about the law that could get him out of being hanged if a woman would take pity on him and make him her husband, so he got down on his knees and prayed to Cupid to touch the heart of some young local beauty, and that's where the posse caught up to him."

"How colorful." Mazey licked honey from her fingers.

"The posse brought Mingus back to face justice, and as he stood at the gallows, looking beseechingly out at the beautiful young women, one angel stepped forward to save him." Natalie paused for dramatic effect.

The guests collectively leaned forward, fully engaged in the story.

"Except she wasn't quite what Mingus was hoping for," Natalie said.

"How's that?" the writer asked.

"A kind way to say it is that Louisa Hendricks was rather plain." Natalie reached across the table to pluck a browning petal from the rose flower arrangement in the center of the table. The leaf crinkled between her fingers.

"Translation," chortled the groom, revealing a row of teeth that were too small for his mouth. "She was fugly."

"Benjy," tittered his beautiful bride, and swatted his shoulder. "Behave."

"Louisa was a spinster and several years older than Mingus," Natalie said. "Her biological clock was ticking and she knew someone like Mingus was her last chance at getting the baby she so badly wanted. Plus, it didn't hurt that he was a good-looking son of a gun. He would give her beautiful babies. Unfortunately, they were never blessed with children."

"Poor guy," the groom commiserated. "Trapped in a loveless marriage with a barren fugly woman."

"Hey," said his bride, "Louisa saved his sorry ass from being hanged, give her some credit, and he could have been the one shooting blanks."

"Mingus *was* disappointed," Natalie continued, "but in spite of all his flaws, he was a man of his word. Cupid had saved him, and he would honor his vow. Over the years, Mingus came to fall deeply in love with Louisa and they ended up having a long and happy marriage in spite of not having kids. Soon after Louisa rescued him, the settlement became a township, and it was named Cupid in honor of the stalagmite that saved Mingus from being hanged."

Poor plain Louisa. How had she felt about being married to a sexy outlaw that so many other women wanted? Had she been proud of snagging him or anxious that someone would steal him from her? Perhaps she'd been self-conscious because she wasn't pretty?

Absentmindedly, Natalie rubbed a hand down her right thigh. She understood what it was like not to fit in the mold of traditional beauty. How much it could hurt.

"But what about the letters to Cupid?" the bride asked. "Where do they come in?"

"That goes back to my own great-grandmother, Millie Greenwood." Natalie's chest puffed with pride.

"Wow, so we're staying in the house of a living legend."

"I'm not the legend," Natalie said. "Here's what happened. In 1924, my great-grandmother was a maid for the Fants, the richest family in Jeff Davis County, and she fell madly in love with their oldest son, John."

"There's nothing more alluring than forbidden love." Mazey sighed longingly.

"John fell in love with Millie too, but he was betrothed to Elizabeth Nielson, the daughter of the second richest man in town. How could a poor maid dare hope for a happily-ever-after with John?" Natalie used a paper napkin to brush crumbs from the table and into her open palm.

"John's family probably thought Millie was a gold digger," said the groom.

The writer cleared his throat. "In those days the working class did not marry above their station. It was unheard of."

"Exactly." Natalie dusted the crumbs from her palm into the top plate on the stack of dirty dishes. "So a romance between them was hopeless and they both knew it."

"How sad." Mazey pressed a knuckle to her eye.

"On the evening before John's wedding, Millie started thinking about Mingus Dill and how his plea to Cupid led him to the love of his life. In desperation, she wrote a letter to Cupid, begging him to find a way for her and John to be together. In the middle of the night, she slipped off to the caverns and put the letter at the foot of the Cupid stalagmite."

"I would have been so scared!" the blonde exclaimed. "Going into a dark cave at night all by myself."

"Love can make you do dangerous things." Her groom lightly tickled her in the ribs. "But you'll never have to go anywhere alone again."

She giggled and ran a palm along his jaw.

Weren't they just the cutest? Would she ever have that? Giggly love that made others around you roll their eyes. That biker sure had lighted a spark inside her. What if…

Quit it!

"What happened next?" asked Mazey.

This was Natalie's favorite part of the story. She went for the brochures advertising the caverns that she kept in the drawer of the sideboard, undid the rubber band holding them together, and passed out the glossy pamphlets printed up by the Cupid Chamber of Commerce.

"John left Elizabeth at the altar, telling her he was in love with another. He went to find Millie, professed his love, and asked her to marry him."

"Seriously?"

"Awesome."

"How romantic."

"I have to see this stalagmite."

The writer looked up from his notes. "Did John know about the letter Millie wrote to Cupid?"

"No, he didn't."

"How did he react when he found out?"

"It caused a bit of a kerfuffle," Natalie admitted. "Someone found the letter in the cave and it got back to Elizabeth. She claimed Millie had bewitched John by summoning up the aid of a pagan god. Everyone took sides and it almost split the town in two. If you want to see it, Millie's letter is on display in the courthouse lobby."

"That must have been rocky for the couple," the writer said.

"If Cupid had bewitched John, he was good and solidly mesmerized. His love for Millie never wavered, even in the face of public outcry." Idly, Natalie reached down to loosen the strap that attached the AFO to her leg. The Velcro made a soft ripping sound as she tugged on it and pressed it back down.

"When you've found the real deal, you'll move heaven and earth for her." The groom stared into his bride's eyes.

"Ah, honey, that's so sweet." She nuzzled her husband.

They canoodled for a long moment until one of the older ladies cleared her throat loudly.

Natalie waited until the amorous couple broke apart before continuing. "The Cupid letter writing really took off when King Edward VIII abdicated the throne."

The writer frowned. "Are you implying that Cupid played a hand in King Edward's abdication?"

"Not implying. It's fact."

"How on earth is that possible?" Mazey planted a palm against her chest.

"Not long before his abdication, King Edward and Wallis Simpson called their romance quits because of his family responsibilities." Natalie glanced at her watch. She needed to wrap up the story.

The writer interjected. "Wallis was twice divorced and their marriage would have caused a constitutional crisis in England."

"That's correct. Brokenhearted, Wallis came to Cupid to visit her dearest friend, Penelope Fant, who was John Fant's older sister," Natalie said. "Wallis and Penelope Fant had both attended a prestigious girls' school in Baltimore together."

"Hard to believe that a social climber like Wallis Simpson would lower herself to visit a place as colloquial as Cupid," Mazey said.

"Which is precisely why she did. She wanted to get away from any and everything that reminded her of Edward. Then when Wallis heard about Millie and John's romance, she decided to write a letter to Cupid to intervene in her love affair with the King of England. Two weeks later, the king showed up in Cupid, got down on one knee, and asked for Wallis's hand in marriage. Shortly afterward, he abdicated to marry the woman he loved."

"That's so romantic, I'm getting goose bumps," the blonde said.

Her husband rubbed his hands along her arms. "I'd give up the throne for you."

Okay, these two were pushing the mushy meter to the limit. If Natalie hadn't experienced the weirdest feelings for a total stranger that very morning, she might have considered a dose of insulin to combat all the sweetness. But even so, her stomach went all melty. She wanted to be like them!

"I can't believe this amazing tale never made it into the history books," Mazey mused. "It's priceless."

"The royal family squelched the story hard, and remember, this was before relentless paparazzi and wiretapping gossip rags. The media had more respect back then for people's private lives. But throughout Texas, the Wallis Simpson story cemented the Cupid legend, and it became the cornerstone of our tourist economy." Natalie folded her hands in her lap.

"There really isn't much of a way to make a living way out here, otherwise, is there?" The bride's question was rhetorical.

"Tourism does have a downside. Because we were getting so many people littering the caverns with let-

ters, the town built a Cupid statue fountain in the botanical gardens and put up an official 'Letters to Cupid'
box there."

"Oh, this is such a good story." The blond bride
turned to her husband, clasping her hands together in
a plea gesture. "Tiger puss, we've just got to visit those
caverns."

"We're supposed to leave for Big Bend this afternoon," he said.

She batted her eyes at him. "Could we extend our
stay an extra day and stay one day less at Big Bend?"

He looked at Natalie. "Would you be able to accom-
modate us another day?"

Natalie smiled. That was why she told them the story.
"I think that can be arranged."

The blonde hugged her young husband, the older ladies went back to the buffet for seconds on the cinnamon rolls, and the writer got on his cell phone.

Natalie bade them all good morning and went about
her business, but once away from people, her thoughts
tracked back to the motorcycle man and his midnight
black hair and his impressively muscled body. She tried
to tamp down the image of him, but it was impossible
to shut down her jumbled mind. That piercing look he'd
sent her, like he knew exactly what she looked like
naked, brought an unwanted burn to her cheeks.

Stop being silly, she scolded herself, and limped to
her office, where she ordered Pearl's flour, and input-
ted the young couple into the computer as staying an
extra night.

Now, she had one more task before returning to the
community center. She had to decide what to do about

Red Daggett. If he wasn't coming back, she needed to get his room rented out, and the sooner the better.

Red had been staying in the carriage house that once upon a time had served as servant quarters. There were two other tenants in the carriage house. One was Lars and the other was a nineteen-year-old computer science whiz kid who went by the nickname of Gizmo. He rarely came out of his room except to attend classes. He'd even managed to sweet-talk Pearl into delivering his meals to his room. Occasionally, Gizmo and Zoey carpooled to Sul Ross together in the Cupid's Rest van.

The room looked out over the duck pond that was situated in the pocket park behind the backs of the houses on Stone Street. When she was a kid, Natalie used to hide in the red-tipped photinia hedges that grew along the fencerow between her house and the park and watch the wild ducks fly in. Most ducks headed for the lake, but a few outcasts and stragglers always ended up in the duck pond.

She pulled a key from her pocket, unlocked the door, and stepped over the threshold. She glanced around the room. Tidy, sparsely furnished, nothing out of place.

It felt like spying. She folded her arms. What should she do? "Red, where are you?"

She tried his cell phone, but it went to voice mail, just as it had the other half-dozen times she'd called him. *Can't leave the room vacant forever.* No, but it felt so cold, just giving up on him. She could put his stuff in storage and use the room for tourists instead of another long-term boarder. That way, if and when Red returned, he could move back in without a long wait. Eventually, she could go back to renting it to long-term boarders if she wanted.

Plan of action. Good. Follow through.

Natalie got a cardboard box from the attic and started clearing Red's meager things from the chest of drawers—an old Timex wristwatch; $4.23 in pennies, dimes, and nickels; a handful of metal washers; a pair of worn-out house slippers; an unopened package of brand-new Hanes boxer underwear; a stack of carefully folded white T-shirts; one pair of faded Wrangler blue jeans; three button-down Western shirts; half a pack of nicotine gum; cheap drugstore sunglasses; six pairs of rolled-up boot socks; empty bottles of both paroxetine and doxepin; and a bus ticket stub. Red hadn't owned a vehicle. He'd kept mostly to himself, walked to his job at Chantilly's bar at the marina, and did odd jobs around the place for Natalie.

Red had lived here for two years, but when it got down to it, she knew hardly anything about him. She remembered their first meeting.

He'd shown up on her front porch, wearing a green windbreaker in spite of the summer heat, and navy blue mirrored sunglasses. He sported a droopy Sam Elliot mustache that hid his upper lip. He was tall and stocky, but stood with his shoulders hunched as if trying to fold in on himself. His long strawberry blond hair had been pulled back into a greasy ponytail. Around his left wrist, he wore a braided black bracelet with a spent bullet casing tied in the middle. He had on blue jeans and a Western shirt, but he didn't really look like a cowboy. His eyes were too wary, his movements too guarded.

"Room?" he'd mumbled.

"For the night?" she'd asked.

"To stay."

At the time, Lars was her only long-term boarder and

she'd hesitated, not sure she wanted to turn the B&B into a rooming house, but then he pulled a money clip from his pocket and started peeling off twenties.

"Follow me," she said, and led him to this room.

Junie Mae had freaked out when she'd first seen Red. "He looks like a felon. Did you do a background check?"

"Looks can be deceiving. He's gentle as a mouse, keeps to himself."

"He could be a serial killer."

"Or he could just be someone who needs a soft place to land."

"You're too empathetic." Junie Mae snorted. "Not everyone is worth your compassion."

"I don't get a bad vibe from him."

"You're also too trusting."

"I've never had it go against me. I believe that, by and large, people live up to your expectations of them."

"Still, have Calvin do a background check on him, just in case."

To keep Junie Mae from nagging her and because she had guests and a sister to consider, she'd gone ahead and asked Cal to do the background check.

She learned Red had been arrested a couple of times for bar fights and that he was an ex–Navy SEAL diagnosed with severe PTSD. Calvin had advised her to evict him, but Natalie didn't have the heart. What kind of person would she be if she turned her back on a military veteran? Red had served his country. He deserved a break.

Red never spoke about his past. A couple of times, she saw him coming out of the little run-down house on Hill Street where AA meetings were held, but she never mentioned it to him.

Had he perhaps fallen off the wagon and gone on a drinking binge? She hoped not.

The sound of frantic quacking came from the duck pond. Were neighborhood dogs after the ducks?

She hurried to the window.

A mallard female was in a panic, flapping her wings like something was chasing her, but Natalie spied no predator. Why didn't she just fly away?

The duck's quacking turned pitiful, doomed. Natalie couldn't bear to see any creature in pain. Moving as quickly as she could, Natalie left the carriage house. Sometimes, her lameness really bothered her. She hated being vulnerable. Zoey used to tease her and say if monsters or vampires or zombies were ever chasing them, she'd be the first one eaten.

Good thing there were no such things as monsters, vampires, or zombies.

Natalie left the perimeter of the McCleary property, pushing aside the short backyard gate to the community area between the surrounding houses. Back in the 1920s, the neighboring homeowners had gotten together, pooled their money, and bought the vacant plot of land behind them and turned it into an oasis. There was no playground equipment—it wasn't that kind of a park—just trees and benches, and a wandering pathway that led in from Dennis Street on the west side and circled around the pond. The round trip made for a nice one-mile walk that Natalie's B&B guests enjoyed.

By the time she reached the flailing duck, the poor thing was so frantic Natalie feared she'd kill herself.

"Hey, there," she soothed, slipped off her Keds at the edge of the pond, and unstrapped her AFO.

The water was murky green with algae. Lilly pads, corkscrew rushes, and cattails grew in profusion. The pond was spring fed and sheltered in the shade of mimosa, desert willows, and mesquite trees. All kinds of squiggly, squirmy things lived there. As kids, she and Zoey had caught tadpoles and kept them in a fish aquarium, watching them grow into frogs.

She took a faltering step.

Mud squished up between her toes, minnows darted underneath the surface, slimy anacharis brushed against her legs as she moved. The water smelled of briny musk.

The female mallard strained to swim away, but she seemed trapped in one place. The closer Natalie came, the more the duck flailed.

"What is it? What's wrong?" Natalie crooned.

Quack! Quack! Quack!

"No need for a heart attack, sweetheart. I'm here to help. What's going on?" Natalie crouched low trying to see what was causing the ruckus, and spotted part of a plastic six-pack ring sticking up behind the duck. Apparently, she'd gotten her feet enmeshed in the plastic ring and couldn't get out.

"Damn litterbugs," Natalie muttered.

Sometimes, late at night, careless teens sneaked back here to drink beer and make out. Zoey used to be one of those teens, but Natalie had never had that luxury. She'd never once sneaked out. Never dated in high school. For that matter, she'd never even had a sip of beer. Goody Two-shoes. That's what Zoey called her. As if she'd had much of a choice.

The duck was bobbing and quacking and flapping.

How was she going to get close enough to help the poor thing out?

"It's okay, Miss Mallard, I'm here to help."

The duck looked skeptical.

"Honestly, it's what I do. Just ask anyone. I've even been accused of being too helpful. Or as my sister likes to put it, sticking my nose in where it doesn't belong, but I bet in the end you'll be grateful for my help." She took another step forward.

Quack. The duck's voice softened.

"That's right, relax."

The duck was no longer trying to swim away. She waited, finally calmed or too exhausted to try to escape, and blindly accepted her fate.

The water was up to Natalie's knees now, dampening the hem of her sundress. The duck was still a few feet away. It had been a long time since she'd mucked around in the pond and she didn't remember how deep it was in the middle.

What if it was over her head? She paused. Maybe she should go back for a change of clothes before plunging ahead.

Honestly, she didn't think that pond was that deep and she was worried what might happen to the duck if she left her alone for too long. If a dog did happen by, the duck would be defenseless. She blew out her breath and took another step. Her ankles sank into the ooze.

Ugh.

She'd never been a tomboy like Zoey, who would throw herself headlong into any adventure without giving a thought to getting dirty or making a mess.

Gram had often said Zoey's middle name should have been Fearless. Did that mean that *her* middle name was Fearful? Cowardly. In her heart, she suspected it might be true. Natalie was afraid of a lot of things— thunderstorms and rattlesnakes, not being able to pay the bills and ending up alone. These fears and many more churned around in her head when she lay in bed at night, but her biggest fear was the fear of heights.

"Completely understandable," Gram had said when she tried to get Natalie on a plane to visit relatives a few years after her parents' death on the mountain and not long after Grandpa's fatal heart attack. The plane was so tiny. All the planes at the Cupid airport were small and the sky was so tall.

Natalie had freaked out worse than the duck with the plastic ring tangled around its legs. She remembered hyperventilating so badly that the copilot had brought her a brown paper bag to breathe into.

"No worries." Gram kissed her on the forehead. "We'll drive."

"I wanna fly!" Zoey had cried. "I wanna go up in the sky."

"How come she's not scared?" Natalie whispered to Gram. "She was in the plane too."

"She doesn't know any better," Gram said, and then with a tinge of admiration in her voice added, "Zoey is fearless."

Shame had rushed through Natalie and she'd longed to be fearless too, but she knew there were some fears you didn't dare face because if you did, you could lose everything.

So they made the nine-hour drive to Fort Worth to see their cousins, and as they drove, Zoey would look up into the sky and say, "We coulda been there already if Natalie wasn't such a chicken." Then she made chicken noises, tucking her hands under her armpits and flapping her arms like wings.

"Ignore her." Gram leaned over the driver's seat to whisper in Natalie's ear. "She doesn't understand."

That made her feel somewhat better, but still, her fear had caused an inconvenience.

Natalie and the duck stared at each other.

"Don't be afraid of the ring. I'm here to help. Be like Zoey. Be fearless and you'll soon fly away," Natalie murmured.

The duck did not move.

"That's it. We're going to do this together. Face our fears." She reached under the water, searching for the plastic ring.

The duck stared into Natalie's eyes, mesmerized, trusting.

"Good girl." She almost had it.

A growling motorcycle engine roared up the circular park path just as Natalie's fingers found the plastic ring.

The panicking duck flew up, the tip of its wings brushing against Natalie's face.

She gasped, lost her balance, and, arms windmilling, fell backward into the water.

Chapter 4

Love at first sight makes absolutely no sense until you experience it, and then everything else is nonsense.

—Millie Greenwood

The woman came up sputtering.

Soaking wet strands of soft brown hair clung to her face and dripped down her shoulders. She swiped at her eyes and then wiped the back of her hand across her mouth and glared at him. Hot as a smoking gun.

But Dade wasn't looking at her eyes.

His gaze was glued to her chest. He slipped off his sunglasses for a better look, folded them, and stuck the shades in the front pocket of his T-shirt.

Yeah, it was rude, but he couldn't seem to glance away. Her dress was soaked, revealing clearly that her nipples were knotted up hard.

Involuntarily, he licked his lips, and then he noticed that she'd noticed that he was staring, just as a realization slammed into his head solid as a two-by-four.

It was the honeysuckle woman.

A single word lit up his brain in bold, red, glowing letters.

HOME.

What the hell? Dade had never in his life had a real home. The military was the closest he'd ever come. Why did he think home when he looked into her eyes?

Shit. This was crazy.

Dade sat astride his Harley. The woman was standing in the middle of the pond, her hands on her hips, looking like a pissed-off water nymph.

Something inside him shifted in a most peculiar way, sort of like an imploded building falling in on itself, leaving behind nothing but a pile of dusty rubble.

Breathe, Vega. Just take a deep breath and hold it.

All well and good in theory, but his treacherous lungs barely stirred air and his head buzzed as if he'd pounded down a couple of shots of tequila in record time.

He didn't know what to say. His pulse hammered so hard and quick that he wondered if he was getting sick. He had hawk-eye vision, and even from this distance, he could see the pulse at the hollow of her throat pounding just as hard as his was.

If he was sick, so was she. The same restless fever.

Even in the best of situations he wasn't a chatty guy. Keep your mouth shut and just act. That was his motto. Too many people dicked around, talking, dissecting, assessing, Monday morning quarterbacking. Not enough people took the bull by the horns and just did what needed to be done.

Except at this moment, his baser instincts were screaming at him to get off the motorcycle, slog through the water, grab the woman around the waist, throw her over his shoulder, drag her off to his lair, and have his way with her.

What the frig is the matter with you? You're here to find Red, not get your rocks off. He could have his pick of women and often did.

What was it about this one that left him speechless? What was this spell she'd cast over him? Honestly, he was surprised to run across her again. The woman in yellow. How could she be here? As if she lived in the pond. As if she'd sprouted there and thrived.

Fairy tale.

He felt as if he was in the grip of some idiotic fairy tale. She was the beauty and he the beast. He thrived on loneliness and anger. It had served him well for thirty-one years. Why mess with what worked?

"Well," she said finally, softly, in a voice as lyrical as a meadowlark's warble. "Well."

He chuckled, and that surprised him too. He wasn't a cheerful guy by nature and she hadn't said anything that was remotely funny, but a strange lightness moved through him, churning up from his stomach into his throat to escape in a laugh.

"It's not funny." A stern glower creased her brow.

He pressed his lips together, trying to stop the laughter, and realized with a start why he was laughing. He was scared!

Why are you scared? You were a frickin' Navy SEAL. What is it about this sweet little bit of honeysuckle that's got you wanting to run as far and as fast as you can in the opposite direction?

He had absolutely no answer to that question.

But he had other questions. Who was she and what was she doing in the middle of the pond?

He swung off his Harley.

She clenched her hands into fists.

He swallowed.

She raised her chin.

For some unknown reason, he thought about Tombstone, Arizona, where he recently completed an assignment—stormy skies filled with voluminous dark clouds, tumbleweed-strewn dirt streets, the taste of gritty sand on the tongue, cowboys with six-shooters hitched onto their hips.

Gunfights? First home and now gunfights? Had his brain misfired? Where were these images coming from? Why did she make him feel both accepted and challenged, throwing down a gauntlet with her eyes. He had no idea what that gauntlet was or why she was putting it out there, but he could not stop staring at her.

A match.

He'd met his match.

He tried to bat the thought away, but it stuck there. Velcro. Duct tape. Super Glue.

Her nipples were tight as head bolts on a factory engine, poking straight up through her wet dress. She seemed rooted, as if her legs were buried deep into the bottom of the pond.

His eyes were back on those breasts, lush and pert and fully round beneath her wet dress.

She crossed her arms over her chest.

His nose burned. His throat tightened. His eyes hooked on to hers and he simply could not look away.

His breathing came out short and hot, and his legs felt oddly weak.

"I'm here," he said, without even knowing he was going to say it.

"I can see that," she answered, as if it was a conversation that they'd long been meaning to have.

How could that be? He didn't know her, and yet he was feeling all these bizarre things. Dade was usually pretty damn good at shutting out unwanted feelings. Why couldn't he do it now?

How must he look to her; his cheeks hollowed with worry over Red, his hair tangled in windblown swirls, his skin ruddied by the desert sun? Could she see exhaustion on him? Feel the violence of his past? Taste the impending grief that something cataclysmic had happened to the only person in the entire world he loved?

Her body might be rigid, but her eyes were soft, accepting, and compassionate. She cared about people. Truly cared.

It made him angry, her gentleness. Didn't she realize it was a cold and vicious world out there? That trusting people opened you up to a whole wide world of hurt? Didn't she get just how damn vulnerable she was?

A crow flew overhead, crying out a harsh caw. Tiny ripples spread over the surface of the pond as a small perch came up to snatch a water strider in its jaws. The scent of fresh-brewed coffee drifted on the air.

Even though he'd changed his clothes and done his best to clean up in the bathroom of a convenience store, he still smelled faintly of gasoline. He'd put on a fresh pair of Wranglers, a black T-shirt, and a weather-beaten straw cowboy hat before he'd gone to Chantilly's bar to apply for Red's old job. He'd found the owner asleep in a hammock on the back patio of the nightclub and he'd roused him.

The old-timer had snorted awake, peered up at Dade with bleary eyes.

"Name's Dade Vega."

The old man squinted at him with tarnished eyes. He was skinny, leathery, and possessed an oversized head that didn't match his body. He had a short snub nose and big ears with attached lobes, causing him to resemble Curious George. "Jasper Grass."

Dade lifted an eyebrow.

"I don't wanna hear no marijuana jokes." He pronounced it *mara-ja-wanna*. "Heard every damn one of them."

"I'm not making any jokes," Dade assured him. "Looking for work. Got anything?"

"You ever tend bar?"

"Yes. Been a bouncer too." And he'd been a security expert and a bodyguard and a mercenary, but he wasn't putting those on his résumé.

"You're hired," Grass said.

"That easy?"

The man shrugged. "I need help, you need work, why mess with red tape? I don't ask questions that I don't want to know the answer to."

"Ostrich policy?"

"I mind my business, you mind yours, okay?"

"Okay."

"Gotta place to stay?"

"No."

"Cupid's Rest B&B might rent you Red Daggett's room. That's the man who used to have this job. He took off without notice. You ain't gonna do that, is ya? Take off without notice." Grass took a red bandana from his pocket and blew his nose.

"No."

"Good. You start tonight," Grass had said, turned over on his side in the hammock, and gone back to snoring.

At the mention of his buddy's name, Dade had experienced a cold, persistent dread. This felt wrong in a hundred different ways. He'd felt this way before. In Afghanistan. He had not listened to his instincts then, but he'd learned a hard lesson.

Always trust your gut.

Right now his gut was telling him something strange and unsettling about this woman.

She's special.

How could he trust that nonsense?

She was still staring at him. Neither of them moved.

For the first time, Dade noticed that she was trembling. "You're cold."

"Yes." She shook her head.

Were those tears in her eyes? Or was it simply water dripping from her hair and clinging to her lashes? Had to be water. No reason for her to cry, but she looked... *touched.*

Finally, she dropped her gaze and slogged from the pond, the soaking dress plastered to her legs, outlining her shapely thighs.

Dade stayed motionless beside his motorcycle. He couldn't take his eyes off her. He couldn't say why she so enthralled him. Yes, she was pretty, but it was a mild beauty, certainly not strong enough to explain why his entire body throbbed for her.

"What were you doing in the pond?" he asked, hoping a return to reality would break the strange spell.

She didn't answer immediately, moved with heavy, plodding steps, not light and effortless the way she'd been on the bike. She stepped free from the pond, and he saw that mud was caked halfway up her calves.

"The duck had a beer six-pack plastic ring around her legs," she said at last. "It kept her from flying."

"Shackles," he said.

"Yes."

"You saved her."

She poked her tongue against the inside of her cheek and pushed a hand through her hair. It was all he could do to keep from ogling her tits again.

Canting her head, she studied him as she wiped her feet on the carpet of grass. "Who are you?"

He loved her voice. Soft but low, sexy, enticing. Dade cleared his throat. "Name's Vega."

"Just one name?" She raised a quizzical eyebrow. "Like Elvis?"

"Dade Vega," he amended.

"Well, Dade Vega, this is a private park. What are you doing driving your motorcycle through here?"

"GPS." He waved at the gadget mounted on his motorcycle. "Technology is great, but flawed."

"Where are you headed?"

"Cupid's Rest B&B. Am I close?"

"You're at my back door." She waved a hand at the house behind the park fence. When she moved, so did her breasts, rising high and perky. If he rested his head there, would they feel soft as pillows?

Dade felt a stirring below his belt, and he steeled his jaw to stave off the erection. "Your back door?"

"I'm the owner of Cupid's Rest."

"Ah," he said, and narrowed his eyes. "My luck has turned."

"Your luck has been unfortunate?"

He shook his head. "Since the day I was born."

"That's a shame."

"Not really. Nowhere to go from the bottom but up."

"A sound philosophical outlook."

He held both arms out in a what-are-you-gonna-do gesture.

"Natalie McCleary," she said with a regal, lady-of-the-manor tilt to her head, extended a hand, and offered him her best hostess smile as if she wasn't standing wet, muddy, and barefoot at the edge of a pond.

He rushed to take her hand, his breath quickening and his heart rising as if it was filled with helium. When they touched, palm to palm and skin to skin, a startling tenderness swept over him, so strong and unrelenting that he almost jumped back on his Harley and sped away. Only his desire to find Red kept him rooted against the onslaught of excitement, pride, desire, and fear.

She smelled like fresh-baked cookies, not honeysuckle as he'd supposed, and the look in her blue eyes was so otherworldly that Dade understood that her delicate image would haunt the recesses of his memory for years to come.

Years? How about for the rest of his life?

Impossible, but unshakable. How was it she seemed the very blueprint of the woman he'd never dared dream existed?

What the frig? This was lunacy and he wanted no part of it. No part of her.

He dropped his hand and it was all he could do not to back up. Dade never backed down. Ever. Instead, he held her wide-eyed stare, determined not to let it show just how much she disturbed him.

"Natalie," he murmured like some love-struck fool. "Pretty name."

"It means born on Christmas Day."

"Were you? Born on Christmas Day?"

"No."

"Neither was I."

Her smile deepened. "Look at that. We have something in common."

He raked his gaze over her again. *That's the only thing we have in common, babe.*

"You looking for a room?" Her lyrical voice stroked him as warm as the arid morning breeze.

"I am."

"I don't have one."

"You were leading me on?"

"I'll have a room tomorrow, but only for a few days. We'll fill up after that for the Fourth of July weekend. Will that do?"

"You already rented out Red Daggett's room then?"

A startled expression skimmed over her face. She hauled in a breath so deep that her chest rose high. He tried not to look at her breasts again, but dammit, he was only human, and she was so delicious that he could eat her up with a spoon. "Where'd you hear about Red?"

"Jasper Grass told me about the vacancy after he gave me Red's job."

"Jasper's already replaced Red?" She frowned, knotted her hands.

"Looks like."

"So you're the new bouncer at Chantilly's?" Her gaze darted to his biceps.

His ego couldn't help flexing his arm. "Bouncer slash bartender."

"How nice for you."

"Any particular reason you're being catty?"

"You did cause me to take an unexpected mud bath." She gestured toward the pond, the plastic six-pack ring still clutched in her left hand.

"I thought we'd already moved past that."

"Because of you, I have to go shower, and my schedule is packed. I really don't have time for a shower, but clearly I have to make time."

"And yet you do have time to rescue ducks in distress."

"I always have time to help those in distress."

Dade pressed his lips together. *I'm in distress. I need rescuing.* Where in God's name did that thought come from? He lowered his eyelids, crossed his arms over his chest. "I apologize for mucking up your day."

"You're forgiven," she relented.

He wanted to ask her a million things. Are you feeling the same way I'm feeling? Does your stomach hurt? Is your chest tight? Does the sun seem incredibly bright? Do you have an irresistible urge to get naked with me?

"So about Red's room?" he prompted.

"He hasn't officially vacated it."

"But he's gone?"

"He left his things. He never checked out."

"So he's missing then?"

She shrugged, but he saw concern on her face. She cared about Red.

"Did you report him missing?"

"How is that any of your business?"

"I need a place to stay."

"Red always comes back." She raised her chin. "It would be disloyal of me to give away his room."

He didn't push it. Although he'd appreciate the opportunity to stay in Red's room while he searched for his buddy, he didn't want to arouse her suspicion. Considering the way he was feeling about her, it was probably better if he didn't stay here. "Do you know who else in town might be willing to rent out a room?"

"How long do you need it for?"

"Can't say for sure."

She made a face, reached up to stroke her chin with her thumb and index finger. Assessing.

"I've got a thousand dollars to put down for a deposit and first month's rent," he enticed.

"Cash up front?" She looked hungry, but conflicted.

"Cash up front."

A long moment of silence passed between them. He could see the tension in her body, felt a corresponding tension tighten in his own.

"I have an ethical dilemma," she said. "I need the money, but what if I rent the room to you and Red comes back?"

"You give me a partial refund and I move out."

She chewed her bottom lip in a gesture that made him want to nibble that lush piece of flesh too. Hell, he wanted to nibble her from head to toe.

He couldn't forget why he was here. Red. He had to keep his mind on Red. His buddy was in trouble and needed his help.

Still, he couldn't stop staring at the mesmerizing

mermaid in yellow with a green streamer of seaweed caught in her hair. He stepped closer.

"I don't know about that."

"This Red character, he just took off without a word to anyone?"

"That's right."

"Did he leave his car behind?"

"He didn't own a vehicle. He walked everywhere he went or hitchhiked."

"Hitchhiked?"

"It's a small town. People don't mind giving their neighbors a ride."

"A regular Mayberry, huh?" he drawled, but Dade knew danger resided as easily in a small town as it did in a big metropolis. They didn't breathe rarefied air in Cupid. Beneath the pretty surface lurked problems and troubles, secrets, and lies.

"We look after our own," she said.

"When was the last time you saw him?" He was pushing it, he knew, walking a thin line, risking giving himself away.

She frowned.

"Trying to gauge when he might come back," Dade hastened to add.

"Red comes and goes as he pleases, so I can't be one hundred percent certain, but I think the last time I saw him was the morning of the nineteenth."

Four days ago. The day before Dade had received the Mayday text. "You didn't think it strange that he disappeared without a trace?"

"He did that occasionally. Took off without notice."

"Did?"

"Yes. Several times."

"You said 'did.' In the past tense. Not 'does.'"

"Oh." Her eyes rounded. "Well, I suppose it's because this time it feels different."

"Different how?"

"For one thing, he's never been gone this long."

"No?" Dade took a step closer. His gaze trained on the pond weeds clinging to her hair. It distracted him. Apparently, she had no idea it was there. "Did you report his disappearance to law enforcement?"

"I did."

"What did they say?"

"Red has some mental health issues."

Dade curled his hands into fists. "If he's got mental health issues, you'd think that would be a stronger motivation to search for him."

She studied him a long moment. "Why do you care?"

"If I rent the room, I'd be disappointed if he shows up to boot me out of it."

"I never said I was going to rent the room to you."

"You need to make up the income for the boarder you just lost."

She bit her bottom lip again, those pearly white teeth sinking into the plump pink flesh. He saw the truth in her eyes. She needed every penny she could scrape together. That intrigued him. What was her story?

"I don't rent long term to just anyone."

"And yet you took in a mental case." *Sorry, Red. No disrespect.*

"I never said he was a mental case." Natalie drew herself up tall, tossed her head. "He served in the armed forces. He suffered from post-traumatic stress disorder. What kind of person would I be if I turned away a former military man who'd suffered the consequences of defending my freedom?"

"A cautious one?"

"I'm not incautious."

"Is that right?"

"It is."

"Then why does a single woman take in boarders?"

She looked perturbed. "Who says I'm single?"

"You don't wear a ring."

She tucked her left hand behind her back. "Not wearing a ring doesn't mean anything. I could be married. I'm plenty old enough to be married and have a passel of kids."

"But you're not married. You're all alone."

"Just because I'm single doesn't mean I'm alone by any stretch. I have three—well, two now that Red's vanished—long-term boarders and a constant turnover of tourists. I have a sister, a maid, a gardener, and a cook. My entire family lives around me—cousins, aunts, uncles. I'm the least alone person you'll ever meet."

"Well, imagine that," he said lightly, feeling that inexplicable tugging in the center of his chest once more.

They were back to square one, not speaking, caught in each other's eyes.

"So if someone wanted to harm you, they'd have to go through a cadre of friends and relatives."

She narrowed her eyes at him. "Who on earth would want to harm me?"

"There's darkness in this world that you have no idea about."

"You underestimate me. I have a permit to carry a handgun and I know how to use it."

Surprised, he arched an eyebrow.

"Rattlesnakes," she said. "Lots of rattlesnakes in the desert."

He couldn't get over this wild attraction beating through him. She was a pretty woman, but what concerned him was the overwhelming pull of attraction that gripped him whenever he looked at her. He hated feeling so out of control. His gaze fixed on the seaweed in her hair again. It was just an excuse to get closer to her, but he couldn't resist. Dade stepped forward.

She backed up, the pulse at her throat thumping wildly. "What are you doing?"

"You've got something…" He reached a hand up to touch her hair.

In that second of that touch, his past disappeared. All the things he'd done wrong, all the wrong paths he'd taken suddenly seemed the exact right paths leading him here—to this woman, this place, this moment in time.

Kiss her! his body screamed at him. *Kiss her! Kiss her!*

Her breath was so shallow that she was scarcely breathing. Their eyes latched together, inseparable, the current between them stronger than electricity. His fingers found the pond weeds and he plucked them from her hair.

"Oh," she said, sounding disappointed. "There really was something in my hair."

"You thought I was lying?"

Her cheeks blushed hotly. She looked so damn cute, he wanted to wrap her into his arms and imprint her lips with his. Brand her. Make her his, forever and ever.

It was an unsettling sensation for a man who'd sworn never to settle down, never to stay in one place for long.

Shocked by his thoughts and feelings, he turned and flung the weeds into the pond.

When he turned around again, she was assessing him coolly, but he could see her trembling. Had he done that to her?

He should cut his losses here, jump on his Harley, and find somewhere else to stay before he got mired in the quicksand of her eyes.

She nodded.

"I'll show you the room," she said. "But that doesn't mean I'm going to rent it to you."

"Thank you."

"I need to change my clothes first. You can follow me inside the house and wait in the kitchen."

"All right," he agreed, feeling so utterly grateful that he was ashamed of himself.

She bent down to pick up her shoes and a plastic leg brace and limped toward the house.

"You're limping," he said.

"It's permanent," she called curtly over her shoulder without looking back.

He felt a stab directly in the center of his heart, and it was all he could do not to rush ahead, scoop her into his arms, and carry her into the house. *Don't, Vega. Don't go there. Not even in your mind.*

Still, he couldn't deny that her vulnerability cut through him as sharp as a bayonet. She possessed a gentle beauty, round and soft and kind. A certain tranquillity that said she led an unblemished life in this safe little town surrounded by extended family.

But the limp belied all that.

The limp—and the labored way she toiled up the hill—told him she'd suffered. Continued to suffer.

Under those circumstances, how had she managed to hold on to her simple elegance?

In that moment, he felt something totally unexpected.

Jealousy.

He was jealous of the way she'd navigated the pain, and while her body had not come out of it unscathed, she'd kept her soul pure. If he'd thought himself unworthy of her before, in the face of her injury, he knew for certain he wasn't good enough to wipe the mud from her resilient feet.

Chapter 5

Love at first sight requires a total leap of faith.
—Millie Greenwood

Natalie couldn't have felt more exposed if she'd been stripped buck naked. Dade stared at her brazenly, lustily, audaciously, as if she *was* naked. His stare set her on fire. No man had ever looked at her in quite the same way.

Her scalp tingled from where Dade's fingers had skimmed through her hair, and her heart was thumping as loud as an orchestra, a rapidly rising crescendo of saxophones, trumpets, bassoons, and trombones. If he were music, he'd be big-band swing—bold, lively, and fast-paced. Looking into his eyes, she had an overwhelming urge to sing, to hop, to dance.

Dance.

He made her want to dance.

She hadn't danced since ballet class, the year before the plane crash, and she would never dance again. Not with her handicap. She would never foxtrot, jitterbug, or do the Lindy hop, and she felt the loss deep within her bones for something she could not have.

It was crazy, this mixed-up jumble of need, longing, fear, hope, and euphoria.

"May I see the room?" His eyes glittered darkly and he looked dead sexy in the morning light. This man had done his share of living.

She wanted to say no. She should have said no, but two things kept her from it. One, she needed the thousand dollars he promised, and two; she couldn't seem to make her mouth form the word. She nodded. "This way."

Her dress was plastered snugly to her body. She turned and, without waiting for him to follow, headed toward the fence separating her yard from the park, moving with precise steps to minimize her limp, fully aware that his intense eyes were gobbling up the sight of her.

She felt him behind her, big and strong. Her pulse skipped through her veins, light and heavy at the same time. She put her tongue to the tip of her upper lip. *This is it. Love at first sight. He's The One.*

Calm down, calm down.

He went ahead of her to open the gate. A gentlemanly gesture. Courtly, but at the same time threatening because it was something she could grow very accustomed to. A man looking out for her. *This* man looking out for her.

She was headed off the deep end.

Truth was, she'd never felt anything like this and he scared the living daylights out of her. Her true love.

Could the legend be true? Did she dare hope it was true? Could she trust it? On the surface, having faith in him was so stupid, but it was too late. No putting that genie back into the bottle. She felt it in every part of her. Magic. Dreams. What if she gave herself over to the fantasy and it turned to dust in her hands? Oh God, what was happening to her?

She stuck her hands in her pockets as she stepped past him with her head down, avoiding his gaze. Her fingers closed over Shot Through the Heart's soggy letter. Dammit. She'd forgotten the letter was in her pocket.

Dade closed the gate behind them, touched her shoulder. His big hand was unexpectedly warm and comforting. She almost jumped out of her skin.

"Are you all right?" he asked.

"I'm fine," she mumbled, abandoning her attempt to walk normally and shambled up the path as quickly as she could, her Keds clutched in the fingers of her right hand, the AFO cradled against her right elbow.

His footsteps echoed behind her, both scary and thrilling at the same time. She was having trouble adjusting to the fact that she was a different Natalie from the one who'd awakened this morning. That Natalie had never felt...this...this...

She had no word for what this was.

Natalie gulped, feeling trapped, challenged, and five hundred other inexplicable things she couldn't even name. Irritated with herself, she clenched her jaw. She was not normally like this, weak-kneed over a handsome man. Then again, she'd never felt this kind of chemistry. If she had, she'd have surrendered her virginity eons ago.

"Have you had breakfast?" she asked, going all B&B hostess on him. That was the way to handle this situation until she could make sense of her feelings. Keep it strictly professional.

"No."

The back door flew open at her light touch, swinging inward with a loud creak.

"That latch is suspect," Dade observed.

"It's an old house."

He paused to look at the door. "It has a skeleton key lock."

"So?" She shrugged.

"This wouldn't keep out a cat, much less a cat burglar. You need a proper lock on your back door," he chided.

"We don't have much crime in Cupid."

"Everywhere has crime."

"If there's something in here that someone wants that badly, they're welcome to it."

"What if they want your life?" he asked.

"My, you're just a little ray of sunshine, aren't you?"

"I could install a lock for you. Wouldn't take me long."

"I'm not worried about it," she told him, and then called out, "Pearl, we have another guest for breakfast. One who apparently has a thing for locks."

"Buffet is still out," Pearl hollered back amid the clanging of pots and pans.

"Just go through there." Anxious to separate herself from him, Natalie pointed to the door leading into the formal dining room. "Help yourself. I'll be back in a minute."

He looked at her with his eyelids at half-mast, a lazy, bedroom expression that constricted her throat. His eyelashes were the color of ink and surprisingly long, softening his devilish eyes. "Don't rush your shower on my account."

Her pulse, which had started to settle down a little, kicked up into a fresh gallop.

The barest hint of a grin tipped the corners of his mouth. She had the most insane urge to ask him to join her in the shower. This was nonsense, but she couldn't shake the thought of the two of them in her shower, steamy water sluicing down their naked bodies, her head tossed back, his mouth nibbling her throat, his hand—

Stop it!

Her body flushed hot all over. She had never had a particularly strong sex drive, which was one of the reasons she'd been satisfied without lovers to meet her needs. A vibrator did the trick.

Until now.

Feeling self-conscious, she clumped up the stairs to her bedroom, determined to tamp down the onslaught of hormones surging through her bloodstream, but her will deserted her. Aching, demanding need pushed low into her belly, building pressure and heat.

Why was she reacting this way? Why now? Why this man? She didn't want to feel this way.

Oh, you liar!

No man had ever ignited her the way he did with nothing more than a sultry look.

For years, she'd secretly felt a little superior to

women who fell willy-nilly into love with first one man and then another. She had seen loving too easily as a weakness, a character flaw, while she smugly clung to her virtue. Now, she'd been infected with it too, consumed by an overwhelming physical need to merge with Dade Vega. It worried her to realize that this man could quickly become an obsession. Payback. Karma.

Cold shower. She needed a cold shower. A cold shower would douse the problem. No hot and steamy water for her.

She pulled Shot Through the Heart's letter from her pocket, opened it carefully, and spread it out on the wide window ledge in her bedroom to dry. Afterward, she stripped off her wet dress and left it lying on the bathroom floor. She turned on the water as cold as she could stand it and stepped under the spray.

Teeth chattering, she soaped up and tried to analyze what it was about him that intrigued her beyond the initial slam-dunk of attraction. Was it more than the novelty of her feelings? She was a twenty-nine-year-old virgin who'd clung for so long to an outmoded belief in one true love for everyone that her belief had created a crisis of faith. So now that it had happened, shouldn't she be over the moon?

Except now that it was finally happening, she was even more muddled and confused and uncertain than ever. Things weren't solid and crystal clear the way she'd imagined they would be. Brakes were needed here. A cautious eye to counter the sizzling desire.

He was a loner. A drifter. A biker. He was decorated with tattoos. He spelled trouble, but at the same time she felt oddly safe with him. Protected. Was it beyond foolish to trust her instincts? So what was he? Dark knight or knight in shining armor?

Gak! She was romanticizing him. She was as hopeless as the lovelorn who wrote letters to Cupid.

She toweled herself dry. Got dressed in dark green walking shorts, a white peasant blouse, and white Keds. She had a pair of the iconic sneakers in every color because they were the only store-bought shoes she could wear in comfort with her AFO.

On the door of her closet hung the shoes she'd bought but could never walk in—black thigh-high boots, a pair of mules, espadrilles, wedges, sling backs, Mary Janes. She'd collected them for years, one pair every Christmas, since she was sixteen. A gift to herself.

Sighing, she closed the closet door.

After pulling her wet hair into a ponytail, she went back downstairs to voices in the kitchen. Dade had entered Pearl's inner sanctum and was still alive to tell the tale?

"Her favorite food is pizza," Pearl was saying. "Pepperoni with black olives."

They were talking about her! Natalie paused outside the kitchen with her hand on the swinging door.

"But she won't ever eat it," Pearl went on. "She never spoils herself. Never indulges." The way her cook said it made self-discipline sound like a fault, not something she took great pride in.

"Why do you suppose that is?" Dade's low voice rumbled. The sound of it sent goose bumps spreading up Natalie's forearms.

"She's scared to death that if she lets down her guard for one little second that everything will fall to pieces and she won't be able to put it back together again. That if she eats just one little slice of pizza, she won't be able to stop, so she won't risk it."

"Control freak, huh?" Dade chuckled.

"It's understandable though." Pearl's voice softened. "She's had it rough."

"How so?" he asked.

Natalie's cheeks burned. No way was she going to stand here and listen to them gossip about her.

"Ahem." Natalie noisily cleared her throat as she pushed into the kitchen.

Dade sat at the small kitchen table looking totally at ease, his long legs stretched out in front of him, the bright morning sun falling across the blue floral tablecloth. He was eating toast smeared with grape jelly. He caught her gaze, and one wolfish eyebrow arched upward.

"If you're ready," she said primly, "I can show you that room now."

He polished off the last bite of toast, washed it down with a swallow of tomato juice, dusted his fingers against a white paper napkin imprinted with Cupid's Rest B&B in pink lettering, and got to his feet. "Thanks for the breakfast, Pearl."

"You're welcome." Pearl beamed.

Natalie couldn't believe her cook liked him. Ornery Pearl got along with very few people. "This way, Mr. Vega."

Without waiting for him, she turned for the back door. His footsteps pattered behind her. Each step escalated the restless jumpiness, coiling her muscles tight as springs. She already regretted agreeing to rent him the room.

She led him to the carriage house, opened the door to Red's room, and stepped inside.

Dade came in after her. His broad shoulders seemed to fill the entire room.

Natalie took a deep breath and faced him. "This is it. If you can leave for a couple of hours I'll send the housemaid over to clean up."

"I can do it. Just give me some cleaning supplies."

"No," she said. "That's not how I do things."

He gave her a wicked half grin that knocked her off kilter. "Stickler for the rules, huh?"

"There's a proper way to do things, and having guests clean their own rooms is not proper."

"I'm a long-term boarder," he said. "Not a guest."

"You can clean your own room after this. I still have to go through Red's things." She picked up the cardboard box, stood stiffly with her back to the window, Dade blocking the exit with his linebacker shoulders.

The expression on his face was enigmatic, but the gleam in his eyes was pure sexual heat. "Everything by the book."

"I have a business to run. It has to be that way."

"Miss Prim," he teased.

"I suppose you pride yourself on being a rebel."

"Snap judgment about me based on the motorcycle?"

"It's not just the motorcycle."

"No?" He took a step toward her.

Her body tightened. She struggled not to let him see how much he affected her. "You came up to the house the wrong way. A rebel comes to the back door."

"Faulty GPS directions, remember."

"That's an excuse."

His fiendish smile told her she'd nailed him. "Maybe

I came to the back door as a surprise attack, not an act of rebellion."

"Why would you want to attack me?"

"Not you personally," he amended. "It's a life strategy."

"For what?"

"Dealing with the world. Life is a battlefield. Every encounter is an opportunity to win or lose."

"That's a bit harsh, don't you think?"

"Life *is* harsh. If you don't have a strategy for dealing with it, you'll end up dead."

"There's just one problem with that philosophy." She toyed with the cord on the window shade.

"What's that?"

"You'll end up dead anyway and in the process turn many people into enemies."

"Many people are enemies to begin with."

She shook her head, clutched the box tighter to her chest. "That's so sad and reductive."

"In what way?"

"Limiting life to a single strategy."

"You've got a strategy too."

"I do not."

"You might not think about it consciously, but you've got a method for making it through the day. We all do."

"Yeah? So what's my strategy?"

His dark eyes burned. "This is just a guess since I don't know you, but from what I can tell, you think life is a rule book. If you follow the rules and don't step outside your comfort zone, you won't get hurt, but because of that, you also never really live."

It unnerved her how accurately he'd summed up her

character. It made her angry too. "How very psychological of you," she retorted dryly.

"I've seen a shrink."

"Oh." That startled her.

"I had a head injury." He patted his temple. "All better now."

"And your shrink encouraged this battlefield metaphor."

He shrugged. "No, but there's nothing he could do about it. I am who I am."

"You don't think people can change?"

"No," he said adamantly. "I do not."

She shook her head. "And you think that *I* have lived a limited life."

"I could teach you a few things." His expression was wickedly sexy, his voice seductive.

She gulped at the idea of all the things he could teach her. "Just because I'm from a small town doesn't mean I'm an ignorant hick."

"I never said that." He stepped closer.

Luckily, the bed was between them, or maybe not so luckily. There they stood, just the two of them, a bed in the middle.

Dade was staring at the bed, the same as Natalie was. Were similar irrational images running through his head as were spilling through hers?

He surprised her by sinking down on the mattress.

Her gaze fixed on the breadth of his thighs. So powerful. She pulled a thin stream of air in through clenched teeth.

He bounced on the mattress. The box springs squeaked.

Natalie's throat convulsed as a dozen downright dirty

images filled her head. She imagined him stripped bare and lying in the middle of the mattress with a big, hard erection. Getting hard just for her.

Immediately, her face burned crimson hot.

"Comfortable." He nodded and leaned back, bracing himself with his palms splayed over the covers.

Her heart was running a dead-heat sprint, rushing blindly down a track that promised nothing but trouble, but as much as she resisted, she couldn't change the visions playing out like a movie—Dade pulling her down on the mattress beside him, stripping off her clothes, letting them drop to the floor, his hot mouth capturing hers.

And his hands!

Oh, his big masculine hands touching her in places and ways that she'd never been touched. She pictured her own hands skating over the rugged masculine angles of his body, deriving pleasure from inducing his needy groans. She imagined what he would taste like. Salty and slick like a raw oyster? Smoky, torrid, and honeyed like barbecue? Or maybe rich, hot, and sugary-sweet like fig-chili balsam?

She wanted so badly to find out.

What was she thinking! She never fantasized like this. Not so graphically, so heedlessly.

This man was a total stranger. He had dark secrets. Rebellious, backdoor secrets. She could feel it in the way his gaze caressed her body. Feel it deep in her bones. He had an agenda, but she had no idea what it was.

Unfortunately, she wanted Dade Vega. Wanted him more than she wanted to take another breath of air. Undeniable fact. It did no good to lie to herself. For the first time in her life, she literally *burned* for a man. Grew wet just thinking about him. Her body was in tumult. Riotous.

He smiled at her. Darkly. Mysteriously. Dangerously. As if he knew every single erotic thought passing through her head.

Dear God, she was in so much trouble! How would she survive having this man sleeping under her roof?

If he's The One, there's nothing to fear. And if he wasn't? What if she was just going batty with sexual need? *Hey, well then maybe he's the one to dispense with your virginity.* Great. *Thanks for that thought.* Now she was even more scared of what she might do. Or not do. How could she want something so much and be so afraid of it at the same time?

She wrapped her arms around herself. "I've changed my mind."

"About what?" he asked.

"I can't rent out Red's room. It doesn't feel right. He could return at any moment."

"Are you sure that's the real reason?"

"Absolutely," she lied.

"What if he never comes back? How long are you going to hold on to the room?"

"That's really none of your business, is it?"

He stood up on her side of the bed.

She stepped back, bumped into the wall. Dammit. Her knees were jelly. If he came any closer, they'd liquefy right out from underneath her.

"I don't think that's the reason at all." He lowered his head. "I think I scare you."

Determined not to be intimidated, Natalie squared

her shoulders, used the cardboard box as a shield. "You do not scare me, Mr. Vega. Not in the least."

"That comfort zone thing. I push you out of it."

She held her breath. "You certainly think a lot of yourself, don't you?"

He laughed, backed up.

Relieved, she exhaled.

He reached into his pocket, pulled out a wallet, counted off ten one-hundred-dollar bills. "Don't worry, darlin', you have nothing to fear from me. You just keep your distance and I'll keep mine."

Dade prowled restlessly at the window, watching Natalie shuffle up the limestone path toward the house. She stopped once and cast a backward glance over her shoulder. When her eyes met his, she quickly looked away and quickened her pace. Peering into her soft sky blue eyes was like sinking into summer.

His pulse skittered.

Hell's bells, he might have pushed her out of her comfort zone, but she'd done the same damn thing to him. He couldn't remember the last time he'd felt so caught off guard.

He followed her with his gaze until she disappeared inside. What he saw was a small-town girl with a lot of responsibility and a big heart. She shouldn't have been the sort of woman to grab him by the short hairs and make him pay attention, but inexplicably, he was mesmerized.

Dade was frightened.

Frightened because she made him feel things he wasn't accustomed to feeling. Nice things, and Dade didn't trust nice. He was also frightened because Red was missing. His buddy had just up and walked away from his possessions. Disappeared. Nice as this town might seem on the surface, he suspected a darker undercurrent ran through it. What in the hell had Red gotten himself mixed up in?

Natalie had accused him of being a rebel, but Red was the real rebel. He was the one who saw rules as a challenge just aching to be broken. Which was why Dade was having trouble wrapping his head around the fact that Red had chosen to settle down in Cupid, Texas, of all places. Why he'd even chosen to settle down at all. In that regard, he and Red were molded from the same clay. They'd both agreed a long time ago that neither of them was cut out for marriage or children. They were both too screwed up.

Red's rebelliousness had gotten him into a lot of trouble in the military, but it had also saved Dade's hide on more than one occasion.

Dade stared out the window, but he no longer saw Natalie's quaint bed-and-breakfast. In its place was the old run-down farmhouse in Durant, Oklahoma, where he'd first met Red.

He was ten years old and freshly removed from his father's house after the cops had confiscated three pounds of crack cocaine from underneath the bedroom floorboards. Dade had been scared, but determined not to show his fear. That was the only useful thing his old man had ever taught him—how to act tough.

He'd been belted into the back of the social worker's gray Chevy Cavalier, scowling at the washed-out-looking woman in a baggy floral dress who'd come to the car, a false smile pasted on her weathered face. Behind her, he'd seen a clutch of kids—all boys—in the dirt yard bare of a single blade of grass.

"Well, well," the foster mother asked. "Who do we have here?"

"This is Dade, he's a really good boy. Right, Dade?" The social worker swiveled her head to give him a please-go-with-me-on-this expression.

He'd folded his arms over his chest, deepened the scowl, and said, "Bite me."

"It's like that is it?" Sighing, the foster mother opened the car door and motioned for him to get out. "Just once couldn't one of them be civil?"

"He's had it rough," the social worker muttered.

"Haven't they all?"

"Yes, but his story is sadder than most," the social worker said in a muted voice and launched into his history about how his heroin addict mother had died of an overdose when Dade was four, leaving him to be raised by his drug-dealing father and his string of junkie whores.

Dade had tuned the women out, climbed from the car, and shifted his attention back to the boys peering at him with a combination of interest, distrust, and hostility. He'd caught the eye of the tallest boy, a stocky redhead with freckles sprinkled over his nose.

Red grinned and gave him the finger.

Unable to help himself, Dade grinned back. Best welcome he'd ever had.

It wasn't a good home. It wasn't a bad one. There was food. Not tasty, but plenty of it. There was a roof over his head and a routine. For most of his life, he'd had neither. Dade was adjusting, getting by, a few fistfights, but carving out a solid niche, until one night, two years later, the foster father came for him.

The man had a bulldog face—smashed in and jowly—and he smelled like whiskey, beef jerky, and motor oil. His name was Tank and he moved like one, heavy and lumbering, fully planting one foot before he moved the other when he walked. He worked for Jiffy Lube, ate corn nuts by the fistfuls, and perpetually carried black grime beneath his ragged fingernails. One hot summer night, he rousted Dade from his bed by slapping a dirty palm over his mouth.

"Shh, we don't wanna wake your roommate." He nodded to the sleeping boy in the upper bunk.

Dade fought, kicking, punching, and grunting, but Tank soon had him in a boa constrictor grip and was dragging him outside the house and toward the barn.

The night was terribly cheerful. Crickets chirping. Lightning bugs flickering through the oak trees. Soft, warm breeze brushed against his skin. A smiley yellow half moon hung high in the sky.

Dread filled Dade. His body was stiff with it, his stomach ice and frost. Goose bumps rippled shivers over his skin. He dug in his heels.

Tank tightened the squeeze around his neck.

He couldn't breathe. Bright sparkles burst behind his eyelids. A hellish fireworks display. He could no longer feel his limbs. His head throbbed and he was only vaguely aware of Tank kicking the barn door closed behind them.

It was hot and airless in the room crammed with rakes and hoses, hammers and saws and chains and car parts. An ancient John Deere tractor sat in one corner. A Chevy engine was perched up on cinder blocks in another. At the very back of the barn lay a rusty old army cot, and that was where Tank lugged him.

The pressure in his head was unbearable. He couldn't scream. Couldn't fight. He was totally helpless.

Tank flung him onto the cot, loomed over him. "This is gonna be fun."

Dade hauled air into his desperate lungs, hungry to breathe, starving to live, terrified of what was going to happen next.

Tank yanked down Dade's pajama bottoms.

No! No!

Weakly, Dade tried to double up his fists.

Tank laughed. "You think that's gonna stop me, you stupid pup?" He cuffed the side of Dade's head with a brick paw.

His ears rang so loudly that he wasn't sure he heard the bam of the barn door clanging open. His vision was still blurry, but he saw Tank jerk his head up, spin around.

Frantically, Dade grabbed for his pajama bottoms, pulling them up as he swung his gaze to the barn door.

There stood Red, shotgun clutched in his hands.

"What the fuck are you doing out of bed?" Tank snarled.

"Step away from the kid," Red growled.

Tank grabbed Dade up and yanked him in front of him, using Dade as a shield. "Or what?"

"Let him go or I'll blow your head off."

"Tough talk. Put down the shotgun, turn around, and walk back to the house, or you'll be next," Tank threatened.

Dade was bathed in sweat, his cotton pajamas sticking to his body. His legs were so weak he could barely stand up.

Red pumped the shotgun.

Tank audibly gulped.

"You wanna die today, fat man?" Red narrowed his eyes, looking like a carrot-topped Clint Eastwood in the making.

Tank splayed his palm to Dade's back, pushed him with a hard shove. "Go on, get out of here. Both of you."

Dade fell to his knees, his heart pounding.

With the shotgun pointed at Tank's beer belly, Red came over and one-armed Dade to his feet, and then put Dade behind him. "Throw me the keys to your car," Red told Tank.

Their foster father swore at them.

Red lowered the gun to Tank's crotch. "Seriously, fucker. Give me the keys or I'll shoot it off."

Something in Red's eyes must have told Tank he meant business, because Tank fished the keys from his pocket and tossed them on the ground. Dade sprang to retrieve them.

"Now lie down on your stomach on the cot," Red instructed.

Sending them a look of pure hatred, Tank did as Red commanded.

"Dade, get that duct tape over there and wrap it around his wrists." Red nodded at the duct tape on the saggy wooden shelf.

Dade taped up Tank, and then he and Red ran to Tank's old pickup truck. Red got in behind the wheel, revved the engine.

"You know how to drive a stick?" Dade asked.

"I can drive anything," Red boasted. He popped the vehicle in gear, and they took off.

"Where did you get the shotgun?"

"Stole it out of Tank's gun case."

"He keeps it locked."

"Like I can't pick a lock?"

"Why did you save me?" Dade asked, always suspicious of the kindness of strangers.

Red shrugged. "You remind me of my kid brother."

"Where is he?"

"Dead." He dropped the word casually but it fell onto Dade like a boulder.

"How did you know that Tank was gonna take me out to the barn?"

"Because I been there," Red said.

The authorities didn't find them until two days later when they got caught trying to shoplift a picnic ham from Wal-Mart. They were sent to a juvenile detention center, which as bad as it was, was better than the place they'd just left.

Dade blinked and he was back in the moment. His muscles were coiled tight and he realized his hands were clenched into fists. Natalie was coming back out of the house again, accompanied this time by a young woman toting a carryall of cleaning supplies.

He blinked, pulled his palm down his face, stepped back from the window. He needed to search the room for clues before the maid cleaned everything up. Quickly, he did a perimeter sweep, opening closet doors, going through the chest of drawers, peering underneath the bed. Nothing but a little dust.

The women came into the room. To keep from looking guilty, Dade grinned wide, but one glance at Natalie and he felt it again—that same overwhelming smack of attraction.

Get over it, Vega. You've been too long without sex, that's all it is.

He could not allow himself to become distracted by Natalie McCleary for so many reasons. Never mind the way she made him feel. He was in Cupid for one purpose and one purpose only. Red had rescued him twice in his life.

Now, it was his turn to rescue Red.

Chapter 6

I was blind until one shot from Cupid's arrow;
now I have 20/20 vision.

—Millie Greenwood

Natalie walked into the community center carrying a platter of Pearl's chicken salad sandwiches with the crusts cut off, trying not to think about Dade and the uproar he'd caused in her life.

The Cupid volunteers took turns bringing lunch for their meetings held every Monday, Wednesday, and Friday at noon when they gathered to answer the week's letters. There were eight permanent Cupid volunteers, plus a dozen others who showed up periodically or filled in for the core group when they went on vacation, experienced illnesses, or had family obligations. Other than Junie Mae Prufrock, Natalie was related to all of them in one way or another.

The Cupid letter-writing tradition had started in the 1930s in response to two events. One, the Depression hit and the town had a desperate need for extra income, and two, a brokenhearted Wallis Simpson made her pilgrimage to Cupid.

Natalie's grandmother Rose had spearheaded the campaign, gathering some of the local women to answer the letters that people left at the base of the Cupid stalagmite. At first, the replies to the letters were left on a bulletin board posted outside the caverns. As tourism grew, so did the pile of letters littering the cave, and the town voted to prohibit the leaving of letters at the stalagmite, and as an alternative, erected the statue of Cupid in the botanical gardens, moved the bulletin board where the answered letters were posted over there, and added the "Letters to Cupid" box.

In the 1940s someone had the idea of doing away with the bulletin board and instead printing the letters and "Cupid's" reply in a free weekly newspaper that was paid for, and distributed by, local businesses. Because of this, tourists would come to town, post their letters, and then hang around for several extra days to read the answers. Cupid's tourism, which had previously revolved primarily around the mineral springs, shifted, and soon just as many people were coming for the Cupid legend as for the health spas. Over the years a list of letter-writing rules had been posted. They currently read thusly:

1. All letters should be submitted using an anonymous pseudonym.

2. Letters will be answered within one week.

3. Letters of a sexually graphic nature will not be published.

4. The letters are for entertainment purposes only.

5. Cupid is not to be held responsible for what the letter writers do with the advice.

The last two items had been added on recommendation of an attorney, just in case some nut job did something crazy in the name of love and blamed it on the town.

In the digital age, there had been talk of accepting letters submitted online, but they quickly realized the volume of the letters would prohibit the volunteers from being able to answer them all. As it was, they received upward of three hundred letters a week. So they voted to keep things old-school. Besides, it added to the mystique. If you wanted to plead your case to the god of love, you had to come to town to do it.

Natalie laid her purse on the long folding table set up in front of the window, positioned so that the group could look out on Main Street and watch the tourists go by as they answered letters. It was a pleasant reminder of their audience and why they were doing what they did.

Generally, each volunteer sat in the same place, unless someone was mad at someone else. Which, considering they were mostly family, happened with some frequency. As the oldest daughter, of the oldest daughter, of the oldest daughter of Millie Greenwood, Natalie's place was at the head of the table.

Aunt Carol Ann, Natalie's mother's younger sister,

was already at the center, busily spreading a cheery paper tablecloth over the buffet table. A five-gallon plastic Igloo beverage dispenser sat to one side, and Natalie knew without having to ask that it was filled with sweet tea.

Her aunt was a sharp dresser, especially for Cupid. She had on a teal green business suit, matching high heels, and a strand of cultured pearls at her neck. She didn't wear pantyhose because she'd read in *How Not to Look Old* that pantyhose made you look like an *old lady*.

Last year, when Carol Ann had turned fifty, the family had misguidedly thrown her a surprise party. With her feelings hurt over the black balloons and over-the-hill signage, Carol Ann had spent the afternoon in the bathroom, staring at her wrinkles in the mirror and plotting a trip to El Paso to get a chemical peel, fillers, and Botox injections. Now, she couldn't frown if she wanted to and she had lips to rival Angelina Jolie's.

"Notice anything new about me?" Aunt Carol Ann turned to smile at Natalie.

Her teeth sparkled as white as Crisco. Natalie wished she hadn't left her sunshades in the basket of her bicycle. "Um…your teeth are very white."

"Thank you! I had them brightened. Dr. Clinton does that Zoom thing. He lightened them seven shades!" Her smile vanished. "But your uncle Davis didn't even notice. I swear I could set my hair on fire and he wouldn't look up from Angry Birds. I wish I hadn't gotten him that iPhone for Christmas."

"Your teeth look beautiful."

"That's kind of you to say." Carol Ann took the platter of sandwiches from Natalie and set it out on the table along with paper plates, napkins, and plastic cups.

Her aunt was lean and long from years of Pilates. She'd had the Pilates machines installed in her house and kept trying to get Natalie to give Pilates a go. She was convinced it would help Natalie's leg, but after years of physical therapy, Natalie knew that this was as good as it got.

"You should try the Zoom. It'll do wonders for your smile," Carol Ann prodded.

"I'm pretty happy with my smile just as it is."

Her aunt shook her head and clicked her tongue. "Tsk."

"What?"

"Honey, why do you settle for so little? You could be so beautiful if you'd just try a bit." She reached over and pulled Natalie's hair back. "For instance, a Brazilian blowout would take care of this frizz."

That needled her, but she didn't like dusting things up, so she let it pass.

"I suppose that's what happens when you grow up without a mother to guide you."

"You've mothered me plenty, Auntie."

Her aunt stepped back. "Your mom would have been so proud of you and all you've achieved, but I know she would have wanted you to spruce yourself up. She'd be disappointed to learn you still weren't married at twenty-nine. If you wait too long to have children you might discover that you can't have them at all."

"Would that be the end of the world?" Natalie asked, feeling defensive. She had chosen to remain single and virginal, but it was her choice. Never mind that she'd just had a mind-altering morning. In this day and age, a woman should be able to choose whatever path was best for her, whether it be marriage or motherhood or even celibacy. One choice wasn't any better than an-other. It wasn't one size fits all.

"Not the end of the world, just sad. It would be the end of a tradition. No more eldest daughter of the eldest daughter of the eldest daughter."

Natalie shrugged off her overreaction, put it down to Dade Vega. "Oh well."

Carol Ann pursed her lips. "I don't know how you do it."

"Do what?"

"Take life in stride."

Natalie shrugged. "What else am I supposed to do? Whine? Complain? Gnash my teeth? Wring my hands? Shake my fist at God? None of that would change any-thing."

"It's just that…" Carol Ann paused, waved a hand, looked pensive a moment. "Oh, never mind."

"How's Melody?" Natalie asked about Aunt Carol Ann's daughter. Melody had escaped Cupid for New York and she was a hotshot Madison Avenue ad ex-ecutive.

"Terrific." Her aunt brightened. "She's heading up Charmin's new ad campaign."

"Charmin the toilet paper?" Okay, that was mean. Natalie was a wee bit jealous of Melody.

Carol Ann proudly raised her chin. "People need toilet paper."

"Turns out not so much. People used to use news-paper, magazines, even leaves to cover the job, and in some other countries they simply use their hands." Oops, where was this tackiness coming from?

"Well, we're not in some other country, are we?"

Carol Ann sniffed. "This is the God-fearing United States of America and we use toilet paper."

" 'Course we do," Natalie placated. Her insurrections were few and far between, and when she was snarky she immediately felt guilty about it. "I'm happy for Melody and Charmin."

Luckily, at that moment the door opened and her cousin Lace Bettingfield dreamily meandered into the room.

Lace was three years younger than Natalie and the only daughter of Lincoln and Colleen Bettingfield. Uncle Lincoln was the middle child sandwiched between Natalie's mom and Aunt Carol Ann. As a child, Lace had battled a severe stutter and it had made her extremely introverted. She'd finally conquered the stutter, but she'd never gotten over the shyness. She was a beautiful girl—the prettiest one in the current crop of Millie Greenwood's granddaughters—with alabaster skin, in spite of the fact she spent most of her days outdoors as a botanist for the botanical gardens; coal black hair; and startling light blue eyes. Everyone said she looked just like Snow White (and the unkind might silently mumble, *If Snow White was thirty pounds overweight*).

If Natalie had to put up with Aunt Carol Ann's unsolicited advice about her limp and her hair, Lace had it worse. Carol Ann was always giving her diet books and signing her up for online weight loss newsletters.

Natalie knew her cousin used the weight as insulation against the opposite sex. Something had happened in high school with a boy that Lace had had an unrequited crush on. As far as Natalie knew, Lace had never had a boyfriend.

While Natalie had had a couple of boyfriends, she

and Lace had something ironic in common. They both answered letters to the lovelorn pretending to be Cupid when neither one of them had ever had a successful love relationship.

Well, that is, until this morning.

Wait a minute. Hold the stallions. She didn't know for sure that she was in love. She couldn't just jump off a cliff because of these feelings. She didn't even know the man.

But when he'd looked into her eyes, when he'd touched her…wow, just wow.

"Natty?" Aunt Carol Ann was at her elbow.

"Uh-huh?"

"Are you okay? You look like you've got a fever." Her aunt placed a palm on Natalie's forehead. "Hmm, cool as a cucumber."

Natalie stepped away, but tried not to let her irritation show. "I'm fine. Thanks for your concern."

"Is something wrong?" Lace asked, temporarily snapping out of her perpetually dreamy state.

Gram used to say about Lace, "I've never seen a child daydream the way that one does. She lives in her own little world." In that regard, to stay with the princess analogies, Lace was more like Sleeping Beauty than Snow White.

And which princess are you?

Natalie shook off the question. She wasn't a princess at all. She was too practical for any of that regal nonsense, but her favorite childhood fairy tale had been Cinderella. She easily identified with hard work and sacrifice, and like Cinderella, she tried to stay cheerful in the face of her responsibilities. She smiled at Lace. "Everything's wonderful. How are you, cousin?"

Lace's face dissolved into a beatific smile. "I got the new adenium hybrid that I ordered six weeks ago from Thailand to bloom. I'm so excited. You have to come by the greenhouse and take a look. It's the color of peppermint candy cane. I hope to transplant it into the garden by the end of next month."

Aunt Carol Ann frowned. "A den what?"

"Adenium is a genus of flowering plants in the dogbane family known as Apocynaceae." Lace gestured enthusiastically.

"Huh?" Carol Ann looked confused.

"It's a rare strain of desert rose," Natalie translated for their aunt.

"Oh. Well, why didn't she just say that?"

Lace rolled her eyes.

Natalie winked at her cousin and gestured toward the buffet table. "Help yourself to some of Pearl's chicken salad sandwiches."

"Limit yourself to two," Carol Ann called after Lace.

The door opened again and Junie Mae came in with Great-Aunt Delia. Delia didn't drive anymore, so Junie Mae always swung by to pick her up.

Delia was Grandmother Rose's younger sister. She toddled in, bracing herself on an ivory-handled cane. At seventy-seven, she was the oldest volunteer. Her body might have been compromised by osteoporosis, but her mind was a steel trap. To keep her mental faculties sharp, she did find-a-word puzzles, practiced water aerobics five days a week at the Cupid senior citizens' center, and took acetyl-L-carnitine supplements. She'd recently heard that learning a foreign language could help stave off Alzheimer's, so she'd bought the full course of Rosetta Stone Spanish.

"*Hola!*" Delia greeted.

"Warning," Junie Mae said. "She jabbered Spanish all the way over here."

"*Todos ustedes deben aprender a hablar a español. Vivimos en Texas.*"

Carol Ann blinked owlishly. "Huh?"

"Learn Spanish and you'll know what I'm saying," Delia said smugly.

"You enjoy being a handful, don't you, Auntie?"

"No more than you, Carol Ann." Delia caught Lace by the arm with the crook of her cane as she walked past. She pushed her glasses down on the end of her nose and peered at Lace's plate loaded with three sandwiches. "Are those Pearl's chicken salad sandwiches?"

"Uh-huh," Lace said.

"I've gotta have some. Pearl makes the best chicken salad in town. It's because she uses tarragon and those seedless Thompson grapes."

"I'll get you a plate, Auntie Delia," Natalie offered. "You go ahead and have a seat."

Delia patted Natalie's cheek. "You're such a good girl. I'll have three halves and some of those ruffled-up sour cream and chive potato chips."

"Chips are full of sodium, Aunt Delia," Carol Ann scolded.

Delia faked a wide-eyed innocence. "My goodness, should we call Channel Nine in El Paso and tell them about the earth-shattering news?"

"I'm just trying to help." Carol Ann sniffed. "Do you want to have to go back on those water pills?"

"*Bese mi asno,*" Delia said sweetly.

Carol Ann frowned. "What's that?"

"She said she appreciates your concern," Natalie lied,

sliding the plate of sandwiches and a small amount of chips in front of Delia as her great aunt sat down. She wasn't about to let Carol Ann know that Delia had just told her to kiss her ass in Spanish.

"Oh well. You're welcome." Carol Ann beamed.

Lace rolled her eyes again and bit into a sandwich. She might be quiet and dreamy, but Lace also had a sarcastic side.

Junie Mae wisely stayed out of it.

Delia crunched a chip. "Where is everyone else?"

"We're here, we're here, sorry to be late."

They all turned as the two cousins by marriage, Sandra and Mignon, entered the room.

Mignon was married to Delia's son, Michael. Mignon had been born in the Loire Valley and she'd met Michael when she worked as a winery tour guide and he'd come to the vineyard for a summer internship. They ran Mon Amour, one of the three wineries nestled in the valley of the Davis Mountains.

Sandra had been married to Delia and Rose's younger brother, Stephen, before he'd passed away six years earlier. Sandra was in her sixties and ran Cupid's Cup, the local coffee shop. She and Stephen had had four sons, none of whom still lived in Cupid, much to Sandra's disappointment. Junie Mae and Sandra had gone to high school together, although Junie Mae had been a senior when Sandra was a sophomore.

There was so much family history to keep up with that sometimes even Natalie got confused about who was related to whom and how.

"You're not too late," Carol Ann said. "Zoey isn't here yet."

Mignon was the most exotic person Natalie knew

and she was responsible for Natalie's fascination with all things French. When Natalie was growing up, Mignon gave her issues of *Elle* and told exciting stories of her numerous love affairs when she lived in Paris.

Even though Mignon drank wine daily, ate her fill of cheese, and never worked out, at forty-five she was as thin as a ruler and almost as tall as Natalie. She wore her hair clipped in a short cap of brown curls, smoked slim brown cigarettes, swore like a stevedore, and did not shave her armpits, but did shave her legs.

That drove Junie Mae nuts. "Either shave or don't shave, pick one," she was fond of telling Mignon. "And for godsakes, if you're not gonna shave those pits, don't wear tank tops. None of the rest of us wanna see that."

Mignon would just laugh at that and raise her arms over her head to show off her au naturel underarms.

"*Mon Dieu*, it's hot out there." Mignon fanned herself with a hand. She had never really adjusted to the southwest Texas heat.

"You'll feel better after a glass of cold sweet tea," Sandra soothed.

As the peacemakers of the group, Sandra and Natalie were more alike than anyone else in the room, although Sandra liked to keep things peaceful because she hated conflict of any kind, while Natalie, on the other hand, was terrified of losing those she loved. When things ran smoothly, Natalie felt more secure.

Sandra was plump, possessed ebony hair sprinkled lightly with gray, and lush caramel skin. Three things differentiated Sandra. She boasted the largest collection of teddy bears this side of the Pecos. She was known far and wide for her banana pudding, for which she refused to part with the recipe, but she hinted she might leave it to someone in her will. And she and Stephen had been the first interracial couple in Cupid.

Oddly enough, considering it was Texas in the sixties, their marriage had barely caused a stir. Mainly because in this town, everyone claimed that when Cupid's arrow struck its target, there was very little you could do about it. Stephen had fallen for Sandra and that was that. Besides, she was one of the nicest people you'd ever want to meet. No one could hold a grudge against Sandra for long. She was an expert at killing detractors with kindness.

"I shall feel better after a glass of chilled Chardonnay," Mignon said, "but sadly, I must wait until I get home for that."

Sandra and Mignon helped themselves to the food and settled in at the table on the same side as Delia. Junie Mae, Carol Ann, and Lace sat across from them.

"We should go ahead and start without Zoey," Natalie said. "Her summer school class runs long."

"Very well," Carol Ann said, reaching into her tote bag for a handful of letters and spreading them out in the middle of the table. She turned on her iPad. By profession, Carol Ann was a CPA, and by hobby, she was a genealogy fanatic, so it was a natural fit for her to keep track of the letters and organize the volunteers.

Carol Ann pulled a pair of snazzy pink and black zebra print reading glasses from her pocket, slipped them on, and consulted the list on her iPad. She smelled of watermelon shampoo and Dial soap. She was a bit OCD and showered two or three times a day.

Their tri-weekly meetings lasted for an hour and a half. They answered what letters they could as a group, consulting with one another, then whatever letters they weren't able to get to, Carol Ann divided up among them and they took them home to answer. Natalie was supposed to have a response today for Shot Through the Heart. She'd already been dragging her feet over the letter—no pun intended—but after what happened that morning, she was even more confused than ever about how she would reply.

"Natalie dear, have you crafted your response to Shot Through the Heart?" Carol Ann asked.

Natalie slowly finished chewing the last bite of sandwich, stalling. It didn't work.

"Well?" Carol Ann prodded.

"Um, not yet." She dabbed at her mouth with a napkin.

"You've had the letter for a week. You know our policy. Answered within a week."

"I know."

"So what's the problem?"

Natalie thought of the letter she'd left drying out on the window ledge after her tumble into the pond. "I'm not sure how to answer her."

"It's not that difficult. Just give her Cupid's standard answer. Follow your heart."

"But the situation is more complicated than that."

Carol Ann twisted her mouth up. "Really, it's not."

"If I tell her to follow her heart and she ends up giving up her scholarship to Oxford, I'd feel responsible."

Her aunt touched her arm. "You're not a guidance counselor. This is just for fun. Like going to a psychic. People don't truly expect us to solve their love problems."

Natalie met her eyes. "Then why do we bother?"

"Someone has to answer the letters."

"Therein lies the problem. I don't know what I'm talking about. I've never been in love, much less fallen in love at first sight," she said, but the minute the words were out of her mouth, Dade's face popped into her head. She saw him exactly how he'd looked that morning, bare-chested, working on his motorcycle. Another flush of heat went through her. Even now, she felt breathless and jumbled.

"Is it irresponsible to encourage someone to believe in a myth?" She posed the question she'd been wrestling with for some time.

The love-at-first-sight feelings she'd experienced for Dade hadn't answered the question as she'd believed it would have. In fact, the feelings only raised more questions, like could she trust her feelings and was he feeling it too and what if he was an outlaw or had a substance abuse problem or—

"It's not a myth, sugar." Junie Mae interrupted Natalie's downward spiral of anxiety. She balled up her napkin and made a free throw at the trash can in the corner. Sank it.

Sandra whistled. "She shoots, she scores. You still got it, Junie Mae."

Junie Mae curled up the fingers of one hand, blew on her nails. "Highest scoring female forward in Cupid High School history," she said to Sandra. To Natalie she said, "True love is as real as you or me."

"But can you prove it?"

Junie Mae shook her head, looked beseechingly around the table. "I can't believe Millie's very own great-granddaughter is so skeptical. Y'all gonna let her get away with that?"

Junie Mae had known Millie personally. She loved to

tell stories of how Millie would open up the Fant home on Pike Street for tea parties and invite the neighborhood girls to attend. Natalie was a bit jealous of that. She would have given anything to have known her colorful great-grandmother.

Junie Mae looked a bit like Dolly Parton, except with less makeup—big-busted, big-haired, narrow-waisted, blond (thanks to Miss Clairol), and she hugged everyone as if they were her long-lost sisters, pressing them into her pillowy chest. She spoke in a soft Southern drawl, sweet as Vidalia onions, and cultivated from an early girlhood in Savannah. She embraced technology. She was the first one in Cupid to own a computer and she was a social networking fanatic. "They invented Twitter just for me," she loved to say, usually while tweeting.

"There's a big difference between sexual attraction and real love," Natalie pointed out, trying to convince herself more than the women around her. "We romanticize the first here in Cupid, downplay the latter."

"Bless your little heart," Junie Mae said. "You just haven't experienced true love yourself, but you will one day. I promise."

Natalie gulped, tried to ignore the fresh sparks igniting inside her as she remembered the way it had felt when Dade touched her. As if the world had come to a complete halt and nothing existed but the two of them. As if she could trust him with her life and he would never, ever betray her.

But was it just a fantasy? Real love was about more than sparks and sparkle. It wasn't just about breathless lungs and racing hearts. When it got down to it, how did you really, truly *know*? She so wanted them to be right, and at the same time, she was terrified of getting plowed under by these feelings.

"Your parents were deeply in love," Carol Ann said.

"Yes, and look how that turned out."

Aunt Carol Ann and Junie Mae gasped at the same time.

Natalie shrugged. "Hey, I'm just being honest here. Love didn't save them."

"You don't know that," Junie Mae whispered.

"Love made them frivolous. Taking an airplane out for a nine-year-old's picnic." It sounded harsh, but she'd thought about it often. If her father hadn't played hooky from work for her birthday, if her mother hadn't indulged him, they might still be here.

"Silly child," Delia scolded. "It wasn't love that killed them, it was wind shears."

"Your parents were soul mates. They were destined. They died together and they are together somewhere right now," Sandra said staunchly.

"Love has led many people astray." Surprised by how angry she suddenly felt, Natalie scooped up a handful of letters and waved them around. Why was she so angry when she was experiencing the very thing she'd longed to experience all her life?

"What do you mean?" Carol Ann asked.

"We have evidence right here. Dear Cupid, I'm in love with a married man. Dear Cupid, I'm in love with a man on death row. Dear Cupid, he hits me but I love him so much, how can I leave him?" She needed reassurance that she wasn't running headlong down a dangerous path.

"*Ma petite*, many of those people are misguided.

Mistaking lust or dependency for love," Mignon pointed out.

"How are you supposed to know the difference?" she beseeched them.

"You're just scared." Junie Mae reached over to stroke Natalie's forearm. "It's understandable, considering what you've been through, but you can't let fear keep you from loving."

"I love," Natalie said, gently putting the letters back down in the middle of the table. "I love all of you."

"That's not the kind of love we're talking about." Sadness tugged down Sandra's mouth. "If you keep closing yourself off to love, you'll never find it."

"I'm not looking for it," Natalie declared, but in her heart she knew why she was being so contentious. Dade Vega. He'd rocked her world. Junie Mae was right. She was scared. She closed her eyes, blew out her breath.

"Are you okay, sugar?"

Natalie opened her eyes, forced a smile. "I'm fine."

"Back to Shot Through the Heart," Aunt Carol Ann said. "We do need to answer her. If you'd rather not answer her, I can give the letter to someone else."

Natalie couldn't say why Shot Through the Heart's letter had gotten such a grip on her, but it had. Now, with this fresh wrinkle in her life, she was more uncertain of her response than ever before, but she hated quitting things in the middle. "I really would like to answer it."

"You'll have a response for me by Wednesday?"

"Could I have another week?" Natalie couldn't help feeling that if she figured out what she was going to say to Shot Through the Heart, it would clarify her own beliefs about love at first sight. There were so many of those bam-it's-kismet! stories floating around in Cupid, but she had started believing they were nothing but stories. Tall tales.

That is, until this morning when she'd felt it too.

Goose bumps waltzed up her arms. Just thinking about Dade and that glorious moment in the rising sun when their eyes had met...

That was the problem. Right there. Those kinds of feelings made people do crazy things like give up scholarships to Oxford.

Dear Shot Through the Heart, get on that damn plane and fly to England. Now!

"I suppose I could give you another week." Aunt Carol Ann didn't look happy. "But if you haven't answered it by next Monday, I'm going to give the letter to Zoey to answer."

"Thank you," Natalie said, grateful for the reprieve.

Carol Ann looked around the table. "Shall we get started?"

Junie Mae took the bull by the horns and opened a letter. "Dear Cupid, I'm afraid my husband is losing interest in me."

"I'll take that one." Mignon waved a hand. She loved telling people how to spice up their love lives.

Carol Ann recorded the letter into her iPad. "Who's the sender?"

"Lost the Spark," Junie Mae said.

"Next," Carol Ann prompted.

Lace opened that one. "Dear Cupid, I'm desperately in love with a man who doesn't love me back." Her pale face colored and she shoved the letter at Sandra. Lace refused to answer letters dealing with unrequited love. "You take that one."

Sandra took the letter and reached over to pat Lace on the shoulder.

They went around the table like that, reading the letters, dividing them up, Carol Ann making note of every piece of correspondence. Forty-five minutes into it, the door burst open and Zoey rushed in. The room lit up the minute she entered. Everyone sat up straighter, smiled bigger. Her sister had that effect on people.

"What's shakin', bacon?" Zoey went around the table and dropped a kiss on everyone's cheek except for Natalie. "Sorry I'm so late. I had a flat and it took me forever to find a cute guy to change it for me."

"You could have called Triple A," Natalie muttered.

Zoey wrinkled her nose. "What would have been the fun in that?"

"How cute was he?" Mignon asked.

"Passable. Nothing to miss lunch for." Zoey sashayed over to the buffet table, piled up a plate with food, and came to plunk down at the end of the table opposite Natalie. "Speaking of handsome, who is our new boarder? He's delish." She licked her lips.

Jealousy burst inside Natalie. Zoey had eyes for Dade? Natalie didn't stand a chance. There wasn't a man alive that Zoey couldn't wrap around her little finger.

Back off! she wanted to growl. *He's mine.*

"You have a new boarder?" Carol Ann perked up. She loved knowing everything that went on in Cupid.

All heads at the table swiveled to stare at Natalie.

Feeling defensive, Natalie shrugged. "It doesn't seem Red is coming back and I need the money."

"He's totally hot." Zoey took a bite of fruit salad. "Where on earth did you find him?"

"He came to me," Natalie answered, realizing it was a strange thing to say.

"What's his name?" Zoey asked. "He's cute enough to change my religion over."

"He doesn't strike me as the pious type," Natalie said dryly.

"You've got a point there." Zoey grinned and wriggled her eyebrows. "But neither am I. He looks wicked bad to me. Any girl thinking about hooking up with him has gotta expect to get burned."

"Don't forget it," Natalie cautioned, but she wasn't talking to her sister, she was warning herself.

Chapter 7

*When it's true love, the only thing that matters is
your beloved's happiness.*

—Millie Greenwood

For the last two days, Dade had done two things: avoid
his pretty landlady and surreptitiously search for his
friend.

The first part wasn't difficult because Natalie seemed
to be avoiding him as much as he was avoiding her. Plus,
he'd started his job at Chantilly's and he'd met all the
players there. He worked from six p.m. to two a.m. and
Natalie got up and went to bed with the chickens. She
was a complication he could not afford, especially given
the way she turned him on.

He'd spent three restless nights tossing and turning
and trying not to think about her. Just when he man-

aged to snag a few zzz's, Natalie would run through his dreams on one long replay loop. In his reverie, he courted her, kissed her, and made love to her with every atom of his being. He jolted awake, bathed in sweat, with a raging hard-on strong enough to cut diamonds.

He had to stay clear of her. If he allowed it, she could easily become an obsession, and if Red hadn't stayed at the Cupid's Rest, he would have already vacated the place. As it was, the B&B and Chantilly's bar were his only connections to his foster brother.

To keep his mind off Natalie, he focused on the reason he was here in the first place.

Red.

But that was another minefield. He couldn't come right out and ask about Red. He'd tried casually asking Jasper about the man who had the bouncer job before him, but Jasper had cut him off. "I'm not a gossiper. You like gossip, go buy the *National Enquirer*."

He'd tried striking up conversations with the other two boarders, the senior citizen and the geeky computer kid. The kid had pretty well ignored him, while the old geezer had bent his ear about some old boat he was having built. He met the next-door neighbor, Junie Mae something-or-other. Dade thought of her as Dolly because she looked a bit like Dolly Parton. She had been willing to talk, but she didn't seem to know much about Red. Finally, he thoroughly searched the room where Red had stayed, looking behind wall plugs and inside the air vent, taking the back off the framed landscape picture on the wall, but he found absolutely no clues to his buddy's whereabouts.

It ate on Dade that he'd made no headway in the past two days. He was scared shitless that Red had gone and done something desperate. Maybe he should go to the authorities and tell them who he was.

He weighed the option, continued to weigh it, but consistently discarded that alternative. For one thing, he'd been on the wrong side of the law enough times in his youth to develop a deep-seated mistrust of law enforcement. For another thing, Natalie had already informed the authorities about Red's disappearance and they'd done little to search for him. Dade had the Mayday text—their one-word secret code for the utmost danger—but no one else would consider it alarming.

Tanked.

Perhaps law enforcement was precisely whom Red was telling him not to trust.

Dade's heart sank.

The pessimist in him feared the worst—that Red had gone off his meds, wandered into the desert, and died.

Intentionally?

But if Red had been suicidal, why had he sent the text message? Had he been in the grips of a delusion? Had he thought he was back in Afghanistan?

The warrior in Dade went on the assumption that Occam's razor was wrong and the simplest theory was not the correct one. The suspicious part of him kept trying to catch a glimpse beyond the friendly smiles and neighborly waves to see what darkness lay beneath.

He knew all too well that looks were deceiving. Besides, this was a tourist town. Cupid's survival depended on its welcoming ways. It was a front, a façade, and he refused to be drawn in by the strong sense of community. His gut told him that something more complicated than PTSD flashbacks had happened to

Red in this town, and he was determined to find out what it was.

On Thursday morning—six days since Red had sent the text—urgency had built to frenzy inside Dade. The longer he went without finding his buddy, the more likely it was that the outcome would be unfavorable.

Pressured by equal doses of worry and lust, and unable to sleep, Dade had gotten out of bed for a five a.m. jog. He dressed in running shorts and sneakers. The only time he ever wore shorts was when he worked out. Short pants made him feel exposed.

Five miles into the run, he'd stripped off his T-shirt and now wore it twisted up and tied around his head like a bandana to keep sweat from dripping in his eyes. He'd been on the Louisiana coast before coming to Cupid and he was still adjusting to the arid heat and altitude, although he didn't miss the humidity.

He ran through town and was just about to lap back to the Cupid's Rest when he caught a familiar sight. A pretty brunette pedaled her blue Schwinn through the town square, the street lamps casting her in an ethereal glow as orange rays of dawn tipped the horizon.

Captivated, Dade stopped in his tracks even though his instincts urged him to pretend he hadn't seen her and take off down a side road. Everything seemed suddenly clear to him, very vibrant and swiftly slow. He could almost smell his own arousal, testosterone swelling slickly through his body, as he watched her progress up Pike Street.

Natalie caught sight of him and a fleeting but unmistakable look of panic crossed her face. Quickly, she snuffed it out and pasted on a smile.

Something loosened inside him at that smile and he

found himself smiling back. No. Not just smiling, but grinning, big and goofy like a kid with his first serious crush.

"Good morning," she called.

He clenched his hands into fists, prayed she'd just keep on riding.

She stopped.

His spirits soared.

"I haven't seen much of you in the past two days," she said.

He looked into her eyes.

Her pupils widened, took him in, open and accepting.

God, how he wanted to capture those pink lips and hold them hostage without ransom, to run his hand up the nape of her neck and cradle the back of her head in his palm, to feel her breasts pressed up tight against his chest. He curled his fingers into fists.

She was staring at his bare chest and he felt both proud and exposed. He wanted to strut like a peacock, flex and pose, show off his muscles for her. It was vanity, he knew it, and that surprised him because Dade wasn't a vain guy, but he wanted Natalie to know he was strong and healthy enough to give her anything she wanted or needed.

Damn this impulse!

"Have you had breakfast yet?" he asked in a rush.

She blinked and her lips parted—sweet, kissable lips. "Um…no."

"Would you like to?" What the frig was he doing? He was supposed to be avoiding her. "Have breakfast, I mean. I've been hearing good things about the eggs at La Hacienda Grill."

"Mmm. You're a bit naked for that, aren't you?"

What? Oh yeah, he'd completely forgotten he was

half dressed and sweaty. "Give me twenty minutes to get home, shower and change?"

Home?

He'd called his room at her B&B home. What the hell was that?

"Are you asking me out?"

"No, not out-out. Just breakfast."

"Pearl is making flapjacks this morning. Don't you want to eat there, save some money?"

"I thought a change of pace might be nice for you. At the B&B you're always taking care of your guests. If you eat somewhere else you'll get taken care of."

She didn't want to have breakfast with him. Drop it.

Natalie tapped her index finger with her chin, but didn't drop her gaze. Here they were in the middle of the quiet street, caught in the throes of an undeniable attraction neither of them was sure they wanted.

He felt his shaft harden, lengthen, and he struggled against the arousal. Sensations streamed through his lower body, and visions of him and Natalie having sex fused in his mind. He saw her legs up in the air as he plunged deep into her. His imagination sparked and a rolling current of energy blasted through him.

"Forget it." He shook his head. "It was a bad idea."

"No, no. It was a good idea. I've just…it's…well…"

He raised a hand, felt as rejected as when Jessica Haddock had shot him down in high school because she was a cheerleader and he was so far on the wrong side of the tracks that people from the wrong side of the tracks looked down on him. He took off jogging again. "Have a good day, Natalie."

"Dade, wait," she called after him, but he just kept running.

* * *

Under a cartouche of fading stars, Natalie pedaled from Dennis Street onto the paved path leading to the pocket park behind Cupid's Rest, the same path that Dade had traversed on his motorcycle on Monday. She maneuvered her bike along at a steady pace, certain and sure in her familiar milieu, but it was the only part of her that was confident.

Dade had asked her out.

And she'd said no.

Was she stupid or brilliant? Natalie had no idea. She wanted to go out with him, longed to go out with him, in fact, but feared it at the same time.

Being twenty-nine and single had never been part of Natalie's life plan. When she was a child, she used to tell her mother she was going to get married when she was twenty-two and have four kids, two boys and two girls.

Her mother would laugh and kiss Natalie's forehead. "We'll see about that."

But after her parents died and she shouldered the responsibility of raising Zoey, her dreams had shifted. Love had started to seem pretty darn dangerous, and she'd realized just how much hard work it took to take care of kids. Those old dreams tattered in the face of real life, and somehow the years slipped away, and with them, Natalie's dreams of finding her one true love.

Part of the problem lay in the fact that the dating pool in Cupid was pretty shallow. She was kin to half the men in town and had known the other half since she was in kindergarten. That left the tourists, but long-distance relationships rarely worked, and besides, she'd never felt the spark, the fire, the unbeatable feeling of romantic love that she'd once believed in so strongly before the years eroded her faith.

That is, until she'd first laid eyes on Dade.

He'd rocked her safe little world, and while the upheaval thrilled her, it bothered her as well.

Love at first sight.

It was a fanciful notion, but every time she thought of him, her breathing sped up and her pulse bounded. He was a very sexy man. He'd make anyone's heart thump.

She had to get the notion of love at first sight out of her head. It was difficult because she'd cut her teeth on the fairy tale, and deep inside of her, she ached for it to be true.

Over the course of the last few days, she'd decided that Dade wasn't really the problem, but rather a symptom. The problem was that she had never had sex. Her virginity had become a serious stumbling block and it was time to dispense with it.

She wasn't in love with Dade Vega. These intense feelings could not be based on anything but the physical. How could they be? She barely knew him. She was not in love.

Not at all.

She was just horny.

Good. It was good to have the diagnosis and admit it. Not love. Lust. She was certain of that now.

The question was what to do about it.

Easy solution. Find someone to have a good time with, someone who was *not* Dade. He made her feel too out of control. She needed a short-term, physical relationship. Maybe with a cute tourist?

Great plan, except for one not so small thing. Natalie had no idea how to flirt and charm, it just wasn't in her makeup, but she certainly knew someone who did.

Zoey.

A loaf of bread lasted longer than most of Zoey's relationships. Maybe she could ask her sister's advice on how to keep things light and relaxed. No pressure. No muss. No fuss. Nothing more than a good time.

Zoey had been dying to give her a makeover for years. Maybe she would finally let her.

Natalie rode up to the duck pond. Two lotus flowers floated on silky green pads atop the murky water. They bloomed incandescent blushing pink cups with creamy ivory centers that drained to ceremonial gold at the bottom. She paused a moment to take in the beautiful sight.

In the soft morning light, she spied Lars and Gizmo standing at the edge of the pool.

"Good morning!" she called out, swung off her bike, and walked it over to where they stood.

Gizmo had his hands stuffed in his pockets. He ducked his head, toed the ground. He was a good two inches shorter than Natalie's five-seven, with skin the color of button mushrooms, pale and washed out. He was pudgy, wore baggy jeans and an oversized Max Payne T-shirt. Greasy auburn hair touched his shoulders, and he wore a brown wool stocking cap pulled down over his ears.

"Mornin'," Gizmo mumbled.

"You're up early."

Gizmo jerked a thumb at Lars. "His fault."

Natalie shifted her gaze to Lars. The ruddy-skinned senior citizen dwarfed the pasty nineteen-year-old. They were the most mismatched pair she could imagine.

"Taking the lad fishing," Lars said smoothly. "He needs to get out of that room once in a while."

"In the pond?"

"At the lake."

Natalie looked at the pond. The lotus blooms were already starting to close in the encroaching heat.

Lars turned his palm up. "We're here for minnows."

"Where's your minnow bucket?"

Lars and Gizmo exchanged a glance. "We're using a Mason jar."

Natalie didn't see a jar. "You'll have to poke holes in the lid so the minnows get air."

"Or not use a lid," Gizmo said.

"Where are your fishing poles?" Natalie's fingers wrapped tight around the bike's handlebars. She had a feeling she'd interrupted a private conversation that had nothing to do with fishing.

Gizmo made a snorting noise that sounded half like a laugh, half like a choke. "Yeah, Lars, where's our poles?"

"We have to stop by the marina to pick up a couple." Lars put his palms to his back, stretched his spine.

"Oh, you don't have to do that," Natalie said. "There are fishing poles in the attic. I keep them there for guests. Let's go get them."

"It's all right." Gizmo scratched his cheek with fingernails that had been bitten to the quick. "I want a pole of my own."

"Are you sure?" Natalie asked. "What if you don't care for fishing?"

Gizmo's shoulders humped up, and then slid back down in a slow shrug. "What's not to like?"

"For one thing—" Natalie smiled "—you have to get up early."

"Yeah, there is that." Gizmo didn't meet her eyes. Then again, he rarely met anyone's direct gaze. He was an odd kid, but he never caused any trouble and paid his rent on time.

"For another thing, you have to stab the minnows on the hook." She shuddered. "I hate that part."

Gizmo's eyes widened. "Dude, you didn't tell me nothin' 'bout stabbing minnows."

"How did you think the minnows were going to get on the hook?" Lars asked. "They don't climb on there themselves to suit you."

Gizmo toed the ground, jammed his hands in his pocket. "It's brutal."

"Sometimes life requires brutality of us." Lars's chiseled mouth pressed into a hard line.

"I'm leaving the minnow stabbing up to you," Gizmo said staunchly. "Got it?"

Lars shook his head. "That's the trouble with young people these days. They want everything handed to them."

"Yo, dude." Gizmo held up his palms, waggled them back and forth in a no-no gesture. "If you're gonna rag on me, I ain't going fishin' with you."

"You're going fishing." Lars's tone was steely and commanding.

Natalie swiveled her head to stare at him. Why did he care whether Gizmo went fishing?

Lars puffed out his chest. "To be fully alive is to feel that everything is possible."

Natalie raised her eyebrows. "Hoffer?"

"Hoffer is very profound," Lars said. "Are you listening, Gizmo?"

Gizmo might not be, but Natalie was. That was exactly what was happening to her. For the first time in her life, Dade made her feel fully, one hundred percent alive. So alive that the faith that had kept her a virgin for so long, before it had grown shaky, returned to settle and gel.

Hope could be a dangerous thing. Maybe there really was such a thing as love at first sight, but just because Dade made her feel alive didn't mean that it was love. The only way to discover the truth was to find someone else who made her feel equally alive and compare the two.

Like that was so easy to do. She'd waited twenty-nine years to feel this way. Mind games. She was playing mind games with herself and she was losing.

"Well," Natalie said, "if you're certain you don't want to use the Cupid's Rest fishing equipment, I'll leave you to your minnow hunting."

"We appreciate the offer, Natty," Lars said. "You're too generous."

"Have you met our new boarder yet?" Natalie asked, interested in knowing Lars's opinion about Dade. Over the years, Lars had become something of a father figure to her, and she valued his opinion.

"Ah, the dark loner who has taken up Red's former abode," murmured Lars.

"What do you think of him?"

"Seems like a hard-ass to me, yo," Gizmo commented. "He glares a lot."

Natalie met Lars's eyes.

"I don't want to prejudice you," Lars said.

Natalie's breath hitched. "But?"

"I'm not sure that I trust him."

"Why's that?"

Lars looked dubious. "It's probably nothing. I just miss Red. He's not Red."

No, Dade certainly was not Red. "He probably won't be staying very long. I just wondered what your impression of him was."

"You're attracted to him," Lars said flatly.

Natalie couldn't deny it. "He's a handsome man."

"You could do so much better. You deserve far better than some transient outsider." Lars shifted, and his eyes narrowed at something he spotted over the top of Natalie's head.

She glanced over her shoulder.

Dade came jogging up the path.

Her stomach did a back flip. God, this was getting ridiculous. Would she ever be able to look at the man without her vital signs going all wonky?

"Morning, folks." Dade's smile was slick, but his eyes were wary, as if he suspected them of some kind of conspiracy.

Well, they *had* been talking about him behind his back, and Natalie's face gave her away when she was guilty. Because of that, she'd never been able to get away with lying. Gram had caught her every time she'd tried to tell a fib.

The heat of Dade's gaze was already starting to burn her. "I better get to work," she mumbled, unnerved, and pushed her bike toward the house.

Dade moved to open the back gate for her. She rushed through, and in her haste, her elbow accidentally clipped his bare, hard-muscled abs.

The power of the contact went through her like an electrical shock. *Oh sweet heaven.* The involuntary sound that came out of her mouth dazed her. It was a moan, low and needy.

Dade made a noise of his own, a startled, sexy grunt.

His face was unreadable. A stone would have shown more emotion, but she could feel the testosterone radiating off him and she had an irresistible urge to plaster herself up against him.

Her heartbeat thundered.

She had to do something about these riotous emotions. Had to stop this lustiness in its tracks. She had to find someone else to get hot and bothered over, because if she didn't, Natalie feared she would give in to temptation and fall heedlessly for him.

Control.

She had to get herself under control.

Tossing her head, she moved forward, determined to appear just as circumspect as he. So what if he turned her on? Big deal.

But it was a big deal because this as the first time she'd ever felt so swept away. A very big deal indeed.

The problem was, you couldn't be both controlled and liberated. If she wanted love, she was going to have to take a risk and let go.

Chapter 8

You can resist all you want, but denial won't make love go away.

—Millie Greenwood

"Natty?" Zoey's voice broke through Natalie's mental fog.

At three o'clock that same afternoon, Natalie stood at the front desk making a to-do list. The Fourth of July was the following Thursday, and it was their biggest holiday weekend of the year. They were booked up, even the smallest room normally reserved for storage. She had so much to get done—decorating, shopping, and cleaning.

"Nat?"

Blinking, she looked up to meet her sister's curious gaze. "Huh?"

"Hello?" Zoey knocked gently on Natalie's temple. "You with me?"

"How do you do it?" Natalie mused.

"Do what?" Zoey opened the lid on the candy jar that Natalie kept on the desk for guests. She took out a bite-sized Twix bar and peeled off the wrapping.

"Juggle so many men without getting hurt."

Zoey shrugged, munched the Twix bar. "Not so many. Just seeing Seth and Ryan right now."

"Do they know about each other?"

"They know I'm not exclusive. I make that clear from the start with every guy I meet."

"You don't want anything long-term?"

"Jeez, Nat, I'm twenty-two. I haven't even finished college, why would I want to settle down?"

"But how do you keep from falling for these guys?"

"Oh, I get it. You're still freaked out about answering Shot Through the Heart's letter. Is Aunt Carol Ann breathing down your neck? I thought she gave you until Monday."

"She did."

"Listen, it's not that big a deal. Tell Shot Through the Heart that true love waits and she should get her education first."

"Really? That's the answer you'd give?"

"Sure. Why so surprised? What did you think I'd tell her to do? Throw away everything for some guy?"

"Honestly, yes."

"You seriously underestimate me, sis."

It dawned on Natalie that one of the reasons Zoey was taking so long getting through school might not be just that she couldn't make up her mind about her field of study. She was delaying growing up. "Does it?"

"What?"

"Does true love wait?"

"How should I know? I've never been in love, but it seems like the kind of answer people like to hear." Zoey fished in the candy jar, and came up with an Almond Joy.

"Those are for the guests."

"Take it out of my allowance." She popped the candy into her mouth.

"You still didn't answer my question. How do you keep from falling in love with these guys you date?"

"Unlike you, my faith in the thunderbolt has never wavered. When it strikes, I'm confident that I'll just *know.*"

"So…you're still a virgin?"

Zoey snorted. "What century are you living in?"

"But you just said you were holding out for the thunderbolt."

"For marriage, not sex."

"There's nothing wrong with waiting to be in love before you have sex," Natalie said lightly.

"C'mon, this isn't the Dark Ages where women give their virginity as a gift to their husband on their wedding night."

"It's romantic though and special."

"Women now days are free to claim their sexuality." Zoey pumped her fist in the air. "We have birth control. We're not hidebound by some archaic patriarchal structure that says only men get to have fun before they settle down."

"Sex has consequences beside pregnancy and genital diseases. That level of intimacy with another person involves a great deal of trust. Treat sex casually and it ceases to have meaning."

"There's nothing wrong with recreational sex as long as you take precautions," Zoey said.

"If being promiscuous is an acceptable choice, then why isn't celibacy?"

"I didn't say it wasn't acceptable, just totally unrealistic. Who today, beyond the most deeply religious, hang on to their virginity beyond their early twenties?"

"Lots of women." Natalie busied herself with stacking papers. Could her sister read her secret on her face?

"Not anyone I know."

"You'd be surprised."

"If you're trying to convince me to save myself for marriage, gotta tell you that ship has already sailed." Zoey gave her a funny look and got really quiet.

Natalie glanced up. "What?"

"Something just occurred to me. Something I never considered before but it would explain a lot. Natalie, are you still a vir—"

"What about the guys you string along?" Natalie rushed to cut her sister off.

Zoey kept staring at her strangely. "I never string them along. They all know I'm not serious. If a guy is the serious type, I don't get involved with him."

"But you *would* get serious. If he was The One."

"Sure. If he's The One. That's what you do when you find The One. You get serious. That's the point."

"What would you do if you found yourself falling for a guy that you really shouldn't fall for? Say Ryan or Seth for instance."

Zoey pondered this while unwrapping a Three Musketeers bar. "I wouldn't."

"For the sake of argument, let's say you did." Natalie took the candy jar off the desk and stuck it in the bottom drawer.

"I'd break things off immediately."

"But what if you weren't even dating the guy you were falling for? Let's say it was someone you sat next to in your anatomy class."

"I'd drop the course and find a new guy to get involved with, pronto."

"How would you do that?"

"Buy some new sexy clothes and hit the town."

"Which means…?"

"Chantilly's. Unless I was in a mood to drive to Alpine, but if I'm going to be drinking, I'd need a designated driver. If I stayed in Cupid, I could just walk home from Chantilly's. Or call you to come get me."

"Not if I went with you."

Zoey's mouth dropped open and her eyes widened with delight. "What?"

"I want to go out clubbing with you."

"When?"

"Tonight."

"Are you serious?" Zoey jumped up and down.

"Dead serious."

"Wow, oh gosh, that's amazing." She paused in her glee. "Wait, aren't you terrified that the world will stop spinning if you take the night off?"

"Only the Fant room is occupied tonight. I can get Lars to watch the front desk."

Nostrils flaring, Zoey sniffed the air. "I smell sardines."

"What?"

"Something's fishy."

"Nothing's fishy."

"You *never* go out."

"That's a bit of an exaggeration. I went to Cousin Gina's bachelorette party."

"Ahem, that was two years ago and you left as soon as the stripper got there."

"I play bingo with Junie Mae once a month at St. Stephen's."

"Hanging with the old ladies does not count."

"I like hanging with them."

Zoey pretended to fall asleep and snore loudly. She opened one eye. "You've got your whole life to be boring."

"Maybe I'm starting to realize that."

"Or maybe..." Zoey scooted her fanny up onto the desk, studied Natalie a long moment. "You're starting to like a guy and he scares you." She snapped her fingers. "Yes, yes. That's it. Why else were you asking me all those questions? Why else do you suddenly want to party with your kid sister?"

"That's not it—"

"Omigod!" Zoey hopped down off the desk. "It's the new boarder. You've got the hots for our new boarder!"

"I do not," Natalie denied, but her face burned crimson.

Zoey grabbed Natalie's shoulders. "Is he The One? Did you feel it?"

"Of course not. I barely know him."

"You're lying. Your left eyelid twitches when you lie."

"It does not." Natalie put a hand to her eyelid. It was twitching.

"Oh wow, I can't believe this, I can't wait to tell—"

Natalie snagged her sister by the arm. "You will *not* tell anyone anything because there is nothing to tell."

Zoey did a little dance, executing a few Zumba moves. "I thought it was never going to happen to you."

"It hasn't happened to me."

"Methinks thou doth protest too much."

"He makes me feel..."

"Yes?" Zoey leaned forward, drinking it in.

Natalie took a deep breath. "I dunno. Restless." That much was certainly true.

"Restless is a great start." Zoey rubbed her palms together.

"It just dawned on me I'm not going to meet anyone suitable by staying home and working 24/7. It's time I got out."

"I'm not going to question whatever it is that caused you to figure this out," Zoey said. "I'm just happy you're willing to do something about it. And you're in luck. They're having a Life Saver relay at Chantilly's tonight."

"What's a Life Saver relay?"

"You'll see. It's a lot of fun."

"But Chantilly's?" That was where Dade worked. She couldn't avoid him if she went where he worked, but if she admitted that, then Zoey would know for certain that Dade was the one she was having these feelings for. "Why not go to Alpine?"

"I don't think you're ready for Alpine. Trust me, you should start small."

There wasn't another club in Cupid. It was Chantilly's or nothing. Natalie hesitated. "I changed my mind. Forget I brought it up."

"No, no, no, sister mine. We're doing this."

Okay, just because Dade was at Chantilly's didn't mean she couldn't scout out other guys. In fact, what better way to prove that he didn't have any power over her, right? If she rearranged her life to avoid him, then *that* would be power. In fact, now she *had* to go to Chantilly's to prove that he did not have power over her.

Zoey picked up the receiver off the cordless phone dock on the desk and passed it to Natalie.

"What's this?"

"Call Lars to come babysit the desk for the rest of the day. It's time for a complete makeover. When I'm done with you, you won't recognize yourself."

"That's what I'm afraid of," Natalie grumbled, but secretly, she was excited to try something new.

When Zoey got finished making her over, Natalie stared in the mirror, stunned by her transformation. Her unruly curls had been ironed flat, her eyes were expertly lined and shadowed, her lips looked plump and pouty. Zoey's shimmery green sheath dress hugged Natalie's body, giving added curves to her lean figure. If it weren't for the blasted AFO and the Keds, she would have been a knockout.

Duh. Just duh. She had no idea that a new hairstyle and a little makeup could make such a big difference.

"Told ya. I've been waiting years for this." Zoey followed Natalie's gaze down to her shoes. "Do you have to wear that darned contraption?"

"You know the answer to that."

"What would happen if you didn't wear it?"

"I'd wake up tomorrow with a horrific backache." She bent to tie her sneakers.

"Wouldn't it be worth it? For just one night?"

"Not really. I have a lot to do tomorrow." She straightened, smoothed her hands over the silky material. She really did look dorky in such a nice dress and Keds.

Zoey picked up her pair of Stuart Weitzmans with kitten heels. "C'mon, just once?"

Natalie reached out longingly to stroke the shoes. "I'd twist my ankle, fall, and break my neck."

"You'd only have to walk from the car into the club.

After that, you just sit at the table and show off those legs."

Natalie shook her head. "This whole thing is beyond stupid. It's not like I can dance or anything. I've changed my mind. I'm not going." She reached around for the zipper on the dress.

Zoey put a hand out to stop her. "Oh, no way. You're just scared."

"You betcha."

"C'mon, you're not going to let that bum leg dictate your life."

"Um, to some degree, it *does* dictate my life."

"Forget the Stuart Weitzmans, but don't back out."

"It doesn't feel right."

"That's because it's something new. Please, sis, do it for me. I'd love for us to go out and have fun together. You know we've never had any fun together," Zoey pleaded.

"We've had fun," Natalie protested. "I've taken you to the movies and picnics in the park and the circus and—"

Zoey yawned. "Pleasant outings to be sure, but not *real* fun."

"Well," Natalie said defensively. "Excuse me for being crippled."

"It's not the limp that's the issue."

"Pretty much. Can't really dance or ski or skate or play slow-pitch softball with this leg."

"It's the excuse you like to hide behind."

"That's not true. Don't you think I want to be like everyone else?" Natalie put on a pair of emerald earrings.

"Then let's go." Zoey picked up her purse.

Natalie stared at her gorgeous younger sister. "There's no way I can compete with you."

"You don't have to," Zoey linked her arms through Natalie's. "Just be yourself. Tonight is about having fun. No pressure. No expectations. Just let your hair down and par-*tay*."

Natalie waved at the mirror. "That is not me."

"For tonight it is."

Natalie hauled in a deep breath and reminded herself why she was doing this: to find some more suitable guy to obsess about. "All right. Let's do this."

By the time they arrived at Chantilly's, the parking lot was packed. The nightclub was situated next door to the marina and directly across the lake from the Cupid's Rest. There was a back porch patio deck that stretched out over the water. White twinkle lights were strung in the trees over the deck. Out on the water, party barges cruised, and the smell of fried catfish scented the air. Alternative rock music vibrated through the open door—the very door that Dade was blocking with a red velvet rope as he checked identification.

He wore snug-fitting jeans, a black Chantilly's T-shirt, and a straw cowboy hat that had seen better days. She'd never seen a more breathtaking sight.

Natalie stalled.

Zoey jostled her elbow. "C'mon."

Adrenaline pumped through her. Run. *Run!* "This is a really bad idea."

"It's a splendid idea." Zoey nudged her forward.

"Don't push!"

"Then get a move on."

Natalie felt both hot and cold at the same time as they

lined up behind the red rope. The two girls in line ahead of them looked all of eighteen. One had vibrantly pink hair. She wore a skimpy little halter top, a sandwich-sized skirt, and an elaborate tattoo of a blue dragon on her lower back. The other girl was total goth, dressed in black from head to toe.

"They're not getting in," she leaned over to whisper in Zoey's ear. "I bet they're still in high school."

Dade gave the giggling girls a stern look. "ID."

They passed him their driver's licenses.

He shone a penlight over the cards and then narrowed his eyes as he looked into their faces. "You young ladies do not look twenty-one."

"We are," said Goth Girl. "It says it right there on our licenses."

"We have good genetics. When we're forty, we'll look thirty," Pink Hair added.

Dade gave the driver's licenses another hard look. Reluctantly, he handed the ID back to the girls and unchained the rope to let them inside. "Behave."

"Does that mean we can't pinch your butt?" Pink Hair asked.

"You may not," he growled. "Scat."

Giggling, they sauntered into the bar, clutching each other's arms.

He shifted his attention back to the line, looked at Natalie, and did a double take. A slow, indolent grin spread across his face. "Natalie? Is that you?"

"Don't act so surprised. I clean up well."

He ran a hot, leisurely gaze down her body.

She shivered involuntarily. It wasn't the least bit cold.

"'Well' isn't the word for it," he corrected. "You look sensational."

Do not blush, she commanded herself, but her cheeks heated anyway. Dammit! Why did she have to embarrass so easily?

"ID please." He held out a hand.

"Seriously? You're going to card me?"

"You look under twenty-one to me."

Natalie rolled her eyes but she couldn't help grinning. She showed him her identification.

His knuckles brushed against her fingers and her body went up in flames. Immediately, she dropped her hand. Her arm felt too weak to hold up.

"Twenty-nine, huh?" He looked surprised. "I never would have guessed it."

"Flattery will get you absolutely nowhere."

"Had to try." He winked and turned to check Zoey's ID.

Natalie's heart was in her throat and her hand still tingled from where Dade had touched her. She was dimly aware of Zoey ushering her into the darkened nightclub.

Wall sconces with red bulbs dimly lighted the way into the main room crowded with people. Couples were on the dance floor. She'd lived in this town all her life and she'd never set foot in Chantilly's.

"I see a table in the far corner." Zoey steered her in that direction. Her sister waved at several people as they went by.

The journey to the table felt a million miles long and Natalie couldn't help feeling that everyone was staring at her. She was so far out of her element. Once she was seated, Zoey said, "I'll go to the bar and get us drinks. It'll take the waitress forever to find us in this corner. What do you want?"

"I'll have a Coke."

Zoey gave her a look. "Seriously?"

"What?"

"You've gotta have a drink-drink."

"I don't drink."

"Tonight you do."

"I don't know what to order."

"Leave it to me." Zoey took off for the bar and she was quickly gobbled up in the throng.

Natalie took a deep breath and settled back in her chair. Someone had put one of the town's ubiquitous love songs on the jukebox. Amy Winehouse belting out "Cupid."

Natalie drummed her fingers on the table. Now what was she supposed to do?

Look around for a hot guy.

Nervously, she licked her lips and surveyed the bar patrons, zeroing in on men without partners. One dark-haired guy caught her eye, but when their gazes met, she glanced away. She didn't want him coming over.

He got up, walked toward her.

Panicked, Natalie fished in her purse for her cell phone, pulled it out, switched it on, and started reading a book on the Kindle app. She did not look up. After a few minutes, she dared to glance around. The guy was talking to another woman. She blew out her breath. Ha! Royal ego buster. He hadn't even been coming for her.

Amy Winehouse bled into 10cc's "I'm Not in Love."

There! That was an anthem she could get behind.

"May I sit down?" A low, deep masculine voice oozed over her like heated butter.

Immediately, Natalie's body responded. See there?

Dade Vega wasn't the only one who could rev her engines. She put on a smile and glanced up.

Only to find Dade grinning down at her.

Fresh tingles started at the top of her head and spread like a rash over her body. Deep in the very center of her, feminine muscles clenched, clamped down. Natalie gulped and gripped the edge of the table with both hands.

Ah, crap.

Without waiting for her reply, Dade pulled out the chair beside her and sat down very close.

Far too close.

Only the thinnest molecules separated them.

The air in her lungs turned to liquid fire and her stomach quivered. She slanted him a sideways glance, too unsettled to squarely meet his gaze.

He didn't say anything.

Neither did she, but her heart was galloping as if she'd just bicycled the thirty miles from Cupid to Marfa in the sweltering summer heat at high noon.

Zoey bebopped back to the table. "Gotcha an appletini and—" Her sister stopped, took a gander at Dade, and a sultry smile came over her face. Her voice lowered instantly. "Hey there."

"Hey." He shifted his weight, turning his shoulder in Natalie's direction, and his knee—oh, his glorious knee—brushed against hers.

Accidental?

She spared a quick glimpse into his devilish eyes. Nothing about this man was accidental.

Natalie snatched the appletini from her sister's hand and took a big gulp. Nice. It tasted like green apples, but immediately afterward, she felt a kick of alcohol speed through her system, and in a nanosecond she was light-headed. Giddy.

Or maybe it wasn't the alcohol at all, but the fact that Dade's knee was still touching hers. But here was the truly terrible thing, she wasn't moving her knee away, did not want to move it away. Why wasn't she moving her knee away?

Zoey glanced from Natalie to Dade and back again. "Um, I see someone I know. Gotta go say hi."

Just like that, her wingwoman disappeared, leaving her wingless with the man she'd come here to forget.

Dade was watching her intently.

She squirmed, finally moved her knee from his, and took another long sip of appletini. Whee! What devastatingly delicious potion was this?

"This isn't your kind of scene," Dade said flatly.

"No," Natalie agreed, trying to appear calm, cool, and sophisticated. She hiccupped loudly, ruining the suave look, and plastered a palm over her mouth. At least she hadn't burped.

"You're not accustomed to drinking."

"No." She wasn't about to tell him it was her first drink ever, other than one time in high school when, in a rare moment of teenage rebellion, she and her cousin Melody had stolen a bottle of Zinfandel from Aunt Carol Ann's wine fridge, drank the whole thing as fast as they could, and promptly threw it up.

"That control thing," he said.

"What?"

"You don't drink because you don't like giving up control."

Damn him for being so insightful. Purposefully, she picked up her glass, took a big slug of appletini. The sweet-tart taste of green apples curled around her tongue as the cool liquid sent a fresh blast of heat rolling through her.

Amusement lit up his eyes. "Have you ever been inside Chantilly's?"

"No."

"Why are you here now?"

It dawned on her that he thought she'd come here to see him. How freaking arrogant!

"I could ask you the same question," she retorted. "Why are *you* here?"

"I work here."

"Not the bar. Cupid."

He shrugged. "Good a town as any."

"You tell me why you're in Cupid and I'll tell you why I'm in the nightclub."

10cc gave way to "Into the Wild" by LP. The lead singer suggested that someone had left a gate open. Hey, shut the damn gate. Too late. Everything had gotten out.

Dade took so long to answer that she didn't think he was going to. Finally, he said, "I'm searching for something."

"Pardon?"

"I'm looking for what's missing in my life," he murmured.

There was so much in that statement that she shied from picking at it. Her head swayed a little, like a willow in the wind. Foggily, she noticed how the black T-shirt emblazoned with the Chantilly's logo stretched taut against his tanned, muscular biceps. He wore snug-fitting black jeans with a sharp crease running down the front legs, and black cowboy boots. Natalie took another swallow of the appletini, ran the tip of her tongue over her lips. It was almost gone. Boo-hoo.

His gaze latched on to hers, clung tight. "You might want to slow down." He nodded at her glass. "Those pack quite a punch."

"You might want to stop telling me what to do."

His grin widened. "So I told you why I'm in town. Why are you in the bar?"

"You didn't tell me. Not really. What's missing in your life?"

His voice lowered along with his eyelids. "Someone special."

Her heart fluttered. Dear God! She was in serious, serious trouble.

"Your turn."

"Not so fast," she said. "You could find someone special in any town in the world. Why Cupid? Why now? What really brought you here?"

Knock it off. Do you really want to know?

"A hunch." He reached out and encircled her wrist with his hand. His hand was so big and her wrist so small, his thumb overlapped far enough to touch the knuckle of his index finger.

Manacled!

Natalie gulped like a fish flopping on dry land, desperate, frantic for air. His touch hit her like a blow to the solar plexus, powerful and draining. She tried to pull her hand away, but he held on tight.

Holy guacamole!

Her stomach took a running jump and landed *splat* in her throat. Her limbs were loose as jelly. And her tongue? It untied itself, rolled out words slippery and easy. "A hunch, huh? You woke up one day and thought,

Gotta go to Cupid, Texas. That's where I'll meet my someone special?"

"Something along those lines." His eyes narrowed to hungry slits, but his gaze belonged to her, one hundred percent.

Her blood bounded in her ears so loudly that she could not hear herself think. "Bullshit."

"It's my story and I'm sticking to it."

"Well," she said. "Thanks for the chat." She wrenched her hand from his grip, and this time, he let her go so easily that she almost toppled over in her chair.

"You all right?"

"Yes." She barely managed to shove the word pass her lips. She pushed up from the table, her head spinning like a whirligig. Her right leg had somehow got tangled around the leg of the chair and it jerked her back down. She tottered.

"Whoa, there." He was out of his seat, his arm going around her waist. "Told you to watch out for that drink. Those appletinis really slip up on you."

"It wasn't the drink," she denied. "It's my stupid leg."

He hovered over her. The T-shirt fit him so snugly she could make out the delineation of his abdominal muscles beneath it. She couldn't say what possessed her, the appletini most likely, tool of the devil that damn drink. She reached out a hand to trace her fingers over his torso.

Steel.

His abdomen felt like pure steel.

He flinched at her touch, hauled in a breath as ragged as her own. "What are you doing?"

"I don't know," she confessed.

"You had better be very careful," he said. "You go

around touching a guy like that and he's going to get the wrong idea."

"And what is that?" she dared, tipping her chin up to meet his stare.

"That you want to take me home with you."

"You already live at my home."

"I do."

The look that passed between them was so scorching that Natalie blistered, burned, boiled, broiled.

"Why did you come here tonight?" he repeated.

Her lips twitched. She gritted her teeth, tried not to tell him. If she told him why she was here, then he would know the truth.

"Natalie," he whispered, so softly she wasn't sure she heard him.

Around them people were laughing and talking and dancing, but she and Dade were encased in their own little cocoon, on another planet that consisted of just the two of them.

"I came here," she said, "to get you out of my head."

Damn you! You had to go and say it. You just had to tell him, didn't you? Stupid woman!

"I'm in your head?"

"Don't look so smug about it. You're in there like a commercial jingle you can't stop humming, but desperately want to."

"That bad, huh?"

"Worse."

"How's that?"

"This is craziness."

"I agree."

"So you go back to bouncing and I'll go back to my appletini."

"Is that what you really want?"

Hell, no. She wanted to whisk off his cowboy hat and plow her fingers through his hair, pull his head down to hers, and kiss him until the end of time. She'd never felt this kind of relentless need. The intensity of it had driven her to go out drinking to forget him and, damn, here the devil was. Grinning at her like he knew every thought that passed through her head.

From the jukebox, Enrique Iglesias started singing "Hero."

Dade manacled her wrist again, led her toward the dance floor.

Natalie balked. She did not dance. Could not dance.

"No." She hooked her head, but clearly, she did not get a vote.

"Yes," he murmured. "Yes."

His arms were wrapped securely around her waist and he was moving her around on the dance floor. Yes, sure, her right leg was dragging a little, but that didn't slow him down one whit. She felt feather light in his arms.

They swayed together. Surprisingly, it wasn't as difficult as she thought, probably because she was a little drunk and he was pressed so tightly against her she couldn't misstep if she wanted to.

A helpless grin spread across her face. Dammit to hell, he made her feel just like Cinderella at the ball.

But just like Cinderella, it was all an illusion. Eventually, midnight would strike, her coach would turn into a pumpkin, her clothes would turn to rags, and she'd go back to cleaning the cinders.

Chapter 9

The first time you kiss your soul mate is like an earthquake, wiping out everything you thought you knew about yourself.

—Millie Greenwood

For four and a half minutes, Cinderella enjoyed the ball as Enrique crooned "Hero."

Who wouldn't enjoy being chest to chest with a handsome, sexy, virile man? A man who was staring her right in the eyes as if she was the only woman on the face of the earth. A man who, in that moment, took away all the pain she had ever felt. A man who made time stand still.

It was the most wondrous moment of her life. Something inside Natalie broke loose and she simply gave way and let it all happen.

His hands slipped from her waist to her hips. The

scent of his cologne filled her nostrils, along with something more—the sexy smell of male skin, all soap and leather.

Enrique pleaded for her to let him be her hero. She did not need Enrique. She had Dade.

They swayed together, barely moving. Natalie rested her outstretched hands on his shoulders, mesmerized by his piercing gaze. One of his hands started a slow journey up her spine, drawing a soft, deep sigh from her lungs, followed by a sharp intake of air as his fingers traced the nape of her neck. Fingers both powerful and gentle. He lowered his head.

She tipped her chin up, daring him to kiss her.

He did not.

Please, she thought. *Please.*

Her body trembled. She felt boneless. Light-headed. Overcome with unfamiliar passion, completely taken off guard.

She reached up to run her fingers over his jaw, lightly stubbled with beard.

A one-sided smile quirked the corner of his mouth and he leaned closer.

He was going to do it. He was going to kiss her!

Natalie stopped breathing. Excitement saturated her every nerve cell.

He tipped his cowboy hat far back on his head and rested his forehead against hers.

The pressure was exquisitely sweet, the joining strange and erotic and intriguingly novel. His forehead was on hers, their eyes drilling into each other. They were barely moving now, in the center of the dance floor as other couples waltzed around them.

"Natalie." His voice was husky.

She stared at his mouth, and a muted, tremulous whimper escaped her lips. "Yes?"

He lowered his eyelids and his pupils dilated. "I feel I should warn you," he said.

"About what?"

"Me."

Hot adrenaline spread through her body, mingled with the alcohol from the appletini, left her feeling both jittery and wrung out. "What about you?"

"I'm no hero."

"That's good," she said breathlessly. "Because I don't need rescuing. I can take care of myself."

"I'm serious," he said. "I'm not the man for you."

"As if I wanted you," she scoffed.

His eyes darkened, glittered. "You want me."

"Arrogant."

"I want you too, but it's not a good idea."

"Agreed," she said, incensed. Who did this guy think he was?

Dade released her easily. Natalie stepped back from him, her mind a crazy jumble.

Enrique stopped singing—thank God—in fact, the music shut off completely as the lights in the bar brightened.

"Boo," complained many patrons, as if they were vampires, their demise hastened by light.

"Don't dis me," Zoey said from behind the bar, her hand on the light switch rheostat. "It's time for the Life Saver relay."

That brought cheers from the crowd.

Disoriented, Natalie made her way to her table. She didn't look back at Dade, but his words rang in her ears.

I'm not the man for you. She already knew that. Why, then, did she feel so *rejected*?

Zoey held up a roll of Life Saver candies and a box of toothpicks. "I'm going to explain the rules for those who've never played. Everyone who wants to play gets a toothpick." She opened up the box. "Come and get one."

Natalie was too confused to play. Plus, she didn't want to have to get up and walk to the bar. Her knees wobbled like homemade jelly that hadn't set.

She told herself she was not going to look around to see where Dade had gone, but something compelled her to turn her head and take a peek. He'd moved to the back of the room, stood against the wall, arms folded, cowboy hat now tipped low over his forehead, his eyes zeroed in on her.

Gulp!

Overwhelmed, she jerked her gaze back to the bar where Zoey, surrounded on all sides by men, slipped a Life Saver onto her toothpick. Her sister attracted men like bees to blossoms.

"Listen up, people," Zoey went on. She loved being the center of attention. "Here's how it works. You hold the toothpick between your teeth. One person has a Life Saver on the toothpick and chooses someone to pass the candy to. You have to keep your hands clutched behind your back. If your hands come forward, you're disqualified and you have to buy drinks for all the people who've preceded you in the relay."

That brought another cheer from the crowd.

"If you drop the Life Saver, you're disqualified and then once again you have to buy a round of drinks for all the people who came before you. In the case where someone drops a Life Saver, the person who successfully passed the last Life Saver must pass a new one to another partner."

"Woot! Woot!"

"Each person can only have the Life Saver passed to them one time. You can refuse to accept the Life Saver from the person who wants to pass it to you, but you're allowed only one refusal."

People were cutting their eyes at each other, grinning and signaling *I'm picking you* or ducking their heads and looking away.

"The relay starts when the music starts and ends when the music ends and the last person left with the Life Saver has to kiss the person who passed it to them. On the dance floor, for everyone to see, and since many of us are related, if you don't want to kiss your cousin, you better be careful who you choose to pass the Life Saver to."

This brought a chuckle from the crowd.

Zoey tilted her head back, stuck the toothpick that the Life Saver was on between her teeth, and signaled to Jasper Grass, who stood beside the jukebox.

Jasper counted off, "Three…two…one…" and put "Cupid" on to play again, but this time it was an elongated, disco-ized version, and yelled, "Go!"

With her hands behind her back, Zoey sidled up to the closest cute guy. He grinned at her and with a toothpick clutched between his teeth and hands behind his back, sank to his knees while Zoey wriggled into position so that the guy could transfer the Life Saver from her toothpick to his.

Amid much giggling, speculation, and taunting chants of "Drop it, drop it," the guy passed the Life Saver on to a woman whom Natalie had gone to high school with. That woman tried to pass it on to Calvin, who was off duty and sitting with his fiancée, Maria. Maria glowered at the woman as Calvin laughed and waved the woman away.

The woman shrugged and passed the Life Saver to Maria instead, who then passed it on to Calvin.

Calvin looked around for someone to pass the Life Saver to, but Maria was glaring so possessively that all the women in the bar shied from Calvin's gaze and he ended up passing the Life Saver to another guy, who promptly dropped the Life Saver and had to buy drinks for everyone who'd already passed the Life Saver along to him, and Calvin had to find a new partner to pass the Life Saver to.

Natalie was enjoying watching the whole thing play out and she was feeling pretty safe from being picked— the "Cupid" song was almost over—when the pink-haired girl passed the Life Saver to Dade.

He didn't refuse her.

Jealousy pushed through Natalie as she watched the girl wriggle and giggle as Dade took off his cowboy hat and set it on a table. Then he maneuvered his body down low enough, limbo style, so that she could pass him the candy.

Natalie gritted her teeth. Now she knew how Maria felt.

Once the Life Saver handoff was successful, Dade straightened, the toothpick with the dangling candy clutched firmly between his teeth. With his hands clasped behind his back, he came straight toward her.

Natalie prayed, *Please let the song end. Please let the song end.*

Um, maybe not. *If the song ends before he gets to*

you, he'll have to kiss Pink Hair. Which was probably Pink Hair's objective. *Keep going, song. Keep going.*

Then there he was at her table, smelling like lightning and trouble.

She could refuse him. She should refuse him. Especially since he'd just told her that he wasn't the man for her, but if she refused him he'd have to kiss Pink Hair.

The final strains of "Cupid" were spilling from the jukebox.

"I don't have a tooth—" Before she could finish, Zoey was beside her, toothpick in her hand.

Dade grinned.

Natalie stood up, took the toothpick from Zoey, and settled it between her teeth.

Dade leaned over her.

"Hands behind your back," Zoey cautioned.

Natalie tucked her hands behind her back and manipulated the toothpick with her tongue. She could feel Dade's warm, minty breath against her skin and smell the flavor of the Life Saver.

Pineapple.

The crowd was making catcalls, but Natalie heard none of it. Her mind was on one thing and one thing only.

Dade's lips.

Her wanton disregard for the people around them alarmed her, but try as she might, she could not rein herself. She tilted her head back, exposing her throat to him, open, vulnerable, waiting.

He hovered, nerves of steel, holding the toothpick steady but not allowing the Life Saver to slip down. Not yet.

She realized why he was hesitating. He was stalling

so she wouldn't have the chance to pass the Life Saver off to someone else before the song ended. He was controlling the timing so that she would have to kiss him.

It was so frustrating to have to keep her hands behind her back when all she wanted to do was thread her fingers through his lush head of thick hair slightly creased from the imprint of his hat. Had a man ever looked so gorgeous?

But what really took her breath away was the way he was looking at her. As if she was a sparkling diamond he'd found lying in the sand.

C'mon baby, let me have it. She boldly telegraphed him the message with her eyes.

Dade looked amused and highly aroused. His cheeks colored and that made her own skin flush hot. Was their attraction evident to the people around them? Was it as blatant as it felt? All hot coals and burning passion?

The crowd was chanting, "Drop it, drop it, drop it."

Natalie was unclear whether they wanted Dade to drop the Life Saver onto her toothpick or for her to fumble it. If the pass-off didn't happen, she'd have to buy a round of drinks for ten people, but she did not care about that. Dade was her focus and only Dade.

The tips of their toothpicks touched, and in that split second, their mouths were connected by two thin pieces of wood. Exaltation shot through Natalie.

The crowd noise swelled, and along with it, Natalie's rising desire, and soon her entire body resounded with sensation.

It was funny and oddly erotic. Natalie's head spun and her right leg wobbled. Oh no! Her leg couldn't give out. Not now.

Dade's eyes caught hers and mentally telegraphed the message. *You're not going to fall. Hang on.*

She could read his thoughts as surely as if he'd spoken them aloud.

The Life Saver fell from his toothpick and slipped down onto hers. The taste of pineapple kissed her lips just as the song ended.

Dade's eyes twinkled.

"Kiss! Kiss! Kiss!"

The next thing she knew, Dade had her around the waist and he was spinning her in a slow circle, his eyes locked on hers.

That's when she realized she had the toothpick and Life Saver still clutched between her teeth. Laughing, she pulled the toothpick from her mouth and tossed it over her shoulder.

Then Dade kissed her and the earth stood still.

It was a cliché, sure, but she had no other way to describe it. She could no longer hear her heart beating, could no longer draw in air. Everything just dropped away—people, sounds, smells.

Nothing existed but Dade.

She kissed him back, thoroughly, completely, and with as much enthusiasm as he kissed her. No man had ever smelled this good. Nothing had ever tasted this good. Not Pearl's fried chicken, not the huevos rancheros from La Hacienda Grill, not even Sandra's famous banana pudding. It was as if she had discovered kissing for the very first time, thrilling to the intoxicating strangeness of it all. She parted her lips and let his tongue pierce her. She was in all the way.

The crowd clapped and chanted, "Go Dade! Go Natalie!"

His arms tightened around her and she wished the moment would never end. She would remember this kiss for the rest of her life, because she knew in her heart that no other kiss would ever compare.

The first time you kiss your soul mate is like an earthquake, wiping out everything you thought you knew about yourself.

It was a Millie Greenwood quote. Instead of lullabies, Millie had passed down sayings of love to her children and they'd passed them on to their children. For the first time, Natalie thought about passing them on to her kids.

Natalie's life had been built on myths and legends of love. She'd always wanted to believe in them, but never dared. Now that it was finally upon her, she was a true believer.

Unfortunately, belief just made things worse. Because now that she'd experienced this mind-blowing chemistry, this deep abiding pleasure, she knew that she would never be satisfied with any other man but him.

Dade alone had the power to break her into a million little pieces.

Dade closed his eyes, one hundred percent goner, rocketing headlong into the sexiest little mouth he'd kissed in years.

Who was he kidding? It was the sexiest mouth he'd ever kissed. Not just sexy, but hot and sweet and wet and delicious.

Perfect.

Natalie possessed the most perfect mouth in the universe.

Do you think you could be overstating things a bit?

You've been without a woman too long and you just forgot about how good it can be.

Yeah, that was it. Nothing cataclysmic going on here.

A kiss is just a kiss.

Unless it's Natalie.

He opened his eyes and her eyes were wide open too, staring at him with awestruck wonder. He raised his hands to cup her face, traced his thumbs over the silky texture of her cheeks.

She sighed, soft and low and dreamy.

He got caught up in the heady sound, taken down like a swimmer trapped in an undertow. He shoved aside the doubts that had been eating at his brain, filed them under "Things to Think About Later." He tightened his arms around her waist and deepened the kiss, taking her down the current with him.

Dade half expected her to break away. They were standing in the middle of the bar, amid good-natured ribbing and cheers. But she did not. In fact, she was running her palms up his bare forearms to his shoulders, reaching higher to thread her fingers through his hair and pull his head down lower as if she was starving for more.

She pressed her body flush against him, her pelvis arching up into him.

You got my attention, darlin'.

Her hips wriggled against his.

What do you want? Anything. Just name it. If I've got it, it's yours. If I can get my hands on it, it's yours. Want that mountain moved? I'm on it. Want the stars brought down from the sky? Let me go get an extension ladder.

Finally, they couldn't keep up the kissing. Oxygen was needed. Lousy need to breathe. They pulled apart simultaneously, and, trembling, lips glistening wet, they stared at each other.

"Mmm, I think we took that a bit too far," she murmured. Her nipples poked out, erect and alert, and her gaze tracked to his hard-on. "You're in a bit of a pickle."

"Hey, you caused it."

"If you move away from me, everyone is going to notice your…er…situation." Humor tinged her voice.

"Then I guess I'll just have to stay right here with you."

"Um…" she said, "wouldn't that escalate the problem?"

"I don't think I can get any more aroused than I already am," he said.

There was no hiding how much he wanted her. No fooling anyone, not even himself. She had a way of making him face things he didn't want to face. She was a straight shooter, honest and forthright, and he was living in her house under false pretenses, lying to her mainly because he didn't have the courage to trust her.

She cocked her head and was studying him with an open, accepting gaze as if she were willing to take a chance on him if he would open up and take a chance on her, but she didn't know him. Had no idea of his shadowy past, had no clue what he was capable of. She was innocent, undamaged by life, and he was both guilty and damned.

He wondered what she saw when she looked at him with those eyes so forgiving and optimistic. Couldn't she see the darkness in him? Couldn't she tell that he was flawed in a fundamental way?

"So what's your…mmm…solution?" she murmured, running a hand over his biceps.

"Let's just dance here for now. They're bound to turn the lights down again soon."

"You forget. I don't dance."

"You do dance. You already danced with me."

"And you already warned me off."

"I know."

"So what's the point?"

"This." Dammit. He kissed her again. Couldn't help himself. He kissed her as the lights dimmed.

It started out soft and sweet. The kind of kiss you were supposed to kiss in public, but it didn't stay that way.

The sweet sigh that seeped from her lips cut straight through him. He felt her arms go around him. She squeezed him tight. Oh God, she felt so damn good.

She was kissing him right back, hot and hard and raw, not the least bit shy in spite of her adorable blushing.

He closed his eyes against the onslaught, fought his urges, but it was no use. He could not resist her.

Dade gave in completely. Surrendered. People were dancing around them, chuckling and intentionally jostling them with their elbows, but it was as if they were on an island of their own and no one could touch them.

How sweet if it were true.

Her tongue skimmed over his lips, tasting him like he was a sugary confection, and a foreign emotion pushed up from the center of his chest and into his head so quickly that his brain spun.

Jesus, what was she doing to him?

"Dade," she whispered.

"Yeah?" His voice came out thick and husky.

"I've got something to tell you."

"Uh-huh?" he murmured, sucking her bottom lip up between her teeth, his hands moving up her spine.

"You might not believe that you're the man for me, but I hate to break it to you."

"What's that?" he rasped.

"I'm precisely the woman for you."

"Oh really?"

She raised her chin. "Yes."

"You really think you can handle me?" he drawled.

He shouldn't be flirting with Natalie when he couldn't mean it. By nature, he wasn't a flirt, but flirting with her was so easy. She made him feel human again, and for a man who'd spent his life avoiding entanglements of any kind it was damn scary. He wished he *could* mean it. That this could lead somewhere, but she was entrenched in this town. Her family was here. Her livelihood. Her heritage.

Natalie studied him, her head cocked at a provocative angle, her face full of sass and curiosity. Her cheeks were pink and her eyes glowed. He wasn't the only one feeling this attraction, but she probably wasn't calculating the distance to the nearest available bed.

Knock it off, Vega.

"How come you're here all alone?" he asked.

"I'm not alone. Zoey is with me."

"I mean why doesn't a woman like you have a date?"

She laughed. "A woman like me?"

"Sexy. Bright. Disarming."

"Don't forget crippled." She waved at her leg.

"You use that as an excuse."

"What?" She looked startled.

"The leg. You hide behind it."

Her tone turned chilly. "You don't know me well enough to make that assessment."

"Sometimes it takes a stranger to really see *you*."

"What's that supposed to mean?"

"Family can take you for granted. They see you the way they've always seen you."

"True enough." She looked pensive. "What do you see?"

"A woman who puts everyone else's needs ahead of her own."

She shook her head. "I'm changing all that."

"Which is why you're here tonight? To have your needs met?"

Her eyes held his. "Are you offering to meet them?"

Hell, yeah! She wasn't the only one with unmet needs. It had been a long time since he'd been with a woman. Months. Lately, he hadn't found anyone that interested him enough to make the effort, but all that had changed from the first moment he'd looked her in the eyes. He moistened his lips and let his gaze drift over her.

The green dress she had on was simple, but that's precisely why it was so sexy. No frills or sequins or sashes to detract from the woman inside it. It had a V-neck that wasn't too low, but revealed just a touch of cleavage, a sweet peek that hinted at so much more beyond the material.

The dress was sleeveless and showed off her toned upper arms. It clung to her body in all the right places, sharpened his desire. She wore those clunky sneakers and that plastic leg brace, but even so, it didn't detract from the shapeliness of her legs. Her soft brown hair was straight as Cleopatra's and it gave her an exotic look. She wore a gold heart-shaped necklace, and a pair of tiny gold earrings nestled at each lobe. Simple, understated, down-to-earth.

Ah, dammit. Natalie McCleary was kind and gentle and sincere. She was apple pie and happily-ever-after. Her family tree ran deep as mesquite taproots. She was the kind of girl you took home to meet the parents.

If a guy had parents. Too bad he was rootless, allergic to apples, and happily-ever-after wasn't in his vocabulary. He was here for one reason and one reason only. To find out what had happened to Red.

So why, when he looked into the depths of those soft sky blue eyes, did he feel such a bone-deep craving for something he could never have? Why did he burn to take *this* woman to his bed and lose himself inside her forever?

Raised voices drew his attention to the other side of the bar where two guys were squaring off, fists raised.

"Duty calls," he said lightly, and took off across the room to stop the altercation before it got started, feeling both relieved and cheated.

He separated the two men, grabbed each by the collar, and dragged them out the side door. "Fight in the parking lot," he said. "But you better make it quick because I'm calling the cops."

Both men snorted and glared and hightailed it for their respective pickup trucks. Dade dusted his hands together and went back inside the bar. Immediately, his gaze went to Natalie's table, but she was gone.

I'm precisely the woman for you.
Dear God, had she actually said that to him?
Back at the Cupid's Rest, safe in her bed, Natalie

cringed and covered her head with a pillow. After she'd made that ridiculous statement, Dade had laughed. Yes, *laughed.* As if it was the funniest thing he'd ever heard.

"Stupid, stupid." She rolled over and punched her pillow.

She sighed and wished her mother were here. There were so many things she wanted to ask her about men, about falling in love.

This shouldn't be so hard, right? If Dade was really The One, shouldn't this be easy? Apparently, it was easy for everyone else. Did that mean that he was not The One?

That made her think about Shot Through the Heart. Falling in love at first sight had been the easy part for the letter writer. Making that love fit into her life was the hard part. No one ever mentioned that.

Natalie threw back the covers, got out of bed. She went over to the desk in the corner, took out a yellow legal pad and a pen. She sat on the window seat ledge in front of the window where Shot Through the Heart's letter—now rippled and warped after drying out from its soak in the pond—lay spread. Folding her legs up, she bent them at the knees and created a makeshift table with her lap. She propped the notepad up and began to write.

Dear Shot Through the Heart,

She paused, and gnawed on the end of her pen.

Falling in love is the easy part.

She ripped the page out, crumpled up the yellow piece of paper, and tossed it to the floor.

Dear Shot Through the Heart,
There's nothing more stimulating than falling
in love at first sight. It takes your breath away.
Steals your reason.

Natalie growled, ripped out that paper, and wadded it in her fist.
Come on. This woman is waiting for a helpful reply. Tell her something she can use. Not platitudes. Nothing vague.

Dear Shot Through the Heart,
While falling in love at first sight seems like such
a blessing, as you've learned, it can cause a
great many complications with your life plans.
The question becomes which is more important
to you? Love or the life path you've chosen?

Rip.
Crumple.
Toss.
She nibbled harder on her pen. She was not the least bit qualified to do this. She was a fraud.

Dear Shot Through the Heart,
I have no idea what I'm talking about.

Another piece of paper joined the others on the floor.
Frustrated, Natalie tossed the pad aside, got up, and tracked over to the framed photographs on her desk. She

picked up the faded black and white picture of Great-Grandmother Millie with her bobbed hair, shapeless flapper dress, long strands of pearls, and blissful smile, standing beside a handsome young man with a Clark Gable mustache and devilish eyes. John Fant, Natalie's great-grandfather. It was their engagement photo.

Natalie traced a finger over Millie's face. "It wasn't easy for you either, was it? I wish I could have known you. Wish I could ask your advice about what to do. This thing with Dade, well, it leaves me mixed up. I can't sleep. I can't eat. Isn't love supposed to make things easier, not harder? Why does it all feel so perplexing?"

Millie's eyes twinkled. She had found her true love. *So have you.*

That's what scared Natalie the most, the idea that Dade was indeed The One. She didn't know if she was ready for that.

"How do I know it's real, Millie?" Natalie whispered. "I think it's real, but that could just be wishful thinking. The truth is, I don't really know him. How can I be in love with someone I don't know?"

You know him. Deep in your heart, you know.

The words popped into her head as loudly as if someone had spoken them. Natalie jumped, unnerved.

He is the other half of you.

Goose bumps spread up her arm. How did she know this to be true? It defied logic. In all honesty, these feelings were probably nothing more than powerful sexual attraction.

What should she do about it? That evening, she'd tried to find someone else to get lathered up over and it had backfired miserably.

You could always put your feelings to the test.

"How's that, Millie?" she asked the voice in her head. Now she was turning well and truly crazy, talking to her long dead great-grandmother as if they could commune through a photograph.

Take him for a test drive.

Natalie's cheeks heated.

Sex.

She should just have a red-hot fling with Dade. If this was nothing but sexual attraction, then the affair was bound to burn out. Anything that sizzled this hotly must cool down. It was a law of physics. Right?

Then again, what did she know? In school, she'd made C's in math and science.

If she and Dade dared to feed the flames scorching between them, they might burn each other down, but what a way to go, huh?

Natalie gulped.

If it wasn't just lust, what was it then?

She stroked her chin pensively. Well, then she'd cross that bridge when she got to it. For the present, she needed a plan. She had to either get Dade completely out of her life, which meant evicting him, or embrace the chaos and just let him lead her into the abyss.

It was so scary and she immediately knew why. She feared losing control. Surrendering to love meant giving yourself over to another person.

Whoa.

Natalie returned to the window seat, picked up the notepad, tore a sheet from it, and began to write.

Dear Cupid,
Please help me. I'm in trouble deep.

Chapter 10

*Sometimes falling in love makes you feel like
you're drowning; just take a deep breath, relax,
and you'll float.*

—*Millie Greenwood*

In the wee hours of Friday morning, four days after he
rode into town, Dade closed down the bar, but he did
not want to go back to the B&B. He didn't trust himself around Natalie.

Jasper had told him if he ever needed it, the hammock on the back patio deck was available to him, just
as long as it wasn't being used by a customer who was
too drunk to drive home.

If he went back to the Cupid's Rest tonight, Dade
didn't trust himself. Natalie would be within reach, and
he wanted her with a relentless fire, and that back door

lock of hers wouldn't hold back anyone determined to get in.

Dade stepped outside, looked up at the dark night sky filled with a million brilliant stars. Usually, the quiet night calmed him. Made him feel part of the universe. But tonight, the sky made him feel isolated, alone. Disturbed, he wandered around the side of the building and walked up on the back porch. The white hammock stood out in the shadows.

It was empty.

Relieved, Dade sank down into the hammock and let out a long breath. He didn't have to go home.

Home.

Why did he keep referring to Cupid's Rest as home?

He kicked off his cowboy boots, rested his hands on his belly, and closed his eyes. The second he did, he saw Natalie's face, sweet, tempting, out-of-this world. He thought about the kisses they'd shared, the provocative taste of her lush lips. No doubt about it. The woman had crawled under his skin and wouldn't get out.

This was dangerous stuff, not only for his peace of mind, but for Red's sake as well. He couldn't afford to give in to the attraction. He had to focus on finding his buddy.

Guilt dug into him then and Dade pulled his cell phone from his back pocket, and as he'd done several times a day since Red had sent the text message, he hit speed dial.

"This is Red, you know the drill."

"Buddy," Dade said, "where the hell are you? What's happened? I'm here in Cupid, can't find a trace of you. Then again you always were good at disappearing, but if you're out there, please let me hear from you. I'm concerned."

Discouraged, he hung up.

Dade stared at the phone and then called the number again just to hear Red's voice. He had an awful feeling that his foster brother might be dead. "Nah, man, no. You can't be dead. You're friggin' invincible."

He blew out his breath, laid his cell phone on the small green table positioned near the hammock. "Swear to God, I don't know what to do next. If I keep lying low, not telling anyone who I am, no one is going to talk to me about you, and I can't blatantly ask without arousing suspicions, but it's getting harder and harder for me to believe that someone in Cupid wanted to harm you. It's a nice place. I can see why you decided to put roots down here."

Paranoid delusions had been part of Red's PTSD diagnosis, but just because you were paranoid didn't mean that someone wasn't out to get you. Dade couldn't afford to assume anything. The "Tanked" Mayday message was serious. It was only to be used in case of an extreme emergency. Red would not use it lightly.

Dade fished in the front pocket of his jeans and pulled out the talisman he carried with him at all times. It was a handmade braided bracelet created of black Afghanistan wool, with a bullet casing threaded through the middle of it.

He closed his fist around the bullet casing, and his mind drifted back four years. He and Red had both just been discharged from the navy and they were sitting in a darkened bar in D.C., neither one of them speaking about what they'd gone through. In fact, they hardly spoke at all, just took periodic sips from their Mich-

elob Lights and stared at the Dallas Cowboys battling
Green Bay on the big-screen TV.

Then out of the blue, Red said, "Gimme your wrist."

"What for?"

"Just give it to me."

Curious, Dade had held out his left wrist.

Red took a small hank of black wool yarn from his
pocket.

The sight of it caused Dade's stomach to pitch.
"Where'd you get that?"

"The girl."

His muscles had tensed. "What girl?"

"Which one do you think?"

Dade's stomach pitched. "She almost got me killed."

"I know. I was there." Red unrolled a piece of yarn,
wrapped it around Dade's wrist to measure, then added
two inches and cut the yarn with his pocket knife. "You
got a damn big wrist."

"You think that's big," Dade had teased, desperate
to lighten things. His thoughts had gone back to the
Afghani girl and he did not want to think about her.

Red rolled his eyes and cut a second piece of yarn
the same length as the first one. He continued to cut
strands of yarn, using the first as a guide, until he had
two piles of black strings.

Dade watched while Red began braiding the strands
of yarns together. He corded all the strings in one pile,
and then started on the other.

The Cowboys and Green Bay were tied, fourth quarter, two minutes to go. Dallas had the ball. It was fourth
down and forty yards from the end zone, but Dade could
not take his eyes off Red.

Red's fingers flew and while the game broke for

commercial, he finished the second braid. From his pocket, he pulled out two bullet casings. A hole had been drilled through the ends.

Dade sucked in air through clenched teeth. "Are those casings from—"

"Yep," Red said, and slipped a bullet casing over each of the braided threads. He knotted the ends of each bracelet. He tied one bracelet around his left wrist, readjusting the knots to fit securely. When he was finished, he glanced at Dade's wrist.

Dade held out his left arm.

The bullet casing was cool against his skin. Red tied the second bracelet around Dade's wrist. They sat in silence, twin bracelets on their left arms.

Red took a sip of his beer. "So Romo," he said, nodding at the TV. "Think he'll take Dallas all the way this year?"

That was all he said. No need to explain what the bracelet meant. Dade knew. *We'll always be connected.* They were brothers of the soul, if not of DNA and they would have each other's backs until the end of time.

He'd worn the bracelet for years, until last week, just before Red had sent the text, the wool strands—frayed and weakened from years of use—had broken.

Dade hadn't seen his buddy in two years, not since Red had left the security firm they went to work for postmilitary, and he regretted that. He hadn't understood why Red left the security detail. It paid well, and after Afghanistan, it was like babysitting. Cushy, well paying, sure they sometimes got mixed up in some gray area misconduct, but that was the nature of the business.

"Why are you leaving?" Dade had asked, feeling a little betrayed by Red's defection.

"This work is too much like war. I need to get the stink of war off me. You can come too," Red had invited.

"Where are you going?"

"To find a place where I can settle down. See if I can become human."

"Do you think that's really possible for guys like us?"

"I have to hope," Red said. "I have to have something more than this."

Much as he loved his friend, Dade couldn't imagine leading a routine life, staying in one place, being tied down. Not him. No way.

Natalie drifted over his thoughts. She was a woman who made him want to stay. He wished things were different. Wished he were different.

Dade reached up to finger his lips, smiled at the memory of their kisses. She was some kind of kisser.

Stop thinking about her. She's nothing but a distraction.

Shifting in the hammock, he stared up at the stars, tried to remember the last time he and Red had a phone conversation. It had been near Easter when Red had called and tried to persuade him to come visit, but Dade had been in Saudi Arabia. He'd promised Red they'd get together whenever he got back to the States, but they hadn't. He hadn't even called Red when he'd gotten the Gulf of Mexico detail. He'd been so close and yet he hadn't made the effort.

It wasn't that he hadn't wanted to see his buddy, because he certainly had. Rather, it was that he didn't want to come to this picturesque community nestled in the crook of the Davis Mountains, and see what had lured Red away from him.

Red spoke so glowingly of Cupid that it made Dade a little jealous that Red had found a place that suited him. And maybe—if he were being honest with himself, he would admit that this was more likely—he was afraid he'd like Cupid and want to stay.

He did like it.

That was the problem.

He simply wasn't the kind of guy who settled down. He had no idea how. He'd never been settled in his life. He didn't belong anywhere, had never belonged, and he liked it that way.

Rolling stone.

He fingered the bracelet, rubbed the spent bullet casing between his thumb and index finger. The Bob Dylan song of the same name reverberated through his head.

"Like a Rolling Stone."

Closing his eyes, he sighed, fought off visions of Natalie. No matter how much he wanted her, he couldn't have her. Not for keeps anyway, and anything else was a complication he simply did not need.

Dade must have fallen asleep, because sometime later, he bolted awake.

His eyes popped open. Dark clouds had moved across the sky, drowning out the light. The black waters of Lake Cupid lapped against the dock below the deck. He lay in the hammock, ears cocked, muscles coiled tight, listening intently. He'd always been a light sleeper, mostly the results of being raised in a house of junkies, never knowing who was going to stumble in or what they might do. Under those circumstances a kid had to stay hypervigilant.

Wind chimes tinkled against each other. A dog

barked. A whippoorwill called. The warm night air ruffled the hairs on his forearm.

He waited, curled his hands into fists, ready for a fight if need be.

A floorboard on the deck creaked.

A shadow moved.

"Who's there?" he commanded.

Someone stepped forward and for one sweet second, he thought it was Natalie and that she'd come to be with him. His heart leaped.

Jackass.

"Señor," whispered an urgent feminine voice. "I desperately need your help."

Dade squinted into the darkness. It was a Mexican woman, neither young nor old, with her hair pulled back off her neck in a single long braid. Dade swung his legs over the side of the hammock, careful not to tip over.

"What can I do for you?"

She stopped mid-step, stared at him, muttered, "Oh no," and immediately spun away from him.

Dade was upon her, grabbed her before she got to the first deck step, clung to her elbow.

She battled him, pounding at him with both hands.

"Stop fighting," he growled, holding her tightly around the waist. "I'm not going to harm you."

Her eyes widened as if she did not believe him. "You are not the gringo I am looking for."

"Who *are* you looking for?" he asked.

She shook her head.

He grasped her shoulders, forced her to look him in the eyes, letting her know that he meant business. "Tell me."

She turned her head away. "I do not know his name."

"Then how do you know I am not the man you want?"

She peeked at him. "I was told the man I am to meet has red hair."

"Red?" His breath stilled in his lungs. At last, a lead on Red's whereabouts! "You came looking for Red?"

She nodded. "*Sí. Rojo.*"

"What do you want with him?"

A frightened expression crossed her face and she squirmed to get away. Dade tightened his grip. "What do you know about Red?" he demanded.

"Nothing."

"Where is he?"

"I do not know," she wailed.

"You're lying." He spit out the words. "What are you up to?"

"Please. My English. Not so good."

"Bullshit. Your English is fine. You came here looking for Red. Who sent you?"

She shied from him. "Please, do not hurt me, señor."

Dade grit his teeth. "I'm not going to hurt you. I just want to know where Red is."

She trembled. "*Por favor*, my arm."

Dade loosened his grip. *Settle down, Vega, you're scaring her.* "Why did you come here in the middle of the night?"

She shrugged her huddled shoulders.

He took her chin in his palm and forced her to meet his gaze, saw stark fear in her eyes. "Tell me."

"Señor, I cannot."

Impatience kicked at him. "You said you needed help. I can help you."

"Not you. No." Violently, she shook her head.

"Give me a chance."

"No."

Frustrated, Dade shoved a hand through his hair. This woman knew something, but she wasn't talking. It might not have a thing to do with Red's disappearance, but this was the first viable clue he'd gotten since arriving in Cupid.

"You're an illegal," he guessed.

She nodded, eyes wide. "Please, please do not tell."

"I'm not going to tell. I just want to find Señor Rojo. Are you Red's…" He paused, searching for the Spanish word for girlfriend. "*Novia?*"

"No."

Okay, so she wasn't there for a romantic tryst. Why then was an illegal immigrant looking for Red? A handful of possibilities popped into his head, none of them pleasant. *You were supposed to settle down, buddy. Stay out of trouble. Not rescue damsels in distress.*

She said something in Spanish that he didn't understand. He didn't know why she was here expecting to find Red, but one thing was clear. She was not going to tell him the reason. Plus, if she had expected to find Red here, that meant she didn't know he was missing.

He released her arm.

She backed up.

"If you find Red, if you hear from him, call me." He took a business card from his back pocket, passed it to her.

She tucked it into the bosom of her blouse, but he could tell from the expression on her face that there was no way in hell she was going to tell him anything.

"Go on." He sighed and waved her away.

Relief flooded her face. She turned and fled down the steps, leaving Dade with even more questions now than he'd had before. Who was the mystery woman? Why was she looking for Red? What in the hell was his buddy mixed up in?

The next morning, Natalie awoke with a lazy smile stretching her mouth wide. She stretched, yawned, remembered. Last night she'd danced with Dade. Kissed him. And it had been amazing. What a beautiful morning! What a glorious day!

Energized, Natalie hopped from the bed, limped through the pile of wadded-up notebook paper on the floor, to reach the window seat. Anxious to embrace her future, she leaned over and threw open the window wide. Dawn, rosy and soft, spilled into the room, fresh and hopeful, but along with it blew a hot, blustery summer wind gusting from the south.

Oops, bad idea.

She moved to shut the window, but the brisk breeze picked up Shot Through the Heart's letter, along with the one Natalie had written to Cupid the night before, asking for his help in sorting out her feelings about Dade, and sent them flying over the roof.

The letters caught against the side of the rock chimney, quivered there in the wind.

Oh, dammit. She could not leave the letters there. What if they flew off? She needed Shot Through the Heart's letter to remember exactly what she'd written, and as for the letter Natalie had written, well, what if someone found it? What if *Dade* found it?

Her face flushed hot at the thought of Dade reading it and discovering exactly what she felt about him. She simply wasn't ready for that. She had to get those letters back.

But how?

The chimney wasn't very far from the window, just a few short feet. In fact, if she stretched really long, she could probably reach out and grab them.

There was just one problem. Her fear of heights.

She stood there, nibbling her bottom lip while the wind flapped against the letters. They made a sound like playing cards pinned to bicycle spokes. Night shadows still darkened the shingles. She could go get a ladder, but the thought of climbing up a shaky ladder was even more intimidating than the notion of leaning out across the pitched roof. She thought about getting Zoey to do it, but her sister would make a big deal of it and insist on reading Natalie's letter to Cupid.

It was high time she conquered her fear. *Just go get the letters.*

Resolutely, she kept her eye on the chimney. *Don't look down.* Gingerly, she crawled up on the window seat and leaned out over the sill.

The wind gusted against her with surprising force.

She sucked in a deep breath, and it was all she could do not to pull back. Clinging to the window with both hands, she eyed the distance to the chimney. It looked no farther than a foot away, but then again, she was terrible at gauging distances.

Well, you can't stay here forever.

Tentatively, she let go with one hand and reached out for the letters. The wind buffeted her hair into her face, the whipping strands stung her eyes, and this time, batting at her hair, she did draw back.

She sank against the window seat. Nausea rose in her throat, and in a flash, she was nine years old again and on that mountain, dangling from a tree.

Oh God, she couldn't do it.

Forget the letters. It wasn't worth this.

Really? Was she going to let her phobia defeat her? At this point, it was no longer only about the letters. It was the principle of the thing. She'd been sheltered and petted for too long. Was she going to spend the rest of her life controlled by fear?

You can do it.

She swallowed, closed her eyes, clenched her teeth, and tried again. This time she was braced for the wind, but no matter how much she stretched, the letters lay inches from her grasp.

If she wanted to reach them, she was going to have to venture out on the roof. Ah, crap. Crawling, she placed her left leg on the slanted roof, the gritty shingles rough against her kneecap.

She paused, needing a moment before she tried to move forward. From the corner of her eye, she spied the ground. It looked a million miles away. If she fell, she could break her neck.

Don't look down.

Natalie closed her eyes. Hung there. Her breathing grew as ragged as a dull saw dragged back and forth across the tough bark of piñon pine. Her muscles seized up.

Move. It's only inches.

The nausea crept up to her throat, but she swallowed it back, opened her eyes, and brought her right knee out onto the roof to join her left.

The sun peeped over the horizon, a happy yellow egg yolk, unbothered by the wind that ruffled the material of Natalie's cotton nightshirt. Sweat popped out on her brow and she shivered the length of her body. Hotly cold? Or coldly hot? Who knew?

Eye on the prize. Grab those letters and get the heck back into the bedroom.

She brought her left knee forward again, moved forward a couple of inches, completely free of the window now. No anchor. No landline.

Don't be silly, the window is right behind you.

It sounded logical. Of course it was logical, but when you were afraid of something, logic didn't enter into it.

She reached out toward the chimney. Her fingertips grazed the paper but she couldn't quite grab it in her fist. *One more inch. Just slide forward. You've got this thing.*

Chuffing out her breath, she scootched forward, knees dragging across the shingles. Her fist closed over the letters just as a particularly strong gust of wind bulleted around the chimney and knocked her off balance.

Natalie toppled over, cried out, and slithered lickety-split down the steep angle of the roof, barreling toward the ground below.

Dade came out of his room at the carriage house, dressed in shorts and running shoes, ready to pound out a good five-mile run.

After the Mexican woman had awakened him, he'd been unable to go back to sleep, so he'd returned to the Cupid's Rest to change clothes in hopes of burning off the restless energy that had dogged him since he'd kissed Natalie.

He rounded the corner, started up the paver stone driveway, and stopped in his tracks.

There, dangling from the roof, was Natalie. She wore a thin white nightshirt, the short hem showing off her legs, and the outline of purple bikini-cut panties showing through. She clutched the gutter tightly in her white-knuckled hands and her breathing came in ragged, panicked gasps.

Instantly, Dade ran to her, reached up, and encircled her waist with his hands. "I've got you," he said. "You're okay. You can let go."

"I can't," she wailed.

"You can. I've got you," he repeated. "You're safe."

The tension seeped from her body into his and he felt her fear. She was terrified. "Natalie," he said firmly. "Let go."

It took her a minute to release the gutter. How long had she been hanging there?

He set her gently onto the ground, but her knees collapsed beneath her weight. Dade gathered her to him, held her against his chest.

She was trembling from head to toe.

"What is it?" he murmured in her ear. "What happened?"

She said not a word, simply clung to him, buried her face against his neck.

He lightly kissed the top of her head, smoothed down her hair with a palm. "Natalie, what is it? Speak to me."

"I...I could have been killed."

"Not really. You were only a few feet off the ground."

"What if I'd fallen on my head?"

"You didn't."

"But I could have." She shuddered against him. "I'm terrified of heights."

He tightened his arms around her like a cocoon. The material of her nightshirt was dangerously thin and the curves of her breasts were mashed against him.

He should let go of her before his body responded in a totally normal way to a smoking hot, scantily clad woman. "It's okay. You're okay now. How long were you up there?"

"It felt like hours, but it was probably only a couple of minutes." Her voice was wheezy.

"I know it's none of my business, but what were you doing up there if you're afraid of heights?"

She waved a fist. She had something clutched in it. Something yellow like notebook paper. "Embarrassing story."

Hmm. He narrowed his eyes. What was she hiding?

She stepped back from him, glanced down at her barely there garment, and immediately wrapped her arms around herself. The wind, which had been blowing hard and steady for the last hour, sent whirling eddies of sand dancing across the street and lifted Natalie's nightshirt all the way to her hips.

And Dade got a great glimpse of her smooth white skin. He gulped, and the boner he'd been battling to hold off poked jauntily against his shorts.

Ah, damn.

Natalie yanked down the hem of her nightshirt while Dade ducked his head.

"Thanks," she mumbled.

"Gotta go," he muttered.

She turned toward the house. He turned toward the street. And they both took off in opposite directions.

Chapter 11

It's usually the skeptics who fall hardest.
—Millie Greenwood

Several hours later, Natalie arrived at the community center still shaken from her tumble down the roof.

"You don't look good," Aunt Carol Ann fussed. "Do you have a fever?"

"I'm fine."

Her aunt put a palm to Natalie's forehead. "You're cool as a cucumber."

Natalie pulled away from her. "I said I'm fine."

"You're not fine. Something's up."

Even though she wasn't hungry, Natalie snatched up a plate and went to the buffet table for the beef brisket that Junie Mae had brought for lunch; anything to avoid Carol Ann's scrutiny.

Sandra walked in carrying an oversized metal bowl

of banana pudding and put it in the community refrigerator. "Don't forget the 'naner pudding, when you leave," she told Natalie.

Although she'd run the risk of galling Pearl, Natalie had ordered the banana pudding from Sandra for tonight's outdoor catfish fry that she was throwing for her B&B guests to kick off a week of Fourth of July celebrations.

Pearl would have her hands full manning the deep fryer on the backyard patio without having to worry about creating dessert. Her cook had pitched a bitch because that was Pearl, but in the end, she acquiesced and grudgingly gave her permission for the order. Even cranky Pearl had to admit Sandra made the best banana pudding in west Texas.

"Thank you," Natalie said, happy to have the focus off her. "I'll get you a check after the meeting."

"No rush." Sandra smiled. "I know you're good for it."

The reprieve was short-lived. Mignon came over, narrowed her eyes. "Are you hungover?"

"You know I don't drink," Natalie said, wishing they'd find another topic of conversation.

"I heard that you drank last night." Mignon grinned. "And that you kissed Chantilly's handsome new bouncer."

"I had to kiss him. I lost the Life Saver relay."

"Why do you say lost?" Carol Ann asked. "It's the object of the relay to be the last one with the Life Saver."

Natalie made a face. "I guess the definition depends on whether you want to kiss someone or not."

"Some people would consider that winning," Mignon said. "He's very handsome."

"I heard you kissed him twice," Lace added.

"Zoey's got a big mouth," Natalie grumbled.

"I didn't hear it from Zoey," Sandra said. "I heard it from Calvin and Maria."

"I heard it from my mailman." Junie Mae poured herself a glass of sweet tea. "I think it's wonderful. Long past time you had a beau."

"He's not my beau!" Natalie protested as she took her seat at the table. "We just kissed. End of story."

"If you say so, dear." Junie Mae's eyes twinkled.

"Leave her alone," Delia defended Natalie. "She's entitled to her privacy."

"Thank you, Auntie Delia."

Delia patted the chair beside her. "Come sit by me and tell me all about him. Junie Mae says he's got muscles to make the Incredible Hulk weep."

"Junie Mae!"

"Well, he does. Just because I'm old doesn't mean I'm blind. I know a good-looking man when I see one, and it's about time you did too."

"Could we please talk about something besides my love life?" Natalie pushed halfheartedly at the brisket on her plate.

"Ooh-la-la," Mignon said. "At least she's admitting she's got a love life."

Oh crap. This was backfiring on her from every angle.

"I don't have a love life. I admit nothing," Natalie declared.

"Ah, *chère*, you should have a magnificent love life. You are young—but not getting any younger."

"We just want to see you happy," Sandra chimed in.

"They need romantic fodder," Lace said. "Heaven knows that no one is living vicariously through *me*."

Natalie looked around the table, spread her arms open wide. "Anyone else want to weigh in? This is your opportunity. Tell me what to do. Should I shag him till I'm blue in the face?"

Delia laughed. "Sounds good to me."

"Woo, Nat, way to get sassy." Lace pumped her fist.

"You're right," Aunt Carol Ann said primly. "We do need to change the subject. Let's talk about Shot Through the Heart's letter. Have you answered it yet?"

Well, that change of subject hadn't helped her any. "Not yet," Natalie admitted.

"Dear, really, it's not an indictment if you just can't do it. Any of us would be happy to take that letter off your hands and answer it today, problem solved."

She should just turn the letter over to one of the other volunteers. If she were being sensible, that's exactly what she would do, but Natalie did the tasks she'd been assigned. She was dependable that way. It was just that this particular task felt impossible. "You said I could have until Monday."

"I have a feeling you're not going to have it done by Monday. You're going to be crazed with getting the B&B ready for the Fourth of July celebrations. Let me ease your burden. I don't mind." Carol Ann smiled.

"If you want to ease my burden, then please give me another week."

Carol Ann pursed her lips. "Natalie, that means it would have taken you three weeks to answer a simple letter. It's unheard of and a violation of our policy, I might add."

"Could we put a humorous, short comment to Shot

Through the Heart in the next newsletter that Cupid is taking her letter under extended advisement, and plead for her understanding?"

"There's no need, if you'd just give over control of the letter." Carol Ann's jaw clenched. Once her aunt got a scenario in her head she tended to become entrenched. She glanced around at the group. "Y'all back me up on this."

"Back you up on what?" Zoey asked, rushing through the door with her book bag slung over her shoulder.

"Carol Ann is pressuring Natalie to answer Shot Through the Heart or give the letter over to one of us," Lace filled her in.

"You say that like it's a bad thing." Carol Ann sniffed. "I'm the one who has to keep this whole show on track. Natalie's being stubborn."

"Take a chill pill, Aunt Carol Ann, how many times has Natalie not done what you've asked her to?" Zoey tumbled into her chair.

"That's not the issue. I—"

"She always does what everyone wants her to do. For godsakes, let her do this one thing in her own time, okay?" Zoey said.

Wow, Zoey was taking up for her? Unbelievable. She smiled across the table at her sister and silently mouthed, *Thank you.*

"How does everyone else feel about this?" Carol Ann asked. "Is this acceptable to you all? Can we all just decide when we'll get around to answering the letters? Is this the precedent you want to set?"

"Take the stick out of your behind, Carol Ann," Delia said. "The world's not going to end if Shot Through the Heart has to wait another week for her letter."

"Fine." Carol Ann pressed her lips into a firm straight line and glared at Natalie. "But I really don't understand what the problem is."

"Don't you get it?" Zoey asked.

"Get what?" Carol Ann's tone was snippy.

"Natalie's fallen in love at first sight and she's wrestling with her beliefs and working it out through her answer to Shot Through the Heart." Her sister ratted her out.

Carol Ann's face transformed. "My gosh." She splayed a hand to her throat. "My goodness. Natalie, why didn't you just say so?"

"Because it's not true," she lied, and felt her eyelid twitch.

"Of course, you can have another week." Carol Ann nodded. "I'll put a little blurb in the newspaper saying that Cupid had to put on his thinking cap for this one."

Oh God.

Natalie groaned and dropped her head to the table. She might have gotten a reprieve on answering the letter, but now the entire town was going to be buzzing with the news that Millie Greenwood's great-granddaughter had finally been struck by Cupid's arrow.

Later that day, while going to the bar to stand in for the day-shift bartender who needed to run some errands, Dade noticed the back door to the Cupid's Rest standing ajar.

Shaking his head, he went over to push it closed. It immediately popped back open. Forcefully, he shoved the door shut, jiggled the latch until it caught with an anemic click. The lock was a joke. Even if it was locked, the most bumbling thief could break in with a credit card and two minutes to spare.

"Natalie," he muttered. "You gotta get this thing fixed." *Hell, you should fix it for her, Vega. Clearly, she doesn't understand how vulnerable she is.*

Dade got on his Harley and took off for Chantilly's. He resented having to go to work at the bar when he wanted to be off looking for Red. He told himself this was the best way to find out about Red, talk to the regular customers where his buddy used to work, but still he ached to spring into action. Do something besides wait around for clues to appear. After his encounter with the Mexican woman, Dade had a renewed sense of urgency, and he was determined to find a lead to Red's whereabouts.

At noon, Milo Birch, who perpetually occupied the last stool at the end of the bar closest to the front door, showed up. Milo was a weathered string bean with sharp features and a habit of wriggling his nose. If you stuck whiskers and a tail on him, he'd look like a desert rat, shifty-eyed and sneaky.

Dade didn't trust him any farther than he could throw him, but he promised to be the best source of information about Red. When Milo was liquored up, his lips loosened like a hooker's knees. Luckily for Dade, Milo was liquored up seventy percent of the time.

"Bud?" Dade asked as Milo settled into the seat.

Milo sniggered for no particular reason and nodded.

While Dade was trying to figure out how to bring Red's name up in conversation, Lars Bakke walked in. Bakke didn't take a seat at the bar, but instead chose a small nearby table and sat with his back to the wall.

It was a seat that Dade himself would have taken in

a similar situation. He always sat with his back to the wall if he could arrange things that way. When you had the wall at your back, no one could creep up on you. He'd met Lars in passing at the Cupid's Rest, but he hadn't really had much of a conversation with him. It was time to rectify that.

Dade slapped a bar towel over his shoulder. "What'll you have?"

"Jack straight up."

Dade poured up a jigger of Jack Daniel's, set it in front of Lars. "Kinda stout for high noon."

"You're pretty ugly to be my mother." Lars smoothly poured the whiskey down his throat, and didn't even wince.

Milo sniggered again.

"Something eating you?" Dade asked Lars.

Lars swiped a hand over his mouth. He was damn fit for a man his age. No belly paunch like the majority of older guys. "Problem with my boat."

"Boat?"

"He's havin' a cherry of a sailboat handcrafted in Mexico," Milo supplied, pronouncing Mexico the way the natives said it, *May-he-co.* "Gonna sail around the world. Show him the pictures, Lars."

Lars shook his head. "Not in the mood to talk about it."

"You want another?" Dade nodded at the jigger.

"Beer. Whatever you've got on tap."

"Got it."

Just then, Jasper came in through the back door. "What's up?" he asked rhetorically.

"Lars's got a glitch with his boat." Milo took a big

swallow of beer, leaving a foam mustache on his upper lip. He snaked out a tongue and licked it off.

"That right?" Jasper asked. "What kinda glitch?"

"He don't wanna talk about it." Milo played with a Chantilly's coaster.

Dade poured Lars's beer. "I slept in the hammock out back yesterday," he said casually. "And in the middle of the night a Mexican woman showed up on the deck."

"Hey," said Jasper, sounding jealous. "How come nothing like that happens to me when I sleep in the hammock?"

Milo snorted. "'Cause you don't look like him."

Lars met Dade's eyes when he settled the beer in front of him. "What did she want?"

"Whaddya think she wanted?" Milo made a lewd gesture.

"Actually," Dade said in a measured, nonchalant tone. "She was looking for the guy whose place I took. Red, right?"

"Hmm," Jasper said. "I didn't know Red had a girl-friend."

"I don't think she was his girlfriend. She said he was supposed to help her with something."

"What was that?" Lars asked.

"I can guess." Milo made another lewd gesture.

Everyone ignored him.

Dade shrugged. "I don't know. She wouldn't elaborate, but she seemed pretty scared."

"No tellin' what Red was up to," Milo said. "He was pretty tight-lipped."

"I'm going to my office." Jasper jerked his head in that direction. "Got some calls to make."

Dade's ears pricked up. What kind of calls was Jasper making? Did it have anything to do with Red?

"Red was something of a character," Lars said. "Of course, most people who come to Cupid tend to be colorful in one way or another. He wore a braided bracelet with a spent bullet casing threaded over it."

"I 'member that ratty old bracelet." Milo scratched his chin. "Red said it was a souvenir from the gun he used to shoot a Talibanny."

"Personally," Lars said, "the story sounded farfetched to me."

Milo kept scratching on down to his neck. "Yeah, but why would he have worn that bracelet it if weren't true? He never took it off."

Dade tensed at the mention of the bracelet. He had to be careful here, couldn't tip his hand. He didn't know whom he could trust, but obviously Red had trusted Lars and Milo enough to tell them the story of the bracelet.

"You don't say?" Dade murmured mildly, as if he wasn't the least bit interested.

Lars lifted his big head. In his youth he must have been one strong son of a bitch. Even now, he was broad and powerful and could give a younger man a run for his money.

"Arm wrestle?" Lars asked.

"What?"

Lars eyed Dade's biceps. "Ever arm wrestle?"

"Sure. When I was a kid."

"Red and I used to arm wrestle."

"Who won?" Dade asked.

Lars shrugged. "Sometimes him, sometimes me."

"Really? You won?"

"A time or two." Lars grinned, showing a row of straight teeth. "Just because I'm an old coot doesn't mean I don't still have some life left in me."

"I can see that."

Lars rested his elbow on the table. "You want to have a go?"

"I don't want to shame you, old man."

"Scared I'll beat you?"

Dade laughed.

Lars nodded toward his arm that he planted on the table and raised his hand. "Show me your stuff."

"I'm on the job."

"The bar is empty."

"Hey!" Milo protested. "I'm here."

Lars flicked him a look that said, *You don't count.*

Affronted, Milo blew a raspberry.

"Jasper," Lars called out.

Jasper poked his head out of his office. "What is it?"

"You mind if I arm wrestle your bartender?"

"Only if I can get in on the action." Jasper bounced into the bar faster than Dade had ever seen him move, pulling a wad of twenties from his wallet. "A hundred on Dade."

"You sure you want to make that bet?" Lars asked.

"Look at him." Jasper waved a hand at Dade.

"Hey!" Milo hiccupped. "I want in on it too. I'll back Lars."

"You got a hundred bucks?" Jasper asked.

"Yep."

"Then pay your bar tab."

"How about this," Milo negotiated, staggering over to the table where Lars sat. "If Dade wins, I pay my bar tab. If Lars wins, you erase my debt."

Jasper stroked his grizzled jaw, considered Milo's proposition. "You got it."

Milo pulled up a chair, turned it around, and straddled the seat with the back against his belly. "Ringside seats. Let's go."

Dade tossed the polishing towel on the bar. This was ridiculous. "I'm gonna smoke you, Grandpa," he told Lars. "You sure you want to be humiliated in front of your friends?"

"Your confidence is commendable," Lars said. "But there is no real freedom without the freedom to fail."

"Huh?" Dade blinked.

Jasper waved a hand. "Never mind. He loves quoting Eric Hoffer. It doesn't make any sense to anyone but Lars."

"Just remember," Dade pointed out to Lars, "you asked for it."

"You've met your match, old man. This one is cockier than Red," Jasper said. "More muscles too."

Dade took the chair across from Lars and locked eyes with his opponent. He was doing this for only one reason, to fit in with this bunch and hopefully get them more willing to open up about Red. He planted his elbow adjacent to Lars's and they clasped palms.

"Ready?" Jasper asked.

Milo hiccupped again.

Dade narrowed his eyes.

Lars squeezed Dade's hand.

"Ready," they agreed in unison.

"Go!" Jasper signaled with a bandana he pulled from his pocket and flung it like he was dropping the flag at a NASCAR race.

Lars's grip was steel, hard and unyielding.

Unluckily for the old man, in the SEALs, Dade's nickname had been Titanium. He pushed back.

Lars grunted, dug in.

Dade set his jaw. This wasn't going to be a slam-dunk. The old man was amazingly strong.

Lars's eyes glistened in the muted lighting. "You're stronger than Red."

"I warned you."

"I'm not scared."

They sat locked in the struggle for a few minutes. Dade's muscles flexed as hard as they did when he lifted weights, while his mind whirled, working on how to broach the topic of Red's disappearance without looking obvious. Finally, he just decided to take the bull by the horns. He was tired of pussyfooting.

"Any speculation on what might have happened to Red?" he ask casually, as if just making conversation, which was kind of hard to do locked in a steel-trap grip with Lars.

"No telling," Milo slurred. "Red was an odd duck. Sometimes likable as hell, sometimes nutty as Pearl's pecan fruitcake."

"I think he just left." Jasper leaned one shoulder against the wall. "Some people ain't long-term folks, you know?"

Like me. He wasn't long-term. Never had been. Never would be.

Dade raised his chin. "But he left without a vehicle? In the desert? Natalie told me he didn't drive."

"Probably hitchhiked," Jasper surmised. "Truckers around here will pick people up even though they're not supposed to. They know how dangerous it is to be out in the desert on foot for too long, especially in the summer."

Dade shifted his gaze to Lars. "You got a theory."

For a long moment, Lars said nothing. He was biting down on his lower lip and sweat was trickling down his temple. The veins in his arm bulged. "Me?" He grunted. "I think he's off on a vision quest."

"Vision quest, huh?" Dade put a bit more muscle into it and Lars's arm trembled on a downward trajectory. "What makes you say that?"

"Red's enamored of Indian culture, especially charmed with the concept of vision quest. He was also fascinated with the Marfa Lights. Went out there a lot. Red was searching for something."

"Something like what?"

"Spiritually."

That was a load of horseshit. Red wasn't given to metaphysical claptrap. Then again, it had been two years since he'd seen his buddy. A guy could change a lot in a short amount of time. "Seems an odd concept for an ex-Navy SEAL."

"He was looking for his place in the world. He was a troubled guy."

Had Red gone off to find his place in the world? But no. There was that Mayday message. He wouldn't have sent it if he wasn't in some kind of trouble. But what?

Lars was chuffing out his breath in short, ragged pants. The sweat was flowing down his head now as he struggled against Dade's hand.

Dade could have taken him down right then if he wanted, but he'd finally gotten the conversation rolling about Red and he wanted to take it as far as he safely could, so he eased off on the pressure just a hair.

Lars pounced on the opportunity and came charging back, the momentum momentarily giving the older man the upper hand.

Milo hopped up, threw the bandana on the floor. "Wipe off my debt, mother effer," he crowed.

"It ain't over till it's over," Jasper said dryly.

"Let's say you're right." Dade stared into Lars's eyes. "How long would a vision quest normally last?"

"Two, three weeks," Lars mumbled, his fingers squeezing tighter.

"How long has Red been gone?"

"Took off over a week ago," Jasper supplied.

"Stop talkin' to him." Milo jumped up and down like a flea with ADD. "He's concentratin'."

Everyone ignored Milo.

"Isn't anyone around here worried about Red?" Dade asked.

Jasper straightened, shrugged. "He's gone off before. I was close to letting him go because of it, but he was such a damn good bouncer. A lot like you. Never had to raise his voice. Just talked real nice and deadly and people always backed down."

"Yep. Red once told me in a smiling whisper that if I didn't calm down he was going to rip my head off and shove it up my ass," Milo supplied.

Lars grunted and gave a hard shove, trying to go in for the kill. "I doubt he'll be back."

"No?" Dade stiffened his biceps, holding in place. *Ain't gonna happen, old man.* "What makes you think that?"

"Feeling I get." Sweat pooled at Lars's lip. "Why do you care so much?"

"Just curious after that Mexican woman visited me in the night."

"Most guys wouldn't be complainin' about finding a pretty señorita in their hammock," Milo said.

"Is that the only reason you want to know?" Lars asked, the loose skin under his chin wobbling.

Dade arched an eyebrow. "Why else would I be asking?"

"You tell me."

"What?" Jasper chortled. "You think Dade is a cop or sumpthin'?"

"Why would a cop be looking for Red?" Dade asked.

Lars and Jasper exchanged a look that Dade couldn't decipher. "Is there something I should know about my predecessor?"

"Nothing," Jasper said. "Just show up, do your job, don't ask too many questions, and all will be well."

Was that a warning? Or was he reading more into the conversation than was truly intended? One thing was clear, if he had any hope of finding Red, he was going to have to confide in someone. The subtle approach wasn't cutting it. He looked from Milo to Jasper and then back to Lars. He wasn't about to trust these guys.

Who could he trust in this town?

Natalie.

If he dared to trust anyone, it was Natalie.

"How long you fellas gonna go at this?" Milo whined. "I'm gettin' bored and Judge Judy is about to come on. Gotta get my fix of Judge Judy. She's hot for an old gal."

"We're finished," Dade said, and while he stared Lars squarely in the eyes, he slammed the other man's hand down onto the table.

Chapter 12

Love makes you feel like nothing else.
—Millie Greenwood

After making up his mind to tell Natalie who he was and why he was in Cupid, Dade went to the B&B, only to find a teenager attending the front desk. The girl told him that Natalie was out for a couple of hours.

Good. That would give him time to run to the hardware store for a new deadbolt lock and start work on making that door safer. After filling in for the bartender who'd had to run a few errands, he didn't have to be back at Chantilly's until six.

Thirty minutes later, he was back and armed with the small tool kit he kept on his motorcycle. He filled Pearl in on what he was going to do.

"Thank heavens," Pearl said. "Natalie's a sweet girl and she thinks everyone is as kindhearted and caring as she is. It never occurs to her that someone might want to break in here. Me?" Pearl picked up a marble rolling pin sitting on the kitchen counter. "I sleep with this. Someone wants to harm this family, they're gonna get a whup knot upside the head."

"She's lucky to have you," he told Pearl.

"I keep telling her that," Pearl said. "Now go do your thing. I've got fresh catfish to skin."

Feeling properly dismissed, Dade went to the back door entryway, mentally rehearsing how he was going to break the news to Natalie that he was Red's foster brother and he'd been deceiving her.

He had cocked his cowboy hat back on his head, crouched down, and was busy wrestling with both his conscience and the new lock that was refusing to come out of the plastic package, when the back door creaked open and whacked into him.

The knob caught him hard in the ribs. Dade grunted just as Natalie let out a bloodcurdling scream.

Instant adrenaline rushed through him. What was wrong? He dropped the lock, doubled up his fists, ready to battle to the death with whoever or whatever was threatening her.

Simultaneously, something metal crashed loudly to the tile floor.

He stepped back, yanked the door all the way open, leaving them face-to-face in the entryway.

Natalie, wearing the cutest little green skirt and crisp white blouse, met his eyes. "You!"

"Me," he confirmed, struggling not to smile.

She seemed pretty pissed off. Anger creased her normally smooth brow and her bottom lip trembled. Yellow goo, white cream, and bananas—and were those vanilla wafers—had splattered just about everywhere.

Banana pudding.

She was covered in banana pudding and looked like she could give Pearl a run for her money in the cranky department. She was *not* happy with him.

Dade searched for something to say to defuse the situation, but Natalie was working up a strong head of steam. He thought about charming her. Compliment her on how sexy she looked with her hair piled on top of her head like that. Tell her how much he wanted to pull the pins out and watch it tumble down her shoulders, but that would be like pitching gasoline on a forest fire.

He had scared her and that made him feel bad, but what she did next stunned him.

Without giving him any time to scramble away, Natalie reached down and scooped up a handful of vanilla wafers, whipped cream, sliced ripe bananas, and sticky yellow filling from what remained in the big metal bowl on the floor. She cocked her arm back and flung the banana pudding right at him.

A big glob hit Dade's chest with a solid *splat*.

"No you didn't!"

She threw another handful and then another, peppering his shirt with it.

He jumped back as if he'd been shot, stared down at his chest dripping with goo. He spread his arms wide. "What the hell?"

"That's for scaring the crap out of me, you bastard!"

"Well, maybe you should have the crap scared out of you," he declared. "I could easily have been an intruder. You need to be more cautious, Natalie."

She glanced down at the lock on the floor beside his

tool kit and sank her hands on her hips. "Who asked you to change the lock on my door, huh?"

"I saw it needed repair so I took matters into my own hands."

Her nostrils flared. "Where do you get off being so damn high-handed, Mr. Dade Vega?"

He pressed his lips together to keep from laughing. In the mood she was in, she was bound to take it the wrong way.

"I don't know how they behave where you're from, but in Cupid, people do not come into other peoples' houses and change their locks without permission!" She flung a hand at him, sending a sprinkle of banana pudding spattering across his face.

He didn't know what track was best. Whether to get mad right back or talk her out of her anger or just pull her into his arms and tell her how sorry he was that he'd scared her, but instead of doing any of those things, a deep throaty laugh rolled from his throat and he found himself issuing a smooth threat.

"Oh-ho, you're in for it now, missy."

Surprised by her own behavior, Natalie stood with her mouth hanging open, banana pudding dripping down her fingers. She was so mad at him for startling her—even as she realized he was only trying to do her a favor by putting a new, stronger lock on her door— that it took her a few seconds to collect her scattered thoughts.

When she'd walked through the back door and seen him crouching there, her mind had lit up INTRUDER and she'd simply reacted. Now the dessert she had planned for tonight's dinner was ruined, plus she had a big mess to clean up.

She'd been so freaked out that she'd completely lost control—something that she seemed to do far too often around him—and she'd just started flinging spilled pudding without thinking it through.

Dade's gaze caught hers, and from the diabolical look in his eyes, she knew she was in trouble. He wasn't going to let her off the hook for this.

In one smooth move, he doffed his cowboy hat, stripped off his shirt, mopped his face with the garment, and then flung it behind him. Then he put his hat back on. Bare chested and with a cowboy hat on? Oh, yeah.

Her knees trembled. What was he doing?

He stalked straight for her.

Natalie gulped, spun around, and raced for the door. Her heart thundered. She was in such a crazy panic, not too different from what she'd felt that very morning when she'd slipped down the roof, that she wasn't watching where she was stepping.

At the best of times, her right leg could not be relied upon, and in the worst of times, it was a downright liability. Her heel caught on the edge of the porch and she wobbled.

Oh no!

Her right leg collapsed underneath her and her hands flew into the air, sending her off balance and tumbling backward over the short wooden railing.

What the hell was this? Natalie's a Klutz Day?

The next thing she knew, she was lying flat on her back on the cushioned patio chaise longue on the porch deck below the steps, staring up at a shirtless Dade standing over her.

"You okay?"

She nodded soundlessly.

"You sure?" He sounded genuinely concerned.

"Uh-huh."

"Good."

"Why do you say that?"

"'Cause karma's a bitch," he said, his tone taking on a seductive note that sent blood pulsing through her veins at the speed of sound. Sun-warmed canvas kissed the backs of her legs and her lungs spasmed, unable to draw in air.

Get up! Quick! You're vulnerable.

Before she could lever herself up off the chaise, Dade was straddling her, one leg on either side of the chaise, right at the level of her waist, the bowl of banana pudding tucked in the crook of his elbow.

"Wh-what are you doing?" she gasped.

"Payback, darlin'."

Defiantly, she raised her chin. "You wouldn't dare."

He dipped his hand into the bowl.

She shook her head, held up her palms like stop signs. "No, no."

He nodded. "Yes, yes."

"A gentleman would not do this."

"See, now there's the problem," he drawled. "I never claimed to be a gentleman."

Natalie's breathing was thready and her heart was pounding and every excited muscle in her body tensed, eager to see what he would do next.

He leaned over to trace a trail of whipped cream over the fluttering pulse at the base of her throat.

She lay frozen, unable to move, to even think.

He dipped his head, planted a hot kiss on her neck, and licked the cream from her skin.

Natalie shivered, pulled the cowboy hat from his head, and sent it flying to the ground.

Dade's hand swept to the hem of her skirt that had ridden up high, his fingertips strumming over her flesh as he edged the material up even higher.

"Those legs drive me crazy," he murmured.

Legs? *Her* legs? Her scarred, mismatched legs.

She felt the summer breeze caress her skin, heard the distant *snap-pop* of firecrackers somewhere across the lake, saw the sheltering arms of the sycamore tree spreading its green canopy overhead, smelled his masculine scent so rich and pure and irresistible.

Little bolts of electricity were hopping up and down her nerve endings, sending all kinds of crazy, heedless messages to her brain—throw caution to the wind, throw away the rulebook, throw away everything because this was new and fresh and intensely glorious.

He lowered his head again and his mouth moved to seize her lips, lay claim to her, while his wicked hand was circling tight swirls along her inner thigh. Her arms went around his neck and she pulled him down on top of her. The chaise creaked under his added weight.

Dade let out a sound of surprised delight and she melted into him, liquid fondue, overcome by a deep-seated sense of rapture. Exalted, she tightened her hold on his neck.

His tongue played with hers, teasing, coaxing. There was little room in Natalie's life for play and she soaked up this ritual, the ceremony of getting to know him even as she knew this was dangerous territory. The closer she allowed him to get, the harder it would be to say good-bye.

But as always with Dade, she couldn't seem to help herself. Whether it was chemistry or that damnable Cupid's doing, she was lost. She was not going to get out of this relationship unscathed, so why not embrace the fall?

Why?

Because her life had already been filled with so much pain. The more she gave to him, the more she had to lose, and loss had defined her life. She could not willingly court more pain.

Not all loss is bad. What about your virginity? Wouldn't that be a spectacular thing to lose to him?

"Dade," she whimpered. "Dade."

"Yes, darlin'?"

"I don't think—"

"Precisely," he said. "Don't think."

"That's not…" she started to say, but trailed off when his fingers slipped up to tug down the waistband of her panties.

His mouth was busy too, kissing back down her throat, headed for her breasts. Her nipples budded hard against the confines of her bra. Sensation after sensation rippled over her in relentlessly pleasurable waves.

For an insane second, she let it all wash over her, absorbing the experience, a sponge. Soaking up every last bit of what he was doing so that she could remember it later in minute detail. Forgetting that she was a B&B owner and any minute one of her guests could wander outside to find them in this compromising position.

Dade unbuttoned the front of her blouse with his teeth, and as each button popped open, a soft sigh escaped her lips. How talented and dexterous his mouth was! She wanted to build a shrine to his tongue and worship at it.

She drifted, ensnared by pleasure. Natalie had never in her life been so reckless and she wanted more.

Free.

With the air on her bare skin and the taste of Dade in her mouth, she felt incredibly, impossibly free. She was giddy with it. Her head spun and a sweet joy tickled the back of her throat. She was bright and shiny, new as a freshly minted penny. What pleasure! Greedily, she wanted more, more, more.

He went for another handful of banana pudding, smeared it over her chest, and lapped it off with a hearty laugh. "Best damn banana pudding I ever ate."

"You're shameless."

"Yep. When it comes to you, darlin', I'm ashamed of nothing." With the skill of a magician, he whisked her panties off her so quickly she barely knew it had happened and he stuck them in the back pocket of his jeans.

Natalie sucked in her breath.

He placed featherlight kisses around her ear, the sound of his raspy breathing pushing her further to the edge. Blood hummed through her veins, setting up a sweet vibration.

Her heart beat against her chest as if it was trying to get out and merge with him. No man had ever been down there before. She was scared and worried and so very excited, and when he spread the pudding over her sensitive skin, she simply sizzled.

His tongue was doing crazy things to her—licking, lapping, tickling.

Oh wow, oh wow. How had she gone so long without ever feeling this?

While he pulled her skirt demurely to her knees with one hand, his other hand audaciously slipped up the inside of her thigh. He eased a finger inside her slick warmth and she let out a startled moan. Oh my, my, my. This was wrong, out here in the open, but it felt so right. What if someone came by?

A new, sharper thrill raced over her.

"Don't…" she whispered weakly, "stop."

"Don't stop," he murmured. "Got it."

"No," she whimpered. She placed her hands on his head, in a vain attempt to hold him back.

"Which is it, darlin'? Don't or don't stop?" He stood up and peered down at her, a dollop of whipped cream on his upper lip. His tongue flicked out to whisk it away, but not before the sight of it escalated the heaviness building low in her abdomen. She burned for him, every part of her, hot and ready and begging for him. He reshuffled her atoms, changed her in some fundamental way.

She peered up into his face. In that moment, he looked so intense, his face half shadowed by the sycamore tree, the other half doused in bright sunshine. The twin faces of Dade. His eyes were unfathomable, the earlier teasing evaporated.

Dark versus light.

Which was he? Her heart told her one thing, her mind another.

Inflamed, she arched her back, lifted her hips up to him. Reckless. This was so reckless and yet she couldn't seem to stop herself. For better or worse, her fate was in his big, strong hands.

"Natalie." His voice was rough, clotted with huskiness. "I'm not going to do anything you don't fully and unequivocally want. I refuse to let you regret this."

She ached to tell him that she wanted him without any doubts, misgivings, or reservations, but her fears had kept her safe for so long. Giving them up was tantamount to diving headlong off a cliff to rocky shoals. She was too scared to do it, to say the words he needed to hear. To take the big step into the abyss she'd avoided for twenty-nine years. Her mouth opened, but she could not speak.

"That's what I thought," he said.

He leaned over and started doing up the buttons on her blouse.

"I'm sorry," she whispered. "I'm sorry."

"Nothing to be sorry for, darlin'." Once she was buttoned up, he picked up his cowboy hat, stuck it on his head, and reached out a hand to help her to her feet.

Instead of getting up, she wrapped her hands around his wrist and pulled him back down on top of her.

"Whoops," he murmured, his big body pressed against her, his dark eyes locked on her lips.

"Do something," she whispered.

He kissed her again.

Natalie gave up the fight, surrendered completely. She could not deny her feelings any longer. Eagerly, she wrapped her arms around him, embraced the myth, solidified her faith, and absorbed his essence deep within her bones. Like it or not, scared or not, foolish or not, she'd fallen helplessly in love with Dade Vega.

The only question was, had he fallen in love with her too?

* * *

Natalie's hands were threaded in Dade's hair when Junie Mae came rushing around the side of the house. "Natalie, I—"

Her neighbor's voice cut through the lust-fueled fog in her brain. Dade reacted at the same time she did. They jumped up, sprang apart.

Junie Mae paused a moment, stared at them—Dade without a shirt on, Natalie guiltily combing her hair into place with her fingers and smoothing down her skirt, both of them covered in banana pudding. If they'd kept going one minute longer, her neighbor would have caught them *in flagrante*.

"Natalie," Junie Mae called out. Her face was pale and a concerned furrow creased her brow. "I'm sorry to interrupt, but I'm deeply worried."

Natalie sank her top teeth into her bottom lip, drew in a deep breath, squared her shoulders, and prepared herself. Junie Mae wasn't an alarmist by nature. If she was worried, there was usually something to worry about. "What's wrong?"

"It's Delia."

Natalie's hand went to her heart. "What's happened?"

"Delia's not answering her phone."

"Maybe she's out in her garden," Natalie soothed.

"She doesn't go outside in the heat of the day and she was supposed to call me at two to let me know if she wanted to go dinner with me and my boyfriend, Marvin, but she didn't call, so I called her and she's not answering."

"I'm sure she's fine. Maybe she was in the bathroom." Natalie put a hand on Junie Mae's forearm.

Junie Mae heaved a little sigh and ran a hand through

her hair. She never did anything to muss her perfectly coiffed hair. There was something more that she wasn't telling.

"What is it?"

"Delia didn't want to bother you and she swore me to secrecy."

"Junie Mae..."

Junie Mae held up both hands in a gesture of surrender. "I know, I know. I shouldn't have promised her I wouldn't tell, but she was scared if you knew that the family would make her move in with someone. That's the reason I've been keeping an extra close eye on her and calling her three or four times a day."

"Junie Mae." Natalie tightened her grip on her neighbor's arm. "What *is* it?"

"Delia's been having vertigo. She fell a couple of times this month, but she wasn't hurt. I didn't tell you this part, but I already drove over to Delia's house to check on her and the door was locked. I rang the bell and waited and waited and, well, here I am now."

"Let's go," Dade said.

"Where to?" Junie Mae asked, owl-eyed.

"To Delia's house."

Natalie whipped her head around. He was standing behind her, big and strong and bare-chested. It would be so easy to let him take charge—to sink into him, to surrender her burdens to him, allow him to carry her load, but she simply could not afford to do that. She had no idea how long he would be in Cupid. She couldn't depend on him because if she ever laid down her burdens, felt freedom on her shoulders, she might never be able to take them back up again, and that was a risk she simply could not take.

"Junie Mae and I will handle this, thank you," she said to Dade, sounding snippier than she intended.

"Don't be prideful, Natty," Junie Mae said. "We might need him to bust down the door."

"Carol Ann should have a key to Delia's house." This wasn't good. Natalie splayed a hand to her chest, trying to still her racing pulse.

"I didn't want to ask her for it. Delia specifically said *not* to get Carol Ann involved if anything should happen."

"Carol Ann has a right to know."

"Only if there really is a need to get her involved."

Dammit. *She* should have a key to Delia's house. Why didn't she have a key? "We'll just have to break your promise to Delia."

"We're wasting time." Dade stalked down the steps toward Natalie's van. "I'll drive."

Natalie was about to argue, but then realized her hands were shaking. *Calm down. Delia is probably just fine.*

Probably, but a forbidding sensation, like long-legged spiders crawling down the nape of her neck, tickled over her. She pulled her car keys from her pocket and tossed them to Dade. He caught them in his palm with lightning reflexes. He slid behind the wheel, let back the driver's seat. Natalie climbed in beside him, riding shotgun.

Junie Mae got into the back of the van. Anxiously, she leaned over the seat, chattering a mile a minute. "I know your Aunt Delia is strong-minded but her body is frail. She thinks she can force her way through anything. That mind-over-matter mantra she chimes doesn't always cut it."

Natalie reached over the seat to pat Junie Mae's arm. "It's going to be okay. We're together, we'll get through this."

Dade made a low noise.

She cast a glance over at him. His eyes met hers and she could read his thoughts. Elderly lady, living all alone, fainting spells, doesn't answer the phone, house locked up tight, what are the odds she's okay?

You don't even know that's what he's thinking. This is your mind drawing conclusions, toying with conjecture. Don't borrow trouble.

That point of view might be fine for Mr. Cynic here, but Natalie couldn't afford to think that way. She crossed her legs, realizing for the first time since hearing about Delia that Dade still had her panties.

"Turn right at the next intersection," Junie Mae directed Dade. "Delia's place is the third house on the left. Blue frame. White trim. It's the one with the pink flamingos in the front yard. You can't miss it."

Dade pulled into Delia's driveway and Natalie was out of the car before it came to a complete stop; Junie Mae was a close second behind her.

Natalie pounded on the door. They waited a second.

"Delia," Junie Mae hollered. "Are you in there?"

"I should have made her get Life Alert," Natalie grumbled. "She said she didn't want to waste the money. I should have insisted."

Dade's hand was on her shoulder. "You did the best you could."

She whirled around, and glared at him. "I did *not* do the best I could. If I'd done the best I could for my great-aunt, this would not be happening."

"Stop beating yourself up. You can't take care of the entire world."

Natalie scowled. "No, but I can take better care of my people."

"You take on too much responsibility."

"It's not your place to tell me what I can and can't take on."

She couldn't really say why she was being so bitchy. She wasn't mad at him. She was mad at herself.

"You're just scared," he said.

True enough.

"Knock down the door!" Junie Mae commanded Dade, pointing at the door.

"That's easier said than done." Dade eyed the door.

"You've got big strong shoulders! Just get a running start." Junie Mae motioned at him like she was a matador waving a red flag at a charging bull.

"I won't be much good to you with a broken shoulder."

"Well don't just stand there!" Junie Mae exclaimed. "Come up with a better plan."

Dade sprang into action. He stripped off his cowboy hat and poked his fist into it. He stepped to the front window, pulled off the screen, and neatly punched a hole through the pane, the hat protecting his fist from getting cut.

The glass fell to the floor inside with a quiet pop. He reached inside, unlatched the window, and slid it open.

"Wow," Junie Mae said, impressed. "You've done this before."

"Misspent youth," Dade replied, and stepped over the windowsill and into Delia's living room. Two seconds later, he opened the door for Natalie and Junie Mae to enter.

They pushed through the house, stuffed with antiques and cardboard boxes of things bought from QVC—a Keurig single-cup coffeemaker, a Montel Williams pressure cooker, nutritional supplements, a crank and tilt patio umbrella. On the walls in the foyer hung movie posters of *Giant* and framed autographed photographs of Rock Hudson, James Dean, and Elizabeth Taylor.

In the den, Delia's cane was propped against an orange leather couch, vintage 1970s, and her reading glasses were folded over a word-find puzzle booklet resting on the coffee table.

They rushed from room to room, calling Delia's name, and finally found Delia unconscious, lying on the floor, a towel wrapped around her waist, the shower curtain half pulled off the rod, one end clutched in her hand. There was a gash on her head, and a small pool of dark blood had spread across the white tile.

"Oh no!" Junie Mae keened and dropped to her knees on the tile beside Delia. "I knew something bad had happened."

An instant headache pounded Natalie's temples. She knotted her hands into fists. She was such a terrible niece. She should have been keeping a better eye out for Delia. Instead, she'd been fooling around with Dade while Delia lay suffering.

"Get something to cover her with," Dade commanded, and stalked to the bedroom.

Natalie obeyed, stepping over Junie Mae, who had Delia's pale, veiny hand clutched in hers and was sobbing softly.

Dade pulled a multitool from his pocket and started taking the bedroom door off its hinge. "Grab the bedspread. You can cover her with that."

Natalie gathered the red satin comforter off the bed. "What are you doing?"

"Go cover her, and while you're at it, strip the top sheet off the bed too."

Fine. He didn't want to explain himself, well fine, then. Natalie blew out her breath. Under any other circumstances this macho crap wouldn't fly, but part of her was so relieved that he'd taken charge that she simply did as he asked and took the comforter into the bathroom and covered Delia up with it.

"Is she alive?" Junie Mae fretted.

Natalie put a finger to Delia's neck, felt for and found a weak pulse. "She's alive."

"Oh, thank God." Junie Mae rocked back on her heels and began to pray.

Dade appeared with Delia's bedroom door in his hands. "Junie Mae."

"Yes sir." Junie Mae jumped to her feet.

"Go put the van's backseat down flat."

"I'm on it." Junie Mae disappeared.

Holding the door sideways, Dade squatted beside Delia's still body now covered with the comforter.

"What can I do?" Natalie asked.

"Help me logroll her onto the door."

"Logroll?"

"We move her body as one unit, in a straight line. In case she has spinal injuries or broken bones."

"Oh my." It fully hit her then. Delia could die. Her stomach fluttered. Natalie squatted beside Dade and he showed her how to keep Delia's body straight.

"I did it." Breathless, Junie Mae appeared in the doorway. "Seat's down."

"Good job," Dade told her. To Natalie, he said, "On the count of three."

Natalie braced her right leg against the bathtub so she couldn't slip. "Ready."

"One...two...three."

In unison, as if they'd been working together all their lives, they rolled Delia onto the makeshift backboard. Delia's body was so limp, and almost lifeless. Tears pushed into Natalie's eyes, but she quickly brushed them away. *Stay strong. Can't afford to cry. Not now.*

With his multitool, Dade cut the sheet that Natalie had brought from the bed into strips. It made a terse ripping sound as the material gave way beneath his big hand. He used the long strips as stays to tie Delia securely to the makeshift backboard.

Then he squatted and power-lifted Delia, board and all, up off the floor. Holding her in his arms, he told Natalie, "Go start the car."

"Shouldn't we call an ambulance?"

"We can get her to the hospital faster than an ambulance can get out here. Move."

Natalie obeyed, going ahead of him to the front door, Junie Mae bringing up the rear.

Junie Mae had left the door of the van open and Dade was able to slide Delia inside on the door. Natalie was amazed at his power, strength, and deep inner calm.

"Who the hell are you?" Junie Mae asked, wide-eyed, echoing what Natalie was thinking. "A superhero?"

Dade didn't answer that, instead he said, "Junie Mae,

ride shotgun with Natalie. I'll ride back here with Delia. Let's roll."

He folded up his big body and crawled up into the back of the van. Leaving Junie Mae to close the door after him.

Natalie was halfway around the van, her mind spinning, when she heard Junie Mae give a little gasp.

"Dade," Junie Mae said, "do you realize you have a pair of women's white lace panties hanging out of your back pocket?"

Chapter 13

If you want to change your entire view of the world, all you have to do is fall in love.
—Millie Greenwood

In the emergency waiting room, Dade felt like a fifth wheel. He waited in the corner with his back to the wall, watching Delia's family and friends arrive. Natalie insisted on introducing him to all of them. Once people had heard the news, through what was apparently Cupid's phone tree, half the town showed up. The emergency room was packed and there wasn't a spare chair in the place. Some of the younger relatives like Zoey were sitting on the floor.

He checked his watch, shifted his weight, and distracted himself by thinking about Natalie's panties tucked in his back pocket.

Natalie sat in a chair, Junie Mae on one side of her, an older African-American woman on the other, both holding her hands. Natalie's legs were primly pressed together, but the thought that she wasn't wearing any underwear under that green skirt was ripping him up inside. It wasn't the time or the place for lusty thoughts, but by God, how did a man turn them off with a woman like Natalie?

Once, she glanced up and met his gaze, and a hint of a naughty smile touched her lips. She blushed prettily and quickly glanced away.

He briefly closed his eyes and in that second, he was back on her patio deck, straddling her in the chaise longue. *Lips. Skin. Heat. Banana pudding.*

She made him think of other things too—which was the truly disturbing part—things like wooden porch swings, cold glasses of sweet lemonade on a hot day, a platter full of buttermilk-battered fried chicken, the evening song of crickets, whippoorwills, and bullfrogs. He didn't know where the impressions came from because they certainly weren't from his memories, but these images of a life with her burrowed into him and wouldn't turn loose.

Fighting for self-control, he opened his eyes. Natalie was so calm amid her family. Some of whom could be quite overly dramatic, like the one called Carol Ann. Natalie seemed to be the family's center, their true north. He admired that about her, while at the same time he flinched from it.

She was everything he'd ever wanted but knew he could never have. He felt a longing inside him, an urge to belong, but he didn't fit in with other people, especially a close-knit community like this one. He realized that. The navy was the closest he'd ever come to a home and even they had eventually turned him out.

Betrayed. All throughout his life he'd been betrayed by everyone he'd ever loved or trusted.

Oh, friggin' boo-hoo for you. Get over it, Vega. You don't fit here, not anywhere, and you never will. Red was the only one who'd never betrayed him. Dade stuck his hand in his front pocket, fingered the frayed yarn of the bullet-casing bracelet. *Where in the hell are you, buddy?*

His instincts told him to leave. He needed to be back at work at 6 p.m.; after all, he had an excuse. He was getting too close to these people, and it would only end in a big lot of hurt on his side, but he couldn't abandon Natalie. Not when she had everyone leaning on her. She needed someone to lean on and he intended on being that someone.

So he stayed.

And waited.

No matter how uncomfortable it felt.

He did take a minute to call Chantilly's and ask the bartender he'd covered for that day to now cover for him, and the man readily agreed because of the emergency situation.

Natalie got up and went around the room, resting her hands on shoulders, murmuring words of comfort, bringing people coffee, passing out Kleenex.

Dade eyed the door and counted off the number of paces it would take him to reach the exit. Twelve if he took long-legged strides; twelve steps to freedom. With the hubbub, probably no one would notice if he left. He readied himself, coiled his thigh muscles, and he was just about to take flight when Natalie came over and wrapped an arm around his waist.

Wrapped her arm around him like it was the most natural thing in the world. A strange lump formed in his throat and he fought to swallow.

Her hand strummed over the seat of his jeans. Oh yeah. She plucked the panties from his back pocket. Not for him. She had come to get her panties back.

Yeah, bullet head, she didn't come over here for emotional support from the likes of you, she just wanted her underwear. Get over yourself.

"Thank you," she whispered, and surreptitiously fisted the panties in her hand and then slipped her fist into the pocket of her skirt. "Thank you so much for being there for me, for Delia."

He shrugged. "Anyone would have done the same thing."

"Don't underestimate what you did."

"I'm no hero."

"You are in my book."

If she only knew! She would not think so highly of him if she knew the things he was capable of, but his desire to be with her was stronger than his self-doubt. It scared him. This neediness. Scared him because it was more than physical. If it were just physical, he could handle that, but when he looked at Natalie, he wanted more, something he'd never wanted before. He wanted what most people in this small town seemed to have— love, belonging, a deep sense of community.

It doesn't work. Not for you. You're marked by your past. A leopard can't change its spots.

Why not? Why couldn't he have happiness?

He looked into her eyes and knew the answer. Because Natalie deserved so much more than what he could offer. She deserved a man with a clear conscience. A man who didn't wake up in the night battling nightmares, a man who could promise to stand by her through thick and thin.

You could promise her that, if you tried.

God, how he wanted to believe that.

She leaned against him and damn him, he just wrapped his arms around her and held her close. Right there in the emergency room. Right in front of her family and friends, and that's when he knew that he was not going to get out of Cupid with his heart intact.

"Listen, Natalie," he said. "We need to talk."

"Okay," she said. "Would you like to go outside?"

He glanced around the room, noticed several members of her family were staring at him. He lowered his voice. "Not here. Not now. Your family needs you. But soon. Very soon."

"Okay." She smiled tentatively and then she stretched up to kiss him on the cheek. "We'll talk when I get home."

Good. He had an appointment to tell her who he really was. So why did he suddenly feel as naked as the day he was born?

It was the next afternoon before Delia awakened in ICU after going through surgery. She'd broken her hip during the fall in her shower. At her age, the hip fracture was worrisome since the elderly sometimes died from complications of a broken hip. She'd also suffered a concussion and mild dehydration.

Guilt gnawed at Natalie. She should have kept a closer eye on her aunt. Delia was the last surviving family member of her generation, and when she passed away, something irredeemable would be lost.

Natalie, Sandra, and Carol Ann had spent the night in the ICU waiting room while everyone else went home. Zoey was going to look after the B&B guests, and Junie Mae promised Natalie she'd pop over to make sure everything was running smoothly. Lars too volunteered to chip in and do what he could to help. The bases were covered on the home front.

For the first visiting hours of the morning, the nurse came into the waiting room. "Miss Delia is asking for Natalie."

Carol Ann got up along with Natalie.

"I'm sorry." The nurse put up a restraining hand. "She asked for *just* Natalie."

Carol Ann looked slightly affronted, but sat back down beside Sandra.

Sandra patted Carol Ann's arm. "It's okay. We can see her next visiting hours. Why don't we go get some eggs in the cafeteria?"

Natalie followed the nurse into the ICU area, and she found herself wishing that Dade were here.

What for? It's not like he was her boyfriend or anything. He was just a sexy boarder that she'd kissed a couple of times.

Oh, you liar. Are you trying to backtrack now? Chicken.

She still remembered how fabulously wicked she'd felt slipping her arm around his hard-muscled waist in the waiting room right in front of everyone and retrieving her panties from his back pocket. How crazy to be turned on over something so simple.

Provocative.

He was provocative and he aroused unfamiliar emotions in her. Emotions she was eager to explore.

Okay, so maybe she did have more expectations from him than she should. Being with him felt good. So good it scared her.

The nurse showed her to her great-aunt's private room. Delia lay propped up in bed, her head resting on a plump pillow. Tubes were everywhere—IVs, monitors, catheters. Natalie's heart stumbled as it hit home how close they'd come to losing her, could still lose her. Her aunt wasn't out of the woods yet.

Delia's skin was ghostly pale, but her eyes were sharp and bright. "Natty," she whispered, and motioned her closer.

Natalie moved to the bedside and took her great-aunt's hand. It felt too cold. She rubbed it between her palms. "You gave us quite a scare."

"Scared myself." Delia laughed weakly.

"I can't imagine what you went through, lying there on the floor all alone."

"But I wasn't alone," Delia said. "Frank was with me."

Natalie cocked her head. Uncle Frank had been dead for ten years. She had heard that sometimes when people were close to death they saw deceased loved ones. She squeezed Delia's hand.

"I could hear him so clearly, talking to me as if he were standing right beside me," Delia went on. "But the main problem with a ghost is that they can't help you up off the damn floor."

Natalie laughed. Even sick and in pain, Delia was still feisty.

"When you love someone, they never die," Delia

said. "They're always with you in your heart no matter what. Just as your parents live on in you, Natalie."

"Shh, don't talk. You need your strength. Rest. Just rest."

"It's just like the way you feel about Dade," Delia went on.

"What are you talking about, Auntie?" Natalie put a hand to her face.

"You love him. He loves you. Cupid has drawn back his bow, flung his arrow. There's no escape."

"Do you really believe in love at first sight?"

"I do," Delia said vehemently. "I know it's out of fashion to believe in such things, but I know it to be true."

"I'm scared of what I'm feeling. It's so strong, but how can you ever be sure?"

"Just listen to your heart." Delia tapped Natalie's chest. "Your heart knows the truth."

"I barely know him."

"That's not true. Your souls speak to each other. You know him, deep down inside. You've always known him on a cellular level."

She'd never heard her aunt talk like this. "Are you telling me that you believe in reincarnation?"

Delia shrugged. "Maybe. Maybe not. But I do believe in soul mates. Someone meant just for you. Dade is your soul mate."

"But how can you know that for certain?" Natalie asked, sounding shriller than she intended.

"Well, for one thing I almost died, so indulge me. It's okay. It's all going to be okay. Just stop being so damn scared."

"What if you're wrong?"

"What if I'm not and you let him get away? You'll regret it for the rest of your life."

"What am I supposed to do?"

"Girl, do I have to spell it out for you? Give yourself to that man. Seal the bond."

"Are you telling me to have sex with him?"

Delia nodded slowly. "A man isn't fully bonded to a woman until he makes love to her, but once he's made her his, if he's the right one, he'll move heaven and earth to be with you."

"That's a pretty generic statement and a bit sexist."

"Hey, I'm an old broad and I broke my hip. That means I get to say what I think."

Natalie kissed the back of Delia's hand. "What if I make love to him and it turns out he's not my soul mate?"

"Well, he is, but just on the off chance that I'm wrong, then at least you will have lived a little, and had a big adventure. If nothing else, you deserve that. But for heaven's sake, use protection, sweetie. Even with a soul mate you don't want to make little ones until you're ready for them."

"You're being a busybody, you know that?"

"That man of yours saved my life, Natty. You should hear the nurses raving about him and if you just give him half a chance, I know he'll save yours."

Meet me @ the B&B dining room.

Dade looked down at the text message from Natalie and smiled. He pocketed the phone and turned his motorcycle for Cupid's Rest. Chantilly's was closed on Sundays and he'd been out driving the roads around town since dawn, pretending to be Red, trying to imagine where his friend might have gone and why. It had been a full week since Dade had first arrived in town and he was no closer to finding Red than he'd been the first day.

He parked the Harley and rushed up the steps, excited to see her again. How had she gotten under his skin in such a short amount of time? It seemed impossible, but he couldn't get to her fast enough.

There was no one in the lobby. Odd. There was usually someone at the front desk during the day. The place was eerily quiet. Maybe Natalie had gotten rid of everyone and she was waiting for him in the dining room wearing something sexy.

His mouth watered as he opened the dining room door.

"Surprise!"

Dade stared at the people in the room, stunned by the party streamers, noisemakers, confetti, and huge red velvet cake positioned in the center of the buffet table. The room was packed with people he did not know. He recognized Pearl and Zoey and Junie Mae. A lot of the folks he'd met at the hospital, but he couldn't remember all their names. Lars was there and so were Gizmo and Jasper.

His chest seized up. It felt like an ambush.

A banner strung across the back of the room read "Dade, You're Our Hero."

Inwardly, he groaned. What the hell was this?

"Look at him," someone said, "he's so surprised he can't speak."

True enough. No one had ever in his life given him a surprise party. In spite of the banner, he still wasn't sure what the surprise party was all about.

"What's this for?" he asked. God, he was out of step

with these people, this life. Too surreal. It was too surreal. As if he had walked into one of those sappy Hallmark commercials.

"We wanted to thank you," Junie Mae said. "For saving Delia's life."

"No thanks needed," he said gruffly, and eyed the door he'd just come through. It was only three feet away. Three steps and he'd be out the door.

But before he could make a break for it, Zoey linked her arm around his elbow from one side while Junie Mae grabbed him on the other and they dragged him toward the buffet table that held Jordan almonds in fancy crystal cups, chocolate chip cookies and punch, cut-up veggies, chips, dips, and little sausages wrapped in crescent rolls. Piggies in a blanket, Red called them.

"We've got homemade ice cream too," Pearl called from across the room.

Someone, he thought it might be Jasper, started singing "For He's a Jolly Good Fellow."

Friggin' hell. He wasn't jolly, nor was he particularly good. He'd just picked an old lady up off her floor and taken her to the hospital. That's all. No big deal.

But apparently, the entire town of Cupid thought it was a big deal.

People were slapping him on the back and shoving a plate in his hand and pushing food at him, and all he wanted to do was run.

Then he spotted her.

Natalie.

Standing quietly in the corner, snapping pictures and watching him with loving eyes. She looked so pretty in a red shirt with pink flowers on it and faded blue jeans. Her hair was pulled back into a swingy ponytail and she wore lipstick the color of fresh watermelon. He licked his lips.

Ah, damn. She was the one thing that could stop him dead in his tracks.

Slowly, she moved toward him in her halting gait that stabbed him in the gut, and the world seemed to stop spinning. Everyone around them disappeared and it was just the two of them.

Her smile lit him up inside, smooth and hot as Kentucky whiskey. "Surprised about the party?"

"You gotta watch out for stuff like this. It could give a guy a heart attack." He rested a palm over his chest.

"You're upset?"

He flicked a gaze over her sexy body. "Not upset. Disappointed."

"Disappointed?" A tiny frown marred her brow.

"I thought you were inviting me over for *you*."

"Oh!" Her eyes rounded and her laugh wobbled. "I didn't mean to mislead you."

"It's okay." He waved a hand like he was batting away a sticky cobweb. "Just had my hopes up since we didn't get to finish what we started before Junie Mae interrupted us."

"My family and friends wanted to do something special for you." She inclined her head toward the crowd lined up at the buffet table. "Cupidites are rather fond of surprise parties."

"I don't like surprises."

She ducked her head, gave him a sidelong glance. "So I gathered from the expression on your face."

He jammed his hands in his pockets, hunched his shoulders. His fingers closed over the bullet casing bracelet. It was his touchstone. Grounded him. Reminded him that Red was the only one he could truly trust.

"You've never had a surprise birthday party?" she asked.

"I can count on one hand the number of birthdays I've celebrated."

"Your parents didn't believe in celebration? Was it a religious thing?"

"My parents believed in only one thing."

She cocked her head. "What's that?"

He shouldn't tell her the truth. It would bust her safe little bubble. "The crack pipe."

She gave a whispered gasp. "Your parents were drug addicts?"

He shrugged.

She looked startled, as if realizing just how little she knew about him. "Oh, Dade."

"It is what it is."

She reached out a hand to touch him. "I can't imagine what that must have been like."

He stepped back before her fingers could graze his hand. Undo him. "Save the pity, darlin'. I don't need it. Got over that shit a long time ago."

She stood there looking at him with so much compassion and understanding that it made his stomach hurt. She felt sorry for him.

"I don't need your pity," he muttered.

"You're right." She held up both hands, and then glanced down at her right leg. "I know how irritating pity can be. So come, let's enjoy the party."

Someone had put music on to play and Adele was singing "Crazy for You."

"I'm not a celebration kind of guy."

"Then you've come to the wrong place."

You can say that again.

He belonged in this place like a badger in a new-born nursery. He was out of place, out of time, out of step with her community. He wasn't used to people caring about him. The closest thing he'd ever come to a real family had been the SEALs, and even they had cut him loose after he'd been injured. He had to admit that after he was discharged, he felt a little betrayed and a lot adrift. It reinforced the message he'd learned as a toddler.

You can't depend on anyone but yourself.

Daring to care left you vulnerable. So he'd concluded that it was better all around not to care or depend on anyone. Red was the only exception to the rule.

"I still need to talk to you," he said. "In private."

Natalie put a hand on his arm. "You're the man of the hour."

"Which means?"

"You have to mingle."

Dade groaned. "I gotta schmooze?"

"You do. You're a hero. And you have to have some of Pearl's red velvet cake. She'll be offended if you don't."

"Okay." He fixed his gaze on her lips. God, he felt like a fool, but damn him, he'd turn cartwheels in a pink tutu if it would please her. "I'll schmooze."

"Twenty minutes. Give it twenty minutes and then slip away and meet me at the duck pond."

"Twenty minutes," he repeated.

So Dade mingled to please Natalie. He ate cake he didn't want to eat, drank punch he didn't want to drink, and made small talk with strangers he didn't want to talk to—people who thanked him repeatedly for saving Delia's life.

He felt a stab of jealousy that Delia had so many people who cared about her. How did Delia manage it? No doubt it was something you were born into. Family. Home. Love. It was a circle of support that a guy like him could not hope to break into.

He took a bite of cake while Carol Ann was bending his ear. Natalie caught his eye and winked. *Thank you*, she mouthed silently.

He felt her smile all the way to the center of his spine and he smiled helplessly in return.

"What was Natalie like as a kid?" he asked Carol Ann, deciding to make good use of being held hostage.

"She was such a serious little thing, but that was understandable of course, considering what happened to her parents. She came at life like it was a problem to solve. She still does. The child doesn't know how to relax." Carol Ann motioned toward Natalie. "Look at her right now, helping Pearl bus the dishes."

"What happened to her parents?" he asked.

"No one has told you?"

He shook his head and Carol Ann launched into the gut-wrenching story of how Natalie's parents had died.

"And the rescue workers found her dragging Zoey down the mountain in her lap," Carol Ann finished, her eyes tearing up. "Her parents' plane crash was one of the biggest tragedies in Cupid's history."

Dade's breathing was fast and shallow. He clenched the plastic fork so tightly in his fist that it broke with a crisp snap. Poor girl. Poor kid. Shit, and here he thought he'd had it bad. He wasn't the only one who'd suffered.

Selfish. He'd been selfish to assume his hurt was bigger than anyone else's.

And the way she'd overcome it. He was damn proud of her. She was some kind of lady.

Yeah, she's way too good for your shaggy ass.

Carol Ann kept talking about Natalie, and he was so hung up on hearing stories of her childhood that it was only when the conversation shifted to Zoey that Dade realized he was late for his rendezvous with Natalie.

"Could you excuse me?" he asked Carol Ann.

"Oh, surely. Please do know how utterly grateful we are to you for what you did for Delia." She touched his hand, smiled at him as if she truly meant every word.

"You're welcome," he said because he didn't know what else to say. He had to get out of here. Had to meet Natalie.

He slipped through the crowd and out the back door. The smell of honeysuckle was ripe in the late afternoon air and full of promise. He tried not to look too eager, but he couldn't stop himself from rushing across the yard and unlatching the back fence.

There was Natalie beside the pond, tossing bits of bread to the ducks.

His entire body lit up.

She didn't glance up as he approached.

"Hey," he said, all the breath leaving his body at once.

"Hey yourself."

"Thank you for the party. I should have said that earlier. It was…*nice*." He was surprised to find he meant it.

"You don't have to lie."

"I'm not lying. I'm just…" He paused, scratched the back of his head. "This is all new to me."

"It's new to me too," she whispered.

"What? Throwing surprise parties?"

"No." She stared him straight in the eyes. "Feeling this way."

His throat went desert dry. "Your aunt Carol Ann told me about your parents. I'm sorry, Natalie."

"Why? You didn't cause the plane crash."

"I'm sorry you had to go through that."

She shrugged. "It made me who I am."

"Our past does shape us."

"So," she said, tossing the last bit of bread to the ducks and dusting her fingers together. "What did you need to talk to me about?"

"This." He toggled his finger back and forth between them.

"Us?"

Us. We. Words he was unaccustomed to using. "I haven't been completely honest with you."

"Oh?" Her voice squeaked, but she tried to look composed.

"I haven't told you the full truth about me."

Alarm creased her brow. "Which is?"

Dade hesitated. Was this the right thing to do?

"I'm listening."

He swallowed. *Just say it.* "I'm Red's foster brother."

She blinked, absorbing what he'd said. "You know Red Daggett?"

"Besides being foster brothers, we were also in the Navy SEALs together."

She said nothing for a long time.

He shifted his weight, interlaced his fingers. *C'mon, say something.*

"So you came to Cupid looking for him?"

"Yes." Slowly, he explained about the Mayday text.

She reached out to run a hand over his upper arm. "This isn't pity," she said. "But empathy. There's a difference. I don't feel sorry for you. I understand about loyalty."

"You're not mad at me for lying to you about who I am?"

"Not at all. I understand. Family comes first and Red is your family."

He nodded. "I'm putting all my trust in you here. Red's message was unmistakable, I was to trust no one."

"Why are you telling me this now?"

"Because I can't do this without help. I've been here a week and I'm not any closer to finding Red than I was the day I rode into town, and I'm scared as hell I'm running out of time. If he's hurt somewhere—"

"He might already be dead," she finished.

"Yes."

"How come you've decided to trust me and not Lars or Jasper or someone else?"

"Because," he said honestly, "I know you didn't harm Red. You're too kind. Too honest." His voice caught. *Too good to be true.*

"Well then, we better get searching for Red."

"We can't tell anyone what we're doing. We don't know who else we can trust." *We.* That word that usually came so hard to him.

"I can't believe anyone in Cupid means Red harm."

"I'm not saying they do. I have to be cautious just in case. Do you have any ideas where we might start?"

"I packed up Red's things in a cardboard box just before you drove up last Monday. Nothing in there meant anything to me, but maybe you can get a clue from it. C'mon."

She led him to the carriage house and they climbed the stairs into the cramped, airless attic. She quickly located the cardboard box.

With sweat sticking his shirt to his body, Dade rifled through the cardboard box. What concerned him were the empty bottles of paroxetine and doxepin. On the surface, it looked like Red was taking his meds, but one glance at the refill date and Dade's blood ran cold.

The pills hadn't been refilled in two months, plenty of time for the therapeutic effects to wear off and for Red to be plunged into deep depression or a manic high. He swore under his breath.

"What is it?" she asked.

He told her.

Nervously, Natalie nibbled her bottom lip.

He turned back to the box and found the bus ticket stub. The destination was Marfa, Texas, and it was dated June 19, the day before Red had sent him the text. Ten days. It had been ten days since Red sent that text. He passed the ticket stub to Natalie.

"Red was fascinated with the Marfa Lights," she said. "He visited them often."

"Lars said Red was interested in the Indian custom of vision quests."

Natalie nodded. "I heard him mention it a time or two. Do you think he's gone on a vision quest in Marfa?"

"I don't know, but I'm headed there."

Natalie put her hand on his arm. "Not without me, you're not. Red was my friend too."

Chapter 14

If you're going to dive into love, headfirst is the only way to go.

—*Millie Greenwood*

Natalie put Zoey in charge of the B&B and hurried to meet up with Dade again. She was still trying to absorb all that he'd told her. He was Red's foster brother and they'd been in the Navy SEALs together. Dade was the buddy that Red had spoken so fondly of.

In fact, Dade was the only thing about Red's past that he'd ever talked about. Red had just never mentioned his buddy's name. She felt honored that Dade had decided to trust her with his secret, while at the same time, her worry for Red escalated. Could someone in Cupid have actually harmed Red? She didn't want to believe it. Couldn't begin to imagine who would want to hurt him or why. She still favored the theory that Red was in the grips of some sort of PTSD fugue state.

Outside, Dade was waiting for her astride the Harley, engine running. Heat radiated off the chrome pipes.

She hesitated. "We're going on your bike?"

"Yep."

"We could take the van."

"What if Zoey needs transportation?"

"Good point, but I have a confession."

He wriggled his eyebrows. "Sounds intriguing."

"I've never ridden on a motorcycle before."

"First time for everything." He grinned. "C'mon."

"Can't. I don't have a helmet."

He settled his helmet on her head. "Now you do."

The weight of the helmet was comforting and his scent surrounded her. When he reached up to tighten the chinstrap for her, Natalie just about came undone at the touch of his fingers on her skin.

"Wh-what are you going to wear?" she asked.

"I'll take my chances."

"I don't like the fact that you're unprotected."

"You have to take some risks in life."

"Risks can get you killed."

"If you never take risks, you're not living."

That was she. She never took risks, and her life was small and tight because of it. She hauled in a deep breath. "Okay. If I get killed at least I will have done something tonight that I've never done before."

"You won't get killed," he said fiercely. "If the Grim Reaper comes for you I'll kick his ass."

If anyone could cheat death, Dade would be the one. Her heart fluttered.

"C'mon, darlin'," he coaxed.

Oh, why not throw caution to the wind? She eyed the Harley. "Um, how do I do this?"

"Ever rode a horse?"

She patted her right leg. "No."

He shook his head. "Poor thing, you've led such a sheltered life."

"So unshelter me."

He chuckled. "Just sling your leg over the seat."

"In case you haven't noticed, my leg doesn't sling so easily."

"I've seen you mount your bike. You do it quite gracefully. It's the same concept."

"This seat is much wider than my bicycle."

"It's still just a seat."

"Yes, but this machine is growling like it's going to eat me."

"If anything is going to eat you, it's not going to be my Hog." He smirked. There was nothing subtle about that innuendo.

Natalie willed herself not to blush. Tentatively, she slung her leg over the rumbling seat. Instantly, the vibrations went up her legs to settle into her groin. It felt highly charged and erotic.

"Now what?" she whispered.

"Wrap your arms around me, darlin', and hang on tight."

It sounded easy enough, but the second her arms slid around his waist, her body was in tumult.

"You ready?" he called over his shoulder.

Was she? She'd paid lip service to wanting adventure, but now that adventure was staring her in the face, fear crept in. "Yes," she declared to keep herself from backing out.

He took off and the force of the launch had her squealing and tightening her grip. She hung on for dear life. This was most definitely *not* her bike. For one thing, on her bike, she did not have the most sumptuous man in the world to hang on to. His leanly muscled back had her nipples hardening. She felt every breath he took, and found herself falling into his smooth, commanding rhythm.

The wind whipped the sleeves of her shirt as they peeled off from the road leading to the marina and headed down U.S. Highway 90 to Marfa, thirty miles away. The moon was starting to rise. The light glimmered off the pavement, guiding their way.

Natalie rested her head against his shoulders, marveling to find herself here with this man. A week ago she hadn't even known him, and now he seemed like destiny. The resistance she'd felt last Monday had, by Sunday, given way to acceptance.

If this was fated, she was all in.

His masculine scent tangled up in her nose and she imagined a million sexy things she wanted him to do to her. She thought about what Delia had told her and she closed her eyes.

Yes. She was ready for sex with him. She was ready for everything!

She let go long enough to slip her hands up underneath his shirt, run her fingers over his ribs to link her hands over his rippled abs. He gave a startled grunt that quickly changed into a growl of pleasure.

Dade kept a steady pace and stayed to the slow lane, which, in this part of Texas where the speed limit was seventy-five, wasn't all that slow. Tires strummed over the asphalt; the landscape of cactus, juniper, and mesquite trees whizzed by in a blur. Behind them, the Davis Mountains lay like slumbering elephants, gray and lazy.

In the expanse of arid land to their right, a herd of leaping pronghorn antelope ran parallel to the highway as if challenging them to a race.

Smiling, Natalie heard the refrains of "Home, Home on the Range" reverberate in her head. This was her land, her country, and her man.

She was flying, having a real adventure. A Harley vibrated beneath her legs. Her arms were strapped around a handsome, hard-bodied man. She felt so alive, so vital.

Shot Through the Heart's Letter flitted through her mind and in that beautiful instant she fully understood what the letter writer meant. Nothing was more exhilarating, nothing more exalted than falling in love. In that moment, everything was crystal clear. This was the man she was supposed to be with, and any lingering doubts she might have had vanished completely.

She was meant for Dade and he was meant for her.

Ten miles out of Cupid a pale yellow-green glow appeared on the horizon that brightened the closer they got.

Dade turned his head toward her. "Are those the Marfa Lights?"

"No," Natalie yelled over the sound of the motorcycle.

"What is it?"

"You'll see."

Dade slowed as they neared a lone square building that was the source of the yellow-green glow in the middle of nowhere, masquerading as a Prada mini boutique. He came to a full stop in the middle of the straight-as-an-arrow highway across from the front of the building and stared at it, slack-jawed. The place had that effect on people. "What the hell is this?"

"Prada Marfa."

"Huh?"

Natalie unstrapped the motorcycle helmet, pulled it off, and shook out her hair. She got off the bike, left the helmet dangling from one of the handlebars, and walked toward the building framed by an old barb-wire fence made with aging, rough-hewn cedar posts. A large tumbleweed sat off to one side of the biode-gradable building made of mud bricks. Across the road, endless train tracks stretched out, leading both every-where and nowhere.

Cool, crisp white awnings shaded two large plate-glass windows flanking either side of an inset nonfunc-tioning door. Above the awnings were twin black signs with the Prada logo in large, white block letters and un-derneath in small type "Marfa." Inside the building were twenty Prada left shoes, evenly, uniformly, and sparsely placed on the shelves, and there were six Prada handbags as well, three on one side of the store, three on the other. The interior was eerily backlit with a greenish-yellow light that instantly made people think UFO.

"But what *is* it?" Dade repeated.

"Art."

"Art? A Prada store?"

"It's not a real store. The front door doesn't work."

"I get that. What I don't get is what's it doing all the way hell and gone out here in the desert?"

"That's the art of it," Natalie said.

"What is Prada anyway?"

"Very high fashion."

"Out of my realm of experience."

"Mine too," she said, but from the minute the art had been erected in 2005, Natalie had gotten it. The piece spoke to her in a way she couldn't explain. In the same way she couldn't explain why she bought designer shoes for herself every Christmas, shoes that she could never wear. "I've always wanted a pair of Prada shoes," she whispered.

"But what does the art mean?"

"Art is in the eye of the beholder, of course. Interpret it any way you want. Juxtaposed against the barren Texas landscape, it's ludicrous and yet infinitely compelling."

"It feels…" He paused. "Lonely."

"Yes."

They stood like that, staring at the art, Natalie in front, gazing at the shoes, Dade standing directly behind her.

"What keeps people from breaking into it and stealing the shoes?" he asked.

"They have," she said. "Three days after the exhibit opened, vandals broke out the windows and graffitied 'Dumb' and 'Dum Dum' on the walls, stole the shoes and handbags. Now the handbags have hollowed-out bottoms to house alarms."

"It is definitely attention getting. I'll give you that."

"And thought provoking."

"Prada is a fish out of water in the desert."

"Uh-huh."

"I'm getting it." He slipped his palms into the back pockets of her jeans, his calloused palms cupping her butt through the denim, and he leaned over to rest his chin on her shoulder.

"What does it say to you?" she murmured.

"There's no telling what kind of beauty you'll find out here."

His breath tickled her ear and a thrill ran the length of her body. He wasn't talking about the art and she knew it. He was talking about her.

Natalie could see their reflection in the glass of the Prada store. Dade's face nestled against the side of her head. Such a ruggedly handsome face with compelling eyes the color of charcoal and those high, mysterious cheekbones. He spied her using the glass to study him, and a slow, one-sided grin lifted the corner of his mouth. Her heart stumbled, crashed.

"I'm beginning to see why Red was so enchanted with this part of the country."

She turned into him.

Simultaneously, they put their arms around each other and he kissed her right there in front of Prada Marfa.

It was a sweet kiss, warm and tender. Natalie sighed at the taste of him. His five o'clock shadow scratched her chin pleasantly.

He pulled back, looked down into her eyes. A variety of emotions—many of them conflicting—flickered across his face. Obviously, he had no idea what to make of her or of the things he was feeling.

She smiled at him, nice and gentle. He was used to fighting his way through life. She wanted him to know that when it came to her, he could lay down his arms and stop warring.

"Maybe Red disappeared inside the Prada Marfa," Dade teased lightly. "It would explain a lot."

"It does kind of look like an alien mother ship."

"Perhaps he just walked right into the store as if it were a painting."

"It could be the portal to a whole new dimension."

In unison, they turned to look at the store and then at each other.

"I'm worried about him," Dade said. "Seriously worried."

"Me too."

"There's a whole lot of isolated territory around here."

"It's not likely that he went on a vision quest, no matter what he told Lars. Not when he sent you that coded text message."

"No," Dade agreed. "Not the least bit likely."

"The simplest explanation is that he went off his medication and started having delusions. That's what Calvin thinks." Natalie brushed a strand of hair from her eyes.

"Calvin?"

"He's my cousin and a deputy sheriff. You met him at the hospital, and he was at Chantilly's for the Life Saver relay."

"Oh yeah, I remember meeting him now, but I don't know if I agree with Calvin's theory."

"What if he..." Natalie swallowed, not knowing how to bring up her greatest fear about Red to Dade.

"Killed himself?" Dade read her mind.

"I hate to believe it."

"I refuse to believe it. He survived a helluva lot. There was no reason for him to take his own life. None at all."

"We can never fully know the demons other people face and what they'll do to be relieved of them."

"Hell, Natalie, the last time I talked to Red he was the happiest I'd ever heard him. He sounded so happy with his life in Cupid that I was actually jealous."

"Okay, let's rule out that he's having delusions and hiding out in the desert from demons in his own mind or that he committed suicide. What happened to him?"

"The Mayday text he sent tells me he thought he was in serious danger."

"Tanked," she said. "That was the word?"

"Yes."

"You care about him a great deal, don't you?"

"He's the brother I never had."

She reached up to touch his cheek and his eyes darkened. "There's something deeper between you."

"Red is the only person on earth I trust one hundred percent."

You can trust me. I would never hurt you. Trust me, Dade!

She looked into his eyes and she could see that he wanted to tell her something so badly, but didn't know how to start. She waited patiently.

In the distance, a lonesome coyote howled. The sun was completely set now and in this dark corner of far west Texas, the constellations caressed the ground. In the foreground of the absurdly incongruous Prada Marfa, Dade begin to tell her the story of how Red had saved him from a child-molesting foster father named Tank and the act of bravery that had set their relationship in cement.

Dade couldn't believe that he'd told her the story. She hadn't pried. Hadn't even asked for it and he spilled like an oil well, gushing out a torrent of dark, turbulent words. Telling her the grim tale he'd never told another soul.

They were on the motorcycle again, continuing their journey to Marfa. He had no idea what they were going to do when they got there. How was retracing Red's steps ever going to help them find him? He had no answer, but one thing was certain, he felt relieved to have

Natalie with him. When she was around he felt stronger, and it was comforting to have her in on his secret.

At last someone he could trust.

They reached Mitchell Flats on the east side of town and pulled into the Marfa Lights View Park located right next to the site of a World War II army airfield. There were a handful of cars in the parking lot, and a couple of RVs had set up camp. Dade parked and they got off the motorcycle. The graveled path led to a sheltered viewing area that also housed restrooms for travelers. There was a plaque in front of the viewing shelter explaining that Apache Indians believed the mysterious lights to be fallen stars.

Beyond the viewing park, the desert stretched out wide and flat.

"The chances of seeing the lights tonight are pretty slim," Natalie said. "Most of the lights that people see are cars on Highway 67 going from Presidio to Marfa. If you see lights off to the southwest, it's car headlights."

They picked their way along the gravel and came upon a man with a tripod, cameras, binoculars and a surveyor's level to measure azimuth angles. The man straightened at their approach.

"Hello, Stan," Natalie greeted him.

The man's face melted into a surprised smile. "Natty McCleary, is that you?"

"I was wondering if I'd see you here tonight."

"You know I'm here every night from June to the middle of August."

She smiled warmly at the man called Stan, too warmly in Dade's estimation. "I didn't know if you were still investigating the lights."

"Always, forever, until I figure out what's causing

them." The man was looking at Natalie as if she was a pork chop and he was a hungry hound dog.

"You're determined to be the one who spoils the mystery, then?" She chuckled. It was an affectionate sound. She *liked* this guy. Dade hated that she liked this guy.

"You know me. I can't stand ambiguity."

"So you ruin it for the rest of us," she teased.

"Knowledge is power." The man stepped closer to her.

Irritation grated against Dade's teeth. He too stepped closer to Natalie.

"Have you seen any lights yet this summer?" she asked.

Stan shook his head. "I'm hoping that means we're due. Fingers crossed it's tonight." He held up two crossed fingers.

"Fingers crossed." Natalie mimicked his gesture.

"It's really good to see you again. How have you been?"

Dade slid his arm around Natalie's waist. "She's been fine. Great. In fact, she hasn't been better."

An eyebrow went up on Stan's forehead. He was a mild-looking guy—long face, balding at the temples, soul patch on his soft chin. Dade hated soul patches. With facial hair you're either in or you're out. A soul patch was a partial commitment. Tiny little scruff of hair looked like he'd just missed a spot shaving.

"Stan Freeman, and you are…?"

"With Natalie." Dade kissed her cheek.

Natalie turned and peered dreamily at him. "Yes, you are."

"And don't forget it." Dade reached for her left hand, interlocked his fingers with hers.

"Oh," Stan said, and then, "*Oh*."

"Listen, Stan," Natalie said, "we're looking for a friend of ours who's gone missing."

Stan put his hands to his spine, stretched. "This isn't the safest place in the world to go missing."

Uneasiness had Dade squeezing Natalie's hand. She might trust this guy, but he certainly did not. "I need to speak to you in private."

"Could you excuse us a minute, Stan?"

"Sure." Stan went back to his tripod.

Dade pulled her over to the side. "What are you doing?"

"I'm going to ask him if he's seen Red. You heard him, he's been here every night this summer."

"How do you know you can trust him?"

"You have a paranoid streak a mile wide, you know that?"

"With good reason. I've been burned more times than I can count."

"Maybe it's because you expect to be burned. Ever think about that?"

"Naive," he muttered. "You're so naive."

"If thinking the best of others is naive—"

"It is," he cut her off. "Most people are rotten to the core. You've been blessed with fairy dust to live in a town surrounded by people who love you. Many people don't have that luxury. Life kicks most of us in the teeth, time and time again."

Natalie looked hurt. "You think I haven't suffered? I was in a plane crash when I was nine years old. I saw my mother die right in front of my eyes. I dragged myself from the wreckage and managed to pull my baby sister out of it too. My leg was broken in twenty-two places. I had to have seven surgeries. I still walk with a limp, and every time the weather changes I get to remember all that. So screw you, Dade Vega, your suffering isn't any more sanctified than mine. I'm sorry no one loved you as a child. That was terrible. I wish I could erase your childhood and give you a bright shiny one, but I can't and you can't keep blaming the past for the way you look at the world. You can't let your history define who you become. That's all it is, history."

Whoa! He'd never heard her go on a rant like that.

She folded her arms over her chest, pressed her lips together in a thin, firm line. "I'm sorry, but you needed to hear that."

"I didn't mean to upset you," he apologized. "I know you're not accustomed to being careful about what you say around people, but if you say the wrong thing to the wrong person Red could end up dead."

"Yes, but if we don't trust someone, sometime, how are we going to find Red?"

Dade ran a hand through his hair. True enough. It was the reason he'd had to finally break down and tell her the truth about why he was in Cupid. He cast a glance over his shoulder at Stan. "Who is this guy?"

"He's a physics teacher at the University of Texas. He comes here every summer to research the Marfa Lights."

"And he could be responsible for Red's disappearance."

Natalie laughed. "Stan?"

"How well do you know him?"

Natalie ducked her chin. "Um, we dated a few years back."

"I see." Dade pressed his lips together in a firm, hard

line. Dated, huh? He imagined Stan kissing Natalie and his blood boiled.

A smiled crooked the corner of Natalie's lips. "Why, Dade Vega, you're jealous."

He pulled her up tight against his chest. "Hell yes, I'm jealous. Just the thought of him putting his hands on you makes me want to smash his face in."

She grinned.

"What? It's not funny."

"It is funny seeing you all hot and bothered over my former lover," she teased.

Dade winced. "Don't say that word."

"What word? Lover? Lover, lover, lover."

"I want to be your only lover," he growled, and planted a punishing kiss on her lips. He hadn't planned this. Didn't really want to be feeling it, but he was feeling it nonetheless—jealousy, lust, possessiveness. He wanted Natalie all to himself.

"Oh!" she exclaimed, and immediately wrapped her arms around his neck.

She kissed him back just as hard as he kissed her, then she whispered, "You've got nothing to be jealous of."

"What happened between you and Stan the man? How come you broke up?"

She shrugged. "He wasn't you."

"Damn straight." He lightly swatted her fanny. She giggled, and the sweet sound went straight through him.

"But we really should ask him about Red."

Dade studied her. "So you really do trust this guy?"

She nodded. "I do."

He hesitated.

"You trust me, don't you?"

"Yeah."

"Well then?" She held her raised palms out at her sides.

Against his better judgment, he agreed. "All right. Ask him about Red, but don't give him any more information than you have to."

"Got it." She saluted him. "Complete paranoia mode."

She ambled away from him, back toward that Stan character. Dade charged after her. He wanted to make it clear to Stan that he had absolutely no chance of rekindling anything with Natalie.

What's going on with you? You're not the possessive type. You don't get jealous. This thing with Natalie...

Yeah, that right there. What was this thing with Natalie?

He had no answer to the question, but he felt compelled to rest his hands on her shoulders as she told Stan about Red and asked if he'd seen him.

"Sure, I know Red," Stan said. "We've had a few interesting conversations about the Marfa Lights."

Natalie canted her head. "We know he came to Marfa on the nineteenth of June. Did you see him that night?"

"Yes, I remember it specifically because I gave him a ride home to Cupid."

"How did he seem to you?" Natalie asked.

Stan shrugged. "Nothing unusual."

"Anything else you can think of?"

"No. I do hope he's okay."

"So do we," Natalie murmured. "Thanks, Stan."

Dade took her hand and guided her back the way they had come.

"Dead end," she said. "The ticket stub is a dead end.

Red took the bus to Marfa but Stan gave him a ride home."

"*If* your pal Stan is telling the truth."

She stopped, dropped his hand, and sank her hands on her hips. "Why would he lie about that? And besides, how would the ticket stub have gotten among Red's things?"

"Why does anyone lie? Maybe he's involved with Red's disappearance. Maybe he put the ticket stub among Red's things. Ever thought about that?"

"Why would he go to all that trouble?"

"To make us think Red came home from the trip to Marfa."

Natalie clicked her tongue. "It's gotta hurt."

"What?"

"Being inside your head. Have a little faith in people."

Dade grunted. "C'mon," he said, and held out his hand to her again.

She hesitated a moment, but finally sank her hand into his. When they were almost back to the bike, Natalie grabbed his elbow. "Dade!" she exclaimed. "Look!"

Similar exclamations came from the people clustered at the viewing shelter, and Dade swung his gaze due east where Natalie pointed. Two basketball-sized fiery orange orbs appeared on the horizon. The orbs bounced up in the sky in unison, then split apart, shimmering and shaking. Then the lights sprang toward each other and merged into one red glowing light. They wriggled and jiggled, split apart again, circled each other twirling and whirling like square dancers.

"Holy shit," Dade said, not believing what he was

seeing. No way could these be car lights or campfires. Something else was going on here to create those lights.

"Isn't it amazing?" she whispered.

"Not half as amazing as you."

She turned to look at him, a happy smile on her face. "You say the sweetest things."

Only to you. "I can see why Red was fascinated with the Marfa Lights. They're something to see."

They stood side by side watching the lights. Natalie slipped an arm around his waist.

"The lights remind me of us," he murmured.

She swallowed visibly as if she had a lump the size of El Paso caught in her throat. "How's that?"

"The way the lights come together, dance for a bit, split apart, and then come back together again."

"We're like that?"

"Have been since day one. Both of us leery of the connection that neither one of us can deny." He couldn't believe he was saying it, but he felt obliged to let her know what he was thinking.

She turned into him. "You feel it too?"

"If you have to ask, then I haven't been doing as good a job of kissing you as I thought."

"Maybe we should work on it some more."

"Maybe we should."

There, in the glow of the mysterious and awe-inspiring Marfa Lights, Dade kissed her thoroughly and completely. "How's that? Any doubts left?"

"Take me home," she whispered. "Take me back to Cupid's Rest and make love to me, Dade."

"Hell, darlin'," he said. "You don't have to ask me twice."

Chapter 15

*Explosive physical love is a natural extension of
a strong emotional connection.*

— *Millie Greenwood*

Tonight, they might not have found a lead on Red's
whereabouts, but Dade and Natalie had discovered each
other. They arrived at the Cupid's Rest shortly after
midnight. The house was dark, the occupants asleep.
A rendezvous moon hung overhead, sinful in its gold-
enness.

"Do you still mean what you said back there in
Marfa?" Dade asked once he'd parked the Harley.

"I haven't changed my mind. Have you?"

"Darlin'," he said, pulling her up against his chest.
"Do you really have to ask?"

Excitement strummed through her as strong as on

the first day she'd seen him. No, stronger, because now she was about to make love to the man of her dreams.

"So where do we go from here?" he murmured.

She laid a finger to her lips. "My bedroom."

The air smelled of summer, honeysuckle, and roses. A fragrance she'd smelled every year of her life and had never really appreciated until now. She inhaled, breathed in summer and the smell of their lust.

Abandoning all caution, driven by the realization that this was probably the wildest adventure she was ever going to have, Natalie moved up the steps. She pushed at the back door. It didn't move. She turned the handle. Locked tight.

Oh yes, Dade had put in a new lock.

She reached in the pocket of her jeans for the key and unlocked the door. He was right behind her and she could feel his breath on her neck. She shivered.

There's no going back once you do it. Once you make love to him it can't be undone.

Good. She didn't want it undone. For once, she wanted to seize life by the throat, take advantage of an opportunity. No regrets.

"Which room is yours?" he asked as soon as she had the door unlocked and they were inside.

"Third room on the left at the top of the landing, why?"

"Because of this." He bent and scooped her into his arms.

"Ooh, put me down."

"Nope, this is me, sweeping you off your feet," he said, and headed for the stairs.

Feeling like Scarlett O'Hara in *Gone with the Wind*

when Rhett Butler whisked her up the stairs, Natalie decided to go with it and hung on to his neck.

He kicked opened the door to her bedroom and carried her inside. He set her on her feet and turned to lock the door. It made a resounding click.

Oh my!

In the dark room, she couldn't see his face. That freaked her out a little. She fumbled in the dark, found the bedside lamp, and flicked it on.

Ack! Now there was too much light.

She crossed the room to light the scented candle on her dresser, turned back to see Dade flick off the lamp. The fragrance of lemon-lime filled the room.

He gazed at her, hair mussed from the wind-blown motorcycle ride.

He grinned wickedly at her, and Natalie's heart rocked. "You have no idea how long I've been waiting for you," he said.

Good heavens, she was so nervous that her hands were shaking. *Be cool. Act like this is no big deal.* But she was nervous as hell. This was her first time and she wasn't ready. She hadn't even shaved her legs. She should be better prepared.

Oh gosh, maybe it was time to rethink this whole thing.

You've had almost thirty years to prepare for this. How much more time do you need?

Excellent point.

He came across the room toward her.

She gulped and backed up.

"Natalie." He breathed her name on a sigh and gathered her in his arms again.

Natalie dissolved in his embrace. She'd been aching for this for days. Dreamed of it. Imagined it. Now here it was and she was feeling a million wonderful and scary things.

"Wait!" She held up a hand.

He stopped.

"Do you have condoms?"

"Couple in my wallet. Bought them the day after we danced at the bar."

"Pretty cocky. Was I that much of a sure thing?"

"Darlin'," he said. "I don't count on anything, but I believe in being prepared."

"Good." She smoothed down her hair with flighty hands. "Shall we get to it?"

"Get to it?" An amused smile twitched his lips.

She reached for his belt buckle to cover her anxiety. She had no real idea what she was doing here. Sure, she'd read steamy novels and *The Joy of Sex*, and she and Stan had done some heavy petting. And she did have a trusty little vibrator tucked into her bedside drawer, but none of those things substituted for the real deal.

Dade stilled her hand. "Hold the phone. I want a little foreplay."

She snorted. "You're a guy."

"And?"

"Guys don't need foreplay." *Because you know so much about it?*

"Wanting and needing are two different things."

"You're already hard," she pointed out.

"That doesn't mean I don't want this seduction to last. It's our first time. It should be special."

Spooked, she backed up. She wasn't sure she could survive prolonged foreplay with him. And what if their first time was just one time? What about that? He was only in town to find Red. Once he found him, what then? Clearly, she had not thought this through.

He snagged her by the elbow. "C'mere, darlin'."

Her pulse skipped.

His hand went around her waist and he drew her to him.

She looked up into his enigmatic eyes. What was he thinking?

He kissed her, and it was sweeter than before, softer. She cupped his face in both her palms and kissed him back.

"Should we talk about this step?" he asked.

"No talking," she insisted. "I want to feel you inside me."

He narrowed his eyes. "You're moving too fast, sweetheart. Slow down. Savor."

"I just want to get this going before I chicken out." She reached down, took his hand, and pressed it to her breasts.

"If you're thinking you might chicken out, then we shouldn't be doing this."

What the hell was wrong with her? One minute she was running hot, the next cold, and then scorching again. She was messing this up. She was no good at seduction. No wonder she was a twenty-nine-year-old virgin. She thought too much.

Instead of answering him, she surprised herself by brazenly slipping her hand lower, moving from his belt to his zipper. Beneath her touch, he turned to stone. Natalie thrilled to the feel of him. *She* made him hard.

Dade groaned and stepped back. "I'm not going to let you sidetrack me. We're doing this my way, got it?"

Hot desire smoldered deep in his eyes and when he looked at her, she caught fire—combusted. "Got it," she whispered.

"So this is your chance. If you want me to leave, say the word and it's over, forgotten. Nothing ruffled or changed."

No, please don't go. She shook her head. "It's not that easy and you know it."

His smile was wicked. "Gotta admit, you've got me wrapped around your little finger."

"So we're doing this."

"Looks like it."

"How do we start?" It wasn't this hard in the movies. In the movies, lovers just gave each other sultry looks and then went at it.

"Here are the rules." He stroked the back of his finger down her cheek.

"There's rules?"

"Oh yeah."

"I didn't know there were rules."

"Don't sweat it. You'll be perfect. You're a great one for following the rules."

"I'm tired of following rules."

"Not these rules."

"Which are?"

"No rushing. No shortcuts. I'm going to make love to you all night long, until the sun comes over the horizon. You're not going to get one minute of rest. Do you understand?"

Wow, oh wow, oh wow. The candle flickered, danced, and scented the air with lemon-lime.

"Do you understand?" he repeated.

"I understand."

He shook his head.

"What?"

"God, Natalie, you are so beautiful."

Goose bumps of pleasure rushed over her. *Beautiful*. Dade had called her beautiful. She smiled, ducked her head. She'd never thought of herself as beautiful, but he certainly made her feel that way.

"You're trembling." He stepped closer, took her hand.

Who wouldn't tremble when they're about to make love to their soul mate for the very first time?

"I'm shaking too," he whispered. "I've never... This is... You are the best thing that has ever happened to me. I wasn't expecting it, but you hit me like a sledge-hammer, woman."

"Dade." Natalie inhaled. Sledgehammer. *She was his sledgehammer*. Floating. She was floating on his words. Had the floor under her feet disappeared? Her head swam and she realized she was holding her breath.

"Breathe. Just breathe." He touched his lips to hers, just barely, and instantly she was wet and hot and ready for him.

She took a slow, deep breath.

"I want you," he said, his eyes fever-bright. "More than I've ever wanted anything in my life."

Omigosh, it *was* true! There were such things as Cupid and soul mates and love at first sight. Every bit of it was there in his eyes for her to see.

Overwhelmed, Natalie lowered her gaze.

Dade ran a hand up the nape of her neck, stabbed his fingers through her hair, and tugged gently, tilting her head, forcing her to meet his gaze. "Look at me."

She raised her eyelids.

"You're an amazing woman," he said. "I am the luck-iest man in the world to be here with you."

I'm the lucky one!

"Come," he said, and led her toward the bed.

In that moment, she saw the only bedroom she'd ever lived in through his eyes. The tall ceilings and thick turn-of-the-century baseboards and elaborately carved crown molding, the walls painted a soft fawn. Her bed was sleigh bed, and instead of a comforter, she used a lace-edged quilt that her gram had hand quilted as a bedspread. Her closet door with the full-length mirror stood up opposite the bed.

Twin Dade and Natalie reflected back at them. The curtains were simple lace sheers and there was an up-holstered window seat, the perfect place to curl up and read. Not that she ever had much time for reading.

She thought of the disparity in the way they were raised, she in the lap of luxury, he in desperation and despair. But he had grown and changed, and she? Well, she had not. Her heart hurt for the boy he'd been, mar-veled at the man he'd become. He and she were differ-ent in so many ways.

Her legs were boiled noodles, soft, weak, unable to hold her up any longer. It was about to happen. The en-counter she'd been waiting a lifetime for, and Dade Vega was her destiny. She knew it. Was certain of it, even if he was not yet one hundred percent certain.

His gaze pinned her into place, holding her up when her legs could not. She pulled thin ribbons of air into her lungs. He reached up to undo the clasp on her neck-lace and then dropped it onto her dresser beside the flickering candle.

Unable to wrench her gaze away, she memorized

his every move, determined to remember this moment forever.

He toed off his cowboy boots, peeled off his socks, tucked the socks inside the boots, and settled the boots side by side near the door. His bare feet were gorgeous in their nakedness. Who knew naked masculine toes could be so sexy?

He removed his wallet from the back pocket of his black denim jeans, slipped out two condoms, and settled the wallet on her bedside table.

Wah! Only two condoms? Would that be enough? He said he was going to make love to her until dawn. Surely they would need more than two condoms.

He sauntered toward her—cocky, eyes wicked, one hundred percent male. Her heart was pounding so hard that each pulsation rocked her entire body. Lusty, desperate need unspooled low in her stomach and spiraled through her veins, consuming her like a raging fever. It would take a thousand fire extinguishers to put out the flame he'd started inside her.

Without a word, his fingers went to the hem of her shirt and slowly, he drew it upward, his knuckles skimming her bare belly. She sucked in her breath, raised her arms over her head.

Surrender.

Heedlessly, he tossed her shirt over his shoulder and she was standing there in a lavender front-clasp bra. His gaze lasered into her. "Natalie," he said, husky and low.

"Uh-huh?" She could barely whisper.

"Do you have any idea what you do to me?"

Transfixed, she stared deeply into his eyes, moistened her lips with the tip of her tongue.

"Or—" his voice deepened "—all the things that I want to do to you?"

She ran her palm up underneath his shirt, touched the hard lines of his taut belly. Her hand tentatively reached out to trace the definition of his abdominal muscles, felt them ripple and contract beneath her fingers.

"I've been wanting to touch you there since the morning I first saw you in the Piggly Wiggly parking lot," she confessed.

"Darlin', not nearly as much as I've been aching for you to touch me."

She paused a moment, looked up into his eyes. "Are we moving too fast?"

"Maybe we are, but I don't care."

"I don't want you to regret this."

He cupped her cheek against his palm. "No matter what happens, Natalie, I will never, ever regret being with you."

She caught her breath as part fear, part hope, and part utter joy took hold of her. "No one has ever spoken to me the way you do."

"Not even Stan?"

"No." It was getting down to it. She was going to have to tell him she was a virgin.

"Good thing you broke up with him."

"Good thing," she echoed. "Listen, there's something I have to tell you before we go any further."

"What's that?" he murmured, lowering his head to nibble the top of her ear.

"I'm... I've never..."

"Uh-huh?" His warm mouth sent tingles shooting throughout her entire body.

She couldn't think. She closed her eyes, savored the

erotic sensation of his hot tongue exploring her ear. "Umm."

"I'm listening," he whispered.

"I…" She squirmed. "You're going to have to stop that if we're going to have this conversation."

His mouth moved lower to her earlobe. "Do we really need to have this conversation?"

"We do."

"Okay." He raised his head.

"I'm not…" *Just say it!* "I've never done this before."

Dade cocked his head, arched a skeptical eyebrow. "Are you saying what I think you're saying?"

She tilted up her chin. "Yes."

"You're a virgin?" he asked, incredulous.

A heavy feeling settled in the pit of her stomach. "I am."

He still looked like he didn't believe her.

"I know. I'm too long in the tooth to be a virgin, but, well, I had a bum leg and no one was knocking down my door to get next to me and I decided, fine, I will wait for just the right guy, but then he never showed up and by then it was way past the time when most women lose their virginity and it was embarrassing and no one ever came along that was worth that kind of effort and—"

"I'm worth the effort?" He sounded gobsmacked.

She couldn't believe that he was stunned. Didn't he get it? Didn't he know? Had his life been so empty of love that he couldn't fully wrap his head around what he'd found with her? "There is no one else."

He reached up to brush a strand of hair from her eyes. "No man has ever cherished you?"

"No." She shook her head. "And I was beginning to

think no one ever would, I was almost ready to give up and then came you."

"All I gotta say is there are some damn dumb men in this town." He cupped her chin in his palm, smiled down at her.

"Hordes."

"But I thought you said that you and Stan were lovers."

"I was trying to make you jealous. I might have overstated that a bit."

"It worked. I was damn jealous. What's a bit?"

"Third base. We went to third base."

"Did he kiss you here?" Dade's hand had drifted to the sensitive spot between Natalie's legs.

She squirmed. "No, not that."

"Did you put your mouth on him down there?"

"No!"

"Then what exactly did you do?"

"Kissing. We kissed. And touched."

"Touched?"

"You know, down there."

"Hand jobs."

"Well, I wouldn't put it so crudely, but yes."

"Hate to break it to you, darlin', but you weren't anywhere near third base," he said, sounding utterly pleased.

"I'm glad."

"Me too."

"But you and me…"

"Yes?" she whispered.

"We're gonna hit a home run."

Every muscle in her body tightened and melted in an alternating rhythm. A sharp, sweet ache speared the very core of her. She sank her top teeth into her bottom lip as her mind spun with a million dizzying erotic possibilities.

Dade bowed his head, pressed his mouth to hers, and sucked her bottom lip up between his teeth, nibbling lightly.

She lit up, a rocket of sensation shooting to the stars.

He placed soft kisses down her jaw to the throbbing pulse in the hollow of her throat. A shudder pushed clean through her. "You taste so good."

His hand flicked to the clasp on the front of her bra; in a second, it was unfastened, dangling open. Dade slipped his fingers underneath the straps of her bra, eased it off her shoulders. She felt him drop it to the floor rather than saw it. Her gaze was adhered to his.

She arched her back, thrusting her breasts forward. She didn't have to tell him what she needed. He just knew!

His unerring mouth found the peak of one hard nipple. He teased it playfully with his tongue until she was moaning softly and then he turned his attention to the other straining nipple. "You have such perfect breasts. Not too big. Not too small. Just right."

Her face flushed in the darkness and she threaded her hands through his thick thatch of hair, tugged gently.

"More?" he murmured, his lips vibrating against her skin.

"More," she croaked, shivered.

While his mouth explored her, her fingers massaged tiny circles up and down the back of his neck. Deep inside, she grew hotter and moister and more desperate— so damn desperate to have him inside her.

He raised his head, went back to her mouth again,

slowing things down. She made a noise of frustration and he laughed. "We'll get there, darlin'. It's about the journey, not the destination."

"Big talk, big man."

"You're not going to provoke me into rashness," he said, squeezing her tightly against him and taking her mouth once more in a fiery kiss.

His fingers moved down her bare spine to her waist and on down to cup her blue-jeaned bottom in his palms. He pushed her firmly into his pelvis and she could feel his rock-solid erection growing against her.

"And you're free to drive me crazy," she gasped, wrenching her mouth from his.

"That's pretty much the idea."

She clung to his muscular biceps, reveled in his strength. He possessed so much self-control! She couldn't wait to drive him wild.

But her plans were foiled when he kissed his way back to her breasts. He lingered, played, driving her completely insane, and then his demanding mouth traveled lower to the flat of her belly as he simultaneously sank to his knees in front of her.

Natalie gasped as his hot tongue explored her navel. Helplessly, she threaded her fingers through his shaggy hair. Oh God, he was so incredibly hot!

He tipped his head up to look at her, his long black lashes softening the hard angles of his cheekbones, his coal-colored eyes searching hers. He looked so vulnerable and endearing in that moment that she touched three fingers to her lips. He might be strong and in control, but her love had the power to shatter him into a million pieces, and that knowledge shook Natalie to the core.

He trusted her!

And she knew how hard it was for him to do that. Her heart liquefied in her chest.

While his eyes stayed fixed on her, watching every emotion that flitted across her face, Dade's fingers plucked at the snap of her jeans. The snap popped open. Millimeter by excruciating millimeter, he eased down the zipper.

Leisurely, he hooked a thumb in the waistband of her jeans at each hipbone and peeled the pants down her legs, his palms skimming the backs of her thighs as he went.

Awed, she stared down at him.

"Mmm," he said. "You smell good enough to eat."

Natalie swooned, had to clutch his hair in her hands to keep from toppling over.

His face was at the V between her legs. She still had her panties and shoes on, the jeans bunched around her ankles. He tugged at her panties with his teeth, and then pushed them down to her knees with his chin, sending a shuddering thrill shooting through her.

"Oh," he said.

"What?"

"You don't remove your hair down there."

"Are you disappointed?" she asked, embarrassed. She wished she'd gone over to Junie Mae's spa and had a wax job, but if she'd done that, Junie Mae would have known exactly what she was up to.

"Hell no," he said. "Nothing about you disappoints me, Natalie. I'm just more accustomed to hairless women."

Her jeans were still around her ankles, her panties at her knees. Gently, Dade pushed her backward onto the mattress. She caught herself on her elbows, sat watching while he took her right foot in his hand. She pulled it back, shying from him. "Don't."

"I thought you trusted me."

"I do. I just don't want you looking at it too closely. It's…" She swallowed. "Ugly."

"Nothing about you is ugly, Natalie McCleary," he declared vehemently.

It took everything she had inside her to nod for him to continue. If she were being honest, she'd have to admit that the leg was the biggest reason she'd never had a lover. It took a lot for her to reveal her greatest wound to intense scrutiny.

Slowly, he undid the laces, slid off the red Keds and matching red sock. Next, he undid the straps on her AFO and slipped that off too.

In the candlelight, he studied her foot, turning it this way and that. Her last two toes were misshapen, and two long parallel scars ran lengthwise across the top of her foot, and there were six smaller round scars on the side of her foot where the pins had been. The scars were faded, silvered with age, but they were part and parcel of who she was.

Dade lowered his head, and one by one, tenderly kissed each scar.

Now who was vulnerable? Now who was in jeopardy of being shattered to pieces by love?

"Never be ashamed of your scars," he said. "I'm not ashamed of mine."

"Can I see them?" she asked, her curiosity piqued.

"What?"

"Your scars."

"We're getting there, darlin', slow down."

He peeled off her other sock and shoe, tugged the

jeans off her ankles, and fished the panties from around her knees. He returned to her right leg, studying each scar he found—and there were a lot of them—kissing each one in turn on his way up her thigh. By the time he reached the last scar, halfway between her knee and her hip, Natalie was a quivering mess.

He stood and stared down at her. It didn't seem fair that she was totally naked and he was still fully clothed.

"I'm at a disadvantage," she pointed out. "It's time for you to get naked."

"There you go again," he murmured. "Rushing things. Let me just look at you a minute."

She squirmed beneath the heat of his gaze, uncomfortable with his cool assessment. She snatched up the corner of the quilt and covered herself with it. "Not until you get naked."

"You drive a hard bargain," he said, and slowly stripped off his T-shirt, giving her full view of his glorious abs.

She sighed happily. "Much better."

His hand went to the snap of his jeans and he shucked them off.

Holy heavens!

He was going commando and he was…he was… Well… His height and broad shoulders weren't the only big things about him. Natalie's jaw unhinged and she stared at him openmouthed.

He held his arms wide. "Here I am."

"Impressive," she croaked.

"Now uncover yourself."

She clung to the quilt, a flimsy barrier between them. He grabbed the opposite end in his fist and began to tug it off her. "C'mon darlin', fair's fair. I got naked for you, time for you to be naked for me."

Yipes!

"I'm feeling shy."

"Past time for that. I've already kissed your leg."

He had at that, but she stubbornly held on to the covers.

"You wanna talk about it?" He let go of the quilt and settled on the mattress beside her, his beautiful penis still standing at attention.

For her!

He stroked her cheek with the pad of his calloused index finger. "We can talk all night if you'd rather do that."

"Really?" She breathed. "You'd settle for that?"

"Absolutely. I'll wait for you as long as it takes."

"A week?"

"Months."

"A year?"

"Ten."

"If you wait ten years for me, that means you'll have to move to Cupid."

"Not necessarily." His finger slipped to her lips. "You could come with me."

Leave Cupid? Here was her golden ticket out, she could follow him anywhere, but she was terrified by the thought of leaving the only home she'd ever known.

Too scary.

Now that it was finally happening, it was all moving too fast. It was too big of a step, and suddenly Natalie could not catch her breath.

Chapter 16

And once the physical bond has been cemented, the emotional knot fully sets.

—Millie Greenwood

"Natalie?" Dade crooned. "You still with me?"

She gaped at him; all the air was trapped inside her lungs and she could not exhale.

Why was she getting cold feet? Ten minutes ago she'd been within inches of raping him and now she couldn't catch her breath and her mouth was dry. What was up with that?

Maybe it was the penis. The thing *was* quite impressive. Not that she had any hands-on experience in measuring erections, but big was big. She was even afraid to look at it.

"You want me to go?" He touched her ankle that was

sticking out from under the cover, and an avalanche of heat pushed the air out of her chest.

"No!"

"All right. Talk to me," he coaxed. "What's bothering you?"

"I'm afraid," she confessed.

"Because it's your first time? I'll be gentle. We'll take our time. Slow and easy."

She cast a sideways glance at his erection. You had to sneak up on something of that magnitude. Quick peek. Look away. Come back again for another sizing up. "It's not that. I trust you in that regard."

"What is it then?"

"I'm afraid that I won't measure up. I don't know what I'm doing. My inexperience was one of the reasons Stan and I broke up. He was afraid I'd be too conservative in bed. Of course we never got far enough along to find out if—"

"Screw Stan," he said vehemently. "No wait, don't screw Stan, screw me."

"It wasn't any better with Joe either."

"Who was Joe?"

"The first guy I almost slept with. I'm too conventional."

"Says who? Stan and Joe?"

She nodded.

"Look at me."

She met his smoldering black eyes.

"Do I look like Stan or Joe?"

"No."

"Well then, stop assuming I'm going to react like those jokers." He reached out to brush a strand of hair from her forehead. "Natty, I like you just the way you are."

Everyone had told her it would be this way when you found The One. He would get you to your core. Why was she testing it? Why was she gumming things up when they'd been moving along so nicely?

"This is our time. Just me and you. No old boyfriends or girlfriends allowed in here. Got it?"

"Got it."

He kissed her sweetly, softly, and very conventionally, and she loved it.

"You set the pace." He kissed her again. "You tell me what feels good." Another kiss. "When you're ready for more adventure, I'm here. I've got your back, Natalie."

This time, he touched the tip of his tongue to her lips and she parted her teeth, letting him slip in, wet and hot. The quilt was the only thing between his naked body and hers.

"Since you don't want to come out from under the covers, I'm going to slip underneath there with you. Will that be okay?"

It touched her to hear this commanding, forceful man asking her permission. She smiled and raised the quilt.

He slipped in beside her.

Gently, he stroked his knuckles over her skin. Everywhere he touched, she ignited. The fabric of their bodies fit beautifully together like denim and silk, an unexpected combination that worked.

Separately, they were inertly innocuous. Dade. Natalie. He on one side of life. She on the other. But together? Dade and Natalie. Natalie and Dade. Datalie. Nade. She giggled. Together, they became something else entirely. Another entity. Active. Dynamic. Explosive.

Her fingers traced over his face, memorizing the texture of him. He cradled her to him and they stared into each other. His intense dark eyes stirred her soul. The moment was sweet poetry full of achy yearning and tremulous hope, a fragile cobweb of delicate intricacy.

His mouth!

Oh, the things he knew to do with his mouth! His sinful mouth seemed to be everywhere at once—on her lips, on her chin, on her belly and her shins. And then he honed in on his target, one central gathering place of erotic tenderness.

He wedged himself between her legs, dipped his head, touched her with his tongue, and began to do unspeakably beautiful things to her. A rumpus of sensation bashed into her like a storm—raw scorched lightning, a loud crack of emotional thunder, a bullwhip of wind.

Dade seized full control of Natalie's body on July first in the wee hours of Monday morning. He loved her with this mouth, and then with his hands, and finally, he tackled the last barrier.

And she finally understood what all the fuss was about as her virginity was delicately, sweetly, painstakingly breached and then she was an innocent no more. This man—her experienced lover—taught her the mysteries of the universe.

A thousand alert nerve endings cheered, spun from synapse to synapse, hummed dizzy tunes of joy, and looted every last ounce of reason she possessed.

In that honeyed night, Natalie learned that the tongue was an amazing utility tool. It could furl and unfurl, flick and lick, curl and flatten. An attentive tongue could stroke and lash, circle and caress, bathe and lave. It could rim membranes, soak up juices, and send an intrepid explorer to Mount Everest heights and then gently set her down on butterfly wings.

Her central nervous system lit up like the ghostly Marfa Lights—mysterious and mystifying, compelling and haunting. When her education on the power of the human tongue was complete, Natalie lay underneath the quilt, shattered and sated and clutching Dade's hair in both hands, as the final rumblings of an earthquake quivered through her.

Dade rose up, peeled back the covers, peered down at her with a glistening grin. "How was that?"

Unable to answer, she closed her eyes and sighed, and when she opened them again, Dade was strutting to the adjoining bathroom, cocky as a rooster. "We're not done yet, darlin', not by a long shot. This is just intermission."

What a beautiful threat!

Her heart thumped as she watched him walk away, his gloriously muscled butt on full display.

On his way back from the bathroom, he cast a sidelong glance into the open door of her closet, did a double take, stopped and switched on the closet light.

"Well, well," Dade said, staring at the rows of pristine high-heeled shoes she'd collected for fourteen years. "What is this? It's Prada Marfa right here in Natalie McCleary's bedroom."

"No Prada. Prada is out of my budget. But I've got Stuart Weitzman and Kate Spade and Michael Kors."

Dade selected a pair of pink Brian Atwood snakeskin sling backs with a three-inch stiletto heel that Natalie had bought half-price from Neiman Marcus online during their last-call sale two Christmases ago, free shipping included.

"We'll start with these." He smiled.

"I don't wear those. I can't wear those."

"And yet." He strolled closer. "They're in your closet. Imagine that."

She sat up. "I just buy them. I can't stand up in them."

"You just plan on letting them go to waste." He clicked his tongue. "Such a shame."

"They're like art to me. My one indulgence. I don't splurge on myself otherwise. So what if I can't wear them?" She tilted her chin up.

He shook his head. "I'm not buying it."

"No."

"You bought them for a reason."

"I did?"

He nodded.

"What reason is that?"

"For me."

"Are you saying I bought them for you to wear? 'Cause if you are, I don't think they're going to fit."

He grinned. "Nope. You're going to wear them *for* me."

"I told you I can't stand up in them."

"You also told me you couldn't dance."

"I didn't dance. You dragged me around the dance floor and we stood there swaying a lot."

"So what?"

"If I put high heels on I topple over and I get instant back pain."

"Not in bed you won't." He looked at her like she was the most desirable woman in the whole world and he had devilish plans for her. "Have you ever even tried them on?"

"No," she admitted.

"We're going to change things around here."

Natalie held her breath.

He reached the end of the bed, paused there for a moment, stroking her with heated eyes. He was a house of bricks, a fluid mountain lion, a stealth ninja, a sex maniac.

And she loved him!

Leisurely, he crawled up on the mattress toward her, the pink snakeskin sling backs clutched in his hand. She scooted backward until she bumped against the headboard. No escape now.

He stretched his body up over hers, trailing delicious kisses as he went until he got to her mouth. He peered down at her. She sank back into the pillow. Dade claimed her mouth, kissed her long and hard.

Then before she knew it, he had whisked the quilt off the bed, leaving her naked and exposed, and he had taken firm control of her right foot.

"Dade! Let me go!"

Natalie wriggled away from him, but Dade held tight, cupping her right heel in his palm. Clearly flustered at his attention on her right leg, she kicked at him with her other leg. He was not going to let her go. He wanted her to understand there was nothing wrong with her. In his eyes there was no damage.

She was perfect.

And she'd just given him the priceless gift of her virginity. He wanted to do something extra special for her.

He slipped the pretty pink shoe onto her foot. It fit like Cinderella's glass slipper. He reached for the other foot. Slipped the shoe on that one too. "Well, look at that, you didn't die."

She met his gaze. "Seriously? Shoes in bed?"

"Why not? Stranger things have happened in bed."

"Not in my bed," she mumbled.

"Like I said, darlin', we're going to change things around here."

She raised her defiant little chin. "I don't like change."

"Yes you do. You're just scared of it."

"You think you know me so well."

"I'm working on it. I want to know everything there is to know about you."

Her beautiful blue eyes widened and he realized it was true. He *did* want to know everything there was to know about her.

"Hmm, let's see if these shoes really were made for walking."

"I told you I can't—"

"Tut, tut." He leaned over to lay an index finger across her lips. "You can just pretend I'm the floor."

He knelt on the mattress at the end of the bed, braced her feet against his knees. "Walk up me."

"This is silly."

"Only because you're not used to having fun. You're always thinking about other people's needs, well, it's high time someone met yours."

"Take off the shoes and then you can meet my needs."

"Not a chance, sweetheart. You're going to have the pleasure of wearing these shoes. I'm beginning to think you buy them just to punish yourself."

"That's twisted psychology."

"Exactly."

"Dade…"

"Natalie," he whispered. "Trust me."

"Oh, easy for you to say, not so easy for you to do. A bit hypocritical, don't you think, Vega?"

"Pay attention, we're getting somewhere here."

"You think?"

"Walk up me, baby." He braced his knees against the bottoms of her feet.

"What's the deal? You got a shoe fetish or something?"

"After seeing your closet, maybe I'll develop one. Walk."

She planted her left foot higher up on his right leg.

"Good girl. Now the other one."

She folded her arms over her chest. "I'm not enjoying this."

"Stop resisting and just relax." He cradled her right calf in his palm. Her hamstrings were clenched tight. "Relax," he crooned, kneading her leg. Slowly, he lifted her right leg and placed it parallel on his thigh with her other leg.

He looked down at her.

God, she was so beautiful, from her slender legs to that dark tuft of hair between her thighs to her firm breasts with the pert nipples. She had the creamy skin of a Scandinavian princess, and her curly pecan brown hair cascaded over the purple pillowcase. The girl must like purple, purple bra and panties, purple sheets. The color of royalty, and she was royal. His princess.

"What is it?" she whispered.

"Huh?" He blinked.

"You're staring."

"Mesmerized," he said. "I don't know how you did it, Natalie McCleary, but you've got me under your spell."

Even in the darkened room, he could see her blush.

She blushed so easily. He liked that about her. Her feelings showed up on her face, real and unguarded. No hidden agendas with this one. What you saw was what you got, and damn, what a sight!

"Walk," he said, getting back to the task he'd set for her. "Climb me, woman."

She moved her legs up his body. With each step she took, he leaned forward just a little bit more. She stopped when she reached the top of his thighs. He was so hard now that it felt as if all the thundering blood through his body had rushed straight to his dick.

"Keep going," he croaked.

She walked those saucy pink shoes up his hips to his belly. He groaned when the spiky stiletto heels dug into his stomach. Immediately, she drew her knees up, but he grabbed her legs and held her in place. "No, no, that was a good groan. Keep going."

"I'm not hurting you?"

"The perfect kind of pain," he said. "So pleasurable it hurts."

"I didn't know there was such a thing."

"Oh yeah, I can't wait to show you."

"Dade…"

"Keep going."

She climbed.

He moved forward with her steps until he was hovering between her knees, bracing his palms against the mattress either side of her shoulders, her sharp heels poking into his nipples, his dick hot and hard as Mediterranean marble aiming straight for her feminine tunnel. All he'd have to do was sink lower a few inches and he'd be inside her.

She peered into his eyes, bit down on that plump bottom lip of hers.

Sweat popped up on his brow. Holy shit, this was erotic.

The heavy aching in his groin was almost too much to bear. It took every ounce of control he possessed not to push into her.

"What now?" she whispered.

"Keep walking."

"I'm stretching like a pretzel."

"Does it hurt? Are you okay?"

"I'm fine. No, that's not true. I'm not fine. I want to feel you inside me so badly that I can't think."

"Don't think, hook your legs around the back of my neck. Lock those heels together."

She did as he asked, and each move she made was a blistering stab to his groin. He could smell the leather of her shoes and the natural, earthy scent of her. He could still taste her on his tongue from before, and now, oh God, now he simply had to have more.

He reached a hand around to stroke her most feminine place, making sure she was ready. A smile curled over his lip when he felt the hot gush of her wetness against his fingers. She was more than ready for him. He'd worked her to a fever pitch, driving her as crazy as he was driving himself.

"Please," she begged.

"You're going to be sore after this sweetheart."

"I don't care. Please. I have to have you inside of me. I have to have you now!"

He had to have her too! Blindly, he fumbled for the remaining condom on the bedside table.

"No," she said. "You concentrate on what you're doing. I'll handle that."

While she stretched to retrieve the condom and ripped open the package with her eager teeth, Dade gently stretched her with his fingers. First one finger, then two, and then finally three, tenderly exploring where he was soon going to be.

They were both breathing heavily. Her legs were locked around his neck, her stilettos spurring into his spine.

"You're amazing," he whispered.

She winked slyly. "Not so bad yourself."

"Do you want me to do that?"

"I might have been a virgin at the beginning of this night, but I'm not uneducated. I can figure out how to put a condom on."

"Have at it."

She rolled the condom onto him, looked up triumphantly.

He peered down into her eyes and the last bit of his control shredded to tatters.

They went at each other as if it was the end of the world and they were the only two people left in it. Fire rolled through his veins, singing through every part of him.

"Woman," he growled. "Do you have any idea how badly I want you?"

"Show me," she whispered. "Just show me."

He needed no more invitation than that. He eased into her snug little warmth.

"Oh, Dade." She clung to him, curled her head in the hollow of his neck, and murmured his name.

What a feeling! He was part of her and she was part

of him. Never in his life had Dade felt so accepted and
so complete.

And to think that he had been resisting this moment
since the first day he'd laid eyes on her. Why? What
had he been so afraid of?

She etched circles over the outside of his arm. Her
touch drove a hard shiver down this back.

Natalie! He was inside her at last.

He felt as nervous and happy as a bridegroom and
just as surely bonded to her as if there had been a ceremony. Once upon a time such a thought would have
scared the hell out of him, but now? Sad. He felt damn
sad that she wasn't *already* his bride.

How had he gotten here so quickly? A loner who'd
sworn never to let anything or anyone tie him down?

"Are you all right?" She reached up to trace a finger over his cheek.

"Never been better."

She sucked his bottom lip between her teeth, lightly
rolled it into her mouth.

A million sensations erupted in his body, heat and
cold, dull and sharp, acute ache and sweet satisfaction.

Natalie didn't stay still. She was going at him the
same way he went at her—frantic, feverish, determined.
She kissed him and nibbled and bucked her hips, wriggled closer to him, trying to get him deeper inside her.

He dove into her, sliding headlong into a deep, warm
pool of pleasure. Dove in and swam around in her feminine pool. And when he came up for air, broke through
the surface, he emerged a new man.

Reborn.

Spellbound in the blue of her eyes, where perfect
order ruled, Dade forgot everything outside of her. In

this sweet, timeless moment, nothing else mattered. Her body was a hallowed playground, a place to both worship and play, a sacred temple tucked away from the ordinary world. Here, they could make their own rules. Have things the way they wanted them to be. Here, he lost all his skepticism. Here, his suspicions disappeared. Here, all doubt vanished and he was a true believer.

She embodied everything he'd ever wanted but never dared dream of—*home*. She was an asylum, sacrosanct territory, a place where rituals were revered and cultivated. He wanted to create traditions with her.

She laughed, a low, warm chuckle that set his head and heart reeling. He could listen to that sweet laugh for the rest of his life. He'd never felt this way about anyone before.

Normally, he kept his romantic relationships light, unfettered. It had served him well. He'd never really felt a need to take things deeper. Knew that doing so meant opening himself up. Trusting. Allowing someone in. No woman had ever been worth the effort before. But for this one? For this one, he'd walk barefoot through the Chihuahuan Desert if need be. For this one, he'd scale the Davis Mountains on his hands and knees. For this one, he would lie down and die.

Shit, Vega, you are in serious trouble here.

He'd heard people talk about feelings like this, thought they were full of bullshit. Now, he was the one who was full of it.

He loved the way she responded to him, so sensitive, so eager, so ready for more. She roused him in a hundred different ways, each unique and new.

Her muscles tightened around him and they were rocketing together, pushing and sweaty and charged up.

"Harder," she begged, "faster. Please."

He could deny her nothing. He quickened their pace, her legs squeezing his neck, those fucking awesome shoes digging into his skin. A minute later, he made a final, hard push and they came together, their climax slamming into them both. It ripped a groan from his throat and a tight little gasp from her.

Finally, he collapsed against her, chest heaving, breath chuffing. He wrapped his arm around her waist, rolled over onto his side to keep his weight off her. He spooned her against him and lay there feeling the wild beating of their hearts, hammering in a perfectly synced tempo.

Chapter 17

There's no force on earth more powerful than love.

—Millie Greenwood

As a meadowlark welcomed the impending dawn outside the bedroom window, Dade lay on his side, pillow tucked underneath his head, listening to Natalie's soft breathing. Her spine was curled against his stomach, her butt at the level of his pelvis. They were both naked. The covers had fallen off the bed sometime during the night, and in the throes of searing hot passion, neither one of them had bothered to draw the sheets up.

After their last lovemaking, he'd gotten up, sneaked down to the kitchen, rummaged through the refrigerator, found some of Pearl's leftovers, and brought them back to bed. He'd gently awakened Natalie and fed her from his bounty—cold fried chicken, potato salad, and strawberry shortcake. They'd kissed, cuddled, and before he even intended it, they were making love again, slower this time, their bellies sated, but their bodies ravenous for each other again.

He tracked his fingers along her rib cage, to the dip of her waist and up the sexy slope of her hipbone. He should have been worn out from all the lovemaking, but damn if he wasn't ready to go again. How was that possible when he could barely hold his eyelids open? Magically, Natalie imbued him with superhuman sexual prowess.

Being with her exceeded all his expectations. Remembering this lovemaking, his breath quickened and his dick stiffened. He touched himself, swallowed back a groan. God, he was insatiable. Disgusted with himself, he closed his eyes, tried to fight off the gathering storm.

"Dade," Natalie whispered, awe in her voice, and rolled over onto her back.

He looked down at her, felt his face turn hot.

She smiled up at him. "Are you thinking what I'm thinking?"

"I seriously doubt it," he croaked.

She turned into him, sank her teeth into his biceps, and her hand—her wicked, sly little hand—went to his shaft.

His dick was so hard he could barely breathe. She turned him to stone. His heart was Thor's hammer in his chest—pounding, pounding, pounding.

"Much as I'd love to, we're out of condoms, darlin'," he murmured.

"That's okay," she said. "You wore me out pretty good. I'm stiff all over."

"Me too."

"My feet are sore."

"You still have those shoes on," he pointed out.

"Hey, what can I say? I never thought of wearing them to bed before. Thanks for the enlightenment."

"I should be thanking you."

"What for?"

"The precious gift you gave me."

"Oh that." She burrowed into the crook of his arm. "You've opened my eyes to so many things."

"Yeah?"

"Yes."

She traced her finger over his arm. "You know what?"

"What," he murmured and tracked a lazy hand over her arm.

"We never did get around to talking about your scars."

"Which ones?" he asked.

"All of them."

"We don't have enough time for all of them. It'll soon be dawn."

"What happened here?" She touched a finger to the nick just under his right ear.

"My dad threw a beer bottle at me. It crashed on the wall over my head and a shard of glass embedded there."

Natalie hissed in her breath through clenched teeth. "Why did he do that?"

Dade shrugged. "Who knows? He was a crack addict. Anything could set him off."

Natalie shuddered. "I can't begin to imagine what that must have been like."

"I'm glad you can't," he said, and kissed the tip of

her nose. "You don't need to know how dark the world can be."

"Whatever happened to your father?"

"Don't know. Don't care. Most likely he's dead or in prison. I haven't seen him since I was eighteen."

"And your mom?"

"She died of a drug overdose when I was four."

"You don't have any family? No grandparents? No aunts or uncles or cousins?" She said it like it was an unfathomable concept.

"Red," he said staunchly. "Red's my family."

That silenced her.

"We're going to find him." She toyed with the hairs on his forearm. "I promise you."

"Yeah, but will he be alive?"

They stared at each other and a long silence stretched between them.

"Red is a survivor," she whispered.

"Everyone has their limits. Even Red."

"What about this one?" Natalie asked, slipping her hand under his back, fingering the long scar that ran the length of his right shoulder blade.

"Long story."

"You don't want to talk about it?"

"It's grim. I don't want to mar a perfect night."

Lightly, she touched his shoulder. "I'd like to hear it if you're in a mood to tell it. If you trust me."

Dade swallowed and gently tousled her hair. "It's not that I don't trust you, but it's part of my past I'm trying hard to forget."

"Maybe talking about it will help you put it away for good. Have you ever tried that?"

If only it were that easy. She had no idea what he'd

seen. The things he'd been forced to do in order to survive. And yeah, he'd talked. To shrinks. More than he wanted to.

"I won't judge you," she said.

"You say that now…"

"Did you get the scar during the war?"

"Yeah." He didn't want to relive it. Not with her. Not now anyway. She was pristine. Special. He didn't want to tarnish her with his dirty knowledge.

"Please," she whispered. "Let me in. Let me share your burden."

"You can't," he said abruptly, and turned away from her.

She sat up, reached for him.

He rolled away from her, dropped his feet to the floor. "Look, Natalie, we had a great time. I don't want to spoil it by talking about things that can't be changed."

"Whatever it is, it has been eating at you for a long time."

True enough, but blabbing about it wasn't going to change a damn thing.

"The reason for the scars is part of why you never stay in one place, isn't it?"

"How do you know that about me?"

"Red. He used to talk about his navy buddy who couldn't put down roots. He said that you had a hole inside you that you couldn't seem to fill. Said you stayed on the move to keep from feeling things."

"Oh he did, huh?"

"Yes."

"How do you know he was talking about me? You said he never mentioned my name. Maybe he was talking about someone else."

"Because when he spoke about you, there was both admiration and concern in his voice. The same admiration and concern that's in *your* voice when you talk about him."

Dade reached down and picked his shirt up off the floor. Wrestled it on. Part of him was desperate to flee Natalie and her questions. Flee the dawn. Flee her safe little world and go back to what was familiar, but he couldn't seem to make himself stand up.

If he stayed, he was going to have to tell her, and if he told her, then she would know his darkest secret. Would she reject him? Turn him away? Shudder with revulsion?

"You can trust me. I accept you unconditionally. I won't betray you," she murmured, saying the magic words he longed to hear but was terrified to believe in.

"I've heard those empty words before."

"From who? A woman?"

"Yes."

"Your mother."

"Well, her dying of a drug overdose was a major betrayal to a four-year-old kid, but she's not who I'm talking about."

"Have you…" She paused. "Been married before?"

"No. I've never let anyone get close enough." *Until you*. "But it's not what you're thinking."

"What is it?"

Dade sighed. Dropped his head in his hands. He was buck-naked except for his T-shirt. The door was right there. All he had to do was put on his jeans and his cowboy boots and walk away. He turned his head, saw Natalie curled up with her knees to her chest, looking wide-eyed and freaked out. He realized then that she might be imagining even worse things than what had really happened.

"I get it if you don't want to tell me," she said. "If it's too intimate. When you get right down to it, we hardly know each other."

"Darlin'," he said, "we know each other as intimately as a man and woman can."

"Physically, maybe," she said, "but emotionally? As long as we have secrets between us, we can never really be intimate."

That brought him up short. "Do you have secrets?"

"Just one."

"Ladies first." He waved an arm. "Be my guest. What's your secret?"

"I'm worried it might scare you off."

"All the better. If your secret scares me off, I won't have to tell you my secret." He was teasing. Sort of. He got up and put on his jeans.

"Which is precisely why you're going to tell me your secret first."

He looked into her eyes. Sat back down on the bed. "How do I know my secrets won't scare *you* off?"

Natalie laid her hand over her heart. "I give you my word."

"How do I know you're a woman of your word?" He grinned, but inside him turbulence swirled.

"On that you'll just have to trust me."

Trust. That word again. The thing he seemed unable to do.

"Your instincts led you to tell me about your relationship to Red. If nothing else, you can trust your own instincts, can't you?"

God, how much he wanted to trust her. Wanting

someone was a basic human need, but he'd been burned so many times. Did he dare try again?

She reached up to stroke his hair, but didn't say another word. "It's okay. You don't have to tell me anything you don't want to. I understand."

Dade blew out his breath. "In country," he finally said. "Afghanistan. Helmand."

She looked blank.

Her innocence was a sweet balm and it was what gave him the courage to go on. "Helmand is a Taliban stronghold."

"Oh."

"Four years ago, my SEAL team was on a mission to root out the Taliban members involved in an attack on a U.S. embassy in India. In a tiny village, I came across a young woman, a girl really, who'd been badly beaten. She was with child."

Natalie pressed a hand to her mouth, but did not interrupt his story. Good thing. If he stopped, he might not be able to pick up the story again.

"I wasn't supposed to help her. It wasn't against direct orders or anything, but we weren't supposed to interfere in the daily lives of Afghans. She was so pitiful, so desperate. She'd been left to die by her people." He clenched his jaw. "I thought it was barbaric, but who the hell was I to judge considering what kind of family I came from?"

"You're a good person, Dade, no matter what kind of upbringing you had. You overcame it."

"Yeah, well." He shrugged. "Some might disagree with you. You're from Cupid, the town of eternal love. You see the world through rose-colored glasses."

She tapped her leg. "We all have our own version

of pain, no matter where we're from. We all suffer. It's part of the human condition."

"So why bother?"

"Because of love," she said softly. "Love is worth all of the suffering."

He hauled in a deep breath. How he wanted to believe that.

Her innocent smile was so full of love. "It is."

Outside the window, meadowlarks sang.

"Go on," Natalie urged.

Dade shoved a hand through his hair. "I helped her. Hid her out in an abandoned building. Brought her food." He winced at the memory of his utter stupidity.

"What happened then?"

"One night they ambushed me."

"They?"

"The Taliban. The pregnant young lady I helped had returned to her people and told them about me."

"She betrayed your kindness."

"In the most fundamental way. Great news for them. Kidnap a Navy SEAL out alone. Execute him on camera. They'd be heroes."

Natalie gasped. "Dade!"

"Yeah."

Neither of them said anything for a long moment. Dade closed his eyes against the dark memories. This was even harder than he'd thought it would be.

"And the scar?" She reached out to finger the scar through the material of his shirt.

He shrugged. "I fought back, but there were seven of them and only one of me. They took me to a secret location. Tortured me for a couple of days. That's this scar…" He pointed to burn marks on his left forearm.

"And the scar on my right knee and the two on my lower back."

"My God." She looked horrified, splayed a hand to her chest.

"They were trying to force me to read a statement on camera renouncing the U.S. I wouldn't. They were going to kill me anyway. I wasn't going to give in to them." He was talking faster now, the words flying out of his mouth. He wanted the story over with. "So they put a black sack over my head and put my head on a chopping block and I knew it was all over."

"I can't imagine how terrified you must have been!"

"Strangely enough, I was very calm. I don't know whether it was my SEAL training, or if I'd detached my mind from my body, or whether I no longer gave a damn if I lived or died. I was just waiting for it to be over."

"I can't begin to imagine what that must have been like."

"I'm glad for that. You should never ever know anything like that. No one should."

Dade paused, moistened his lips. "Then I heard machine-gun fire—*bap, bap, bap, bap*. My hands were tied behind my back and my legs were bound so I couldn't run."

He could still smell the gunpowder. Hear the screams. Taste his own fear in his mouth.

"What happened next?" she asked breathlessly.

"Someone yanked the bag off my head and I looked up into Red's face. I was never so glad to see anyone in my life. After he untied me, Red tossed me a gun and we got out of there, but as we were leaving the compound where I was being held, we found ourselves surrounded."

"It sounds like something from a movie."

"No. This was no movie. This was real life. Ugly and brutal and nasty."

"I'm sorry, I'm sorry." She wrapped her arms around his neck. "I'm sorry I prodded you to talk about it."

He loosened her arms from around his neck, gently guided her back down on the bed. "You were right. I do need to talk about this. You need to know what kind of man you're involved with."

Her eyes went wide and she drew her legs up underneath her. "I'm listening."

"Red and I had to shoot our way out of the compound. As we made it to the exit, I stepped over one of the gunmen I'd had to kill." Dade closed his eyes, massaged his temple. He could see the gunman's face as clearly as if he was in the room with him.

Natalie rubbed his arm. "It's okay."

He opened his eyes. "It wasn't okay. The gunman was just a kid. No more than fifteen or sixteen. I killed a kid, Natalie. A child died at my hands. It doesn't get any worse than that."

She swiped at a tear trickling down her cheek. "You didn't know he was a child. He had a gun and he would have killed you if you hadn't killed him. It was self-defense."

"Maybe it would have been better if he *had* killed me."

"Dade!" Natalie said sharply. "Don't *ever* say that!"

"I tried to give the kid CPR, but Red pulled me out of there. The kid was gone, but I couldn't accept it. Taliban enforcements were converging and we escaped by the skin of our teeth. It was the second time Red rescued me." Talking about his buddy brought a lump to his throat. "I gotta find him, Natalie. I owe him my life."

"We *will* find him." She squeezed Dade's hand and he took comfort from her. "I'll call my cousin Calvin. Reiterate how important it is that—"

He shook his head. "We have to be careful."

"Honestly, we can trust Calvin. He's a deputy sheriff."

"Red's message was clear. Trust no one."

"You took a chance on me. We need help, Dade. We can't do this alone."

"Just promise me for now that you won't tell anyone who I am or why I'm here. Please."

"I don't—"

"Promise."

"All right," she agreed. "I promise not to say anything to anybody until you give permission."

Silence fell over the room as rays of light pushed through the curtains. The candle on the dresser barely flicked, it had burned down the wick, the scent of lemon-lime lingered in the air.

"So," he said. "I'm betting you wish you'd gone first after all. Can't really top that for a secret, huh?"

"My secret is the opposite of yours. It's about hope instead of despair."

"Hey, I could use all the hope I can get. Let's hear it."

She took both his hands in hers. "This might sound weird, but from the minute I laid eyes on you, I knew."

"Knew?"

"Just one look, as the saying goes."

"Just one look?"

"This thing between us that we felt on that very first day, the very second our eyes met, the out-of-body, out-of-this world experience that seized us both. I *know* you felt it too."

He tightened his jaw. He couldn't deny it, but confirming it felt so dangerous.

"It's not about the sex," she said. "Although it is damn fine sex."

"It was, wasn't it," he said, trying to derail her. Quick! Think of something to divert her attention. If she said what he feared she was going to say there would be no denying it, no going back, no unsaying it. If he could just stop her before she said the words—

"I fell in love with you. I don't know why it happened. I can't explain it. Maybe there is something to the Cupid lore, but I just had to tell. I'm in love with you, Dade Vega, no matter what. Completely and unconditionally. I know this will probably freak you out, but if I'm right and you're the one I'm supposed to be with, then it's okay for me to say it."

Tears shone in her eyes and she was smiling at him like he was the most wonderful person in the world.

His chest constricted and he was having trouble drawing in a deep breath. *Natalie loves me.* She *loves me. She loves* me.

It was an impossible dream—the white picket fence, two kids, maybe three, the dog and the cat and the minivan. But he wasn't like normal people. He never had been. He couldn't fit in, would never fit in. No matter how much he wanted it. He would only bring her heartache in the end. He would only disappoint her.

"Natalie," he murmured. "You barely know me."

"I trust you, Dade. With my heart, my soul, my body, every part of me."

Her faith snatched him up by the throat, seized him

in a chokehold, and wouldn't let go. She assumed the best of people and she wasn't afraid to let down her guard and show her tender underbelly. She didn't allow doubt to hamstring her. Why was her belief in him such a powerful turn-on?

Mmm, could it be because you're too damn wary, too afraid to take a chance on love?

Love.

It was such a hard word to say, such a powerful feeling to experience.

Love.

When he looked at Natalie, the word welled up in him, silent but unrelenting.

Love.

He could see it in her eyes. Feel it throbbing from her into him. Filling him up with a wondrous glow. Making him feel whole at long last. But how could he depend on it? How could he say the word? How could he know for sure? Love was unfamiliar to him and scary in its expectations.

He didn't know how to say it, so he showed her the only way he knew how. He reached into his pocket, and pulled out the bracelet that Red had given him. The bracelet that meant, *We'll always be connected.*

"Let me have your wrist."

Natalie watched Dade tie the strings of the frayed handmade bracelet around her wrist. "Red had a bracelet just like this one."

"I know," he said. "Red made one for both of us after we came back from Afghanistan."

The braided yarn was soft against her skin, a sharp contrast to the cool metal of the bullet casing. She ran her index finger over the string. "This means something important to you."

"Yeah," he said quietly. "It means we're connected. Always."

Natalie looked into his dark eyes, searched his face. "Dade, this is your bracelet, your connection to Red."

"And now," he said, "it's my connection to you."

The bracelet spoke for him. He couldn't say the words "I love you." She understood how hard this must be for him, a cautious, practical man with a heart-wrenching childhood. A man who'd spent his life moving around because he feared settling down. Feared he couldn't do what ordinary people did. Love at first sight was scary enough for someone willing to embrace the concept, but for a guy like Dade, it must seem impossible.

There was so much she didn't know about this man. Common sense asked how she could possibly love a man she did not know. Natalie wished she could explain her certainty, but her feelings defied explanation. She might not know all the details about Dade's life, but she knew him. Knew him as surely as she knew her own name.

When they made love and he looked deeply into her eyes, well, she could see clear through to his soul. He'd suffered, yes. She could see that too, but the suffering had not damaged him beyond repair. It had made him kind and empathetic, but being a man, he tried to cover it up with gruffness.

He didn't want to appear weak, but that was his mistake. Empathy did not weaken you. It made you stronger. He put on a tough front without ever realizing how truly tough his tenderness was.

"Are you sure you want to give it to me?" she asked.

"I've never been more certain of anything in my life."

Her heart quivered. She moved the bracelet around on her wrist, felt tears of joy sting her eyes. He might not be able to say it yet, but he loved her. She saw it on his face, felt it in the way his calloused hands touched her so gently. It was soon, but this was right. She had no doubts about him.

She kissed his cheek tenderly, but things didn't stay tender. He gathered her into his arms and kissed her deeply, passionately. It was with reluctance that she sighed and finally pushed away. "I have to go. It's Monday and I pick up the letters to Cupid every Monday and you should sneak out of the house before anyone sees you. Oh heavens, it's five till six now. You've got to go."

"Ashamed of me?" he teased.

"No, I'm just not ready for the entire world to know that we consummated our relationship."

"Darlin', one look at your face and the cat's out of the bag."

Her hand flew to her face. "What?"

"Other than the fact your lips are puffy from all the kissing and you've got beard rash on your chin. I'm sorry about that, I hair up fast. You're glowing."

"You're pretty impressed with yourself," she said.

"So are you." He winked, slipped on his socks and cowboy boots, but still he lingered, his gaze on her.

"Shoo." She motioned for him to go, even as she longed to pull him back into her bed again. She was sitting in the middle of the bed naked except for the bracelet he'd given her.

"When can we meet later?" he asked.

"Seriously? You're that ready to go again?"

"With you, Natalie, I'm always ready, but I meant to talk strategy about finding Red."

"I won't be free until this afternoon."

"This afternoon then. Two o'clock? Meet at the pond?"

"It's a date," she said.

He gave a deep sigh, tracked back to the bed for another kiss. "The night was too damn short."

Then with one last look at her over his shoulder, he left her with a happy smile on his face.

Chapter 18

Love is the strongest force in the universe.
— *Millie Greenwood*

An hour later, after Natalie had retrieved the Cupid letters, and passed them on to Aunt Carol Ann, she returned to the B&B to greet her guests as they came downstairs for breakfast.

She was humming "Cupid" under her breath and couldn't seem to keep from smiling. She told her usual stories, passed out flyers about the town's Fourth of July celebration events, and wished her guests a pleasant day.

She headed to the kitchen to consult with Pearl about the week's schedule, but stopped to speak to Lars, who was sitting in the breakfast alcove with a bran muffin, a cup of coffee, and the *Alpine Gazette* Sunday crossword puzzle.

"Mornin'," she greeted him. A lazy fly crawled on

the back of a chair. Natalie waved it away. Where was the fly swatter?

Lars sat down his paper, peered at her over the rim of his reading glasses. "You look radiant."

Natalie raised a hand to her hot cheeks. "How's the boat coming along? Get everything worked out?"

"Yes. Production has resumed."

"That's good." Natalie reached over to straighten the tablecloth that was slightly askew.

"I noticed your new boarder didn't sleep in his room last night," Lars said.

Oh great. Lars suspected something was going on between her and Dade. She straightened. "You keeping tabs on him?"

"Just to be safe. He is a stranger and you are a trusting soul. You think everyone means you well."

She smiled. "You mean they don't?"

"It's not a pretty world outside the boundaries of Cupid." Lars slipped off his reading glasses. "Not everyone is trustworthy."

"I appreciate your concern." The fly was back, trying to land on her arm. She shooed it.

"I saw Dade coming out of the main house at dawn," Lars went on. "I couldn't help wondering why."

That was the downside of living in a small town. Everyone stuck their noses in your business. "Did you? He must have come in for breakfast."

"Pearl wasn't even up yet. I think he's up to no good."

The heat in Natalie's cheeks flamed into a five-alarm blaze. Had Lars been spying on them? She fingered the bracelet at her wrist, thought of Dade and how he'd looked at her when he'd tied it to her arm, as if she was the most precious thing he'd ever seen. Her heart clutched at the memory. She loved him so much!

Lars tracked her movements. "What's that?"

She blinked, her mind still focused on Dade and the wonderful night they'd spent together. "What?"

"What is that on your wrist?"

Natalie couldn't stop grinning. "Dade gave it to me."

Lars made an O with his mouth. "I see."

"He really is a great guy." She twirled the bracelet on her wrist, remembered when he'd tied it on her.

Without another word, Lars got up, pushed in his chair, a look of consternation on his face. "Is he? How can you know? He's a stranger."

"Dade is a—" Natalie bit down hard on her tongue. She was just about to tell Lars he was a former Navy SEAL. It was hard monitoring her conversation. She wasn't accustomed to suspecting everyone of something. Was this how Dade lived his life? On a constant level of alert? That thought made her feel sad for him all the way down to her toes.

Lars frowned, rolled up his newspaper, and slammed it down hard on the table.

Natalie jumped.

"Killed that pesky fly," Lars explained, and tossed the paper, fly and all, into the wastebasket.

Dade crouched beside his motorcycle underneath the portico between the carriage house and Cupid's Rest, changing the oil and thinking about what he and Natalie had learned the previous night.

Stan had given Red a ride home from Marfa on the night of June 19, the day before his buddy had sent Dade the alarming text message.

If Stan's account could be trusted. So what had happened from the night of the nineteenth to the afternoon of the twentieth? Today was the first of July. Red had been missing for eleven days.

He would check out the local newspapers for that date and the days immediately after the nineteenth to see if he could find some kind of clue to where Red might have gone. Happy to have a direction to pursue, he stood up, and wiped his hands on the bandana he plucked from his back pocket.

The back door of the B&B opened and Lars came out on the porch.

He raised a hand to the older man. "Morning."

"Good morning." Lars moved down the steps toward him.

"Looking forward to the Fourth?" Dade asked. He was lousy at small talk.

Lars's eyes narrowed in the glare from the morning sun. "Bunch of tourists, parades, and fireworks. Seen it all before."

"There's Pearl's barbecue to look forward to."

"There is that." The gravel crunched under the older man's feet as he stepped closer. "How about yourself?"

"Pardon?"

"Are *you* looking forward to the holiday?" Lars's gaze tracked back to the B&B. "Since you've got a real reason to celebrate."

Dade cocked his head, tucked the oil-stained bandana into the back pocket of his jeans. "What do you mean?"

Lars's stare was sharp. "Natalie."

The hairs on the back of Dade's neck stood up. What had she told him?

Lars shrugged. "It's easy to see on both your faces. Love alters a man."

"We haven't known each other long enough to be sticking that kind of label on things."

"It only takes a second to fall in love," Lars said.

Was it Dade's imagination or was tension tugging at the Norwegian's mouth. Was he upset that Dade and Natalie were an item? Why should he care?

"Whether you want to admit it or not, I think you're already smitten." Lars cracked his knuckles. "I guess you'll be staying at the Cupid's Rest awhile longer."

"Depends on when Natalie's previous boarder returns."

"*If* Red returns."

"Why wouldn't he?"

"Unpredictable, that one."

Dade weighed how to dig further without giving himself away, but before he could think of the best way to phrase his question, Lars started toward the carriage house. *C'mon. Say something. Keep him talking.*

"Hey Lars."

The older man paused, pivoted on his heel. "Yes?"

"You take the newspaper, don't you?"

"I do, even though print news is a dying art form. Us dinosaurs have to stick together in the digital age. I subscribe to both the daily *Alpine Gazette* and Cupid's weekly."

"Do you save the copies?"

"I do."

"Would you mind if I borrowed the last two weeks' worth of issues?"

One gray eyebrow shot up on his ruddy forehead. "Why?"

Hmm. So Dade wasn't the only suspicious one in

town. He flashed a reassuring smile. "I'd just like to familiarize myself with the town and surrounding area. Since I'm going to be staying awhile."

"Why settle for the past two weeks? Why not a year's worth?"

"I think two weeks' worth is enough to give the flavor of a town without information overload."

Lars swallowed visibly. "All right. I'll get them to you."

"Could we go get them now?"

"Where's the fire?"

"No fire. Just thought while my mind was on it and we're both here. No time like the present."

Lars looked as if he was about to refuse, but then nodded. "Let's make it quick. I've got something I have to do."

"Thanks."

He followed Lars to the carriage house. The older man didn't invite him into his room, just left Dade standing in the hallway while he slipped inside, mumbling, "It's a mess in here." And shut the door.

Fine. Dade understood about treasuring privacy.

A few minutes later the door opened and Lars handed him a stack of papers. "Let me know if you need more issues."

"Appreciate it."

Lars leveled him a hard stare. "You really sure you shouldn't get on your motorcycle and ride out of here before it's too late?"

"Why would I run out on the best thing that's ever happened to me?"

"Because," Lars said as he shut the door, "maybe you're not the best thing that's ever happened to her."

* * *

Chewing on the old man's words, Dade took the papers back to his room. Was Lars right? Was he bad for Natalie? Was it stupid of him to believe that he could settle down, quit his rambling ways, and find happiness in her arms?

Someone to love.

The elusive dream that had evaded him since he was a kid. He'd honestly felt as if he didn't deserve happiness. He was too screwed up. Too soiled and sullied, but Natalie's innocence had transformed him. She gave him hope that he could live the dream.

Hope was such a damn dangerous thing.

Kneading his temple, he sank down on the bed and restlessly leafed through the papers, starting with June 19. He had no idea what he was looking for or even what he hoped to find. He was grasping at straws and he knew it, but what else did he have?

Most of the *Alpine Gazette* was little more than a list of births at the local hospital, the obituaries, the crossword puzzle, the TV programming grid, and readers' favorite recipes. On the front page was an article about a Marfa artist who'd gotten a gallery showing in New York City, along with blurry color photographs of some of the artwork.

On the second page was a feature about a local vineyard that won honorable mention in some wine award. It wasn't until the third page that he finally found some real news. The chancellor at Sul Ross announced they'd discovered several students with fake drivers' licenses that were so professionally forged even law enforcement had difficulty telling the false identification from the real thing. The FBI and Homeland Security were investigating.

Huh. Maybe that explained why some of the kids coming into Chantilly's had looked much younger than the stated age on their IDs. From now on, if he suspected someone wasn't twenty-one, he was notifying law enforcement.

He went through all the papers for the past two weeks but found nothing that might have caused Red alarm. Maybe he was missing something. Then again, maybe there was nothing there.

Another dead end.

Reluctant to give up, he went through the papers again, this time paying special attention to the classifieds. Again, he found nothing that raised a red flag. Discouraged, he fisted his hands on his knees and gazed down at the back page of the last paper. An ad for Cupid Caverns caught his eye.

Need a cool respite from the Texas sun? Come to Cupid Caverns for a tranquil escape.

During a mission in Afghanistan, he and Red and some other SEALs had been surrounded by al-Qaeda and they'd been forced to hole up in a cavern for several days before they could be rescued. Staying in those dark caverns had made everyone edgy except for Red.

"I like caves," Red confessed to Dade. "I get why Afghanis hide out in them. They make you feel safe. Like a womb."

It hit him all at once and he could have kicked himself for not thinking about it sooner. The caverns were the perfect place to hide if you'd gone off your medication and were in the traumatic throes of PTSD delusions.

Before Natalie went to the community center, she stopped by the hospital to check on Aunt Delia. Her aunt was sitting up in bed, a tray of hospital food in front of her. She broke into a smile when Natalie came into the room.

"Hi, are you here all by yourself?"

"I sent everyone home. People need to get some rest. They've fussed over me enough." Delia poked at reconstituted eggs with her fork. "Damn, I wish I had a Denver omelet from La Hacienda Grill."

"I'll see if I can smuggle one up for you tomorrow."

"Watch out for Nurse Ratched out there. She's a pistol and she's gunning for me. Keeps carrying on about my cholesterol. I don't care. I'm seventy-seven years old. If I want a pint of Butter Brickle ice cream when I watch *Dancing with the Stars*, I'm gonna have it. I was eating Butter Brickle before she was born."

"She's just trying to do her job," Natalie placated.

"Hmph." Aunt Delia sniffed. "Never mind her. How'd it go with the hunk?"

Natalie couldn't stop a grin from spreading across her face. "It went."

"You naughty girl you." Aunt Delia's eyes twinkled. "At least I hope you were naughty."

Natalie cast a glance over her shoulder, lowered her voice. "Very naughty."

"Oh goody." Aunt Delia clapped her hands. "It's about time you had some fun."

"It's more than that."

"I suspected as much. He's The One, isn't he?"

Natalie nodded. "How did you know?"

"I've seen it happen enough times. Happened to me too."

"It's an unbelievable feeling."

"You're floating on clouds." Delia smiled.

"Yes."

"The sky is bluer, food tastes better—"

"Yes, yes."

"You ache deep down inside when you're not with him."

"That's it."

"I'm so happy for you, child. You deserve this more than anyone I know."

"But, well, he can't tell me he loves me. I told him, but he didn't say it back."

"It's hard for some men to say those words. Doesn't mean they don't feel it."

"He gave me this." She held up her wrist, showed off the bracelet like it was the Hope Diamond.

Delia inspected it. "Bullet casing bracelet, huh? Now that's unique."

"It has an emotional significance attached."

"I assumed. Honey, are those tears in your eyes?"

"Uh-huh."

"Here. Take a tissue."

Natalie plucked a tissue from the box on Aunt Delia's over-the-bed table.

"Happy tears are good, baby." Delia patted her hand. "You gonna break the news to the girls?"

"Not yet."

"I gotcha. You want to keep this special time just between the two of you for now."

"And you." She smiled.

"It's gonna be kinda hard keeping this on the down low as Zoey would say, considering you're glowing brighter than the sun. All I've got to say is that he better be good enough for you."

"Oh, Auntie, there's nobody better."

* * *

The park attendant was just opening the gate of the chain-link fence guarding the entrance to Cupid Caverns when Dade drove up on his Harley. He parked and stepped to the kiosk to pay the five-dollar admission fee and noticed the sign announcing the hours.

"Open 10 a.m. to dusk. Monday-Saturday. Closed Sundays and all national holidays."

Dade struck up a conversation with the red-faced, thick-waisted man with chin jowls that wobbled when he spoke. "Do people ever get lost in the caverns?"

"People get turned around now and again," Wobble Jowls said. In spite of his jowls, he had a thin neck and eyes the size of marbles. "But we only have the front portion of the caverns open to the public. It's got a well-lit path. Stay with the crowd and you'll be fine."

Dade glanced around at the empty parking lot.

"There's a parade in town this morning. Others will be along soon." Wobble Jowls passed Dade his receipt and a brochure.

"So there's no way to see parts of the cavern where the public isn't allowed?"

"Nope. It's off-limits except to law enforcement or researchers who have special permissions."

"No provisions for avid spelunkers?" Or ex-Navy SEALs on vision quests?

"None that I know of. You'd have to check with the town council."

"So there's no way someone could sneak into the caverns at night?"

"Don't even try it," the man said. "It's dangerous. Not to mention you'd be breaking trespass laws. If you want to see deeper into the cave, talk to the town council."

"Thanks. I'll do that."

Dade entered the caverns. It was cool inside, a nice respite from the July heat. The slow, steady dripping off stalactites echoed in the large cavern. There was a smooth path that diverged in two directions.

He consulted the map. Following the left-hand path would take him to the cave that housed the Cupid stalagmite.

He headed in that direction, ducking his head as the cavern gave way to a series of smaller caves. Jagged stalactites jutted down like monsters' teeth. The colors of the rock formations were an amazing blend of orange, yellow, brown, and green, a *Phantom of the Opera* world down here. It was just the sort of place where Red would feel safe.

Pausing near one of the lighted wall sconces, Dade read about the lore and history of the caverns. It was a fairly small cavern system, even including the part that was off-limits to the public, but it had a colorful and romantic past. Besides the legend of the Cupid stalagmite, there were rumors that during Prohibition, gangsters had smuggled liquor in from Mexico and hid it here.

A quarter of a mile into the cavern, he came upon the Cupid stalagmite inside a small cave all its own. A path wove in a spiral circle around the stalagmite, a dead-end cul-de-sac with Cupid in the center. The way Dade had entered the cave was the only route in or out.

The stalagmite was much larger than he expected. It stood over seven feet tall and almost touched the ceiling of the cave. Indeed, it looked like Cupid was standing on one leg, with the other leg bent at the knee as if he were running, a bow cocked in his arms, arrow ready to be flung into unwitting hearts.

Of course, Cupid didn't really have a face. It was just a blob of stone formed from hundreds of years of steady drip-drip-drip, but it was easy to see how the town founders could be seduced into naming their little burg after the Roman god of erotic love.

"Pretty impressive, is it not?"

Dade whirled around to see Lars Bakke standing behind him. He'd been so absorbed with studying the stalagmite that he hadn't heard the approaching footsteps.

Uneasiness rippled over him. "Yeah. Impressive."

Lars peered around. "You all alone?"

Dade's muscles tensed. "Yes."

They stood looking at each other. Lars had his hands behind his back, and Dade's uneasiness bloomed into full-blown suspicion. Something was very off about the old man.

"Nice statue. I see what all the fuss is about," Dade said mildly.

"Ah yes, Cupid. The god of love."

The hairs on Dade's arms were standing at full attention and his gut squeezed tight. He moved toward the exit.

Lars sidestepped, blocking his way. "Where you going so fast? You just got here."

"I've got somewhere to be. If you'll step aside, I'd appreciate it." He gave Lars his coldest stare.

"I'm sorry, Vega, but I'm afraid I just can't let you leave." Lars swung his arms around.

Dade glanced down, and he was not the least bit surprised to see a snub-nosed revolver clutched in Lars's hand.

Chapter 19

Never give up on love.

—Millie Greenwood

"**W**hat's this all about?" Dade asked evenly as his mind raced.

Tanked.

Red's Mayday message. Trust no one. Lars was the person his buddy had been trying to warn him about.

"Raise your arms and turn around slowly."

"Let's talk about this."

"Arms in the air." Lars raised the gun and pointed it in his face.

"All right." Dade raised his arms and faced away from the Norwegian. Was the old dude going to shoot him in the back? Why?

"Walk forward."

"We'll be going around in circles."

"Just do it." Lars's voice was pure steel.

Slowly, Dade raised his arms over his head and pivoted on his heel. His reflexes were faster than the old man's, but Lars was twenty feet away and he could get off a shot before Dade reached him. Dade would bide his time, play along. Maybe he could find out what Lars had done with Red and why.

"Walk," Lars commanded.

"Take it easy."

"I know you're a SEAL, so don't try any crap with me. Don't think for one second that I will hesitate to shoot you."

"Calm down. This is a public place, Bakke. Someone could walk in here at any moment. We don't want any innocent bystanders hurt."

"Then you better start walking. Put your hands on the back of your head."

Dade put his hands on his head and started walking forward; four feet and he was going to have to turn to follow the circular path or walk into the cave wall.

Lars made a scuffling noise behind him. It was all Dade could do not to glance over his shoulder and see what the man was up to.

A few seconds later, his question was answered when the cave wall in front of Dade started moving inward. He blinked. It was a secret door built into the cave wall, and camouflaging a hidden passageway. Bootleggers. It must have been bootleggers who built this during Prohibition.

"Move," Lars commanded.

Dade stepped into the narrow, dank passageway. Was Lars going to shut him up in here?

"Keep going and keep your hands on your head. Do anything funny and I won't hesitate to kill you."

"What's this all about, Bakke?"

"Shut up."

Dade moved down the narrow passageway. His raised elbows brushed against the cave walls on either side. He could see a light beyond. He heard the secret door shut behind him. Was Bakke still back there? He stopped.

"Keep going."

The passageway widened into a room. There was a second door on the far side of the room. Were there more secret caves and passageways beyond? At first glance, the room looked like an office. There was a table set up with a Mac computer and a printer, but a closer look told Dade this wasn't just any printer, but a state-of-the art security ID printer. On the desk were baskets filled with drivers' licenses and identification cards. Off to one side sat a bicycle-powered generator that provided electricity to the equipment.

It was not unlike the al-Qaeda setups the SEALs had found in the cavernous mountains in Afghanistan, except this one was far more sophisticated.

Slowly, Dade turned to face Lars. "You're counterfeiting IDs. It's you."

Lars did not look the least bit contrite. "It's very lucrative."

"Where did you get the printer? That's high-tech stuff."

"Anything can be had for the right price."

"Who are you working for?"

"No one," Lars said. "I'm running this outfit myself."

"All by yourself? Sorry, I'm not buying it. You don't

strike me as having the computer skills to pull this off. Besides, how do you ride the bike and run the computer at the same time?"

"I am pulling it off. I'm making twenty thousand a month, but I got a lot of expenses and the installment loans on my boat are a hundred grand each, so I have to keep at it until I can pay for my boat."

"Supplying fake identification to teenagers?" Lars was a pretty damn good counterfeiter. Dade thought about the article he'd read in the June 19 issue of the *Alpine Gazette*. Had Red read the same article? Had his suspicions been aroused and he'd decided to investigate? "Among other things."

"Supplying IDs to illegal immigrants?"

"That too."

"Are you also providing fake IDs to potential terrorists?"

Lars shrugged. "Could be. I don't ask their politics as long as their money is green."

Dade couldn't wrap his head around this. Natalie's senior citizen boarder was running a counterfeit identification ring right here in Cupid, Texas? "But why?"

"Money. What else?"

"Money for what?"

"Not that it's any of your business, but the sailboat I'm having built cost a million five."

"And counterfeiting is the only way you could do it."

"Hey, try living on social security. You won't have enough to buy cat food."

"You look pretty healthy to me."

"The great crimes of the twentieth century were committed not by money-grubbing capitalists, but by dedicated idealists. Lenin, Stalin, and Hitler were contemptuous of money. The passage from the nineteenth to the twentieth century has been a passage from considerations of money to considerations of power. How naive the cliché that money is the root of evil!"

"What the hell is that supposed to mean?"

"It's one of my favorite quotes of Eric Hoffer. It means money is a good thing and the more the better."

"I'm not sure it means that."

"Who are you?" Lars bellowed. "I knew Eric Hoffer. He was a great man."

"Do you think he would approve of your counterfeit scheme?" Dade had no idea who Eric Hoffer was, but apparently Lars was quite enamored of the man.

"Hoffer believed in the concept of meaningful work."

"And you consider this meaningful work?" Dade waved his hand at the basket of forgeries.

"Hoffer would say, 'It is the pull of opposite poles that stretches souls. And only stretched souls make music.'"

"That doesn't even make sense."

"Of course it does. It makes perfect sense."

Dade rolled his eyes. "Whatever."

"No, not 'whatever.'" Lars's glower deepened and rage infused his voice. "Hoffer was a genius."

"Genius. Got it."

"You understand nothing," Lars ranted.

I understand you're a friggin' lunatic.

Dade's mind spun with options as he tried to figure out how best to disarm Bakke without getting shot in the process. Bakke was wisely staying across the room from him. Dade's back was to the second door. Maybe he could just make a run for the second door, see if he could escape that way, but what if the door was locked?

Nothing ventured, nothing gained. Would he be any worse off for having tried?

"Red didn't stop taking his meds, did he?" Dade asked. "That must have been an old pill bottle I found that he'd neglected to throw away, and he kept his new prescription on his person. He didn't wander off. He didn't commit suicide. He stumbled across your little operation here."

"Alas," Lars said. "And now, so have you. I wanted to give you the benefit of the doubt. I really did, because I like you. Then when you asked me for those newspapers I knew that you'd see the article about the counterfeit IDs, but I hoped you wouldn't understand the significance."

He hadn't. It was the ad for the Cupid Caverns that had brought him here, not the news article.

"You came here armed and looking for me."

"I followed you, yes. If you'd gone somewhere else, then all would have been well and I could leave you be, but oh no, you had to come to the caverns. Just like your buddy Red did."

Dade moistened his lips. "How do you know that Red was my buddy?"

"Your little girlfriend gave you up."

"What?"

"Natalie. She spilled the beans."

Dade's veins iced up. Natalie had told Lars who he was? And after she promised she would not reveal his identity to anyone until they'd had a time to formulate a plan. Betrayal bit into him. This was just like with that Afghan woman he'd tried to help.

Ah hell, no, this was worse. Given the culture of fear the girl had lived in, he should have expected betrayal from the Afghan woman, but from Natalie? The woman who claimed to love him? The woman who said she had his back? The woman he'd given his most prize possession to as a symbol of his connection to her?

Dammit, Natalie, you've ruined us.

It felt as if someone had jabbed a knife straight into the thick meat of his heart.

He snorted, shook his head. *Snap out of it. You need all your focus if you're going to get out of this alive. Bakke knows if you leave here he's going to prison for the rest of his life. He can't afford to let you leave here.*

"She was so happy over that tacky bracelet you gave her." Lars shook his head. "Just glowing over the damn thing. Like it was solid gold."

"Natalie didn't tell you who I was?"

"No, she didn't have to. The bracelet you gave her was the twin to the one Red wore. Red told me the story of the bracelet. He wore it all the time. It didn't take a rocket scientist to put two and two together. The minute I saw it on her wrist, I knew who you were."

All the air left his lungs. Natalie hadn't betrayed him! He'd betrayed himself.

"Still, I had hoped we could have avoided all this. If you just hadn't asked for those papers. Once you asked for those papers, I knew you were not going to let this lie. Loyalty and stubbornness. That's your downfall, Dade Vega."

"Where's Red?" Dade growled. "What have you done to him?"

"He's in a better place."

Lars's words were a sledgehammer to the heart. Red was dead? "You son of a bitch. You better kill me then, because if you don't, I'm going to hunt you down and kill you."

Lars looked regretful. "I was so afraid you were going to say that. Why did you have to say it like that? If you hadn't said that I could just tie you up and leave you in here until I have time to clear out, but now, you leave me with no choice."

"You're not going to get away with it." Dade gauged the distance between him and Lars. Fourteen feet. There was no way he could cross that distance before Lars got a shot off.

"Oh, but I am. In fact, my escape is in the works as we speak. Turn out your pockets."

"What?"

"You heard me. Empty your pockets."

Glowering, Dade turned out his pockets. His utility knife, penlight, cell phone, motorcycle key, and the key to his room at the Cupid's Rest clattered to the floor.

"Ah, the room key. That's very important. Last time I made the mistake of not getting Red's room key. This time, your room is going to be cleared out lock, stock, and barrel, and your little girlfriend will assume you ran out on her after you had your night of fun. No one is even going to come looking for you."

"You're not going to get away with this," Dade repeated through gritted teeth.

"Sure I am. Drifter biker. Soldier of fortune. Ex-SEAL probably had PTSD just like his buddy Red. You've got no family. No one's going to give a damn when you're gone."

Dade was ready to lunge for Bakke's throat, revolver in his hand be damned, when the door behind Dade opened. He spun around to face the newcomer.

It was Gizmo, the auburn-haired computer whiz who also boarded at the Cupid's Rest. He was in on this with Bakke?

It dawned on Dade then that the Mexican woman who'd shown up the night he'd slept in the hammock on the deck at Chantilly's hadn't been looking for Red, but for Gizmo. He had red hair too. She'd been seeking counterfeit identification. No wonder she'd been so scared to find him there instead of a red-haired man.

Dade didn't hesitate. He lunged for the kid, planning on using him as leverage, forcing Lars to put down the gun, but before he could reach him, Gizmo pulled out a stun gun and zapped him.

For over an hour, Natalie waited for Dade by the duck pond. By three o'clock she was starting to get worried. She tried to call the cell number he'd given her when he'd leased the room but it went to voice mail.

"Hi, Dade, did we get our wires crossed? I thought we were supposed to meet at the duck pond at two p.m. I'm going back to work. Call me when you get this or just come on into the lobby."

When she hadn't seen or heard from him by the six p.m. dinnertime, she started to get worried. She left a second voice mail for him. Then at seven, she left another. His motorcycle wasn't under the portico, but she went to his room anyway, and knocked on the door.

"Dade?" she called. "Are you in there?"

There was no answer.

She knocked again.

When he didn't answer on her third knock, she took the master key from her pocket and unlocked the door.

The room was completely empty, the bed tidily

made. She rushed into the room, started opening dresser drawers.

Empty, every one of them.

She flew to the closet, flung it open.

Empty.

Numbly, she drooped onto the mattress as the realization hit. Dade was gone.

Water splashed on Dade's face—*plop, plop, plop.*

He opened his eyes, stared into malignant darkness. Blackness. Complete blackness. Black as black as black can be.

Where the frig was he? He was lying on something hard and the water smelled dank and musty. He struggled to sit up, discovered his hands were bound at the wrist with zip ties.

Everything came flooding back to him.

The cave. He was somewhere in the far recesses of the caverns. Lars and Gizmo were forgers wanted by the FBI and Homeland Security. And he'd been stungunned.

Son of a whore.

Mostly, Dade tried to keep his cussing to a minimum. He'd been raised around foulmouthed junkies and he believed excessively vulgar language diminished a person. They'd made fun of him for it in the SEALs, sometimes calling him Preacher or even Titanium Preacher, and he'd accepted the teasing good-naturedly, but now he uttered every foul word he'd ever heard and then he made up a few more for good measure.

How long? How long had he been out and trussed up like a self-basting Butterball? Hours? A day? Longer?

He'd better get used to it. The zip tie was not going to untie itself.

Grunting, Dade wriggled around, searching behind him for a craggy surface to rub the plastic zip tie against. Friction. He needed friction.

Friction made him think of last night.

Last night made him think of Natalie.

Thinking of Natalie made him smile.

Briefly.

The smile disappeared when he realized that if Lars cleaned out his room at the B&B and removed his Harley from the caverns parking lot, Natalie would believe he'd left town. Run out on her. She would not alert the authorities. She would not come looking for him. She would assume that he was Mr. Wham-Bam-Thank-You-Ma'am. That he'd stolen her virginity and left her cold.

That killed him. He was hurting her and he'd never intended it. *Ah shit, Natty. I'm so damn sorry.*

He cursed Lars again, sawed the zip tie vigorously against a sharp rock formation behind him. Sawed and cursed, cursed and sawed. Abraded his wrists until they were raw and bleeding, but he didn't stop until finally the plastic zip tie weakened and gave way.

"Arrr." He growled in triumph and leaped to his feet.

Instant dizziness hit him. His ears rang. He saw stars.

Dade put out a hand to the cave wall to steady himself. He'd once had a dog named Taser. A pit bull mix. God, he'd loved that dog, but his junkie daddy had traded Taser for a teenth of crack. God, his life had been messed up. Hell, maybe it was better if Natalie did think he'd just run out on her.

A hollow sadness dug into him and he sank back down on the ground, completely overcome by despair.

He'd lost her, the shining gold star that was Natalie Mc-Cleary. Lost her before he'd had the chance to tell her how much he loved her.

He'd been afraid to love her for this very reason. Afraid that if he allowed himself to love, he'd lose her just like he lost Taser. *Boo-hoo, Vega. You gonna sit there like a whiny girl, or are you gonna do something to get out of this and go claim your woman?*

Dade gritted his teeth and pushed up from the cave floor, slowly this time, prepared for the ascent.

He felt around with his foot, trying to get his bearings, and discovered he was on a rock ledge about three feet wide. Below him was a sharp drop-off.

How far down? Damn, he wished he had his penlight. He felt around for a pebble, found one, tossed it off the ledge, and listened to it fall.

Six feet down at least.

What about in front of him? How far did the ledge run before it too dropped off? Which direction led out of the cave and which led deeper into the cave?

Dade hesitated, trying to get his bearings and formulate a plan.

A faint sound caught his attention. Rats. Probably rats. Cocking his head, he strained to listen. His raspy breathing filled his ears.

There it was again, a faint tapping noise.

Probably just water dripping off stalactites. Or rats. He kept listening, waited.

There it was again. Rhythmic tapping.

It wasn't his imagination. Three quick taps, followed by three taps spaced further apart, followed by three more quick taps. A smile spread across his face.

Morse code. SOS.

Red?

Hope surged through him. "Red," he called out. "Red, is that you?"

The tapping sound came again, faster this time.

His smile widened. It *was* Red. It had to be his buddy. "Hang on, I'm coming for you."

More tapping, but lower, fainter this time. Red probably couldn't speak. Was no doubt weak as hell if he'd been trapped in here for eleven days.

"Buddy, I don't have a flashlight. Can you keep tapping so I can find you? Doesn't have to be a lot. A couple of taps every few minutes or so."

Tap. Tap.

The sound echoed off the cave walls, making it difficult to figure out precisely where the sound was coming from.

The right. It was coming from his right. At least he hoped it was. Dade steeled his jaw and set his course. Keeping one hand on the wall, he moved forward, pausing every so often to wait for the next tap. At times, he called to Red, encouraging his friend to hang in there.

The farther he went, the thinner the ledge grew. It was painfully slow going in the dark. After about a half hour, the ledge became so narrow, his foot slipped.

Rocks slid under his feet and he kicked at them. The rock fell with a sharp echo. The drop-off was deeper now, from the sound of it, twelve feet or more. A tumble off the ledge could impale him on a stalagmite. Happy thoughts.

Was that what had happened to Red? He cringed. What kind of shape was his buddy in?

"Red," he called, and waited for the tapping.

It didn't come.

"Red? You still with me?"

A long minute passed. Two. Three.

Ah, shit.

Dade held his breath. "Red!"

Red, Red, Red, his voice echoed back to him.

Finally, there came a faint tapping.

"Got it. Save your strength. I'm on the way." He was on the move again, forced by the narrowing ledge to walk toe to toe. The ceiling of the cave was getting lower too. Occasional stalactites skimmed the top of his head.

Gingerly, he put out his foot to take another step and felt nothing. The ledge was completely gone.

Immediately, he tried to retreat, but the remaining rocks crumbled and Dade plunged headlong into the black abyss.

Chapter 20

Trust that love will sustain you in your darkest hour.

—Millie Greenwood

It was the Fourth of July and three days had passed since Dade abandoned her. Natalie still couldn't wrap her mind around it. Yes, she could believe that he'd flaked out. The man was terrified of his feelings, but what she could not accept was that he'd left town without finding Red. What if Dade had found Red and they'd left town together?

Her heart ached. She'd been so stupid to tell him that she loved him. She'd spooked him and he'd run away. *You don't know that for certain.* She'd told Dade she trusted him. Now was the time to prove it.

Luckily, the Fourth of July celebrations kept her from dwelling on it too much. She had responsibilities, obligations—to her B&B guests, to her family. Everyone expected something of her. So she buried herself in work and for short stretches of time, she didn't think about Dade.

But the nights, oh, those long, miserable nights where she had nothing to do but think, they were the worst.

For the most part, sleep escaped her. She would lie in bed, staring at the ceiling, twisting the bracelet around and around on her wrist (she couldn't bring herself to take it off), and remembering. She recalled in crystal-clear detail everything about him—his delicious masculine scent, the taste of his lips, his lopsided smile, the scars.

So many scars.

He was right. She was naive. Naive and foolish. For believing in love at first sight, for thinking she could have a happily-ever-after with him. He'd tried to warn her. She'd give him that, but she'd ignored the signs and she'd trusted him anyway and he'd betrayed her in the most fundamental way that a man could betray a woman—abandoning her after she'd given him her heart, soul, mind, and virginity.

And yet, she loved him still.

She could no more stop her love for him than she could dam up a river with her body, and it hurt so much. She been raised on the Cupid legend, and although she'd cut her teeth on the concept of love at first sight, her belief had faltered until it happened to her. Now, she *knew* love at first sight was real, but what no one told her was how much damn pain was involved.

Love hurt.

She bought "Love Hurts" on iTunes (several versions, but her favorite was the hard, soulful rendition by Nazareth), and she played it over and over on her iPod. She cursed Cupid—the town, the stalagmite, and the Roman god.

When her family asked questions about Dade, she quickly changed the subject and distracted herself with work, and when Carol Ann asked if and when she would have an answer for Shot Through the Heart, Natalie just up and left the community center.

She had her own grief to deal with. She couldn't handle Shot Through the Heart's dilemma. At least Shot Through the Heart had a decision to make. When Dade left, he had taken away Natalie's choice.

On the morning of the Fourth, she awoke with a pounding headache and her heart was heavier than it had been on the previous days. Time had worsened the pain, not improved it, as it was finally sinking in that he truly was not coming back.

The B&B emptied out early, everyone headed for the activities at Lake Cupid with picnic baskets Pearl had packed. Even Lars and Gizmo were gone. It was just Natalie rambling around the house. Zoey tried to get Natalie to come boating with her and some of their cousins, but she turned down the offer.

Listlessly, she ambled out to Dade's room, stood in the door, with her arms crossed over her chest. She thought of Mingus Dill and Millie Greenwood and Wallis Simpson. They'd all gone to see the Cupid stalagmite and asked for heavenly intervention in their love affairs. It had worked for them, but was it simply happy coincidence? What about all the people who had written to Cupid or visited the statue whose dreams of love had *not* come true? *Those* stories never got any press. People only talked about the happily-ever-after tales.

Maybe Mingus's and Millie's and Wallis's pleas had simply been self-fulfilling prophecies?

Why not go see the stalagmite? Give it a shot. It's not like she had anything to lose.

Yes, but wasn't that holding on to desperate hope when she should instead be trying to move on? She should forget Dade. Except she knew there would be no forgetting him.

Ever.

The Cupid Caverns were closed on holidays, but as one of Millie Greenwood's direct descendants, Natalie had a key to the padlock that secured the front gate.

She went to the front desk, opened the desk drawer, and reached for the key. It wasn't in its usual slot. She rifled around in the desk and finally found it. Zoey must have used it. No doubt sneaking in after the caverns were closed with some of her friends. Had Zoey had copies made? She'd have to check on that.

Pocketing the key, she then went to put a flashlight, a bottle of water, and a couple of PowerBars in her tote bag. Because Zoey and her cousins had taken the van, she walked next door and asked Junie Mae to give her a ride up to the caverns.

"Sugar, why are you going up there?" Junie Mae asked.

"I need to be alone."

"It's about Dade, isn't it?"

Natalie nodded mutely. If she said anything, she'd burst into tears.

Junie Mae pulled up into the cavern parking lot. "When do you want me to come back and get you?"

"I've got my cell phone. I'll call Zoey to come get me when I'm ready."

"You sure? We could go back to my place and get drunk on margaritas."

"I'd be poor company."

"Sweetie, I'm so sorry things didn't work out between you and Dade." Junie Mae squeezed her arm.

"Thanks." Natalie hopped out of the car quick before she broke down. She waved as Junie Mae pulled out of the parking lot.

She trudged to the front gate and unlocked it and then clicked the lock closed again behind her. She didn't want anyone else coming in. She needed solitude. Hopefully, Zoey hadn't had copies of the key made and distributed among her friends.

The caverns were eerie in their silence. She'd been visiting this place since before she could walk, and it still moved her every time she entered nature's cathedral. The wall sconces stayed on all the time, so she wasn't in the dark. She inhaled the musty air, and with a heavy heart, limped down the path toward the Cupid Cave.

She imagined her great-grandmother Millie walking this same path, in similar despair. History. Tradition. Her blood ran thick with it.

The Cupid formation looked as ancient as Roman ruins. The sight of the stalagmite never failed to move her. Pretty damn majestic. It was easy to understand the town's fascination with the thing. In the hushed quiet, it felt like hallowed ground.

Natalie knelt at the stalagmites, closed her eyes, and clasped her hands. "Dear Cupid, please, please let him come back to me."

She knelt there waiting, but the despair did not lift. She did not feel comforted.

Slowly, she opened one eye, and stared at Cupid. "Work with me here. I've been answering letters on your behalf for ten years, the least you could do was give me some kind a sign."

A drop of water dripped on her from a stalactite.

"That's it? That's all I get?"

Another plop of water hit her square on her upturned forehead.

"Message received loud and clear. I get it. You're trying to tell me I'm all wet. Thanks for nothing." She dragged herself to her feet, sighed, and turned to leave.

And that's when she saw something she'd never before seen in the cul-de-sac cave—an open passageway leading deeper into the caverns.

Pain.

So much friggin' pain.

Dade lay in the darkness engulfed in pain.

His shoulder felt like a giant had taken him by the arm and pulled it from his socket the way little boys dismantled grasshopper appendages. He kept drifting in and out of consciousness. Was he dreaming? If he was dreaming, he'd better wake the hell up.

Nausea roiled in his stomach. Hard, sharp objects poked into his back. Fear and worry and hopelessness closed around him.

He heard tapping again. Red. His buddy was tapping.

Days had gone by. He didn't know how many. He'd lost all track of time. He knew Red was nearby, but he had no idea how close. Dade had talked to Red, but his buddy was too weak to do more than utter an occasional soft whisper that he could barely understand.

Since his fall into the pit Dade had slowly pieced together over time that Red had grown suspicious about the number of kids coming into Chantilly's who appeared to be underage, and yet they all had what appeared to be valid driver's licenses. Red's suspicions had also been aroused by the number of illegal immigrants who came to the back porch at the bar looking for Lars or Gizmo.

Early one Sunday morning when he was out for a walk, he'd seen Lars and Gizmo opening the padlock and slipping into the caverns on a day they were closed. He had wondered about it, but it hadn't really seemed suspicious until June 19, the night he'd gone to Marfa.

Stan had told him he'd heard from a friend of his in law enforcement that there was an investigation into drivers' licenses and ID forgeries in southwest Texas. Red didn't have anything concrete to take to the authorities other than his Navy SEAL sixth sense, so he'd decided to follow Lars and Gizmo and see if he could find out what they were up to.

That's when he'd found their secret room inside the Cupid Cave. They'd caught him, but he'd managed to get off the "Tanked" Mayday text to Dade before escaping deeper into the cave.

He'd only had the light of his cell phone to guide him, but it hadn't been enough to keep him from plunging off the ledge. He'd lost his phone in the fall and Dade had been his only hope of rescue. Lars and Gizmo had left him for dead. He'd survived this long only because the SEALs had taught him to always be prepared and he always carried a package of peanuts and beef jerky in his pocket. He'd rationed out the food, nibbling a bit every day until it was gone, and he drank the moisture that dripped down the cave wall.

Now, Dade was in the exact same predicament.

Odd how irony was usually not the least bit funny.

"Hey, now we can die together." Red had given a raspy cough when he finally concluded the story that had taken days to tell, before lapsing into a silence so long that Dade got scared. Red had been down here for two weeks with a broken leg. He had to be close to death. Only his stubbornness and strength of will had kept him alive this long.

Dade had tried to drag himself from the pit, but with a dislocated shoulder and no flashlight, his attempts had been quickly defeated. He'd been lying here trying to formulate some kind of plan, but his brain wasn't cooperating. He hadn't had anything to eat since his last meal with Natalie in her bed, although he'd taken Red's cue and drank the water tracking down the cave walls. His reasoning was fuzzy and he kept dozing off, and then through the mist of shifting consciousness, he thought he heard something.

Footsteps.

Was he hallucinating?

Grunting against the pain in his shoulder, he forced himself to sit up. Was Lars or Gizmo coming back to finish them off? Once the blinding pain eased off a bit, he concentrated on listening.

Yes, footsteps.

"Red," he whispered. "You hear that?"

Red tapped weakly.

"Christ, it's got to be Bakke or the punk kid. Who else could it be?" Dade asked.

The footsteps grew louder.

All his muscles tensed. The person—it sounded like one set of footsteps—was moving in a slow, halting gait, clearly having trouble navigating the narrow rock ledge.

Several long moments passed.

Dade's pulse slammed through his head. They were sitting ducks. God, he hated this. He gritted his teeth. Had Bakke come to shoot them? Maybe that wouldn't be so bad. Put them out of their misery.

Except that he would never see Natalie again. His gut wrenched. He'd had three days to adjust to that reality, and yet, he had not. The thought of never touching her again ripped him apart.

There was a thin play of light on the cave wall above the pit where he and Red were lying.

Desperately, he felt around for a weapon, a rock, anything to throw at whichever captor was about to appear, and the hand of his good arm closed over a baseball-sized stone. *C'mon you son of a bitch, I'm not going down without a fight.* He had to get back to Natalie or die trying.

The flashlight beam bobbled directly above their heads. As the footsteps grew closer, they became more defined, and Dade identified a slight dragging sound.

He knew that gait! It was very dear to him.

Then a beloved face appeared in the darkness.

It wasn't Bakke or Gizmo on the narrow ledge above them, but Natalie!

A few feet ahead of her, the ledge path that she'd been following dropped off into darkness.

Natalie paused, confused. After seeing the opening in the Cupid cave, she'd found the lever mechanism inset into the cave wall and camouflaged as a rock formation.

The second she saw it, Natalie knew this had to be the mythical secret room the old-timers whispered about, the place where bootleggers had stored illegal bottles of alcohol during Prohibition. She'd never really believed in that rumor, but she was proven wrong.

She'd followed the narrow passage, and several feet inside found an empty room. There was a second door on the opposite side of the room. What she couldn't figure out was how the passageway had gotten opened in the first place. Had the lever mechanism somehow just sprung open on its own?

"Hello?" she'd called out into the darkness.

There had been no answer.

Hitching her tote bag up on her shoulder, she'd opened the second door.

It led deeper into the cavern. Excitement had raced through her. This looked like the place where Mingus Dill supposedly holed up from the posse. The lure of Cupid's history drew her deeper inside.

She tugged her flashlight from her tote, happy to have something to think about besides her ruined love affair with Dade. The path was littered with rocks and pebbles. There was no upkeep back here. No caretakers to clear the way. This was raw, original, unsullied by visitors. It was an adventure.

The temperature inside was much cooler than in the main cavern. She shivered and wished for a sweater. *Go back. You're not prepared for spelunking.*

She didn't know what compelled her to keep moving forward, but she did. Traveling at least a quarter of a mile, maybe farther. Maybe having been with Dade had made her unafraid to take chances. Nothing could hurt as much as his abandonment, right? *It's great news that you're ready to grab life by the throat and all that, but there's daring and then there's stupid. Turn back.*

But still, she kept going until she came to the end of the line where the rocky ledge played out. Game over. Head back.

She turned.

"Natalie!"

The sound of Dade's voice rushed over her like a soothing balm on a hot sunburn, and it stopped her in her tracks. Had she really heard him call to her or was it her imagination?

"Dade?"

"Down here, Natalie. Be careful. That ledge is precarious."

Tentatively, she shone the light over the edge of the ledge. Fourteen feet below her lay a body. She gasped, focused the light beam on the still form.

It was Red. He was motionless on his back with his eyes closed, and from this distance, she couldn't tell if he was breathing or not. His face was deadly pale and his right leg was at an odd angle. Clearly broken. Her own right leg twinged in empathy and her chest tightened.

"Dade? Where are you?"

"To your left."

She shone the light to the left and found him about six feet from Red's still form. He was propped up against the cave wall, surrounded by massive stalagmites. It was a miracle he hadn't been impaled in his fall from the ledge, because obviously that was what had happened. He'd fallen off the ledge while searching for Red. His face was etched with pain.

Her heart leaped into her throat. He hadn't run out on her! But he *was* in deep trouble. "What's happened?"

"Dislocated shoulder. I'll live." He quirked a wry grin. "Now that you're here."

"I'm going to toss my tote bag down to you. It's got water in it and two PowerBars."

"Thanks," he said gratefully, his voice raw and raspy.

She pitched the tote down, aiming to get as close to him as possible. It landed at his feet. He had to lean for it and he cried out in pain.

Natalie slapped a palm over her mouth. His pain was a knife to her gut.

He grimaced, but managed to snag the tote bag. He had to lean back against the wall and rest for a minute.

It was so hard having to stand here and watch him suffer, to be unable to go to him. Her arms ached to hold him.

"How did you find us?" he asked.

"There was an opening in the cave wall. I followed the passageway and it led me here, but I had no idea you were down here. I was just exploring."

"The secret door was left open? Did you find the room?"

"Yes."

"Did you see the fake IDs?"

"What? No. The room was completely empty."

"They've cleared out their equipment."

"What equipment?"

"Is it the Fourth of July?"

"Yes."

"The cavern is closed on holidays. How did you get in?"

"I'm a Greenwood direct descendent. The cave is on family land. I have a key."

"Do you keep your key where Lars could have access to it and make copies of it for himself?"

"Yes," she admitted. "I keep it in the front desk and sometimes Lars watches the desk for me, but I don't understand what you're getting at."

"They must have been waiting for the holiday so that they could move their operation without interruption."

"I'm confused. Who are you talking about?"

Dade told her a story then that she could scarcely believe about Lars and Gizmo and high-quality identification forgery. Was it true? Or was his thinking skewered from being in a cave for three days with a dislocated shoulder?

"Are you sure?" She nibbled her bottom lip. "Lars and Gizmo involved in counterfeiting?"

"Lars pulled a gun on me and Gizmo Tasered me and they did that to Red." Dade motioned in the direction where his buddy lay.

Natalie put a hand to her forehead. "I can't wrap my mind around this."

"How is Red?" he asked.

She shone her light in Red's direction again. He still hadn't moved. "He looks bad. I'm going for help."

"Be very careful, Natalie. I'm not kidding when I say Bakke and Gizmo are armed and dangerous."

Moving as fast as she dared, Natalie went back the way she'd come.

It seemed as if she'd been walking for days. Natalie's leg hurt up into her hip from maneuvering the rough terrain. She was cold and damp and her head ached. Every step was torture as her mind kept stirring up terrible possibilities for what lay both ahead and behind her.

Natalie gritted her teeth. *Keep moving.* It was the only option. She had to get help. And what would happen if she got back to the room and found Lars or Gizmo waiting with a gun?

But there's no way they could know she was in the caverns. Junie Mae had brought her here, so she'd left no vehicle in the parking lot to give her away, and her neighbor was the only one who knew she was at the caverns. Still, even if they didn't have a gun on them and they caught her coming out of the cave, they would know something was up.

Don't let them catch you coming out of the cave.

She had tried to call Calvin on her cell phone and tell him what was going down, but she couldn't get any reception this deep inside the cave.

How far *had* she walked? Shouldn't she be getting close now?

She stopped a moment to rest, leaned her back against the wall, and ran a hand down her leg. The flashlight battery was growing dim so she switched it off and tucked it into her pocket. It was so dark without the flashlight beam to guide her. So very dark and lonely.

To comfort herself, she thought of Dade. He had not run out on her after they'd made love. She couldn't wait for him to hold her in his arms again. *Get a move on. The sooner you get out of here, the sooner that will happen.*

She pushed off from the wall, debating whether to walk in the darkness for a while and save the flashlight battery or turn it on again, when she heard muted voices.

Her heart somersaulted into her throat. She recognized the voices as belonging Lars and Gizmo. They were close. She must be near the second door of the secret room.

Panic spread through her, wildfire quick. What to do? Go back and wait for them to leave?

The stupid, trusting part of her balked. Even though Dade had told her what Lars and Gizmo were involved in, she found it difficult to accept. These two men had lived in her home. How could they want to harm her? Maybe she could reason with them.

Don't be naive, Natalie. For godsakes, listen to Dade. He knows what he's talking about.

Pulse racing, she turned to go back the way she came, but she couldn't move quickly in the dark and she was too afraid to turn the flashlight back on in case they saw the beam.

They were arguing now, their voices angry, but the cave warped the sound and she couldn't make out what they were saying. She kept moving away from them, trying to be as quiet as possible.

She heard a clanging sound and more arguing. Her fist knotted around the flashlight and she forced herself not to turn it back on. Her breath slipped shallowly over her lips. There was a strange scent in the air. Stranger than the normal musty cave smell. Her nostrils twitched.

Lars and Gizmo were making more noises, banging things around. What were they doing?

Then all at once there was complete quiet.

She stopped walking. Held her breath. Strained to hear something. Nothing.

But instead of putting her at ease, their sudden silence bothered her even more than the noise had.

One minute passed. Nothing. Then two minutes. Three.

The hairs on the back of her neck lifted and the most ominous feeling passed through her.

And then came the explosion.

Chapter 21

Love can bridge any gulf.

—Millie Greenwood

The blast shook the cave. The force knocked Dade from his sitting position against the wall. Rubble rained around him and dirt filled his mouth.

In utter shock, he let out a terse curse as his mind scrambled to deduce what had happened. Whatever explosive had caused the detonation had to be something fairly small or it would have brought the whole cave down. From the sound of it, maybe a quarter of a stick of dynamite or even just a blasting cap. Just enough of a blast to seal off the back caves behind the secret room, but not enough to destroy the entire caverns.

It hit him then, exactly what was going on. That son of a bitch Bakke had set off a detonation to cause a cave-in, entombing inside the two people who could send him to prison on forgery or counterfeiting charges. Two loners without family who would never really be missed.

Natalie!

Dear God, where was Natalie?

His blood ran cold. Where was she? Had she interrupted Bakke's explosion? Had he killed her too? Maybe she'd gotten out. He clung to the hope. Prayed she'd gotten out alive before Bakke and Gizmo had come back to cause the cave-in.

"What the fuck was that?" Red croaked.

"Bakke," Dade said. "He's making sure we don't get out."

Fresh worries washed over him. What if Natalie had been hurt by the blast? If she was still in the cave at the time of the explosion, she would be much closer to the source of the blast than he and Red were. She might even be dead.

Dade clamped his teeth together. No. He refused to think like that. He had to get out of here. Had to go after her. He tried to stand but the pain in his shoulder knocked him to his knees. Waves of nausea washed over him. Dade whistled in air through convulsing lungs.

He tried to stand again.

An aftershock ran through the cave. More rubble fell. Something hit him on the head, and that was the last thing Dade knew.

Consciousness returned to Natalie in degrees.

First, it felt as if she were swimming up from a dark pool, air-hungry and desperate. Hours later, her eyes popped open and she stared into total darkness.

"Dade," she whispered, and fell into the fog again.

Finally, the incessant ringing in her ears roused her enough to sit up and rest her spinning head in her hands.

An explosion. There'd been an explosion. Had Lars and Gizmo set it off?

Impossible.

This had to be some kind of horrible dream.

Natalie groaned. No dream. The dirt in her mouth and nose certified it.

With shaky hands she groped around for the flashlight and flicked on the thin, fading beam of light and saw to her horror that her escape route was completely blocked by boulders humped up like camel backs.

There was no way out. Absolutely none.

As she studied the massive pile of rocks going all the way to the ceiling of the cave, that last gasp of light winked out, plunging her into inky blackness.

She shook the flashlight. Heard the battery rattle. Clicked the switch off and on. Nothing.

This was it. They were all done for. She and Dade and Red. Bested by a senior citizen and a computer geek. It was all over. They would never get out of here.

She wondered how long it would take to die of starvation and dehydration. Apparently, Red had somehow managed to stay alive for two weeks, but he was an ex–Navy SEAL. He had survival skills. He could last longer than most people. If she was lucky, it would take her less time to die.

Lovely thought.

Way out. She needed a way out.

Options. What were her options? She could go back to where Red and Dade were.

In the dark? Risk falling to her death?

Either way, she was dead. What did the method matter? Or she could sit here and wait for rescue. Someone would have surely heard the explosion. People would be here soon. Emergency workers. Volunteers. The smart thing to do was stay put.

But what if help didn't arrive immediately? People were out at the lake, celebrating the Fourth, shooting off fireworks. If it was indeed still the Fourth. She had no idea how much time had passed.

Junie Mae knew she was here. Someone *would* come looking. The whole town of Cupid would come looking. That's what her community did. Rally about one another. She held on to that knowledge. They would be rescued.

But in time to save Red's life? The man was hanging on by a strand as thin as a spider's silk. He might already be dead.

Natalie brought her knees to her chest and rested her head on her knees. The muscles in her right leg jumped and twitched involuntarily.

Rest.

She needed to rest. Regroup. Think this through.

She wished she had a bottle of water. Wished she had a PowerBar. While she was wishing, why not wish for a T-bone steak and an appletini? Why not wish for her pillow-top mattress and goose-down pillow?

None of those things was going to come true so she might as well wish for the stars. Why not wish that Dade would tell her that he loved her? Why not wish that he wasn't terrified of loving her the way she loved him? Why not wish for an elaborate wedding held in the botanical gardens beside the Cupid statue? Why not wish for three children, all of whom had Dade's dark good looks? Why not wish for the world?

Pity isn't going to solve your problem.

Right. Suck it up.

Except when she tried to stand, her leg was so exhausted she could barely lever herself up. She'd pushed herself to her limits. Like it or not, she was going to have to rest.

Sometime later, Natalie awakened again.

The tiny stream of light drilling down through the top of the cave shone a small spotlight on her lap.

Joyously, she turned her face upward. There was a way out!

Except the cave ceiling was a good fifteen feet above her. Cool air blew against her face. Her throat was parched, her leg numb from being curled up underneath her. Getting to the ceiling meant scaling fifteen feet of unstable boulders.

With a bum leg.

With a deep-seated fear of heights.

Suddenly, her salvation seemed like utter damnation. It might as well be Everest. Dread lodged in her throat. She had no alternative. She had to face her greatest fear. She had to climb that mountain.

"Sir Edmund Hillary," she muttered. "Here I come."

Natalie stumbled to her feet, shaking her numb leg to get the pins and needles out. Slowly it came to life, tingling painfully. She tried to put her weight on the leg, but her knee gave way and she fell forward.

She thrust out her hands to catch herself, her palms ramming into sharp rock points. *Ow, ow.*

Her left palm was bleeding, lacerated. Not seriously, but painful, messy. Resolutely, she wiped her palm against the side of her jeans and glanced up at the pile of rocks again.

C'mon. You can do this. You dragged yourself down a mountain with a broken leg at nine years old, how hard can it be to drag yourself up one?

Hard as hell.

Her leg was finally coming around. She tested it again and it held her weight. *Just think, in a few minutes you could be out of here and going for help. Keep your eye on the prize.*

Dust motes danced in the pencil-thin light shining down on her. It had to be late morning. She had only a few hours before the sun moved down the horizon and she lost the light.

Get moving.

She obeyed, going along to the far side of the boulder pile that seemed to offer the easiest path up. Carefully, she positioned her feet, hiked her right leg up, and dragged it over a bottom boulder. The stretch was almost more than she could handle, and when she pushed off with her left foot, she sent herself falling over the boulder. She lay there a moment, stunned at how difficult that had been, and it was only the first step.

Keep going.

She pulled herself up, found a handhold in the rock above, and took another step.

The stones were slick and smooth. It would be so easy to lose her balance.

She cast a terrified glance down. It was only a foot but it felt like a mile. She gritted her teeth. *Don't look down.* She took another step and another. By the time she was halfway up the pile, her arms were trembling so bad that she had to stop and catch her breath.

Don't look down, don't look down, don't look down.
She looked down.

Big mistake.

The floor of the cave yawned below her, big and dark and deadly.

A crushing sensation pressed in on her chest, squashed her lungs. She curled her fingers around the rock she clutched, frozen by fear. She hung there for the longest time, stymied by fear. She could not move forward, could not slide back. She was stuck.

A metaphor for her life. She smiled. What a stupid time to get amused by her predicament. But it was true. Her fear had kept her stuck. She had been too afraid to dare to dream. She'd taken the safe path. Done what was expected. She'd been admired for it, lauded for it, but deep down, she'd been disappointed in herself.

Now was the time to get over that fear. It was here. It was real. *Move forward. Prove you're not stuck. Prove you can take charge of your life. Face your fears. You are in control of your destiny, Natalie. Nothing can hold you back.*

Emboldened by that pep talk, she tightened her jaw, let go of the rock with one hand, and reached higher. Taking the risk. Taking the gamble.

What if you get to the top and you can't dig your way out of the cave? What then?

She cringed. She couldn't think about that now. It was all she could do to scale this damn pile of rocks.

The thin beam of sunlight was waning. She had to hurry.

C'mon, c'mon. You can do this. For Red. For Dade. For yourself.

One hand followed the other. She pulled up her right

leg. The damn thing had held her back so many times. Her wound was at the root of her fear. She refused to let it pull her down.

With a heavy grunt, she moved her leg to the next boulder.

The rock pile wavered.

Natalie gasped, paused.

Please don't fall.

The rock stabilized.

She tried again, skimming quickly over one unstable rock to the next one. She was higher now than she'd ever been since the accident, a good ten feet off the ground. Halfway. She was halfway to the light.

Keep moving.

Her arms were trembling. Her leg was heavy. Her stomach was queasy, but her resolve was strong. Dade. She was doing this for Dade. He was counting on her and she would not let him down.

Dizziness gripped her. If she fell now, she'd be dead.

You won't fall. You can't fall. You are strong. You will make it.

Another step and then another. Her fingers clawed at the rocks. She broke nail after nail, didn't care. All that mattered was getting to the top before the light vanished.

An hour passed.

Two.

Her toil continued. Slowly, methodically. Every time a fresh fear surfaced, she'd tamp it down by remembering Dade's face. He needed her. Red needed her. She had to do this.

On and on she climbed.

When pebbles skittered beneath her feet and dropped

to the ground, she would stop, wipe the sweat from her brow, and keep going. She felt like an ant pushing a rubber tree plant. She had high hopes. Rescue.

Finally, the impossible happened, and she reached the pinnacle.

She paused to haul in hungry gasps of air. She rested her head on the top rock. Pressed her lips to it. Success. After all she'd been through. She'd faced her greatest fear and won.

But the victory was short-lived.

Now came the hard part. Balancing on the top boulder, which was about the size of a hassock, while investigating the crack in the ceiling.

She inhaled sharply, glanced down.

Blackness lay below. The rocks were nothing but dark humps in the shadows. Cold, hard stone awaited her if she fell.

Turning her face toward the diminishing light, she reached out a hand, touched the cave ceiling, and rejoiced. It wasn't stone but earth as she hoped. The outside world was only a few inches of dirt away.

She poked at the ceiling with a finger. Dirt shifted in on her, filled her mouth. She spat, winced. Ugh. Dug in with all five fingers of her right hand while her left hand held steady to the last boulder, her feet positioned in a wide stance.

Her fingers widened the hole, and hope soared.

Greedily, she grabbed for another handful, digging the dirt, dropping it to the floor, hearing it spatter. There was grass now. Handfuls of it. Faster and faster, she snatched handfuls of earth and dried grass. More dirt fell in her face, burned her eyes. She spat again, swiped at her face, closed her eyes, and kept digging.

She went back for another handful, her fist broke through, and she felt warm air and sun on her fingers. Blinking, she opened her eyes. She'd made a hole the size of a saucer. She arched her back, reaching for another handful of dirt to widen the opening.

Big mistake.

Her right leg slipped from its toehold and she hung suspended. Her left arm and left leg clinging to the rock, her right arm and right leg swinging in mid-air.

She threw down the dirt, scrambled to find something to grab on to with her right arm, found a spot.

Gravity tugged at her.

She wobbled. Her blood stampeded through her veins, pounded in her ears.

No! She would not lose this battle. She would not fall!

She wobbled, hanging twenty feet above the cave floor. Inches from freedom.

Can't fall. Won't fall.

She hung, swung, unable to move. Her limbs were exhausted. She was tapped out. This was how it was going to end. The story of Natalie McCleary over in a mere twenty-nine years.

Turn out the lights, the party's over.

And then she heard a voice, far away, but familiar.

"Natalie!"

"Mommy?" she mumbled. "Mommy, is that you?"

"Natalie!"

The voice was coming closer. Was she already gone and hearing dead relatives? Her arms trembled, defeated. This was it. She could just let go and fall into the arms of her mother. Let go and be free.

"Natalie!"

She cocked her head. The voice was almost upon her now, but even though it was familiar, it was not her mother. She was not dead.

It was Zoey!

"Here!" she cried out. "I'm down here."

Relief gave her the strength to hold on, to pull herself up and over that top boulder. She lay there gasping, thanking God, and trying to wrap her mind around the idea that she'd been saved.

Chapter 22

Love at first sight is a rare gift indeed.
                                        —Millie Greenwood

In the emergency room at Cupid General, Natalie refused treatment. There was nothing wrong with her beyond a few scrapes and bruises. She wanted the staff to give all their attention to Dade and Red. She sat with her family and friends packing the waiting room.

Red had been taken into surgery to repair his broken leg and they'd sedated Dade in order to put his dislocated shoulder back into its socket. It had been out of the joint for so long that the muscles had started to stiffen.

Calvin came in while they were waiting, holding his patrol hat in his hands. "They caught Lars and Gizmo trying to cross the border into Mexico at Presidio. Texas Rangers are bringing them back here to face charges."

"Did they admit what they'd done?"

"We caught them with hundreds of fake IDs on them, so they couldn't deny it. They even told us the reason they waited until the Fourth of July to cause the cave-in. They didn't want to hurt any innocent bystanders so they picked a day the caverns would be closed. Plus with the fireworks from the Fourth of July, people wouldn't notice the explosion. That, and they needed time to get their hands on the dynamite."

"But they were okay with leaving Red and Dade in the cave to suffer in the meantime?" Natalie shuddered.

"Just for the record, Lars feels really bad that you were in the cave when they imploded it. They'd just meant to seal in Red and Dade. Since you hadn't left a vehicle in the parking lot of the caverns because Junie Mae gave you a ride, they had no idea that you'd gone inside."

"Would it have stopped Lars if he had known?"

Calvin shrugged. "Maybe. He did say he was happy that you were alive."

"So he was brave enough to kill Red and Dade, but not ruthless enough to kill me?" Natalie snorted. "Why? Because I'm the helpless crippled girl?"

"There's nothing helpless about you, cuz." Calvin crossed the room to rest a hand on Natalie's shoulders. "How are you holding up?"

"I'm hanging in there."

"Thanks to you and Red and Dade, we've busted the biggest counterfeit ID operation in southwest Texas."

"How badly were the caverns damaged?"

"Miraculously, the Cupid stalagmite is intact, although there's some argument that Cupid's arrow slipped a bit in the blast."

Natalie breathed a sigh of relief. "Thank heavens for that."

"But the bootleg room is history."

Natalie stabbed her fingers through her hair. "There is one thing that's been bothering me."

"What's that?"

"How did Lars even know the secret room was there? I mean we're Greenwoods and we didn't know about it."

"Apparently Jasper Grass told him."

"How did Jasper know about the room?"

"Jasper's great-granddaddy was the biggest bootlegger west of the Pecos and he passed that little tidbit of information on to his kinfolk. A family secret."

"Was Jasper involved in the counterfeiting?"

"No. We checked him out. He's clean."

"That's good."

"I do have some bad news for Dade. I was thinking maybe you could break it to him for me."

Natalie's stomach clenched. "What's that?"

"Lars and Gizmo admitted that they put his Harley in the secret room just before they blew it up. It's gone."

"Oh no. He is going to be heartbroken. He loves that motorcycle."

A nurse popped her head into the waiting room. "Natalie, you can go in to see Dade now. He's a little dopey, but asking to see you."

Natalie hopped up and followed the nurse.

"He's in behind there." She pointed to one of the curtained areas.

Natalie pushed back the curtain to find Dade resting on a gurney and covered by a green sheet. He had an IV in his arm.

"Hi." He gave her a drunken little smile.

"Hey, big guy." She walked over to the bed.

"You did it. You got us rescued."

"But you saved Red. If you hadn't been so suspicious of Lars, he and Gizmo would have gotten away with it and Red would be dead."

"How is Red?"

"In surgery. He's malnourished and dehydrated and he's got a long road to recovery, but the doctors say he's going to make it."

"That's good." His words slurred a bit.

She wanted to touch him, to kiss him, but she didn't know how to begin.

"You know what," he said cheerily.

"What?"

"That medication is good stuff."

She smiled. "I'm just happy you're feeling better, but I'm afraid I've got some bad news."

"What's that?"

She told him about the motorcycle.

"Hey, it's just a motorcycle."

"That represented freedom to you."

He reached for her hand. "Maybe freedom isn't so important to me anymore."

Her heart skipped a beat. "Beau Jenkins is trying to selling his Harley. Maybe you could buy his."

"Maybe we should just take the money and buy a trip to Paris."

"We?" Her voice went up an octave.

He rubbed his thumb over her knuckles. "As in you and me."

Natalie gulped, moistened her lip. This was her dream. Paris. And she'd overcome her fear of flying. Why not?

"I was thinking maybe we should make it a very special, once-in-a-lifetime trip," Dade murmured. "Include a visit to a real Prada store where I buy you your first pair of Prada shoes."

"What are you saying?" Her heart was a butterfly in her chest.

"I'm thinking boots. For the honeymoon. Black. Thigh-high. Stilettos."

"What?" She blinked, scarcely able to believe what she was hearing.

"Okay, scratch the boots. That's my fantasy. You tell me what kind of shoes you want."

"The boots are fine. But are you sure we should be having this conversation? You're drugged up. You don't know what you're saying." Her pulse was at a full gallop, and her heart! Oh, her crazy heart was soaring high on the wings of love.

"I've been thinking more clearly," he said. "I should probably wait and do this the right way. Get a ring first. Get down on one knee. But I can't wait one more minute to ask this question. Natalie McCleary, will you marry me?"

Natalie's eyes widened and Dade's heart stopped as he waited for her answer.

A few hours ago, as they'd carried him from the caves on a stretcher in the wee hours of the morning of July 6, amid the hullabaloo of rescue workers, firefighters, policemen, and medics who had saved him and Red, Dade had been startled to see that the parking lot was slick black from an unseasonal summer rain.

It felt surreal, and he experienced the same dulled, apathetic sensation he'd experienced when he'd been taken prisoner by the Taliban, but as they loaded him into the back of the ambulance, dawn had peeped tentatively through the tunnel of darkness, revealing ghostly wisps of fog skimming above the asphalt.

And then there was Natalie, battered and bruised, rushing up to him. He was fading in and out of consciousness, but he heard her repeat what she'd told him the night they'd made love.

"I'm in love with you, Dade Vega, no matter what. Completely and unconditionally."

The paramedics carrying the litter paused and let her kiss his cheek. At that very same moment, a double shiny rainbow slowly unveiled itself in the rising light, shifting to reveal shimmering stripes of blue, purple, orange, and yellow, and twin arches straddling the Davis Mountains like a glorious crown.

The truth was there right in front of him, invisible to touch, taste, sound, sight, smell, but as wide and alive as the Chihuahuan Desert.

He loved her, but he had no idea how to express it. How to form those words. He'd never uttered them to anyone. What did love mean except you had so much more to lose?

Salty tears were in his throat. Oh hell no. He wasn't going to cry. He would not cry. He was a tough Navy SEAL. He hadn't cried since that night Red had saved him from Tank.

He'd been wrong in believing that never staying in one place was what kept him safe. He wasn't safe. He was stunted. Arrested development. You couldn't fully trust a stranger and he *was* that stranger. Flowing in and out of towns and cities alike, no anchor, no home, no place to call his own. He hadn't saved himself. Instead, he'd cut himself off, left beauty and love for only one reason.

He was terrified.

Afraid of being hurt. Afraid of loss. Afraid of love.

He was a coward.

Dade realized that he had two choices open to him. He could face forward and keep moving, or he could take the biggest gamble of his life, but that meant taking a giant leap of faith. That meant believing in this love that he'd felt for Natalie the second he'd first laid eyes on her.

Trust that it was real and solid. Something that they could build a future on.

The fog evaporated in the sunrise and he could see the village nestled in the valley, quiet and welcoming. The vineyards shone green as emeralds. Orange tile roofs glistening bronze in the dawn. The church steeple rose tall and majestic into the sky. Streetlamps flickering off one by one, letting the morning take over. The town yawned, stretched, awoke.

Home.

This place could be his home. He could be loved. All he had to do was reach out and accept it, but before he could do it, he'd been loaded into the ambulance and whisked away.

He squeezed her hand. "How long are you gonna leave me hanging here, Natty?"

She smiled.

Love.

It was all over her for anyone to read.

She truly loved him.

Just one look one summer dawn was all it had taken, and they'd fallen in love at first sight.

"I'm not going anywhere."

"I can see that," she said. "You're strapped to a gurney."

He reached up to cup her face with his palm. "As crazy as this love-at-first-sight thing sounds, I'm a believer. I love you, Natalie McCleary. I don't want to live another day without you and this nutty town."

Her eyes shone with joy. She was the most beautiful sight he'd ever seen.

"I'm in love with you but I'm so scared I'm going to screw this up. I don't know how to stay in one place. I don't know how to be part of a community. Will you teach me? Will you show me how to trust?"

"Dade," she whispered. "You just showed yourself."

"No," he said. "It's all you. You lift me up. Cleanse me. Make me a better man, and I want to spend the rest of my days living up to your expectations of me."

"You will," she whispered. "You've been in my blood since the beginning of time."

"You never did answer my question. Will you marry me, Natalie McCleary?"

"Dade Vega," she said. "There never has been and never will be another man for me. Yes. Yes. Of course I will marry you."

He tugged her down on the gurney beside him, kissed her with every ounce of love he had in him. He'd come to Cupid to find a friend but he'd found much more than that. He'd also discovered his one true love and a whole new life.

"Let's have it," Aunt Carol Ann said the following Monday when Natalie walked into the community center. "Your time is up. You do have an answer, don't you?"

"Absolutely," Natalie said. Grinning, she pulled the letter from her pocket and passed it to her aunt.

Dear Shot Through the Heart,
Love at first sight is indeed a rare gift. Cherish it because you and your beloved have something special that many people will never know. And while love at first sight is thrilling, it can also be a bit disorienting.

If you know it in your heart that this love is strong and true, then you have nothing to fear. His love will not waver and neither will yours. You can go to Oxford and his love will be with you whether he is near or far away. His thoughts will always be on you, and yours on him.

He is in your heart, your mind, your soul, your blood, and you are in his. Together you are stronger, better, richer because of your love. Trust it. Love never diminishes you, but always lifts you up. Let love guide you. Love will find a way. Have no worries because love is always enough.
Yours in love,
Cupid

* * * * *

The Marfa Lights

The Marfa Lights are a mysterious phenomenon that has baffled scientists for centuries. Often dubbed "ghost lights," these mischievous nocturnal illuminations appear unpredictably in the night sky, mostly east of Marfa, Texas, in a region known as Mitchell Flats. This location is also the site of an old army airfield where, during WWII, tens of thousands of pilots were trained. The lights pulse and shine, dance and change colors, and the patterns are different with every sighting. The lights can last from a few minutes to several hours.

Believers in paranormal activities have attributed the lights to everything from otherworldly spirits to space aliens, while cynics say it's nothing more than atmospheric reflections of car lights or campfires. Still others claim that the lights are a mirage caused by sharp temperature gradients between layers of hot and cold air. While Marfa is in the Chihuahuan Desert plateau, it is also at an elevation of 4,688 feet above sea level, so rapid shifts in temperature are quite common.

But in spite of the Marfa Lights having been heavily investigated by scientists and ghost hunters alike, no consensus on the cause of the phenomenon has been reached. The site is so popular that the State of Texas has created a viewing park for visitors who are hoping to catch a glimpse of the mysterious Marfa Lights.

At Avon Books, we know your passion for romance—once you finish one of our novels, you find yourself wanting more.

May we tempt you with . . .

- **Excerpts** from our upcoming releases.

- Entertaining **extras**, including authors' personal photo albums and book lists.

- Behind-the-scenes **scoop** on your favorite characters and series.

- **Sweepstakes** for the chance to win free books, romantic getaways, and other fun prizes.

- Writing **tips** from our authors and editors.

- **Blogs** from our authors on why they love writing romance.

- **Exclusive content** that's not contained within the pages of our novels.

Join us at
www.avonbooks.com